# Vintage Vampire Stories

EDITED BY

*Robert Eighteen-Bisang*

*&*

*Richard Dalby*

Skyhorse Publishing

A HERMAN GRAF BOOK

Skyhorse Publishing books may be purchased in bulk at special discounts
for sales promotion, corporate gifts, fund-raising, or educational purposes.
Special editions can also be created to specifications. For details, contact
the Special Sales Department, Skyhorse Publishing, 307 West 36th Street,
11th Floor, New York, NY 10018 or info@skyhorsepublishing.com.

Skyhorse® and Skyhorse Publishing® are registered trademarks of Skyhorse
Publishing, Inc.®, a Delaware corporation.

www.skyhorsepublishing.com

10 9 8 7 6 5 4 3 2 1

Library of Congress Cataloging-in-Publication Data is available on file.
ISBN: 978-1-61608-234-5     DEC 2 0 2011

Printed in the United States of America

# Table of Contents

# Introduction

## by Robert Eighteen-Bisang and Richard Dalby

The first four chapters of *Dracula* are narrated by Jonathan Harker, who introduces us to Transylvania, Count Dracula and the three vampire women in Dracula's castle. Our access to his diary informs us that vampires exist before the other major characters in the novel are aware of this. Our knowledge heightens the suspense as, one by one, Lucy, Mina, Seward, Morris and Holmwood (a.k.a. Lord Godalming) are forced to acknowledge that a supernatural force has invaded the mundane world. Their lives, indeed, their immortal souls, depend on their response.

In chapter eighteen, Professor Abraham Van Helsing calls the newly-formed vampire hunters together and informs them in broken English: "Take it, then, that the vampire, and the belief in his limitations and his cure, rest for the moment on the same base. For, let me tell you, he is known everywhere that men have been. In old Greece, in old Rome, he flourish in Germany all over, in France, in India, even in the Chermosese, and in China, so far from us in all ways, there even is he, and the peoples for him at this day. He have follow the wake of the berserker Icelander, the devil-begotten Hun, the Slav, the Saxon, the Magyar."

The modern vampire is part of popular culture. Most children can tell you that "Dracula" is a vampire from "Transylvania" and recite bits and pieces about vampires' strengths and weaknesses. Whether they know it or not, most of their knowledge about vampires is based on the rules laid down by Bram Stoker's masterpiece in 1897.

As marvelous and important as *Dracula* is, other writers have established different sets of rules by which their creations must live, hunt and die. Anne Rice, Buffy the Vampire Slayer and

Stephanie Meyers' Twilight Series have made important modifi-
cations to Bram Stoker's formula.

The stories in this book take place before Stoker's Count
became the "King of the Vampires." Most of the tales were
written in or unfold in Victorian England, but some stories open
in Australia, China, Germany, France, Portugal or the United
States of America.

As readers move from tale to tale they will become literary
vampire hunters who, like Van Helsing and company, must
discover what a vampire is and how to control it as they turn
the pages.

Let the hunt begin!

# Pu Songling:
# The Blood-Drinking
# Corpse (1679)

Pu Songling (a.k.a. P'u Sung-ling) [1640—1715] is best-known as the author of *Strange Stories from a Chinese Studio* (a.k.a. *Strange Tales from Liaozhai*). He spent most of his life as a private tutor in Zibo, in the province of Shadong. During this time, he collected almost five-hundred stories which were published posthumously in *Strange Stories from a Chinese Studio*.

Their content varies, and some of the stories are less than a page long. Pu borrowed many supernatural elements from folktales that blur the boundaries between the dream world and waking life. His tales about revenants, ghosts and fox women—who are often vampire-like vixens—have inspired many Chinese films, including those by King Hu (*Painted Skin*) and Ching Siu-tung (*A Chinese Ghost Story*) as well as the television series *Dark Tales* and *Dark Tales II*.

There are several different versions of the following tale. Herbert Giles translated it as "The Resuscitated Corpse" in 1926, while John Minford titled it "Living Dead" when he chose it for Penguin Classics abridged edition of *Strange Stories* in 2006.

George Soulié de Morant (1878-1955) was a French scholar and diplomat who played a key role in introducing acupuncture to the West. "The Blood-Drinking Corpse" is taken from his *Strange Stories from the Lodge of Leisures*, which contains twenty-five stories. His translation was published by Constable in 1913 and reprinted by the Houghton Mifflin Company in Boston and New York.

"The Blood-Drinking Corpse" underscores the vampiric elements of the story.

Night was slowly falling in the narrow valley. On the winding path cut in the side of the hill about twenty mules were following each other, bending under their heavy load; the muleteers, being tired, did not cease to hurry forward their animals, abusing them with coarse voices.

Comfortably seated on mules with large pack-saddles, three men were going along at the same pace as the caravan of which they were the masters. Their thick dresses, their fur boots, and their red woollen hoods protected them from the cold wind of the mountain.

In the darkness, rendered thicker by a slight fog, the lights of a village were shining, and soon the mules, hurrying all together, jostling their loads, crowded before the only inn of the place.

The three travelers, happy to be able to rest, got down from their saddles when the innkeeper came out on the step of his door and excused himself, saying all his rooms were taken.

"I have still, it is true, a large hall the other side of the street, but it is only a barn, badly shut. I will show it to you."

The merchants, disappointed, consulted each other with a look; but it was too late to continue their way; they followed their landlord.

The hall that was shown to them was big enough and closed at the end by a curtain. Their luggage was brought; the bedclothes rolled on the pack-saddles were spread out, as usual, on planks and trestles.

The meal was served in the general sitting-room, in the midst of noise, laughing, and movement—smoking rice, vegetables preserved in vinegar, and lukewarm wine served in small cups. Then everyone went to bed; the lights were put out and profound silence prevailed in the sleeping village.

However, towards the hour of the Rat, a sensation of cold and uneasiness awoke one of the three travelers named Wang Fou, Happiness-of-the-kings. He turned in his bed, but the snoring of his two companions annoyed him; he could not get to sleep. Again, seeing that his rest was finished, he got up, relit the lamp which was out, took a book from his baggage, and stretched himself out again. But if he could not sleep, it was just as impossible to read. In spite of himself, his eyes quitted the columns of letters laid out in lines and searched into the darkness that the feeble light did not contrive to break through.

A growing terror froze him. He would have liked to awaken him companions, but the fear of being made fun of prevented him.

By dint of looking, he at last saw a slight movement shake the big curtain which closed the room. There came from behind a crackling of wood being broken. Then a long, painful threatening silence began again.

The merchant felt his flesh thrill; he was filled with horror, in spite of his efforts to be reasonable.

He had put aside his book, and, the coverlet drawn up to his nose, he fixed his enlarged eyes on the shadowy corners at the end of the room.

The side of the curtain was lifted; a pale hand held the folds. The stuff, thus raised, permitted a being to pass, whose form, hardly distinct, seemed penetrated by the shadow.

Happiness-of-kings would have liked to scream; his contracted throat allowed no sound to escape. Motionless and speechless, he followed with his horrified look the slow movement of the apparition which approached.

He, little by little, recognized the silhouette of a female, seen by her short quilted dress and her long narrow jacket. Behind the body he perceived the curtain again moving.

The spectre, in the meantime bending over the bed of one of the sleeping travelers, appeared to give him a long kiss.

Then it went towards the couch of the second merchant. Happiness-of-kings distinctly saw the pale figure, the eyes, from which a red flame was shining, and sharp teeth, half-exposed in a ferocious smile, which opened and shut by turns on the throat of the sleeper.

A start disturbed the body under the cover, then all stopped: the spectre was drinking in long draughts.

Happiness-of-kings, seeing that his turn was coming, had just strength enough to pull the coverlet over his head. He heard grumblings; a freezing breath penetrated through the wadded material.

The paroxysm of terror gave the merchant full possession of his strength; with a convulsive movement he threw his coverlet on the apparition, jumped out of his bed, and, yelling like a wild beast, he ran as far as the door and flew away in the night.

Still running, he felt the freezing breath in his back, he heard the furious growlings of the spectre.

The prolonged howling of the unhappy man filled the narrow street and awoke all the sleepers in their beds, but none of them moved; they hid themselves farther and farther under their coverlets. These inhuman cries meant nothing good for those who should have been bold enough to go outside.

The bewildered fugitive crossed the village, going faster and faster. Arriving at the last houses, he was only a few feet in advance and felt himself fainting.

The road at the extremity of the village was bordered with narrow fields shaded with big trees. The instinct of a hunted animal drove on the distracted merchant; he made a brisk turn to the right, then to the left, and threw himself behind the knotted trunk of a huge chestnut-tree. The freezing hand already touched his shoulder; he felt senseless.

In the morning, in broad daylight, two men who came to plough in this same field were surprised to perceive against the tree a white form, and, on the ground, a man stretched out. This fact coming after the howling in the night appeared strange to them; they turned back and went to find the Chief of the Elders. When they returned, the greater part of the inhabitants of the village followed them.

They approached and found that the form against the tree was the corpse of a young woman, her nails buried in the bark; from her mouth a stream of blood had flowed and stained her white silk jacket. A shudder of horror shook the lookers-on: the Chief of the Elders recognized his daughter dead for the last six months whose coffin was placed in a barn, waiting for the burial, a favorable day to be fixed by the astrologers.

The innkeeper recognized one of his guests in the man stretched on the ground, whom no care could revive.

They returned in haste to find out in what condition the coffin was: the door of the barn was still open. They went in; a coverlet was thrown on the ground near the entrance; on two beds the great sun lit up the hollow and greenish aspect of the corpses whose blood had been emptied. Behind the drawn curtain the coffin was found open. The corpse of the young woman evidently had not lost its inferior soul, the vital breath. Like all beings deprived of conscience and reason, her ferocity was eager for blood.

# William H. G. Kingston:
# The Vampire; or, Pedro Pacheco and the Bruxa (1863)

William Henry Giles Kingston (1814–1880) was born in London but spent much of his youth in Oporto, Portugal, where his father was a merchant.

His first book for boys, *Peter the Whaler*, was published in 1851. It was such a success that he retired from his father's business to devote himself to writing. He travelled widely, and described many of his adventures for young readers.

"The Vampire; or, Pedro Pacheco and the Bruxa" is taken from his collection *Tales for All Ages* which was published by Rickers & Bush in 1863. As collectors of juvenilia who have hunted down this *rara avis* have discovered, the following story is *not* intended for children.

———————

T he most terrific of all the supernatural beings in whose existence the peasants of Portugal believe, is the *Bruxa* (pronounced Broocha). She is similar in her propensities to the Eastern Ghoul or Vampire. Indeed there can be no doubt that she was introduced into Portugal by the Moors during the time that they held sway in the country. The Bruxa is to all appearance a woman, but a woman possessed of an evil spirit. She may be the daughter of honest good parents; she may marry and have children, and she is often very beautiful, though there is a certain fierce expression in her eye and an ominous wrinkle in her otherwise smooth brow.

Nobody can tell who are Bruxas and who are not. They never allow any mortal to discover their dreadful secret, and woe betide the mortal who shall attempt to pry into it. Sometimes their own daughters become Bruxas, or else they keep up their numbers by inveigling some hapless maiden whose heart has been turned from the right path, and who has deserted her whole religion to join their association. She knows not whither she is to be led or what is to be her fate till it is too late to retract, when the fatal compact is signed with her blood; then, miserable girl! Her shrieks, he cries are of no avail. Truly there is a deep moral—an awful warning in the legend. From sunset to sunrise the demoniacal power possesses the Bruxas. During the day they return to their families, no one suspecting the dreadful truth. When darkness overspreads the world and the rest of the household are wrapped in slumber, they noiselessly rise from their couches, and after joining the orgies or their sisters in crime, are transformed into the shape of some noxious creatures of night—owls or gigantic bats. Away they fly at a prodigious rate, far from their homes, over hill and dale, but especially across marshes, stagnant pools and lakes; unwillingly they skim along the surface, gazing on their hideous forms reflected in the water and perfectly conscious of their fate.

They occasionally, on these nocturnal rambles, encounter some friend or relation, and either by allurements or by force will lead him far away from the point towards which he was proceeding. Many a poor wretch has thus been led across the country, over rough rocks and through brambles and briars, which have scratched his face torn his clothes till, almost worn to death, wet, weary, and bloody, he has at length returned home, complaining that the horrible Bruxas have thus led him astray and maltreated him, and that the wine shops are in no way to blame.

But this is not the only harm the Bruxas do. After their orgies and these long wanderings on the wing, they, with vampirish hunger, fly back to their peaceful homes, where, in calm repose, sleep their innocent offspring. Though feeling a human loathing for this terrific task, their horrible propensities overcome their maternal love, and seizing on their babes, their black wings fanning them to repose, they suck the life-blood from their veins—dreadful fate!—conscious all the time that they are destroying the only ones they love on earth. When they have thus murdered their own children, they enter the cottages of their neighbours and friends whose sleeping infants they in like manner deprive of life, and often when a child is found dead, livid, and marked with punctures, the sage women whisper to each other with fear and trembling, "a Bruxa has done this," casting eyes of suspicion on each other, for no one knows who the Bruxa may be.

As the first streaks of the grey dawn appear, the miserable females return to their mortal forms, awaiting the time when they must perform their dreadful orgies, never for an instant forgetful of the fate to which they are doomed. Truly it would be difficult for the most poetical and fertile imagination to conceive a more horrible lot than that of the hapless Bruxan.

But to commence our tale.

Portugal has on several occasions been placed under the ban of the Pope, and on these occasions, so the monks affirmed the spirits of evil bad peculiar power. On one occasion the thunders of the Vatican were launched against the whole nation in consequence of the marriage of the Princess Theresa with her cousin Alfonso, King of Leon. At that time there lived near the town of Aveiro, situated on the shores of the Atlantic, a sturdy farmer, Pedro Pacheco by name. It must be known that close to the town there is a long shallow lake, which in those days was a wide extending marsh, fell of tall reeds and surrounded by a thick underwood.

Pedro Pacheco lived in a cottage of his own, with his wife and several children, whom he looked upon as paragons of perfection, in which sentiment Senhora Gertrudes, his better half, evidently joined him, as is not unusual in married couples with respect to their own handy work; though greater, according to the importance of the subject—that is to say, the more trifling the matter the louder they talked and the more they wrangled, as if their whole existence depended on the result; indeed the neighbours whispered that Senhora Gertrudes, whose voice was none of the sweetest, invariably had the best of the argument, if she was not in truth the better horse of the two. Notwithstanding their slight disagreements, Pedro loved his wife. He was a jovial fellow, of an excellent disposition, rather short and very fat, with well-filled cheeks and black rolling eyes. He was a welcome guest at every Romaria, or merry-making, when his ringing laugh was sure to be heard above all the others, or the sound of his voice as he touched his tinkling viola.

One day it happened that, leaving his wife at home to take care of the children, he joined a fiesta which took place in honour of the marriage of one of his friends, who lived on the opposite side of the marsh to where his cottage was situated. Pedro enjoyed himself to the utmost. He laughed and talked, and ate and drank enough for everybody; he cracked his best jokes, he told his best story, and sang his best song. There was nothing to damp his spirits; when the dance began he snapped his fingers, nodded his head, and toed and heeled it with the youngest of them, every now and then taking a pull at the wine-skin just to prevent his mouth from getting dry. At last, the shades of evening coming on, the guests began to separate, and at the same time it struck Pedro that if he did not make haste to return home, he would receive rather a warmer reception than might agree with his ears when he got there. For some part of the way a considerable number of the revelers accompanied him, he walking at their head as proud as a peacock with open tail, with his guitar in hand, improvising songs in honour of the newly-made bride, the rest of the party taking up the chorus. One by one, however, dropped off on the road as they proceeded, till at last he was left to find his way home by himself as best he could. But that mattered little to friend Pedro; he knew the way perfectly, as well he might, for he had traversed it frequently, both day and night; his heart was stout, and he had a tough bow at his back, with plenty of arrows, and a sword by his side, for those were not times when a man could walk abroad without arms. On he went for some time, caring little for the stones and puddle in his way, singing at the top of his voice, though there was nobody to hear him except the frogs, who kept up a not very melodious concert in the neighbouring marsh. At last he remembered that there as, for his sins it might be said, such a person as the Senhora Gertrudes, his wife, who, it was more than probable, would make his ears tingle if he were not at home at the time she desired him to return. In those good old days, watches, steam-engines, political economy, and most other of the wicked inventions of the free-masons, were unknown, so he could only guess that he had no time to spare, and just as he arrived at this conclusion, he came to a path which made a short cut across the marsh, by which he should save a quarter of a league at the least. That there were several very soft places in it he knew, but he felt so light, airy, and active, that he fancied he could easily skip over them as he had often seen a daddy-long-legs do over a stagnant pond. The sky was clear, the moon was bright, so that he could not by any possibility, miss the path. One thing, though, he did not take into consideration, the differences of his own figure and that of a daddy-longlegs; indeed, honest Pedro was not the only person in the world who had not a true perception of himself, what-ever may be the case at present—times have changed since then. Well, he boldly turned off from the broad well-beaten path, and took the narrow footway across the marsh, over which he had not proceeded far, singing louder than ever, for the cool air of the evening put him in spirits, when, on a sudden, up got before him a large bird, flying slowly along, as if perfectly heedless of his presence.

"A wild duck, as I live!" exclaimed Pedro to himself; "if I can manage to send an arrow into that gentleman's neck, to stop his flight, I will take it home to my wife for supper, and thus save my own ears."

Whereupon, throwing his viola over his shoulder, he seized his bow, and let fly a bolt directly at the bird. The creature uttered a cry just like a wild duck, and continued its course as slowly as before. Pedro felt certain he had hit it; indeed, he fancied that he could hear the arrow strike, it was so near; he probably had broken one of its legs and another bolt would bring it down. Again he let fly, but with equal want of success; the bird turned off a little on one side, and Pedro followed. He was not a man to be deterred by disappointments, particularly in his present humour; arrow after arrow he shot away ineffectually; the bird kept the same distance before him; and so eager was he in the pursuit that he quite forgot the direction he had taken. The ground beneath his feet became every instant more wet and swampy, but on he splashed through the water, his ears already tingling at the thoughts of returning home without a peace offering to his dear Gertrudes. What a blessing it is to have a wife to keep one in order!

"The next shot must bring the beast down, to a certainty," he cried, as he let fly his seventh arrow; but the bird only uttered a loud, derisive, "quack, quack, quack!" and flew on at an increased speed.

It now appeared to honest Pedro to be a larger bird than he had at first thought it; but this only made him the more anxious to have it for his supper. On he ran, almost out of breath, not quite so lightly as he expected, for he was frequently up to his knees in mud and water, now and then he sank still deeper, and more than once came down on his face; but he was a true sportsman, not to be thrown out by such trifling accidents. Again he shot, and he was certain that he saw some feathers fly off from the bird, which went "quack, quack, quack," louder than ever.

"Ah! Senhor Goose, I'll have you now," exclaimed Pedro; "clever as you think yourself, you are no match for Pedro Pacheco, let me tell you."

"Quack, quack, quack!" went the goose, and flew on, Pedro pursuing.

In a few minutes more, poor Pedro was thoroughly wet through, now up to his middle in water, now sprawling like a tortoise, on his back with his legs in the air, now with his face in the mud, but he somehow or other always contrived to get on his feet again. Have the goose he would, if he went on all night, he was determined. Pedro now lost his temper, as well he might, for it was provoking to run such a chase when he wanted to get home. To add to his difficulties, the sky, which had hitherto been clear, was now obscured by clouds: and when, while once on his back, he looked up to see what had become of the moon, he could no where behold her. There was, however, just light enough to see the strange creature which he still persisted in considering a goose or a duck, for he was, as may have been seen, in rather an obstinate humour. Whatever it was, it had now grown larger than ever, and every arrow Pedro shot stuck it, but it cared no more for them than if they had been so many toothpicks, only giving vent to more unearthly quack, quack, quacks. A man in his calm senses would have been suspicious of evil, but poor Pedro only thought of getting a goose for supper.

There was, indeed, little use in thinking of going home, for when he looked north, south, east, or west, he had not the remotest idea which way to take. The highest object he could see was a line of bulrushes, and the gigantic bird just above them.

After going on in this way for an hour or more, when he had not a dry rag upon him, he came to a change of scene, namely, a thick mass of low trees and shrubs, which extended on each side as far as he could see. He thought that perhaps the bird would fly against them and be caught in their branches, but no such thing, over it flew just above the highest, and went skimming along as before. Pedro had no help for it but to follow, or, after all his labour, give up the pursuit. I shall be dry, at all events, he thought, as he entered among the underwood. He soon, however, found to his cost that he had fallen from the frying-pan into the fire. Before he had tumbled in soft mud and merely got wet, now his hands and face were scratched by the brambles, and his clothes were torn into shreds. Still there was the strange bird flying unconcernedly on, just above his head, among the trees. Every now and then it turned round its head with a knowing look, as if just to see whether he was following, and Pedro could see the malicious glitter of its eye.

"I'll have you, my fine bird, never fear," he cried and dashed on. Just then he tumbled plump into a pit filled with briars and covered over with dry leaves. He had great difficulty in getting out, the blood streaming down from every limb, and he made sure the bird must have escaped him, but there was the creature stopping quietly on the top of a tree as if to wait for him. He had not time to draw breath after all his exertions, when away it again flew; and now, being scratched and seamed all over (it was a miracle his eyes still remained in his head), he found himself clear of the wood. Whether he had changed for the better or worse was now to be seen. A wide extent of rocky ground lay before him, with hills in the distance, towards which the bird directed its course, quacking louder than ever to attract him onward.

Poor Pedro! Down he tumbled and broke his shins; then he scraped all the skin off his elbows; then down he came on his seat, black and blue in every part, till he found himself slipping over a wet smooth slab of stone, off which he fell splash into a rapid stream. Fortunately he could swim, though not very well, so his head went under several times till he was half full of water, and at length, by dint of great exertion, he reached the other bank, spluttering and blowing. A steep hill was before him, up which the bird flew, he following, climbing from rock to rock; now he caught hold of the branch of a tree, which gave way in his hand and let him fall down a dozen yards or so—he did not stop to measure the distance. He was up again in a moment, catching hold of trees, shrubs, tufts of grass, rocks, or whatever came in his way, till at last he was only a few feet from the crea-ture on the top of the hill. He now saw its immense size, but undaunted at the sight and furious with rage, he drew his sword, and rushed at it to cut it down. The bird rose as he approached; so headlong was his speed that he could not stop his way, and over he went down a steep precipice—bounding from rock to rock, the bird quacking and screeching in his ears all the time, every bone in his body cracking, till he bounded on to a smooth rock, down which he slid, slid, slid, every instant expecting to find himself in the ocean, which he could hear roaring beneath him; but a comfort it was, though a small and cold one, when instead, he was shot right into the soft sand on the sea shore. He looked up, there was the creature flying round and round and round, which remained uninjured; so he tried to rise, for he was, as has been seen, a plucky little fellow, a true Lusitanian of those days; but though he could not stand he lifted himself up on his knees, drew his last bolt, a louder shriek, which sounded like the derisive laughter of a hundred Pedro, "A pretty night's work I have had for nothing; I have got only a certainty when I get home. There is no use being drowned into the bargain, so I'll try and get out of this."

He accordingly crawled along till he found some soft, dry sand above high-water mark, and there he went to sleep to wait for the morning light to enable him to find his way home. At last he was awoke by a rough shake on the shoulder.

"What are you doing here, my friend?" said a loud voice; and looking up, Pedro beheld a fisherman standing over him.

"I've been sleeping," said Pedro.

"I see you have," said the other.

"But where am I, Patricio?" asked Pedro.

"Upon the sea shore, about six leagues from Aveiro," was the answer.

"Impossible," muttered Pedro to himself, "six leagues in one night!"

"And what's your name, friend?" said the fisherman.

"Pedro Pacheco," said Pedro.

"You Pedro Pacheco!" exclaimed the fisherman. "I don't believe it. Pedro Pacheco is a quiet, sober man, and you, to say the best of it, look like a good-for-nothing drunken beast, who has been getting into some scrape or other and received a broken head."

"And so I have got into a terrible scrape, which has taken all the skin off my shins, and my head has been broken into the bargain," answered poor Pedro. "But it was all owing to a terrible Bruxa, which led me astray, oh, oh, oh," and Pedro fell back from exhaustion.

Now the fisherman was a kind-hearted man, so he lifted Pedro into his boat and rowed him back along the cost to the spot nearest his house, where he landed and carried him home. Poor Pedro's troubles were not over, for no sooner did Senhora Gertrudes catch sight of him than, thinking he had got tipsy at the merry-making, without stopping to inquire the truth of the fisherman, she darted at him, nearly scratching out his eyes and pulling his ears, till they were black and blue all over.

"Oh, oh, oh," uttered poor Pedro; but being very weak, he resigned himself to his fate, as many another better man has done before under like circumstances.

The fisherman, however, published the story which Pedro told him, and as he was a great favourite, the neighbours did him justice; some, indeed, going as far as to hint to each other that perhaps his wife was the Bruxa who so cruelly beguiled him.

These whispers of course honest Pedro did not hear, but owing to his adventure he was one of the loudest in demanding the separation of the Princess Theresa and King Alfonso, that the ban of the church might be removed, till when, he affirmed, the people could never hope to get the land rid of Bruzas and other evil spirits. The removal of the excommunication had not, however, the desired effect: Bruxas having been met with at a much later date in Portugal.

# Mary Fortune:
## The White Maniac:
## A Doctor's Tale (1867)

Mary Helena Wilson (1833-1910) was born in Belfast, Ireland. Her family moved to Montreal, Canada, where she married Joseph Fortune in 1851. Shortly thereafter, Mary's father immigrated to Melbourne, Australia, and she joined him there in 1855.

She was a prolific writer whose career began in 1855 with pseudonymous contributions to local newspapers. She began to write for *The Australian Journal* in Melbourne under the pseudonyms "W. W." and "Waif Wander" in 1865. Fortune was one of the first female crime writers in the world. Her most important series was "The Detective's Album" which ran from 1868 to 1908.

"The White Maniac: A Doctor's Tale" was first published in *The Australian Journal* 2:98 in 1867 under the pseudonym "Waif Wander."

———————

In the year 1858 I had established a flourishing practice in London; a practice which I owed a considerable proportion of, not to my ability, I am afraid, but to the fact that I occupied the singular position of a man professional, who was entirely independent of his profession. Doubtless, had I been a poor man, struggling to earn a bare existence for wife and family, I might have been the cleverest physician that ever administered a bolus, yet have remained in my poverty to the end of time. But it was not so, you see. I was the second son of a nobleman, and had Honourable attached to my name; and I practised the profession solely and entirely because I had become enamoured of it, and because I was disgusted at the useless existence of a fashionable and idle young man, and determined that I, at least, would not add another to their ranks.

And so I had a handsome establishment in a fashionable portion of the city, and my door was besieged with carriages, from one end of the week to the other. Many of the occupants were disappointed, however, for I would not demean myself by taking fees from some vapourish Miss or dissipated Dowager. Gout in vain came rolling to my door, even though it excruciated the leg of a Duke; I undertook none but cases that enlisted my sympathy, and after in time the fact became known, and my levees were not so well attended.

One day I was returning on horseback toward the city. I had been paying a visit to a patient, in whom I was deeply interested, and for whom I had ordered the quiet and purer air of a suburban residence. I had reached a spot, in the neighbourhood of Kensington, where the vines were enclosed in large gardens, and the road was marked for a considerable distance by the brick and stone walls that enclosed several of the gardens belonging to those mansions. On the opposite side of the road stood a small country-looking inn, which I had patronised before, and I pulled up my horse and alighted, for the purpose of having some rest and refreshment after my ride.

As I sat in a front room sipping my wine and water, my thoughts were fully occupied with a variety of personal concerns. I had received a letter from my mother that morning, and the condition of the patient I had recently left was precarious in the extreme.

It was fortunate that I was thought-occupied and not dependent upon outward objects to amuse them, for although the window at which I sat was open, it presented no view whatever, save the bare, blank, high brick wall belonging to a house at the opposite side of the road. That is to say, I presume, it enclosed some residence, for from where I sat not even the top of a chimney was visible.

Presently, however, the sound of wheels attracted my eyes from the pattern of the wall-paper at which I had been unconsciously gazing, and I looked out to see a handsome, but very plain carriage drawn up at a small door that pierced the brick wall I have alluded to; and almost at the same moment the door opened and closed again behind two figures in a most singular attire. They were both of the male sex, and one of them was evidently a gentleman, while the other waited on him as if he was the servant; but it was the dress of these persons that most strangely interested me. They were attired in white from head to heel; coats, vests, trousers, hats, shoes, not to speak of shirts at all, all were white as white could be.

While I stared at this strange spectacle, the gentleman stepped into the vehicle; but although he did so the coachman made no movement toward driving onward, nor did the attendant leave his post at the carriage door. At the expiration, however, of about a quarter of an hour, the servant closed the door and re-entered through the little gate, closing it, likewise, carefully behind him. Then the driver leisurely made a start, only, however, to stop suddenly again, when the door of the vehicle was burst open and a gentleman jumped out and rapped loudly at the gate.

He turned his face hurriedly around as he did so, hiding, it seemed to me, meanwhile, behind the wall so as not to be seen when it opened. Judge of my astonishment when I recognised in this gentleman the one who had but a few minutes before entered the carriage dressed in white, for he was now in garments of the hue of Erebus. While I wondered at this strange metamorphosis the door in the wall opened, and the gentleman, now attired in black, after giving some hasty instructions to the servant, sprang once more into the carriage and was driven rapidly toward London.

My curiosity was strangely excited; and as I stood at the door before mounting my horse, I asked the landlord who and what were the people who occupied the opposite dwelling.

"Well, sir," he replied, looking curiously at the dead wall over against him, "They've been there now a matter of six months, I dare say, and you've seen as much of them as I have. I believe the whole crew of them, servants and all, is foreigners, and we, that is the neighbours around, sir, calls them the 'white mad people.'"

"What! do they always wear that singular dress?"

"Always, sir, saving as soon as ever the old gentleman goes inside the gate he puts black on in the carriage, and as soon as be comes back takes it off again, and leaves it in the carriage."

"And why in the name of gracious does he not dress himself inside?"

"Oh, that I can't tell you sir! only it's just as you see, always. The driver or coachman never even goes inside the walls, or the horses or any one thing that isn't white in colour, sir; and if the people aren't mad after that, what else can it be?"

"It seems very like it, indeed; but do you mean to say that everything inside the garden wall is white? Surely you must be exaggerating a little?"

"Not a bit on it, sir! The coachman, who can't speak much English, sir, comes here for a drink now and then. He doesn't live in the house, you see, and is idle most of his time. Well, he told me himself, one day, that every article in the house was white, from the garret to the drawing-room, and that everything *outside* it is white I can swear, for I saw it myself, and a stranger sight surely no eye ever saw."

"How did you manage to get into the enchanted castle, then?"

"I didn't get in sir, I only saw it outside, and from a place where you can see for yourself too, if you have a mind. When first the people came to the place over there, you see sir, old Mat the sexton and bell-ringer of the church there, began to talk of the strange goings on he had seen from the belfry; and so my curiosity took me there one day to look for myself. Blest if I ever heard of such a strange sight! no wonder they call them the white mad folk."

"Well, you've roused my curiosity," I said, as I got on my horse, "and I'll certainly pay old Mat's belfry a visit the very next time I pass this way, if I'm not hurried."

It appeared unaccountable to even myself that these mysterious people should make such a singular impression on me; I thought of little else during the next two days. I attended to my duties in an absent manner, and my mind was over recurring to the one subject—viz. an attempt to account for the strange employment of one hue only in the household of this foreign gentleman. Of whom did the household consist? Had he any family? and could one account for the eccentricity in any other way save by ascribing it to lunacy, as mine host of the inn had already done. As it happened, the study of brain diseases had been my hobby during my noviciate, and I was peculiarly interested in observing a new symptom of madness, if this was really one.

At length I escaped to pay my country patient his usual visit, and on my return alighted at the inn, and desired the landlord to have my horse put in the stable for a bit.

"I'm going to have a peep at your madhouse," I said, "do you think I shall find old Mat about?"

"Yes, doctor; I saw him at work in the churchyard not half an hour ago, but at any rate he won't be farther off than his cottage, and it lies just against the yard wall."

The church was an old, ivy-wreathed structure, with a square Norman belfry, and a large surrounding of grey and grass-grown old headstones. It was essentially a country church, and a country church-yard; and one wondered to find it so close to the borders of a mighty city, until they remembered that the mighty city had crept into the country, year by year, until it had covered with stone and mortar the lowly site of many a cottage home, and swallowed up many an acre of green meadow and golden corn. Old Mat was sitting in the middle of the graves; one tombstone forming his seat, and he was engaged in scraping the moss from a headstone that seemed inclined to tumble over, the inscription on which was tin but obliterated by a growth of green slimy-looking moss.

"Good-day, friend, you are busy," I said. "One would fancy that stone so old now, that the living had entirely forgotten their loss. But I suppose they have not, or you would not be cleaning it."

"It's only a notion of my own, sir; I'm idle, and when I was a lad I had it sort o' likin' for this stone, Lord only knows why. But you see I've clean forgotten what name was on it, and I thought I'd like to see."

"Well, I want to have a look at these 'white mad folk' of yours, Mat, will you let me into the belfry? Mr Tanning tells me you can see something queer up there."

"By jove you can, sir!" he replied, rising with alacrity, "I often spend an hour watching the mad folk; faith if they had my old church and yard they'd whitewash 'em, belfry and all!" and the old man led the way into the tower.

Of course my first look on reaching the summit was in the direction of the strange house, and I must confess to an ejaculation of astonishment as I peeped through one of the crevices. The belfry was elevated considerably above the premises in which I was interested, and not at a very great distance, so that grounds and house lay spread beneath me like a map.

I scarcely know how to commence describing it to you, it was something I had never seen or imagined. The mansion itself was a square and handsome building of two stories, built in the Corinthian, style, with pillared portico, and pointed windows. But the style attracted my attention but little, it was the universal white, white everywhere, that drew from me the ejaculation to which I have alluded.

From the extreme top of the chimneys to the basement, roof, windows, everything was pure white; not a shade lurked even inside a window; the windows themselves were painted white, and the curtains were of white muslin that fell over every one of them. Every yard of the broad space that one might reasonably have exported to see decorated with flowers and grass and shrubberies, was covered with a glaring and sparkling white gravel, the effect of which, even in the hot brilliant sun of a London afternoon, was to dazzle, and blind, and aggravate. And if this was not enough, the inside of the very brick walls was whitewashed like snow, and at intervals, here and there, were placed a host of white marble statues and urns that only increased the, to me, horrible aspect of the place.

"I don't wonder they are mad!" I exclaimed, "I should soon become mad in such a place myself."

"Like enough, sir," replied old Mat, stolidly, "but you see it *didn't* make they mad, for they did it theirselves, so they must 'a been mad afore."

An incontrovertible fact, according to the old man's way of putting it; and as I had no answer for it, I went down the old stone stairs, and having given my guide his donation, left the churchyard as bewildered as I had entered it. Nay, more so, for then I had not seen the extraordinary house that had made so painful an impression upon me.

I was in no humour for a gossip with mine host, but just as I was about to mount my horse, which had been brought round, the same carriage drove round to the mysterious gate, and the same scene was enacted to which I had before been a witness. I drew back until the old gentleman had stopped inside and performed his toilet, and when the carriage drove rapidly toward the city, I rode thoughtfully onward toward home.

I was young, you see, and although steady, and, unlike most young gentlemen of my age and position in society, had a strong vein of romance in my character. That hard study and a sense of its inutility had kept it under, had not rendered it one whit less ready to be at a moment's call; and, in addition to all this, I had never yet, in the seclusion of my student life, met with an opportunity of falling in love, so that you will see I was in the very best mood for making the most of the adventure which was about to befall me, and which had so tragic a termination.

My thoughts were full of the 'White mad folk,' as I reached my own door; and there, to my utter astonishment, I saw drawn up the very carriage of the white house, which had preceded me. Hastily giving my horse to the groom I passed through the hall and was informed by a servant that a gentleman waited in my private consulting room.

Very rarely indeed had my well-strung nerves been so trouble-
some as upon that occasion; I was so anxious to see this gentleman,
and yet so fearful of exposing the interest I had already conceived
in his affairs, that my hand absolutely trembled as I turned the
handle of the door of the room in which he was seated. The
first glance, however, at the aristocratic old gentleman who
rose on my entrance, restored all my self-possession, and I was
myself once more. In the calm, sweet face of the perfectly dressed
gentleman before me there was no trace of the lunacy that had
created that strange abode near Kensington; the principal expression in his face was that of ingrained melancholy, and his deep
mourning, attire might have suggested to a stranger the reason of
that melancholy. He addressed me in perfect English, the entire
absence of idiom alone declaring him to be a foreigner.

"I have the pleasure of addressing Doctor Elveston?" he said.

I bowed, and placed a chair in which he re-seated himself,
while I myself took possession of another.

"And Doctor Elveston is a clever physician and a man of
honour?"

"I hope to be worthy of the former title, sir, while my position
ought at least to guarantee the latter."

"Your public character does, sir," said the old gentleman,
emphatically, and it is because I believe that you will preserve the
secret of an unfortunate family that I have chosen you to assist
me with your advice."

My heart was beating rapidly by this time. There was a secret
then, and I was about to become the possessor of it. Had it
anything to do with the mania for white?

"Anything in my power," I hastened to reply, "you may depend
on; my advice, I fear, may be of little worth, but such as it is-".

"I beg your pardon, Doctor," interrupted he, "it is your
medical advice that I allude to, and I require it for a young
lady—a relative."

"My dear sir, that is, of course, an every day affair, my professional advice and services belong to the public, and as the public's
they are of course yours."

"Oh, my dear young friend, but mine is not an every day affair, and because it is not is the reason that I have applied to you in particular. It is a grievous case, sir, and one which fills many hearts with a bitterness they are obliged to smother from a world whose sneers are poison."

The old gentleman spoke in tones of deep feeling, and I could not help feeling sorry for him at the bottom of my very heart.

"If you will confide in me, my dear sir," I said, "believe that I will prove a friend as faithful and discreet as you could wish."

He pressed my hand, turned away for a moment to collect his agitated feelings and then he spoke again.

"I shall not attempt to hide my name from you, sir, though I have hitherto carefully concealed it, I am the Duke de Rohan, and circumstances, which it is impossible for me to relate to you, have driven me to England to keep watch and ward over my sister's daughter, the Princess d'Alberville. It is for this young lady I wish your attendance, her health is rapidly failing within the last week."

"Nothing can be more simple," I observed, eagerly, "I can go with you at once—this very moment."

"Dear Doctor, it is unfortunately far from being as simple a matter as you think," he replied, solemnly, "for my wretched niece is mad."

"Mad!"

"Alas! yes, frightfully—horribly mad!" and he shuddered as if a cold wind had penetrated his bones.

"Has this unhappy state of mind been of long duration?" I questioned.

"God knows; the first intimation her friends had of it was about two years ago, when it culminated in such a fearful event that horrified them. I cannot explain it to you, however, for the honour of a noble house is deeply concerned; and even the very existence of the unfortunate being I beg of you to keep a secret forever."

"You must at any rate tell me what you wish me to do," I observed "and give me as much information as you can to guide me, or I shall be powerless."

"The sight of one colour has such an effect on the miserable girl that we have found out, by bitter experience, the only way to avoid a repetition of the most fearful tragedies is to keep every hue or shade away from her vision; for, although it is only one colour that affects her, any of the others seems to suggest that *one* to her mind and produce uncontrollable agitation in consequence of this she is virtually imprisoned within the grounds of the house I have provided for her; and every object that meets her eye is white, even the ground, and the very roof of the mansion."

"How very strange!"

"It will be necessary for you, my dear sir," the Duke continued, "to attire yourself in a suit of white. I have brought one in the carriage for your use, and if you will now accompany me I shall be grateful."

Of course I was only too glad to avail myself of the unexpected opportunity of getting into the singular household, and becoming acquainted with the lunatic princess; and in a few moments we were being whirled on our way toward Kensington.

On stopping at the gate of the Duke's residence, I myself became an actor in the scene which had so puzzled me on two previous occasions. My companion produced two suits of white, and proceeded to turn the vehicle into a dressing-room, though not without many apologies for the necessity. I followed his example, and in a few moments we stood inside the gate, and I had an opportunity of more closely surveying the disagreeable enclosure I had seen from the church belfry. And a most disagreeable survey it was; the sun shining brilliantly, rendered the unavoidable contact with the white glare, absolutely painful to the eye; nor was it any escape to stand in the lofty vestibule, save that there the absence of sunshine made the uniformity more bearable.

My companion led the way up a broad staircase covered with white cloth, and balustraded with carved rails, the effect of which was totally destroyed by their covering of white paint. The very stair-rods were of white enamel, and the corners and landing places served as room for more marble statues, that held enamelled white lamps in their hands, lamps that were shaded by globes of ground glass. At the door of an apartment pertaining, as he informed me, to the Princess d'Alberville, the Duke stopped, and shook my hand. "I leave you to make your own way," he said, pointing to the door. She has never showed any symptoms of violence while under the calm influence of white; but, nevertheless, we shall be at hand, the least sound will bring you assistance," and he turned away.

I opened the door without a word, and entered the room, full of curiosity as to what I should see and hear of this mysterious princess. It was a room of vast and magnificent proportions, and, without having beheld such a scene, one can hardly conceive the strange cold look the utter absence of colour gave it. A Turkey carpet that looked like a woven fall of snow; white satin damask on chair, couch, and ottoman; draped satin and snowy lace around the windows, with rod, rings, and bracelets of white enamel. Tables with pedestals of enamel and tops of snowy marble, and paper on the walls of purest white; altogether it was a weird-looking room, and I shook with cold as I entered it.

The principal object of my curiosity was seated in a deep chair with her side toward me, and I had an opportunity of examining her leisurely, as she neither moved or took the slightest notice of my entrance; most probably she was quite unaware of it. She was the most lovely being I had ever beheld, a fair and perfect piece of statuary one might have thought, so immobile and abstracted, nay, so entirely expressionless were her beautiful features. Her dress was pure white, her hair of a pale golden hue, and her eyes dark as midnight. Her hands rested idly on her lap, her gaze seemed intent on the high white wall that shot up outside the window near her; and in the whole room there was neither book, flower, work, or one single *loose* article of ornament, nothing but the heavy, white-covered furniture, and the draping curtains. I advanced directly before her and bowed deeply, and then I calmly drew forward a chair and seated myself. As I did so she moved her eyes from the window and rested them on me, but, for all the interest they evinced, I might as well have been the white-washed wall outside. She was once more returning her eyes to the blank window, when I took her hand and laid my fingers on her blue-veined wrist. The action seemed to arouse her, for she looked keenly into my face, and then she laughed softly.

"One may guess you are a physician," she said, in a musical, low voice, and with a slightly foreign accent, that was in my opinion, a great improvement to our harsh language.

"I am," I replied, with a smile, "your uncle has sent me to see about your health, which alarms him."

"Poor man!" she said, with a shade of commiseration clouding her beautiful face, "poor uncle!" but I assure you there is nothing the matter with me; nothing but what must be the natural conse-quence of the life I am leading."

"Why do you lead one which you know to be injurious then?" I asked, still keeping my fingers on the pulse, that beat as calmly as a sleeping infant's, and was not interested by a single throb though a stranger sat beside her.

"How can I help it?" she asked, calmly meeting my inquisi-torial gaze, "do you think a sane person would choose to be imprisoned thus, and to be surrounded by the colour of death ever? Had mine not been a strong mind I would have been mad long ago."

"Mad!" I could not help ejaculating, in a puzzled tone.

"Yes, mad," she replied, "could *you* live here, month after month, in a hueless atmosphere and with nothing but *that* to look at," and she pointed her slender finger toward the white wall, "could you, I ask, and retain your reason?"

"I do not believe I could!" I answered, with sudden vehe-mence, "then again I repeat why do it?"

"And again I reply, how can I help it?"

I was silent. I was looking in the eyes of the beautiful being before me for a single trace of the madness I had been told of, but I could not find it. It was a lovely girl, pale and delicate from confinement, and with a manner that told of a weariness endured at least patiently. She was about twenty years old, perhaps, and the most perfect creature, I have already said, that I had ever beheld; and so we sat looking into each other's, eyes; what mine expressed I cannot say, but hers were purity, and sweetness itself.

"Who are you?" she asked, suddenly, "tell me something of yourself. It will be at least a change from this white solitude."

"I am a doctor, as you have guessed; and a rich and fashionable doctor," I added smilingly.

"To be either is to be also the other," she remarked, "you need not have used the repetition."

"Come," I thought to myself, "there is little appearance of lunacy in that observation."

"But you doubtless have name, what is it?"

"My name is Elveston—Doctor Elveston."

"Your christian name?"

"No, my christian name is Charles."

"Charles," she repeated dreamily.

"I think it is your turn now," I remarked, "it is but fair that you should make me acquainted with your name, since I have told you mine."

"Oh! my name is d'Alberville—Blanche d'Alberville. Perhaps it was in consequence of my christian name that my poor uncle decided upon burying me in white," she added, with a look round the cold room, "poor old man!"

"Why do you pity him so?" I asked, "he seems to me little to require it. He is strong and rich, and the uncle of Blanche," I added, with a bow; but the compliment seemed to glide off her as if it had been a liquid, and she were made of glassy marble like one of the statues that stood behind her.

"And you are a physician," she said, looking wonderingly at me, "and have been in the Duke's company, without discovering it?"

"Discovering what, my dear young lady?"

"That he is mad."

"Mad!" How often had I already ejaculated that word since I had become interested in this singular household; but this time it must assuredly have expressed the utmost astonishment, for I was never more confounded in my life; and yet a light seemed to be breaking in upon my bewilderment, and I stared in wondering silence at the calm face of the lovely maiden before me.

"Alas, yes!" she replied, sadly, to my look, "my poor uncle is a maniac, but a harmless one to all but me; it is I who suffer all."

"And why you?" I gasped.

"Because it is his mania to believe me mad," she replied, "and so he treats me."

"But in the name of justice why should you endure this?" I cried, angrily starting to my feet, "you are in a free land at least, and doors will open!"

"Calm yourself, my friend," she said, laying her white hand on my arm, and the contact, I confess, thrilled through every nerve of my system, "compose yourself, and see things as they are; what could a young, frail girl like me do out in the world alone? and I have not a living relative but my uncle. Besides, would it be charitable to desert him and leave him to his own madness thus? Poor old man!"

"You are an angel!" I ejaculated, "and I would die for you!"

The reader need not be told that my enthusiastic youth was at last beginning to make its way through the crust of worldly wisdom that had hitherto subdued it.

"It is not necessary that anyone should die for me; I can do that for myself, and no doubt shall ere long, die of the want of colour and air," she said, with a sad smile.

There is little use following our conversation to the end. I satisfied myself that there was really nothing wrong with her constitution, save the effects of the life she was obliged to lead; and I determined, instead of interfering, with her at present, to devote myself to the poor Duke, with a hope that I might be of service to him, and succeed in gaining the liberation of poor Blanche. We parted, I might almost say as lovers, although no words of affection were spoken; but I carried away her image entwined with every fibre of my heart, and in the deep sweetness of her lingering eyes I fancied I read hope and love.

The Duke was waiting impatiently in the corridor as I left the lovely girl, and he led me into another apartment to question me eagerly. What did I think of the princess's state of health? Had she shown any symptoms of uneasiness during my visit? As the old gentleman asked these questions he watched my countenance keenly; while on my part I observed him with deep interest to discover traces of his unfortunate mental derangement.

"My dear sir, I perceive nothing alarming whatever in the state of your niece; she is simply suffering from confinement and monotony of existence, and wants nothing whatever but fresh air and amusement, and exercise; in short, life."

"Alas! you know that is impossible; have I not told you that her state precludes everything of the sort?"

"You must excuse me, my friend," I said, firmly, "I have conversed for a considerable time with the Princess d'Alberville, and I am a medical man accustomed to dealing with, and the observation of lunacy, and I give you my word of honour there is no weakness whatever in the brain of this fair girl; you are simply killing her, it is my duty to tell you so, killing her under the influence of some, to me, most unaccountable whim."

The duke wrung his hands in silence, but his excited eye fell under my steady gaze. It was apparently with a strong effort that he composed himself sufficiently to speak, and when he did his words had a solemnity in their tone that ought to have made a deep impression upon me; but it did not, for the sweetness of the imprisoned Blanche's voice was still lingering in my ears.

"You are a young man, Doctor Elveston; it is one of the happy provisions of youth, no doubt, to be convinced of its own infallibility. But you must believe that one of my race does not lie, and I swear to you that my niece is the victim of a most fearful insanity, which but to name makes humanity shudder with horror."

"I do not doubt that you believe such to be the case, my dear sir," I said, soothingly, for I fancied I saw the fearful light of insanity in his glaring eye at that moment, "but to my vision everything seems different."

"Well, my young friend, do not decide yet too hastily. Visit us again, but God in mercy grant that you may never see the reality as I have seen it!"

"And so I did repeat my visits, and repeat them so often and that without changing my opinion, that the Duke, in spite of his mania, began to see that they were no longer necessary. One day on my leaving Blanche he requested a few moments of my time, and drawing me into his study, locked the door. I began to be a little alarmed, and more particularly as he seemed to be in a state of great agitation; but as it appeared, my alarm of personal violence was entirely without foundation.

He placed a chair for me, and I seated myself with all the calmness I could muster, while I kept my eyes firmly fixed upon his as he addressed me.

"My dear young friend; I hope it is unnecessary for me to say that these are no idle words, for I have truly conceived an ardent appreciation of your character; yet it is absolutely necessary that I should put a stop to your visits to my niece. Good Heavens, what could I say—how could I over forgive myself if any—any—"

"I beg of you to go no farther, Duke," I said, interrupting him. "You have only by a short time anticipated what I was about to communicate myself. If your words allude to an attachment between Blanche and myself, your care is now too late. We love each other, and intend, subject to your approval, to he united immediately."

Had a sudden clap of thunder reverberated in the quiet room the poor man could not have been more affected. He started to his feet and glared into my eyes with terror.

"Married!" he gasped, "Married! Blanche d'Alberville wedded! Oh God!" and then he fell back into his chair as powerless as a child.

"And why should this alarm you?" I asked. "She is youthful and lovely, and as sane, I believe in my soul, as I am myself. I am rich, and of a family which may aspire to mate with the best. You are her only relative and guardian, and you say that you esteem me; whence then this great distaste to hear even a mention of your fair ward's marriage?"

"She is not my ward!" he cried, hoarsely, and it seemed to me angrily, "her father and mother are both in existence, and destroyed for all time by the horror she has brought around them! But, my God, what is the use of speaking—I talk to a madman!" and he turned to his desk and began to write rapidly.

There I sat in bewilderment. I had not now the slightest doubt but that my poor friend was the victim of monomania; his one idea was uppermost, and that idea was that his unfortunate niece was mad. I was fully determined now to carry her away and make her my wife at once, so as to relieve the poor girl from all imprisonment, to which there seemed no other prospect of an end. And my hopes went still farther; who could tell but that the sight of Blanche living and enjoying life as did others of her sex, might have a beneficial effect upon the poor Duke's brain, and help to eradicate his fixed idea.

As I was thus cogitating, the old gentleman rose from his desk, and handed me a letter addressed, but unsealed. His manner was now almost unearthly calm, as if he had come to some great determination, to which he had only been driven by the most dreadful necessity.

"My words are wasted, Charles," he said, "and I cannot tell the truth; but if you ever prized home and name, friends and family, mother or wife, send that letter to its address after you have perused it, and await its reply."

I took the letter and put it into my pocket, and then I took his hand and pressed it warmly. I was truly sorry for the poor old gentleman, who suffered, no doubt, as much from his fancied trouble as if it were the most terrible of realities.

"I hope you will forgive me for grieving you, my dear sir; believe me it pains me much to see you thus. I will do as you wish about the letter. But oh, how I wish you could see Blanche with my eyes! To me she is the most perfect of women!"

"You have *never* seen her yet!"—he responded, bitterly, "could you—*dare* you only once witness but a part of her actions under one influence, you would shudder to your very marrow!"

"To what influence do you allude, dear sir?"

"To that of colour—one colour."

"And what colour? have you any objection to name it?"

"It is red!" and as the duke answered he turned away abruptly, and left me standing bewildered, but still unbelieving.

I hastened home that day, anxious to peruse the letter given me by the duke, and as soon as I had reached my own study drew it from my pocket and spread it before me. It was addressed to the Prince d'Alberville, Chateau Gris, Melun, France; and the following were its singular contents :-

DEAR BROTHER.-A terrible necessity for letting another into our fearful secret has arisen. A young gentleman of birth and fortune has, in spite of my assurances that she is insane, determined to wed Blanche. Such a sacrifice cannot be permitted, even were such a thing not morally impossible. You are her parent, it is then your place to inform this unhappy young man of the unspoken curse that rests on our wretched name. I enclose his address. Write to him at once.

Your afflicted brother,<br>"DE ROHAN"

I folded up this strange epistle and despatched it; and then I devoted nearly an hour to pondering over the strange contradictions of human nature and more particularly diseased human nature. Of course I carried the key to this poor man's strangeness in my firm conviction of his insanity, and my entire belief in the martyrdom of Blanche; yet I could not divest myself of all anxiety to receive it reply to this letter, a reply which I was certain would explain the Duke's lunacy, and beg of me to pardon it. That is to say if such a party as the Prince d'Alberville existed at all, and I did not quite lose sight of the fact that Blanche had assured me that, with the exception of her uncle, she had not a living relative.

It seemed a long week to me ere the French reply, that made my hand tremble as I received it, was put into it. I had abstained from visiting my beloved Blanche, under a determination that I would not do so until armed with such a letter as I anticipated receiving; or until I should be able to say, "ample time for a reply to your communication has elapsed; none has come, give me then my betrothed." Here then at last was the letter, and I shut myself into my own room and opened it; the words are engraven on my memory and will never become less vivid.

"Sir,—you wish to wed my daughter, the Princess Blanche d'Alberville. Words would vainly try to express the pain with which I expose our—our horrible secret—to a stranger, but it is to save you from a fate worse than death. Blanche d'Alberville is an *anthropophagus*, already has one of her own family fallen victim to her thirst for human blood. Spare us if you can, and pray for us.

"D'ALBERVILLE"

I sat like one turned to stone, and stared at the fearful paper! An anthropophagus! A cannibal! Good heavens, the subject was just now engaging the attention of the medical world in a remarkable degree, in consequence of two frightful and well authenticated cases that had lately occurred in France! All the particulars of these cases, in which I had taken a deep interest, flashed before me, but not for one moment did I credit the frightful story of my beloved. Some detestable plot had been formed against her, for what vile purpose, or with what end in view I was ignorant; and I cast the whole subject from my mind with an effort, and went to attend to my daily round of duties. During the two or three hours that followed, and under the influence of the human suffering I had witnessed, a revolution took place in my feelings, God only known by what means induced; but when I returned home, to prepare for my eventful visit to the "white house," a dreadful doubt had stolen into my heart, and filled it with a fearful determination.

Having ordered my carriage and prepared the white suit, which I was now possessor of, I went directly to the conservatory, and looked around among the brilliant array of blossoms for the most suitable to my purpose. I chose the flaring scarlet verbena to form my bouquet; a tasteless one it is true, but one decidedly distinctive in colour. I collected quite a large nosegay of this flower, without a single spray of green to relieve its bright hue. Then I went to my carriage, and gave directions to be driven to Kensington.

At the gate of the Duke's residence I dressed myself in the white suit mechanically, and followed the usual servant into the house, carefully holding my flowers, which I had enveloped in newspaper. I was received as usual, also by the Duke, and in a few seconds we stood, face to face in his study. In answer to his look of fearful inquiry I handed him my French epistle, and stood silently by as he read it tremblingly.

"Well, are you satisfied now?" he asked, looking me pitifully in the face, "has this dreadful exposure convinced you?"

"No!" I answered, recklessly, "I am neither satisfied nor convinced of anything save that you are either a lunatic yourself, or in collusion with the writer of that abominable letter!" and as I spoke I uncovered my scarlet bouquet and shook out its blossoms. The sight of it made a terrible impression upon my companion; his knees trembled as if he were about to fall, and his face grew whiter than his garments.

"In the name of heaven what are you going to do?" he gasped.

"I am simply going to present my bride with a bouquet," I said, and as I said so I laughed, an empty, hollow laugh. I cannot describe my strange state of mind at that moment; I felt as if myself under the influence of some terrible mania.

"By all you hold sacred, Charles Elveston, I charge you to desist! Who or what are *you* that you should set your youth, and ignorance of this woman against my age and bitter experience?"

"Ha ha!" was my only response, as I made toward the door.

"By heavens, he is mad!" cried the excited nobleman, "young man, I tell you that you carry in your hand a colour which had better be shaken in the eyes of a mad bull than be placed in sight of my miserable niece! Fool! I tell you it will arouse in her an unquenchable thirst for blood, and the blood may be yours!"

"Let it!" I cried, and passed on my way to Blanche.

I was conscious of the Duke's cries to the servants as I hurried up the broad staircase, and guessed that they were about to follow me; but to describe my feelings is utterly impossible.

I was beginning now to believe that my betrothed was something terrible, and I faced her desperately, as one who had lost everything worth living for, or placed his last stake upon the cast of a die.

I opened the well-known door of the white room, that seemed to me colder, and more death-like than ever; and I saw the figure of Blanche seated in her old way, and in her old seat, looking out of the window. I did not wait to scan her appearance just then, however, for I caught a glimpse of myself in a large mirror opposite, and was fascinated, as it were by the strange sight.

The mirror reflected, in unbroken stillness, the cold whiteness of the large apartment, but it also reflected my face and form, wearing an expression that half awoke me to a consciousness of physical indisposition. There was a wild look in my pallid countenance, and a reckless air in my figure which the very garments seemed to have imbibed, and which was strangely unlike my usual calm propriety of demeanour. My coat seemed awry; the collar of my shirt was unbuttoned, and I had even neglected to put on my neck-tie; but it was upon the blood-red bouquet that my momentary gaze became riveted.

It was such a contrast; the cold, pure white of all the surroundings, and that circled patch of blood-colour that I held in my hand was so suggestive! "Of what?" I asked myself, "am I really mad?" and then I laughed loudly and turned towards Blanche.

Possibly the noise of the opening door had attracted her, for when I turned she was standing on her feet, directly confronting me. Her eyes were distended with astonishment at my peculiar examination of myself in the mirror, no doubt, but they flashed into madness at the sight of the flowers as I turned. Her face grew scarlet, her hands clenched, and her regards *devoured* the scarlet bouquet, as I madly held it towards her. At this moment my eye caught a side glimpse of half-a-dozen terrified faces peeping in the doorway, and conspicuous and foremost that of the poor terrified Duke; but my fate must he accomplished, and I still held the bouquet tauntingly toward the transfixed girl. She gave one wild look into my face, and recognised the sarcasm which I *felt* in my eyes, and then she snatched the flowers from my hand, and scattered them in a thousand pieces at her feet.

How well I remember that picture today. The white room—the torn and brilliant flowers—and the mad fury of that lovely being. A laugh echoed again upon my lips, an involuntary laugh it was, for I knew not that I had laughed; and then there was a rush, and white teeth were at my throat, tearing flesh, and sinews, and veins; and a horrible sound was in my ears, as if some wild animal was tearing at my body! I dreamt that I was in a jungle of Africa, and that a tiger, with a tawny coat, was devouring my still living flesh, and then I became insensible!

When I opened my eyes faintly, I lay in my own bed, and the form of the Duke was bending over me. One of my medical *confreres* held my wrist between his fingers, and the room was still and dark.

"How is this, Bernard?" I asked, with difficulty, for my voice seemed lost, and the weakness of death hanging around my tongue, "what has happened?"

"Hush!" my dear fellow, you must not speak. You have been nearly worried to death by a maniac, and you have lost a fearful quantity of blood."

"Oh!" I recollected it all, and turned to the Duke, "and Blanche?"

"She is dead, thank God!" he whispered, calmly.

I shuddered through every nerve and was silent.

It was many long weeks ere I was able to listen to the Duke as he told the fearful tale of the dead girl's disease. The first intimation her wretched relatives had of the horrible thing was upon the morning of her eighteenth year. They went to her room to congratulate her, and found her lying upon the dead body of her younger sister, who occupied the same chamber; she had literally torn her throat with her teeth, and was sucking the hot blood as she was discovered. No words could describe the horror of the wretched parents. The end we have seen.

I never asked how Blanche had died, I did not wish to know; but I guessed that force had been obliged to be used in dragging her teeth from my throat, and that the necessary force was sufficient to destroy her. I have never since met with a case of anthropophagy, but I never even read of the rare discovery of the fearful disease, but I fancy I feel Blanche's teeth at my throat.

# G. J. Whyte-Melville: Madame de St. Croix (1869)

George John Whyte-Melville (1821-1878) was a Scottish novelist who was born at Mount Melville, near St. Andrews. He was educated at Eton and became a Captain in the Coldstream Guards. After retiring from the army, he published his first novel in 1853. Like most of his subsequent works, *Digby Grand* was a historical romance that revolved around fox-hunting.

*Bones and I; or, the Skeleton at Home* is an anomaly. This episodic novel is narrated by a recluse who lives in the heart of London, but whose only companion is a skeleton. Their "conversations" range from amusing adventures to reflections on religion and philosophy.

The fourth part of *Bones and I* revolves around a mysterious Hungarian woman who calls herself "Madame de St. Croix." This segment, which Whyte-Melville titled "A Vampire," is excerpted here for the first time in more than a century.

———

Leaning idly against the chimney-piece the other night, contemplating my companion in his usual attitude, my elbow happened to brush off the slab a Turkish coin of small value and utterly illegible inscription. How strangely things come back to one! I fancied myself once more on the yellow wave of the broad Danube; once more threading those interminable green hills that fringe its banks; once more wondering whether the forest of Delgrade had been vouchsafed to Eastern Europe as a type of Infinity, while its massive fortress, with frowning rampart and lethargic Turkish sentries, was intended to represent the combination of courage and sloth, of recklessness and imperturbability, of apparent strength and real inefficiency, which distinguishes most arrangements of the Ottoman Empire.

"Bakaloum" and "Bismillah!" "Take your chance!" and "Don't care a d—n," seem to be the watchwords of this improvident Government. It lets the ship steer herself; and she makes, I believe, as bad weather of it as might be expected under such seamanship.

Engrossed far less, I admit, with political considerations than with the picturesque appearance of a Servian population attending their market, I rather startled my friend with the abruptness of the following question:

"Do you believe there is such a thing as a Vampire?"

He rattled a little and almost rose to his feet, but re-seating himself, only rejoined,

"Why do you ask?"

"I was thinking," I replied, "of that romantic-looking peasantry I used to see thronging the market-place of Belgrade. Of those tall, handsome men, with the scowl never off their brows, their hands never straying far from the bellyful of weapons they carried in their shawls. Of those swarthy wild-eyed women, with their shrill, rapid voices, their graceful, impatient gestures, carrying each of them the available capital of herself and family strung in coins about her raven hair, while on every tenth face at least, of both sexes, could not fail to be observed the wan traces of that wasting disease which seems to sap strength and vitality, gradually, and almost surely, as consumption itself. Yes, I think for every score of peasants I could have counted two of these 'fever-faces,' as the people themselves call their ague-ridden companions, though I ascertained after a while, when I came to know them better, that they attributed this decimation of their numbers, and faded appearance of the victims, rather to supernatural visitation than epidemic disease. They believe that in certain cases, where life has been unusually irregular, or the rites of religion reprehensibly neglected, the soul returns after death to its original tenement, and the corpse becomes revivified under certain ghastly conditions of a periodical return to the tomb and a continual warfare against its kind. An intermittent existence is only to be preserved at the expense of others, for the compact, while it permits reanimation, withholds the blood, 'which is the life thereof.' The stream must therefore be drained from friends, neighbours, early companions, nay, is most nourishing and efficacious when abstracted from the veins of those heretofore best beloved. So the Vampire, as this weird being is called, must steal from its grave in the dead of night, to sit by some familiar bedside till the sleeper shall be steeped in the unconsciousness of complete repose, and then puncturing a minute orifice in the throat, will suck its fill till driven back to its resting-place by the crimson streaks of day. Night after night the visits must be repeated; and so, week by week, the victim pines and droops and withers gradually away. There is no apparent illness, no ostensible injury, but the frame dwindles, the muscles fall, the limbs fail, the cheek fades, and the death-look, never to be mistaken, comes into the great haggard, hollow, wistful eyes. I have repeatedly asked the peasants whether they had ever met any of these supernatural visitants, for they spoke of them so confidently, one might have supposed the famished ghouls were flitting about villages nightly; but though presumptive evidence was forthcoming in volumes, I was never fortunate enough to find an actual eyewitness. The sister of one had been frightened by them repeatedly; the cousin of another he had himself carried to her tomb, drained of her last life-drops by a relative buried some weeks before; and the grandmother of a third had not only met and talked with this inconvenient connection, expostulating with it on its depraved appetites, and generally arguing the point on moral as well as sanitary grounds, but hand induced it by her persuasions, and the power of a certain amulet she wore, to abstain from persecuting a damsel in the neighbouring village for the same ghastly purpose, or, at least, to put off its visits till the horrid craving should be no longer endurable. Still I could meet nobody who had actually seen one in person; and that is why I asked you just now if you believed there was such a thing as a Vampire?"

He nodded gravely. "They are rare," said he; "but I believe in such beings, because I have not only seen one, but had the advantage of its personal notice, and a very pretty, pleasing acquaintance it was! You would like to know something more? Well, it compromises nobody. You will not quote me, of course. Indeed I don't see how you can, for I still mention no real names. I don't mind telling you the story of a life, such as I knew it; a life that by some fatality seemed to drag down every other that came within the sphere of its attractions to sorrow, humiliation, and disgrace. I have no brain to swim, no pulses to leap, no heart to ache left, and yet the memory stirs me painfully even now.

"In early manhood," he continued, bending down, as though to scan his own fleshless proportions, with an air of consciousness that was almost grotesque, "I paid as much heed to my personal appearance, and flourished it about it public places as persistently as others of like age and pursuits. Whether I should do so if I had my time to come again, is a different question, but we will let that pass. Being then young, tolerably good-looking, sufficiently conceited, and exceedingly well-dressed, I had betaken myself one evening to your Italian Opera, the best, and I may add the dearest, in Europe. I was fond of music and knew something about it, but I was fonder still of pretty women, though concerning these I enjoyed my full share of that ignorance which causes men so to exaggerated their qualities both good and bad; an ignorance it is worth while to preserve with as much care as in other matters we take to acquire knowledge, for there is no denying, alas! that those who know them best always seem to respect them least.

"I rose, therefore, from my stall at the first opportunity and turned round to survey the house. Ere I had inspected a quarter of it, my glasses were up, and I will tell you what they showed me—the most perfect face I ever saw. Straight nose, thin and delicately cut, large black eyes, regular eyebrows, faultless chin, terminating a complete oval, the whole set in a frame of jet-black hair. Even my next neighbour, who, from an observation he let fall to a friend, belonged apparently to the Household Troops, could not refrain from ejaculating, 'By Jove, she's a ripper!' the moment he caught sight of the object on which my gaze was fixed.

"I saw something else too. I saw that the lady by her side was a foreigner with whom I had long been acquainted; so edging my way into the passages, in two minutes I was tapping at their box-door like a man who felt pretty sure of being let in.

"The foreigner introduced me to her friend, and as the second act of the opera was already in progress, told me to sit down and hold my tongue. We were four in the box. Another gentleman was placed close behind the lady who first attracted my attention. I had only eyes just then, however, for the wild, unearthly beauty of my new acquaintance.

"I had seen hundreds of pretty women, and even in youth my heart, from temperament, perhaps, rather than reflection, was as hard as my ribs; but this face fascinated me—I can use no other word. My sensations were so strangely compounded of admiration, horror, interest, curiosity, attraction, and dislike. The eyes were deep and dark, yet with the glitter in them of a hawk's, the cheek deadly pale, the lips bright red. She was different from anything I had ever seen, and yet so wonderfully beautiful! I longed to hear her speak. Presently she whispered a few words to the man behind her, and I felt my flesh creep. Low as they were modulated, there was in every syllable a tone of such utter hope-lessness, such abiding sorrow, regret, even remorse, always present, always kept down, that I could have imagined her one of those lost spirits for whom is fixed the punishment of all most cruel, most intolerable, that they can never forget they are formed for better things. Her gestures, too, were in accordance with the sad, suggestive music of her voice—quiet, graceful, and somewhat listless in the repose, as it seemed, rather of unhappiness than of indolence. I tell you I was not susceptible; I don't think boys generally are. In love, more than in any other extravagance, 'there is no fool like an old one.'

"I was as little given to romance as a ladies' doctor; and yet, sitting in that box watching the turn of her beautiful head as she looked towards the stage, I said to myself, 'I'll take good care she never gets the upper hand of *me*. If a man once allowed himself to like her at all, she is just the sort of woman who would blight his whole life for him, and hunt the poor devil down to his grave!' Somebody else seemed to have no such misgivings, or to have arrived at a stage of infatuation when all personal considerations had gone by the board. If ever I saw a calf led to the slaughter it was Count V—, a calf, too, whose throat few women could have cut without compunction. Handsome, manly, rich, affectionate, and sincere, worshipping his deity with all the reckless devotion, all the unscrupulous generosity of his brave Hungarian heart, I saw his very lip quiver under its heavy moustache when she turned her glittering eyes on him with some allusion called up by the business of the stage, and the proud, manly face that had never quailed before an enemy grew white in the intensity of its emotion. What made me think of a stag I once found lying dead in a Styrian pass, and a golden eagle feasting on him with her talons buried in his heart?

"The Gräfinn, to whom the box belonged, noticed my abstraction. 'Don't fall in love with her,' she whispered; 'I can't spare you just yet. Isn't she beautiful?'

"'You introduced me,' was my answer, 'but you never told me her name.'

"'How stupid!' said the Gräfinn. 'At present she is a Madame *de* St. Croix, an Englishwoman, nevertheless, and a widow, but not likely to remain so long.' And with a mischievous laugh she gave me her hand as I left the box, bowing to Madame *de* St. Croix and also to the Hungarian, who in his happy pre-occupation was perfectly unconscious of my politeness.

"I saw them again in the crush-room. The Gräfinn had picked up an *attaché* to some legation, who put her dutifully into her carriage. The Hungarian was still completely engrossed with Madame *de* St. Croix. I had not yet forgotten the look on his handsome face when she drove off with her friend. 'He's a fool,' I said to myself; 'and yet a woman might well be proud to make a fool of such a man as that.'

"I left London in the middle of the season and thought no more of Madame *de* St. Croix. I had seen a pretty picture, I had heard a strain of sweet music, I had turned over the page of an amusing romance—there was an end of it.

"Thy following winter I happened to spend in Vienna. Of course I went to one of the masked balls of *The Redouten-Saal*. I had not been ten minutes in the room when my ears thrilled to the low, seductive accents of that well-remembered voice. There she was again, masked, of course, but it was impossible to mistake the slim, pliant figure, the graceful gestures, the turn of the beautiful head, and the quiet energy that betrayed itself, even in the small, gloved hand. She was talking to a well-known Russian magnate less remarkable for purity of morals than diplomatic celebrity, boundless extravagance, and devotion to the other sex. To be on terms of common friendship with such a man was at least compromising to any lady under sixty years of age; and it is needless to say that his society was courted and appreciated accordingly.

"Madame *de* St. Croix seemed well satisfied with her neighbour; and though in her outward manner the least demonstrative of women, I could detect through her mask the same cruel glitter in her dark eyes that had so fascinated me, six months before, in the Gräfinn's opera-box. The Russian talked volubly, and she leaned towards him, as those do who are willing to hear more. *Château qui parle* furls its banner, *femme qui écoute* droops her head. Directly opposite, looking very tall and fierce as he reared himself against the doorway, stood Count V—. The Hungarian was pale as death. On his face, so worn and haggard, so cruelly altered since I saw it last, was set the stamp of physical pain, and he gnawed the corner of his brown moustache with that tension of the muscles about the mouth which denotes a paroxysm bravely kept down. As friends accosted him in passing, he bowed his head kindly and courteously while his whole face softened, but it was sad to see how soon the gleam passed away and the cloud came back, darker and heavier than before. The man's heart, you see, was generous, kindly, and full of trust—such a heart as women like Madame *de* St. Croix find it an interesting amusement to break.

"I think he must have made her some kind of appeal; for later in the evening I observed them together, and he was talking earnestly in German, with a low pleading murmur, to which I thought few women could have listened unmoved. She answered in French; and I was sorry for him when she broke up the colloquy with a little scornful shrug of her shoulders, observing in a hard, unfeeling tone not like her usual voice, 'Que voulez-vous? Enfin, c'est plus fort que moi!'

"The Russian put her into her sledge, for there was a foot of snow in the streets, and Count V— walked home through it, with a smile on his face and his head up, looking strangely elated, I thought, for a man, the last strand of whose moorings had lately parted and left him adrift.

"I had not then learned there is no temporary stimulant so powerful as despair, no tonic so reviving as a *parti pris*.

"Next day, lounging into the *Chancellerie* of the Embassy for my usual gossip, I found little Hughes, an unpaid *attaché* (who earned, indeed, just as much as he received), holding forth with considerable spirit and energy.

"'Curse him!' said this indomitable young Briton. 'If it had been swords, I should like to have fought him myself. I hate him! I tell you. Everybody hates him. And V— was the best chap between here and Orsova. He was almost like an Englishman. Wouldn't he just have polished him off if they'd had swords. That old muff, Bergheimer of the Cuirassiers, ought to hanged. Do you think, if *I'd* been his second, I'd have put him up with pistols against the best shot in Europe?—and at the barrier too! It's not like at home, you know. I never knew such a mull as they made of it amongst them. This cursed Calmuck gets the pull all through, and poor V—, who had lost his fortune already, loses his lady-love and his life. What a rum world it is!'

"Here the orator rolled and lit a cigarette, thus affording me a moment to inquire into the cause of his indignation. I then learned that, in consequence of a trifling dispute after last night's ball, a duel had been fought at daybreak, in the snow, between Count V— and a Russian nobleman, in which the former was shot through the heart.

"'Never got *one* in at all!' said Hughes, again waxing eloquent on his friend's wrongs. 'I've seen both the seconds since. They were to walk up to a handkerchief, and the Russian potted him at forty yards the first step he made. They may say what they like about the row originating in politics—I know better. They quarreled because Madame *de* St. Croix had left V— and taken up with this snub-nosed Tartar. First, she ruined my poor friend. I know all about it. He hadn't a rap left; for if she'd asked him for the shirt off his back, he'd have stripped like beans! Then she broke his heart—the cheeriest, jolliest, kindest fellow in Europe—to finish up by leaving him for another man, who kills him before breakfast without a scruple; and if the devil don't get hold of *her* some fine day, why he's a disgrace to his appointment, that's all! and they ought to make him Secretary of Legation here, or pension him off somewhere and put him out of the way! Have another cigarette!'

"Ten years afterwards I was sitting in the gardens of the Tuileries, one fine morning towards the middle of May, wondering, as English people always do wonder, on a variety of subjects—why the cigars were so bad in Paris, and the air so exhilarating—why the tender green leaves quivering over those deep alleys should have a sunshine of their own besides that which they reflected from above—why the *bonnes* and nursery-maids wore clean caps every day—why the railings always looked as if they had been re-gilt the same morning, and why the sentry at the gate should think it part of his duty to leer at every woman who passed, like a satyr?

"Indeed I believe I was almost asleep, when I started in my chair, and rubbed my eyes to make sure it was not a dream. There, within ten paces of me, sat Madame *de* St. Croix, if I was still to call her so, apparently not an hour older than the first time we met. The face was even paler, the lips redder, the cruel eyes deeper and darker, but in that flickering light the woman looked more beautiful than ever. She was listening quietly and indolently, as of old, to a gentleman who sat with his back to me, telling his own story, whatever it might be, in a low, earnest, impressive voice. I raised my hat when I caught her eye, and she bowed in return politely enough, but obviously without recognition. The movement caused her companion to turn around, and in two strides he was by my chair, grasping me cordially by the hand. He was an old and intimate friend, a colonel in the French army, by whose side I had experienced more than one strange adventure, both in Eastern Europe and Asia-Minor—a man who had served with distinction, of middle age, a widower, fond of society, field-sports, speculation, and traveling; essentially *bon camarade*, but thoroughly French in his reflections and opinions. The last man in the world, I should have thought, to be made a fool of by a woman. Well, there he was, her bounden slave! Absurdly happy if she smiled, miserable when she frowned, ready to fetch and carry like a poodle, perfectly childish about her, and utterly contemptible. If she had really cared for him, the temptation must have been irresistible, and she would have bullied him frightfully. But no, there was always the same repose of manner, the same careless kindness, the same melancholy, the same consciousness of an unquestionable superiority. One of his reasons, he soon confided to me, for being so fond of her was, that they never had an angry word! For a week or two I saw a good deal of them. Paris was already empty, and we did our plays, our Opéra Comique, and our little dinners pleasantly enough. She was always the same, and I found myself, day by day, becoming more conscious of that nameless charm about her, which I should despair of being able to describe. Yet as often as I met the glance of those deep, dark, unearthly eyes, a shudder crept over me, such as chills you when you come face to face with a ghost in your dreams. The colonel, I have said, was devoted to her. He was rarely absent from her side, but if by chance alone with me, would talk of her by the hour.

"He had found, he declared, fortunately before he was too old to appreciate it, the one inestimable treasure the earth contained. He had cherished his fancies, committed his follies, of course, *tout comme un autre*, but he had never experienced anything like this. It was his haven, his anchorage, his resting-place, and he might glide down into old age, and on to death, perfectly happy, because confident, that her heart and her force of character, she would never change. Oh no! She was so frank, so confiding, so sincere. She, too, *passé par lá*, had told him so; unlike other women, had confessed to him not only her last, but her former attachments. He knew all about poor V—, who was shot in a duel, and the Russian general, banished to Siberia. How fortunate she had broken with him before his disgrace, because, in the loyalty of her nature, she would surely have followed him into exile, although she never cared for him in her heart, never! No, nor for any of the others; never had been fairly touched till now. Him, the colonel, she really *did* love. He had proved his devotion so thoroughly (I found out afterwards, though not from him, that my friend had been fool enough to sacrifice both fortune and profession for her sake), he was so reliable, she said, so kind, and so *good*. In short, he was perfectly happy, and could see no cloud in his horizon, look which way he would.

"Six months afterwards 'Galignani' informed me that my friend the colonel had been reinstated in the French army and appointed to a regiment of Chasseurs d'Afrique then serving in Algeria, where, before the Tuileries Gardiens were again green, I learned from the same source he had already solved the great problem in an affair of outposts with the Khabyles. Long years elapsed, and there were streaks of grey in my hair and whiskers ere I saw Madame *de* St. Croix again. I had heard of her, indeed, at intervals both in London and Paris. I am bound to say her name was always coupled with those who were distinguished by birth, talent, or success. She was very choice, I believe, in the selection of her victims, despising equally an easy conquest and one of which the ravages could be readily repaired. The women hated her, the men said she was charming. For my part I kept out of her way: we were destined to meet, nevertheless. I had embarked in a Peninsular and Oriental steamer at Marseilles very much indisposed, and retiring at once to my berth never quitted it till we were entering the Straits of Buoni-faccio. Here I came on deck, weak, exhausted, but convalescent, drinking in the sunshine and the scenery with that thirst for the beautiful which becomes so fierce after the confinement of recent illness. I literally reveled in the Mediterranean air, and basked in the warmth of those bright colours so peculiar to the shores of that summer sea. I was approaching middle age; I had ventured body and mind freely enough in the great conflict; and yet, I thank heaven, had hitherto been spared the crushing sorrow that makes a mockery of the noblest and purest enjoyments of earth, causing a man to turn from all that is fairest in sight and sense and sound with the sickness of a dead hope curdling at his heart. But then I had kept clear of Madame *de* St. Croix.

"When my eyes were at last sated with the gaudy hues of the coast and the golden glitter of the water, I was a little surprised to see that lady sitting within three paces of me reading a yellow-bound French novel. Great heaven! what was the woman's secret? She looked younger than ever! Even in the searching glare of a southern noon not a line could be detected on the pure, pale forehead, not a crease about the large, wistful, glittering eyes. That she was gifted with perennial youth I could see for myself; that she was dangerous even to the peace of a grey-haired man, I might have found out to my cost had our voyage been retarded by contrary winds or any such unavoidable delay, for she was good enough to recognise me on this occasion, and to give me a large share of her conversation and companionship. Thus it was I learned to own the spell under which so many had succumbed, to appreciate its power, not to understand, far less describe, its nature. Fortunately for me, ere its work could be completed, we arrived at Athens, and at Athens lay a trim, rakish-looking English yacht, with her ensign flying and her foretopsail loosened, waiting only the steamer's arrival to spread her wings and bear off this seductive sorceress to some garden of paradise in the Egean Sea.

"The owner of the yacht I had often heard of. He was a man remarkable for his enterprise and unfailing success in commerce as for his liberality, and indeed extravagance, in expenditure. He chose to have houses, pictures, horses, plate, everything of the best, was justly popular in society, and enormously rich.

"I never asked and never knew the port to which that yacht was bound. When we steamed out of the harbour she was already hull-down in the wake of a crimson sunset that seemed to stain the waters with a broad track of blood; but I saw her sold within eighteen months at Southampton, for her late owner's name had appeared in the 'Gazette,' and the man himself, I was told, might be found, looking very old and careworn, setting cabbages at Hanwell, watching eagerly for the arrival of a lady who never came.

"You may believe I thought more than once of the woman whose strange destiny it had been thus to enslave generation after generation of fools, and to love whom seemed as fatal as to be a priest of Aricia or a favourite of Catharine II. Nevertheless, while time wore on, I gradually ceased to think of her beauty, her heartlessness, her mysterious youth, or her magic influence over mankind. Presently, amongst a thousand engrossing occupations and interests, I forgot her as if she had never been.

"I have driven a good many vehicles in my time, drags, phae-tons, dogcarts, down to basket-carriage drawn by a piebald pony with a hog-mane. Nay, I once steered a hansom cab up Bond Street in the early morning, frightened with more subalterns that I should like to specify of her Majesty's Household Troops, but I never thought I should come to a bath chair!

"Nevertheless I found myself at last an inside passenger of some of these locomotive coaches, enjoying the quiet and the air of the gardens at Hampton Court in complete and uninter-rupted solitude. The man who dragged me to this pleasant spot having gone to 'get his dinner,' as he called it, and the nurs-ery-maids, with their interesting charges, having retired from their morning, and not yet emerged for their afternoon stroll, I lay back, and thought of so many things—of the strength and manhood that had departed from me for ever; of the strange, dull calm that comes on with the evening of life, and contents us so well we would not have its morning back if we could; of *the gradual clairvoyance* that shows us everything in its true colours and at its real value; of the days, and months, and years so cruelly wasted, but that their pleasures, their excitements, their sins, their sorrows, and their sufferings, were indispensable for the great lesson which teaches us *to see*. Of these things I thought, and through them still, as at all times, moved the pale presence of an unforgotten face, passing like a spirit, dim and distant, yet dear as ever, across the gulf of years—a presence that, for good or evil, was to haunt me to the end.

"Something in the association of ideas reminded me of Madame *de* St. Croix, and I said to myself, 'At last age must have overtaken that marvelous beauty, and time brought the indomitable spirit to remorse, repentance, perhaps even amendment. What can have made me think of her in a quiet, peaceful scene like this?'

"Just then a lady and gentleman crossed the gravel walk in front of me, and took their places on a seat under an old tree not a dozen yards off. It was a lovely day in early autumn; the flowers were still ablaze with the gaudiest of their summer beauty, the sky was all dappled grey and gold, earth had put on the richest dress she wears throughout the year; but here and there a leaf fell noiseless on the sward, as if to testify that she too must shed all her glories in due season, and yield, like other beauties, her unwilling tribute to decay.

"But there was nothing of autumn in the pair who not sat opposite my couch, chatting, laughing, flirting, apparently either ignoring or disregarding my proximity. The man was in all the bloom and beauty of youth; the woman, though looking a few years older, did not yet seem to have attained her prime. I could scarcely believe my eyes! Yes, if ever I beheld Madame *de* St. Croix, there she sat with her fatal gaze turned on this infatuated boy, leading him gradually, steadily, surely, to the edge of that chasm into which those who plunged came to the surface nevermore. It was the old story over again. How well I remembered, ever after such an interval, the tender droop of the head, the veiling eyelashes, the glance so quickly averted, yet, like a snapshot, telling with such deadly effect; the mournful smile, the gentle whisper, the quiet confiding gesture of the slender hand, all the by-play of the most accomplished and most unscrupulous of actresses. There was no more chance of escape for her companion that for a fisherman of the North Sea, whose skiff had been sucked in the Maëlstrohm, with mast unshipped and oars adrift half a mile astern. By sight, if not personally, I then knew most of the notabilities of the day. The boy, for such I might well call him in comparisons with myself, seemed too good for his fate, and yet I saw well enough it was inevitable. He had already made himself a name as a poet of no mean pretensions, and held besides the character of a high-spirited, agreeable, and unaffected member of society. Add to this, that he was manly, good-looking, and well-born; nothing more seemed wanting to render him a fit victim for the altar at which he was to be offered up. Like his predecessors, he was fascinated. The snake held him in her eyes. The poor bird's wings were fluttering, its volition was gone, its doom sealed. Could nothing save it from the destroyer? I longed to have back, if only for a day, the powers which I had regretted so little half-an-hour ago. Weak, helpless, weary, and worn-out, I yet determined to make an effort, and save him if I could.

"They rose to go, but found the gate locked through which they had intended to pass. She had a way of affecting a pretty wilfulness in trifles, and sent him to fetch the key. Prompt to obey her lightest wish, he bounded off in search of it, and following slowly, she passed within two paces of my chair, bending on its helpless invalid a look that seemed to express far less pity for his condition than a grudging envy of his lot. I stopped her with a gesture that in one more able-bodied would have been a bow, and, strange to say, she recognised me at once. There was not a moment to lose. I took courage from a certain wistful look that gave softness to her eyes, and I spoke out.

"'We shall never meet again,' I said; 'we have crossed each other's paths at such long intervals, and on such strange occasions, but I know this is the last of them! Why time stands still for *you* is a secret I cannot fathom, but the end must come some day, put if off however long you will. Do you not think that when you become as I am, a weary mortal, stumbling with half-shut eyes on the edge of an open grave, it would be well to have one good deed on which you could look back, to have reprieved one out of the many victims on whom you have inflicted mortal punishment for the offence of loving you so much better than you deserve? Far as it stretches behind you, every footstep in your track is marked with sorrow—more than one with blood. Show mercy now, as you may have to ask it hereafter. Life is all before this one, and it seems cruel thus to blast the sapling from its very roots. He is hopeful, trustful, and fresh-hearted—spare him and let him go.'

"She was fitting the glove on her faultless little hand. Her brow seemed so calm, so soft and pure, that for a moment I thought I had conquered, but looking up from her feminine employment, I recognised the hungry glitter in those dark, merciless eyes, and I knew there was no hope.

"'It is too late,' she answered, 'too late to persuade either him or me. It is no fault of mine. It is fate. For him—for the others— for all of us. Sometimes I wish it had not been so. Mine has been an unhappy life, and there seems to be no end, no resting-place. I can no more help myself than a drowning wretch, swept down by a torrent; but I am too proud to catch at the twigs and straws that would break off in my hand. I would change places with you willingly. Yes—you in that bath chair. I am so tired sometimes, and yet I dare not wish it was all over. Think of me as forbear-ingly as you can, for we shall not cross each other's path again.'

"'And this boy?' I asked, striving to detect something of compunction in the pitiless face that was yet so beautiful.

"'He must take his chance with the rest,' she said. 'Here he comes—good-bye.'

"They walked away arm-in-arm through the golden autumn weather, and a chill came into my very heart, for I knew what that chance was worth.

"A few months, and the snow lay six inches deep over the grave of him whose opening manhood had been so full of promise, so rich in all that makes youth brightest, life most worth having; while a woman in deep mourning was praying there, under the wintry sky; but this woman was his mother, and her heart was broken for the love she bore her boy.

"His death had been very shocking, very sudden. People talked of a ruptured blood vessel, a fall on his bedroom floor, a doctor not to be found when sent for; a series of fatalities that precluded the possibility of saving him; but those who pretended to know best affirmed that not all the doctors in Europe could have done any good, for when his servant went to call him in the morning he found his master lying stark and stiff, having been dead some hours. There was a pool of blood on his carpet; there were ashes of burnt letters in his fireplace; more, they whispered with meaning shrugs and solemn, awe-struck faces—

'There was that across this throat
Which you had hardly cared to see.'

"You can understand now that I believe in Vampires."

"What became of her?" I asked, rather eagerly, for I was interested in this Madame *de* St. Croix. I like a woman who goes into extremes, either for good or evil. Great recklessness, equally with great sensibility, has its charm for such a temperament as mine. I can understand, though I cannot explain, the influence possessed by very wicked women who never scruple to risk their own happiness as readily as their neighbours'. I wanted to know something more about Madame *de* St. Croix, but he was not listening; he paid no attention to my question. In a tone of abstraction that denoted his thoughts were many miles away, he only murmured,

"Insatiate—impenetrable—pitiless. The others were bad enough in all conscience, but I think she might have spared the boy!"

# Sabine Baring-Gould:
# Margery of Quether (1884)

Sabine Baring-Gould (1834–1924) was a prolific novelist, poet and squire-parson who wrote numerous British and European travelogues. His vampire stories include "A Dead Finger," "Glamr" and "A Professional Secret," but he is usually remembered today for his hymn "Onward Christian Soldiers."

His seminal *Book of Werewolves* (1865) was one of Bram Stoker's primary sources of information for *Dracula*. Stoker appropriated many of the werewolves' features—including canine teeth, pointed finger nails and the ability to change shape—for his literary vampire.

On 1 June, 1867, the *Daily Mail* compared *Dracula* to five classics of gothic literature: *The Mysteries of Udulpho*; *Frankenstein*; *Wuthering Heights*; "The Fall of the House of Usher" and "Margery of Quether." The first four of these stories have remained in print and are easily available today, but Baring-Gould's story has been all but neglected. "Margery of Quether" was first published in the *Cornhill Magazine* in April and May of 1884, with original illustrations by Harry Furniss. It was reprinted in *Margery of Quether: And Other Stories* (London: Methuen, 1891) and enjoyed limited edition in 1999. However, the following presentation marks its American debut.

———

This is written by my own hand, entirely unassisted. I am George Rosedhu, of Brinsabatch, in the parish of Lamerton, and in the county of Devon—whether to write myself Mister of Esquire, I do not know. My father was a yeoman, so was my grandfather, idem my great-grandfather. But I notice that when anyone asks of me a favour, or writes me a begging letter, he addresses me as Esquire, whereas he who has no expectation of getting anything out of me invariably styles me Mister. I have held my acres for five hundred years—that is, my family, the Rosedhus, have, in direct lineal descent, always in the male line, and I intend, in like manner, ti hand it on, neither impaired nor enlarged, to my own son, when I get on, which I am sure of, as the Rosedhus always have had male issue. But what this Nihilism, and Communism, and Tenant-right, and Agricultural Holdings legislation, threatened by this Gladstone-Chamberlain Radical Government, there is no knowing where a man with ancestral acres stands, and, in the general topsy-turvyism into which we are plunging—thanks to this Radical Government, God bless me!—I may be driven to have only female issue. There is no knowing to what we landed proprietors are coming.

Before I proceed with my story, I must apologize for anything that smacks of rudeness in my style. I do not mean to say that there is anything intrinsically rude in my literary productions, but that the present taste is so vitiated by slipshod English and effeminacy of writing, that the modern reader of periodicals may not appreciate my composition as it deserves. Roast beef does not taste its best after Indian curry.

My education has been thorough, not superficial. I was reared in none of your 'Adademies for Young Gentlemen,' but brought up on the Eton Latin Grammar and came at the Tavistock Free Grammar School. The consequence is that what I pretend to know, I know. I am a practical man with a place in the world, and when I leave it, there will be a hole which will be felt, just as when a molar is removed from the jaw.

There is no exaggeration in saying that my family is as old as the hills, for a part of my estate covers a side of that great hog's-back now called Black Down, which lies right before my window; and anyone who knows anything about the old British tongue will tell you that Rosedhu is the Cornish for Black Down. Well, that proves that we held land here before ever the Saxons came and drove the Bristish language across eh Tamar. My title-deeds don't go back so far as that, but there are some of them which, though they be in Latin, I cannot decipher. The hills may change their names, but the Rosedhus never. My house is nothing to boast of. We have been yeomen, not squires, and we have never aimed at living like gentry. Perhaps that is why the Rosedus are here still, and the other yeomen families round have gone scat (I mean, gone to pieces). If the sons won't look to the farm and the girls mind the dairy, the family cannot thrive.

Brinsabatch is an ordinary farm-house substantially built of volcanic stone, black, partly with age, and partly because of the burnt nature of the stone. The windows are wide, of word, and always kept painted white. The roof is of slate, and grows some clumps of stone-crop, yellow as gold.

Brinsabatch lies in a combe, that is, a hollow lap, in Yaffell— or as the maps call it, Heathfield. Yaffelll is a huge elevated bank of moor to the north-west and west, and what is very singular about it is, that at the very highest point of the moor an extinct volcanic cone protrudes, and rises to the height of about twelve hundred feet. This is called Brentor, and it is crowned with a church, the very tiniest in the world I should suppose, but tiny as it is, it has chancel, nave, porch, and west tower like any Christian parish church. There is also a graveyard round the church. This occupies a little platform on the top of the mountain, and there is absolutely no room there for anything else. To the west, the rocks are quite precipitous, but the peak can be ascended from the east up a steep grass slope strewn with pumice. The church is dedicated to S. Michael, and the story goes that, whilst it was being built, every night the devil removed as many stones as had been set on the foundations during the day. But the archangel was too much for him. He waited behind Cox Tor, and one night threw a great rock across and hit the Evil One between the horns, and gave him such a headache that he desisted from interference thenceforth. The rock is there, and the marks of the horns are on the stone. It is said also that there is a depression caused by the thumb of S. Michael. I have looked at it carefully, but I express no opinion thereon—that may have been caused by the weather.

Looking up Brinsabatch Coombe, clothed in oak coppice and with a brawling stream dancing down its furrow, Brentor has a striking effect, soaring above it high into the blue air, with its little church and tower topping the peak.

I am many miles from Lamerton, which is my parish church, and all Heathfield lies between, so, as Divine service is performed every Sunday in the church of S. Michael de Rupe, I ascend the rocky pinnacle to worship there.

You must understand that there is no road, not even a path to the top; one scrambles up over the turf, in windy weather clinging to the heather bushes. It is a famous place for courting, that is why the lads and lasses are such church-going folk hereabout. The boys help the girls up, and after service hold their hands to help them down. Then, sometimes a maiden lays hold of a gorse bush in mistake for a bunch of health, and gets her pretty hand full of prickles. When that happens, her young man makes her sit down beside him under a rock away from the wind, that is from the descending congregation, and he picks the prickles out of her rosy palm with a pin. As there are thousands of prickles on a gorse bush, this sometimes takes a long time, and as the pin sometimes hurts, and the maid winces, the lad ahs to squeeze her hand very tight to hold it steady. I've known thorns drawn out with kisses.

I always do say that parsons make a mistake when they build churches in the midst of the population. Dear, simple, conceited souls, do they really suppose that folks go to church to hear them preach? No such thing—that is the excuse; they go for a romp. Parsons should think of that, and make provision accordingly, and se the sacred edifice on the top of moor or down, or in shay corners where there are long lanes well wooded. Church paths are always lovers' lanes.

When a woman gets too old for sweethearting—if that time ever arrives, in her own opinion—she goes to church for scandalmongery, and, of course, the further she has to go, the more time she ahs for talk and the outpour of gossip. I know the butcher at Lydford kills once a week. Sunday is the character-killing day with us, and all our womenkind are the butchers.

Well!—this is all neither here nor there. I was writing about my house, and I have been led into a digression on church-going. However, it is not a digression either; it may seem so to my readers, but I know what I am about, and as my troubles came of church-going, what I have said is not so much out of the way as some superficial and inconsiderate readers may have supposed. I return, for a bit, to the description of my farm-house. As I have said once, and I insist on it again, Brinsabatch makes no pretensions to be other than a substantial yeoman's residence. You can smell the pigs' houses as you come near, and I don't pretend that the scent arises from clematis or weigelia. The cowyard is at the back, and there is plenty of mud in the lane, and streams of water running down the cart ruts, and skeins of oats and barley straw hanging to the hollies in the hedge. There is no gravel drive up to the front door, but there is a little patch of turf before it walled off from the lane, with crystals of white spar ornamenting the top of the wall. In the wall is a gate, and an ascent by four granite steps to a path sanded with mundic gravel that leads just twelve feet six inches across the grass plot to the front door. This door is bolted above and below, and chained and double-locked, but the back door that leads from the yard into the kitchen is always open, and I go in and out by that. The front door is for ornament, not use, except on grand occasions.

The rooms of Brinsabatch are low, and I can touch the ceiling easily in each with my hand; I can touch that in the bedrooms with my head. Low rooms are warmer and more homelike than the tall rooms of Queen Anne's and King George's reigns.

On the other side of Heathfield is Quether, a farm that has belonged to the Palmers pretty nigh as long as Brinsabatch has belonged to the Rosedhus. Farmer John Palmers pretty nigh as long as Brinsabatch has belonged to the Rosedhus. Farmer John Palmer is a man of some substance, one of the old sort of yeomen, fresh in colour, with light blue eyes and fair hair; he is big-made and stout. He is a man who knows the world and can make money. He has a lime-kiln as well as a farm, but the lime-kiln is not his own, he rents it. His daughter Margaret is a very pretty girl. He has several sons, and a swarm of small children of no particular sex. They are all in petticoats. So Margaret can't take much with her when she marries. Margaret used to go to chapel, but her religious views underwent a change since one Sunday afternoon she visited Brentor church. This change in her was not produced by anything in the parson's sermon, but by the fact that I was there, aged three-and-twenty, was good-looking, and the sole owner of Brinsabatch. I accompanied her back to Quether. Since that Sunday she has been very regular in her devotions at S. Michael de Rupe; she has, I understand, returned her missionary box to the minister of the chapel, and no longer collects for the conversion of the heathen to humbug. As for me, I became a much more regular attendant at church after that Sunday afternoon than I had been before. When the day was windy, I helped Margaret up the rock, and held her hand very tightly in mine, for had she missed her footing she might have perished. When the day was rainy, we shared one gig umbrella. When the day was windy and rainy, it was better still; for the gig umbrella could not be unfurled, so I folded my wide waterproof over us both. When the day was foggy, that was best of all, for then we lost our way in the fog, and could not find the church door till service was ended. On sunshiny days we were merry; in rain and fog, sentimental.

One Sunday she and I had gone round to the west end of the church after service. I told her that I wanted to show her Kit Hill, where the Britons made their last stand against King Athelstan and the Saxons; the real reason was that there is only a narrow ledge between the tower and the precipice, on which two cannot walk abreast, but on which two can stand very well with their backs to the wall, and no one else can come within ye and ear shot of them. Whilst we stood there, a sudden cloud rolled by beneath our feet, completely obliterating the landscape, but we were left above the vapour, in the sunlight, looking down, as it were, on a rushing, eddying sea of white foam. The effect was strange; it was as thought we were insulated on a little rock in a vast ocean that no bounds. Margaret pressed my arm and said, "We two seem to be alone in a little world to ourselves."

I answered, looking at the fog, "And a preciously dull world and dreary outlook."

I have not much imagination, and I did not at the moment take her words as an appeal for a pretty and lover-like reply. I missed the opportunity and it was gone past recall. She let go of my arm in dudgeon, and when I turned my head Margaret had disappeared. With a step she had left the ledge, and a few paces had taken her to her father. The fog at the same time rose and enveloped the top of the Tor and the church, so that I could no longer see Margaret, and the possibility of overtaking her and apologizing was lost.

Next Sunday she did not come to church. This made me very uncomfortable. I like to have the even tenor of neither my agricultural nor my matrimonial pursuits disturbed. I had been keeping company with Margaret Palmer for seven or eight months, and I had begun to hope that in the course of a twelve-month, if things progressed, I might make a declaration of my sentiments, and that after the lapse of some three r four years more we might begin to think of getting married. This little outburst of temper was distasteful to me; I knew exactly what it meant. It showed an undue precipitancy, an eagerness to drive matters to a conclusion, which repelled me. My sentiments are my own, drawn from my own heart, as my cider is from my own apples. I will not allow anyone to go to the tap of the latter and draw off what he likes; and I will not allow anyone to turn the key of my bosom and draw off the sentiments that are therein. On the third Sunday, I did not go to church, but I sent my hind, and he reported to me that Margaret Palmer had been there. I knew she would be there, expecting to find me ripe and soft to the pitch of a declaration. By my absence I showed her that I could be offended as well as she. That next week there came a revivalist preacher tot eh chapel; he was a black man, and went by the name of "Go-on-all-fours-to-glory Jumbo.' I heard that

Margaret Pamer had been converted by him. The week after there came a quack female dentist to Tavistock, and I went to her and had one of my back teeth out. Margaret Palmer learned a lesson by that. I let her understand that if she chose to be revived by Methodies, I'd have my teeth drawn by quacks. I'd stand none of her nonsense. My plan answered. Margaret Palmer came round, and was as meek as a sheep and as mild as buttermilk after that. Next Sunday I went as near a declaration as ever a man did without actually falling over the edge into matrimony. Brinsabatch is a property of 356 acres 2 roods 3 poles, and it won't allow a proprietor to marry much under fifty; my father did not marry till he was fifty-three, and my grandfather not till he was sixty. Young wives are expensive luxuries, and long families ruin a small property. One son to inherit the estate, and a daughter to keep house for him till he marries, then to be pensioned off on 80l a year, that is the Rosedhu system. Now you can understand why I object to being hurried. Brinsabath will not allow me to marry for twenty-seven years to come. But women are impatient cattle. They are like Dartmoor sheep; where you don't want them to go, there they go; and when you set up hurdles to keep them in, they take them at a leap. I've known these Dartmoors climb a pile of rocks on the top of which is nothing to be got, and from which it is impossible to descent, just because the Almighty set up those rocks for the cheep not to climb. To my mind, courting is the happiest time of life, for then the maiden is on her best behaviour. She knows that there is many a slip between the cup and the lip, and she regulates her conduct accordingly. I've heard that in Turkey females are real angels; they never nag, they never peck, they never give themselves airs. And the reason is, that Turkish husband can always turn his wife our of the house and sell he in the slave market. With us it is otherwise; when a woman is a wife she has her husband at her feet in chains to trample on as she pleases. He cannot break away. He cannot send her off. She knows that, and it is more than a woman can bear to be placed in a position of unassailable security. As long as a man is courting, he holds the rod, and the woman is the fish hooked at the end; but when they are married, the positions are reversed.

Well, to return to my story. We made up our quarrel and were like two doves. Then came the event I am about to relate, which disturbed our relations.

I had been the custom on Christmas Eve from time immemorial for the sexton and two others to climb Brentor, and ring a peal on the three bells in the church tower at midnight. On a still Christmas night the sound of these bells is carried to a great distance over the moors. I dare say in ancient times there may have been a service in the church at midnight, but there has been none for time out of mind, and the custom being unmeaning would have fallen into disuse were it not that a benefaction is connected with it—a field is held by feofees in trust to pay the rent to the sexton and the ringers, on condition that the bells are rung at midnight on Christmas Eve. Of late years there has been some difficulty in getting men together for the job. Wages are so high that laboring men will not turn out of a winter's night to climb a tor to earn a few shillings. Besides, the sexton has been accused of disseminating a preposterous, idle tale of hobgoblins and bogies to frighten others from assisting him, so that he may pocket the entire sum himself.

Be this as it may, it is certain that on the Christmas Eve that followed the quarrel I have spoken of, no additional ringers were forthcoming. The sexton, who was also clerk, Solomon Davy, worked for me and occupied one of my cottages. I beg, parenthetically, to observe that the cottages that belonged to me would do credit to any owner. My maxim is, look to your men and horses and cows that they be well fed and well hosed, and they are worth the money. Solomon Davy was an old man. His work was not worth his wages, but I kept him on because he had been on the farm all his life, and had married late in life. During the afternoon of Christmas Eve, Solomon Davy sent for me. He was taken ill with rheumatism and could not leave his cottage.

"I've ventured on the liberty of asking you to step in, sir," said he, when I entered his door, "because I've been took across the back cruel bad, and I can't crawl across the room."

"Sorry to hear it, Solomon. Who will do the clerking for you tomorrow?"

"I'm not troubled about that, master, as Farmer Palmer do the responses in a big voice. That which vexes me is about the ringing bells this night."

"It can't be done," said I.

"But, sir, meaning offence, it must be done, or I don't get the money. The feofees won't pay a farthing unless Christmas be rung in."

"You must send somebody else to do it."

Solomon shook his head. "Then that person pockets the money, and I get naught." He remained silent awhile, and then added, "Besides, who'd go?

"Make it worth a man's while, and he'll do anything," said I.

Again he shook his head, and this time he said, "There's Margery of Quether."

"What do you mean?" I asked, flushing. "What has Miss Palmer to do with the bells? Oh, I understand; she likes to hear the peal, and you would not disappoint her."

Solomon looked up at my slyly. "I didn't mean she."

"Then who the deuce do you mean?"

"Her as never dies."

"Solomon, the lumbago has got into your brains. I'll tell you what I'll do. I will ring the bells for you, and you shall draw the fee for having done it. That, I hope, will content you, my good man."

"Now that be like you, master, the nest and kindest of your good old stock," exclaimed Solomon. "I never heard of a master as was of such right good stuff as you. You don't turn off an old man because he is past work, nor grudge him a bit of best garden ground, took out of one of your fields, nor deny him skimmed milk because you want it for the pigs and calves, nor refuse him turnips and pertatees out of the fields as many as he can eat."

So he went on. I do not hesitate to repeat what he said, because he confined himself strictly within the bounds of truth. I flatter myself I always have been a good master, and just, even generous, to my men. I have been more, I have been considerate and kind. Lights were not made to be put under bushels, and I am not one of those who would distort or suppress the truth, even when it concerns myself. I know my own merits, and as for my faults, if I light on any at any time, I shall not scruple to publish them.

The old sexton jumped at my offer—I mean metaphorically, for his lumbago would not allow him to jump literally. I had made the offer out of consideration for him, but without considering myself, and I repented having made it almost as soon as the words had left my lips. However, I am a man of my word, and when I say a thing I stick to it.

"Where is the key?" I asked.

"Her be hanging up on thicky [that] nail behind the door," answered the old man.

As I took down the great church key, Soloman said, in a hesitating, timid voice, "If you should chance to meet wi' Margery o' Quether, you won't mind."

"I do not in the least expect ot see her," I said, getting red, and hot, and annoyed.

"No—meb-be not, but her has been seen afore on Christmas Eve."

"Margaret on the tor at midnight!" I exclaimed; then, highly incensed at the idea of the old man poking fun at me, and even alluding to my weakness for Margaret Palmer—love is a weakness—I said testily, as I walked out swinging the key on my forefinger, "Solomon, I object to Miss Palmer's name being brought in in this flippant and impertinent manner. What with the Gladstone-Chamberlain general-topsy-turvyism of the Government, the working classes are forgetting the respect due to their superiors, and allow themselves liberties of speech which their forefathers would have turned green to think of."

If I was regular in my devotions every Lord's Day, a laboring man in one's employ earning eleven shillings a week had no right to suppose that I did not ascend Brentor from the purest motives of personal piety. It is a duty of one in his position to think so. His insolence jarred my feelings, and I already regretted the offer I had made. It is a mistake to be good-natured. It is lowering in the eyes of inferiors; it is taken for weakness. The man who is universally respected, and obtains ready attention and exact obedience, is he who cares for nobody but himself, is loud, exacting, and self-asserting. The good-natured involves a man in endless troubles. I had undertaken to ring the bells at midnight in mid-winter in the windiest, most elevated steeple in England; I had to ascend a giddy peak on which one false step would precipitate me over the rocks, and dash every bone in my body to pieces. I am not on to shrink from danger, or to shirk a responsibility, freely in inconsiderately undertaken. I have already said that I would frankly admit my faults when I noticed them; and now the opportunity arises. I admit without scruple that I am too prone to do kind acts. This is a fault. A man out to consider himself. Charity begins at home. In this instance I did not think of myself, of the discomfort and danger involved in ascending Brentor at midnight.

I took a stiff glass of hot rum and water about half-past ten or quarter to eleven, and then turned out.

There was no snow on the ground; we are not likely to have seasonable weather so long as this Gladstone-Chamberlain-Radical topsy-turvy Government remain in power. Our sheep get cawed with the wet, the potatoes get the disease, the bullocks get foot-and-moth complaint, and the rain won't let us farmers get in our harvest. If only we had Beaconsfield back! But there, politics have nothing to do with my story.

The evening was not cold, it was raw, and the night was black as pitch. I had a lanthorn with me (I spell the spell the substantive advisedly in the old way, lanthorn and not lantern, for mine had horn, not glass, sides). I knew my road perfectly. The lane is stony, wet, and overhung. Stony it must be, for it is worn down to the rock, and the rock breaks up as it likes and stones itself, just the coats of the stomach renew themselves. Wet it is, because it serves as main drain to the fields on either side. Overhung it is, because tress row on either side. If the trees were not there, it would not be overhung. You understand me. I like to be explicit. Some intelligences are not satisfied with a hint, everything must be described and explained to them to the minutest particular.

By the lanthorn light I could see the beautiful ferns and mosses in the hedge, and the water oozing out of the sides, and the dribble that ran down the centre of the lane and then spread all over it, then accumulated on one side, and then took a fancy to run over to the other side. I notice that a stream in going down a hill zigzags just as a horse does in ascending a hill, and as a woman docs in the aiming at anything. The road rises steeply from my backyard gate to the church porch. When I say road, I mean way. For after one comes out on the moor, there is not even a track.

I knew my direction well enough, so I went straight over the heath to the old volcano, and as I ascended the peak I thought to myself, if an y traveler were on Hearthfield to-night, what a tale he would make up of the Jack-o'-lanthorn seen dancing in and out among the rocks, and winding its way up the height, till at last it hopped in at the church door of S. Michael on the Rock, and then a faint glimmer was visible issuing from all its windows. Probably he would suspect some witches' frolic was going on there such as Tam o' Shanter saw on All Hallowe'en, when Kirk Alloway seem'd in a bleeze, though the 'bleeze' could not be bright that issued from my tallow candle in a lanthorn.

The sky was overcast. Not a star was visible; only in the S. W. was a little faint light, and a thread of it ran round the horizon. The simile is not poetical, but it is to the purpose, when I say that the earth seemed under a dish-cover which didn't quite fit.

I reached the church in safety, dark as the night was; the few gravestones lit up with a ghastly smile as the lanthorn and I went by them in the little yard. I set down the clickering article on the stone seat in the porch, turned the key, resumed my lanthorn and went into the tower.

The church was not in first-rate repair. I believe the Duke of Bedford, who owns all Heathfield, did intend to do something to the church. He brought an architect there, and the architect said he must pull down the old church that dates from the thirteenth century, and build a sort of Norman Gothic cathedral in its place. You see the architect thought only of the Duke's pocket from which to draw; he gets five per cent on the outlay. But when the parson heard that, and I too, being churchwarden, we put our foot down and said, No! We loved the little old church; it was seen by Drake and Raleigh as they sailed into Plymouth Sound, just the same as we see it today, and we would not have a stone changed of the carcase. They might do what they liked with the vitals inside, that we conceded. Since that day we have heard nothing more of the restoration of Brentor church. Consequently, the sacred edifice has been getting more and more out of repair.

The rain had driven for centuries through the joints of the masonry, even throught he stone itself, and had streamed down inside, rotting the joists of the ebll-chamber where they rested in the wall. I don't blame the builders, they did their best. The walls are thick, but there is no stone in the country that is impervious to a south-western wind charged with rain. Granite is worst of all. You might as well build of sponge. Brentor church is built of the stone of the hill on which it stands, a sort of pumice, full of holes, and therefore by nature spongy. It holds the wet, and weeps it out at every change of weather. Now the belfty joists had given way, rotted right off, and had brought the planking down with them, and lay a wreck at the bottom of the tower. By day, I have no doubt, anyone looking up would see the three bells, and the holes in the lead roof above them. It was difficult for me to get at the ropes, so encumbered was the floor with fallen beams and boards that smelt of mildew and earth. I fancy the floor had given way since last Sunday, and that was why the litter lay there. Some of the sexton's tools had been knocked over by the falling beams. He wants strong tools, for the graves have to be hewn in the rock.

After I had removed some of the rotten timber, I made myself space, and stood in a pool of coffee-coloured water that had leaded from the roof, and drained from the sodden joists, and then I began to ring the bells. As I rang I looked round now and then. It was, of course, possible, though hardly probable, that the blacksmith or Luke Petherick might come up and take a turn at the ropes. I did not expect anyone, but I thought one might come; and I almost wished I had knocked the blacksmith up on my way, and asked him to join me a s personal favour. He couldn't have refused, for he does all my blacksmithing for me. But itmight have seemed as if I were afraid to go alone, and it would have deprived Solomon of half the ringer's fee. Looked at in another light, it would not have done, for one in my position is hardly the person to be seen ringing a church bell, and to be known to have done it out of good-nature.

I soon found that, for on unaccustomed to bell-ringing, the exertion was great; it brought into play muscles not usually exercised, and I began to feel the strain. I paused and wiped my forehead. My hands were getting galled. I did not moisten them in the customary way, which vulgar; but I dipped my palms in the coffee-coloured solution on the pavement at my feet. I had hitherto rung the 'cokck,' as Solomon designates one old heavy bell that has a curious Latin inscription on it, which begins 'Gallus vocor.' Now, as I rose from moistening my palms, I looked at the rope of the tenor bell, intending to pull that next. As I did so, I noticed something dark, like a ball of dirty cobwebs, hanging to the cord, rather high up. I elevated my lanthorn to see what it was, but the light afforded by the tallow dip was not sufficient to enable me to distinguish the outline of the object. I supposed it might be a great mass of filthy cobweb, or perhaps a piece of broken flooring which had remained attached to the rope, caught when the rest fell away. I considered that if I pulled the rope, I should probably bring the thing—whatever it was—down on my head. You will understand that my desisting form touching that cord was prompted by the wisest discretion, not by inane fear. SO I rang the treble bell, and ever and anon cast up my eye at the remarkable mass above.

Presently, I desisted from ringing altogether. I thought that the object was descending the rope slowly. I say I thought so, I did think so at first, but very soon I was certain of it. So certain was I, that I stepped back, and in so doing fell over a balk. When I had picked myself up the thin had reached the bottom. I should have liked to leave the church, but to do this I must step past this creature; I must do more; it was in the only clear space between me and the tower arch, so that to get out I must lift it from its place to make a passage for myself, and this I did not feel inclined to do. I never have believed in the supernatural. I do not believe in it now. Ghosts, goblins, and pixies are the creations of fevered imaginations and illiterate ignorance. It puts me out of patience to hear people, who ought to know better, speak of such things. I did not for a moment, therefore, suppose that the object before me was a denizen of another world. As far as I can recollect and analyze my sensations at the time, I should say that blank amazement prevailed, attended by a dominating desire to be outside the church and careering down the flank of the hill in the direction of Brinsabatch. I had no theory as to what the thing was; indeed the inclination to theorize was far from me. The creature I could now see had a human form. It was of the size of a three months' old baby. I have had no experience in babies myself, and am no judge of ages, so that when I say three months I do not wish to be tied down to that period exactly. In colour the object was brown, as if it had been steeped in peat water for a century, and in texture leathery. It scrambled, much as I have seen a bat scramble, out of the puddle on the pavement to the heap of broken timber, and worked its way with its little brown hands and long claws up a rafter, and seated itself thereon, holding fast by a hand on each side of what I suppose was the body, and then blinded, much in the same way as a monkey blinks, drawing a skin over the eyes different in colour from the skin of the face.

"I be Margery Palmer of Quether," it said in strange, far-off, mumbling words. "I couldn't bide up yonder no longer; the word be that rotten, it is all giving way, and I be afeard I may fall and break my bones. That 'ud be a gashly state o' things, my dear, to hev to bide up there year after year with a body o'bones all scatted abroad [broken to pieces], and never no chance of the bones healing."

"Who are you?" I asked, perhaps not as loudly or with as firm a voice as that in which I usually accost a stranger. The creature did not hear me. It went on, however, in its mumbling voice, and with a querulous intonation, "I be Margery Palmer of Quether. I reckon there be someone there, but my dear, I cannot see you, and if you speak I cannot hear you. I be dear as a post, and I've the eyes white wi' caterick."

"Are you a spirit?" I inquired. She did not hear me; so, waxing bolder, I put my hands to my mouth and shouted, as through a speaking trumpet, "are you a spirit?"

"Spirit—spirit!" she echoed. "Lauk a mussy! I wish I was! Spriti! No such luck comed to me yet. If I was I'd be thankful. Ah! Wishes don't fulfill themselves like as prayers do."

"How came you here?" I called.

"Here!" she repeated. "Can't hear. I be got too old for that I reckon I be Margery Palmer o' Quether."

"Impossible," I said. Were my senses taking leave of me? "This is a sheer impossibility." She did not hear my protest, but went mumbling on. "I lives up yonder among the bells. I've lived there these hundreds of years. I reckoned it were the safest place I could be in. I'd not ha' come down now, but that I were feared the bells would give way and all fall together, and my bones would ha' broke. It 'ud be a gashly thing to live on for hundreds o' years wi' broked arms and legs, and mebbe also a broked neck, so that the head hung down behind, and with no power to move it, not a bit and crumb. There ain't no healing power in my old bones now; they be as ancient as they in the graves, and no more power of joining in them, than the dead and mouldering bones hev."

I held up the lanthorn to inspect this curious creature squatted before me on a beam. It was, as I said, of the size of a baby;

but otherwise it was a grown woman very aged and withered. The face was not merely wizen, it was dried up to leather, quite tanned brown, the colour of the oak beams; the hands and arms were shriveled and like those of a bat. There was actually no flesh on them, they were simply dry, tanned skin about bone. The garments seemed to have been tanned like the hide by liquor distilling from the oak. The eyes were blear.

"I can't see, and I can't hear," she went on, "except just a little scrap o' light which I take to be a link. I gets blinder and ever blinder, till in time I shall look into the sun and see only blackness and darkness for ever. I gets deafer and deafer, but I can hear the bells still. I can also feel a little with my skin, but not much. I've one tooth remains in my head, and I hang on by that. I drive it into the oak beam, and cling round the beam wi' my arms, and strike my nails in too, and so I hold fast. But I knowed very well that the wood were rotten; I knowed it by a sort of instink, and sp I've a-comed down to-day. I reckon my hair be all falled off now; I can't tell by the feel, my hands be that numbed wi' clinging, that the feel be most gone from them. But you can see for yourself." She put her hand to her head and thrust back a leathery hood that had covered it. The little skull was bald. I opened the door of my lanthorn and took out the candle to inspect her better. The head was as if cut out of a thornstick. Only at the back at the junction with the neck was a little frizzle of ragged white hair. I observed as she moved that her neck creased like old hide that threatened to crack at the creases. The flexibility was gone from it. "Hold the candle before my eyes," she said; "I like the light. I can feel it shining though my dull eyes down into my stomick. What be your name, now?"

"George Rosedhu." I yelled my name into her ear.

"Ah, George! George!" exclaimed old Margery, "you put off and off too long. You should have married when the fancy first took you. Now it be too late; we be scrumped up [dried up] like old apples."

What could this extraordinary creature mean?

"Ah, George! George!" she went on. "That were a cruel, unkind act of yours, keeping company with me so long, and them giving me the clip after all. Do you mind how we used to meet here of Sundays, and how on the windy days you helped me up the rock, and on windy and rainy days you wrapped your clock round the both of us, and how, when the days were foggy, we used to lose out way in the mist, and never were able to find the church door till the service were over? And do you recall how one day you took me round to the west end of the church, after service, where we could stand at the edge of the rock, wi' our backs to the tower, and you said you wanted to point out Kit Hill to me-"

I sprang forward and put my hand over her mouth.

"Good heavens!" I exclaimed. "Will you drive me mad? What do you mean? Who are you?"

She went on, when I withdrew my hand, "Ah, George, George, you know there was not much to be got with me. There were my brothers and a swarm of little ones coming on, and so you left me out in the cold, and took up with Mary Cake, of Wring-worthy, who was twenty years older than me. You said I were tooyoung; and now Mary Cake that become Mary Rosedhu be dead and mouldered these hundreds of years, and I—I be alive and old enough even for a Rosedhu."

Then the old creature began to laugh, but stopped with a short scream. "I must not do it. I dare not laugh. I be too old, and I shall crack my sides and tear my skin. Then what is cracked bides cracked, and what is tore bides tore."

What did the creature mean by her allusion to Mary Cake? That was my great, great—I am afraid to say how many times removed—grandmother. She died about two hundred years ago. She brought an addition to the property of fifty-three acres, which I now possess. I have the marriage settlements in the iron deeds-chest under my bed, the date 1605.

"Well, well" the little old woman went on, "we all make mistakes. Life is but a string of them. Coming into the world is the first; courting, marrying, everything in succession is a mistake.

You, George, made a mistake in taking Mary Cake instead of me. Her led you a cruel, sour life, to my thinking. Her had a vixenish temper as would worry any man out of conceit with life. I, on the other hand, was all lightsomeness and fun. You knew that; but what cared you for a pretty face and sunny temper alongside of a few acres of moorland? You Rosedhus are a calkelating family, and you reckon up everything wi' a bit o' chalk on the table. I hadn't the land Mary brought, but I'd youth and energy and a cheerful disposition. But, Rosedhus, you are all afraid of long families, and are a grasping and a keeping set. You always marry late in life, and oldish women, lest a lot of children should eat the property as mice eat cheese. It be a mistake, a gashly error. But there, now, I won't aggravate you. Now tell me this: How come you alive at this time? I thought you'd be dead these two hundred and fifty years. Can't you find your rest no more nor I? Did you also pray that you might never die?"

I could not answer. I have no imagination, and I was unable to follow her, mixing up the past and the present in such an unaccountable manner. As far as I could understand, she confused me with a remote ancestor of the same name who died in 1623. That was the George Rosedhu who married Mary Cake, of Wringworthy, in 1605.

"I made my mistake when I prayed for life," said the old woman. "I was so joyous and fond of life and full of giddiness that I used to pray every Sunday when I came to church, and every evening when I said my Matthew, Mark, Luke, and John, that I might never die. I were also mortal afraid of death. The graves here be digged out of living stone, and be full of water afore they coffins be splashed into them, and the corpses don't moulder; they sop away and go off the bones hust as if they was boiled to rags. That terrified me, so I always prayed for one only thing, that I might never die, and my prayer hev been heard and answered. I cannot die, but I can grow older and more decrepit and drier. I get older and older, and shrump [wither] up more and more, and get drier and blinder and deafer. I can no longer taste, and I cannot smell, and I can hardly fell. I have no pleasure in life at all now, and the only feeling in me is fear—fear lest I should get broke or tore, for I be past mending; if I be broke or tore I must bide to the end of time. On a very hot day, when the sun shines, I seem to have a sort o' a sense of warmth, and the frost must cake me up in ice before I knows I'm cold. I reckon in another hundred years my tongue will have dried up, and then I sha'n't be able to talk no more; but that is the last organ to go in a woman, as her temper is the first; her mind may go, her teeth may go, her sight may go, her hearing may go—but her tongue dies hard. In another hundred years I shall not be able to feel the streak of midsummer sun that falls on my back, nor the winter icicle that hangs from my nose. I sit bunched up on a beam above the bells, and hold on with a tooth drove fast into the wood right home to the gum, and my nails hev grown till they go round the beam I clutch. The dry rot has got into the wood, and it be turned to powder, so that the crust has given way and I've sunk into the dust and mildew. You must put me away where I can be safe for another two or three hundred years out o' the way of dogs and rats and boys. Dogs would tear my skin, and rats gnaw holes in me, and boys pelt me wi' stones and break my bones. What is broke is broke, and what is tore is tore—I be past all healing. I were put up in the belfry above the bells as the place where I might be safest, but now that the rafters and joists be rotten and falling about me, it b'aint safe no more."

She ceased, and sat blinking at me. The skin of her eyelids was the only part of her that retained any flexibility, and any likeness to human skin in colour and texture. The eyelashes were white like frost needles. I was touched with compassion. As I have already said, I have no intention of disguising or hiding my faults, and I frankly confess that a too great readiness to be moved by a tale or stirred by a spectacle appealing to human sympathy is one of my worst faults. I fear it is ineradicably ingrained in my constitution; I was born with this just as some unfortunates come into the world with the germs of scrofula in their blood and tubercles in their lungs. I remembered now to have heard, when a boy, of a certain girl who was said to have been so much in love with life that she had prayed she might never die, and who, accordingly, was doomed to live for ever; but I thought that she raced on stormy nights with a white owl hooting before her over the moors in the train of the Black Hunter and the Wisht Hounds. I know my old nurse had told me such a tale to draw a moral from it of content with what Providence disposes; but it was news to me that this Undying One had been put away to wither up among the bells of Brentor Church. What a wretched existence this poor creature had dragged on! My ancestor, who had flirted with her and then jilted her, had lived over two hundred years ago, and she would be alove, drier and more wretched two hundred years hence, when Margaret and I are fallen to dust, and our lineal descendant in the male line reigning at Brinsabatch. My kindly disposition was touched—my heart softened. In a sudden access of pity, I put my arms round the poor old creature—she was as light as a doll—and crooking my finger through the ring of the lanthorn, I said, "I will carry you home, old Margery! You shall feel a Christmas fire, and taste Christmas beef and plum-pudding."

She did not understand. I do not think she heard me, but she laid hold of me tenaciously, as she had laid hold of the beam on which she had crouched for two centuries; she drove her single tooth through my coat and waistcoat, even cutting my skin, and her bat-like hands and claws clutched me, the nails going into me like knife-blades. I left the church with her, and carried her home; that is to say, she adhered to me so tenaciously—I might say, voraciously—that I had no occasion to use my arms for her support; she was like a knapsack slung on the wrong way, and quite as securely fastened—faster, for a knapsack with oscillate, but old Margery stuck to me as tight as a tick on a dog.

When I got home I said, "Now, old Margery, shake yourself off and sit by the brave big fire, and I'll give you something warm to drink that will cheer the cockles of your leathery heart." But, not a bit would she budge. I shouted into her ear, but she could or would not hear. Her tooth, which was driven into my chest like a proboscis of a mosquito, held her fast, and her hands were no more to be unlocked from my arms than the laces of old ivy from an oak. There was nothing for it but for me to sit down in my armchair, nursing her. The situation was almost grotesque, and always in vain; and I thought I should have next morning to get a man with a knife to slit up my coat and waistcoat behind so as to let the old creature slip off with the garments. But I was saved this annoyance by her tooth gradually being withdrawn, and her fingers relaxing. She fell off, and dropped on my knees, and lay there like a sleeping infant after its meal.

I threw a bunch of gorse on the fire, and it roared up the chimney in a sheet of golden flame, filing the little parlour with light. I was able now to study the face of the little creature on my lap, entirely at my ease. It struck me now that old Margery looked younger than I had taken her to be when I saw her in the belfry. She was a very old woman indeed, still, but there was a human-like moisture on the leathery skin, which also looked less liable to part at the folds, and there was even a rosy tinge on the lips. I suppose that from holding her so long I was somewhat more able to appreciate her weight. It was not that of a doll stuffed with bran, but of a baby with milk and flesh and blood in it adapted to its age. I thought her also rather larger than I had at first supposed, but that may be because she was now asleep on my knees, and there is a gain of an inch or two in repose, owing to muscular relaxation.

I put her down very gently on my sofa, and set a chair against the side, lest she shold roll on the floor; then I went in quest of a clothes basket, which I filled with soft pillows. This I set in the ingle nook, and laid old Margery in the maund. I covered her over with an eider-down quilt taken from my own bed, and she seemed very cozy in the extemporized cradle. I did more. I got a Florence flask that had contained sweet oil, and rinsed it well out with a strong solution of soda. When it was quite clean, I filled it with hot strong rum and sugar and water. I wished I could find a flexible india-rubber tube, but I was unprovided with such things. There had been no call for them hitherto, in my house—Hold! There was though! I recollected that one of the cows after calving had died of mild-fever, and the calf had been brought up by hand. I remembered a vulcanized india-rubber contrivance that had been tried but had not answered, as the calf disliked the taste of the sulphur. I now found this, and with some little ingenuity adapted it to the Florence flask, and then put it into the basked beside Margery. I put my finger into her mouth first to encourage her, but she only played with it, and then I inserted between her almost toothless gums the vulcanized india-rubber contrivance—I forget its proper name. I thought it would keep her quiet, but she dragged so hard at it that the tube came out, and all the rum and water ran among the pillows. So I had to take her out again, and dry the cushions before the fire, and make up the bassinet with fresh pillows. Poor little thing, she slept through it all, like an angel.

All this took me a long time, and gave me great exertion; it called into requisition faculties of the mind and heart that had not been previously exercised. I was very tired; I sat back in my chair and fell asleep. I did not dare to go to bed lest old Margery should wake and want me. When I opened my eyes, it was Christmas Day. The clerk was ill, I was churchwarden, and must be at S. Michael de Rupe on that sacred festival, to give the good day and the best wishes of the season to all my neigh-bours—sweet, blooming Margaret Palmer of Quether included. I went upstairs and dressed myself in my Sunday suit, and a blue neckcloth, and put on my cairngorm pin with a terrier's head in it, put some pomatum on my hair—that I always do on Sunday that last thing before going to church—and before I left I drew down the coverlet and looked at old Margery.

She was sleeping still—bless her!—with her old brown thumb in her mouth. I was uneasy because the nail was so long, I thought it might scratch her palate or irritate the uvula, so I got a pair of scissors and cut it. I felt strangely moved with pity, and with that pity there awoke in me a sort of sense of personal property in old Margery. Also, I presume, because of that, I was aware of some pride in her. I knew that she was wizen and old and hideous, and I knew also, that if any woman had come into my house with her baby in her arms and had asked me to admire it, and then had looked disparagingly at Margery, I should have hated that woman ever after. As it was, that day a child was christened in the church. I looked at its soft pink skin, and went away from the sacred edifice with envy and enger rankling in my heart.

## II.

I left Brinsabatch that morning with great reluctance, and all the time of divine service I was thinking far more of old Margery than of young Margaret, as I ought—and I do not mind confessing my fault openly. My seat is a little forward of the Quether pew on the other side. Usually, when standing for the psalms and hymns, I stand sideways, that the light may fall on my book, and look over the top at Margaret, who does the same; but as she is on the other side and the window opposite mine, she turns towards me that she may get the light on her print, and so our eyes are always meeting. When the parson is praying to us, I lean forward with my head on the book board, and so my eyes go diagonally backward, Margaret leans her head in an opposite fashion, and so her eyes go diagonally forward, and our eyes are always meeting in the prayers, as in the psalms. During the sermon I am obliged to turn round on my seat, as I am hard of hearing in my right ear, owing to a cricket ball having hit it when I was at the Tavistock Grammar School. Margaret always somehow has her bonnet string over her left ear, so she is fored to sit roundabout on her seat and expose the hearing ear to the preacher, and so it always comes about that during the sermon our eyes are meeting. This Christmas Day it was other with me; I could think of nothing but my poor little old Margery in her bassinet by the fire, and I kept on wondering whether she would wake up in my absence and fret for want of me. Then I had through the sermon a pricking feeling in my chest—I suppose where her tooth and nails had held so tight—and I was restless and uncomfortable to be back at Brinsabatch.

After service, as I was shaking hands all round, feeling eager to get it over and be off, Farmer Palmer said to me, "Come home to Quether with us, Rosedhu, and eat your Christmas dinner there. We are old friend and hope to be closer friends in time than we are now. I don't like, nor does Margaret here, to think of you sitting lonely down to your meal on Christmas Day. There is a knofe and fork laid ready for you, and I will take no refusal."

I made a lame sort of excuse. I said I was unwell.

"That is true enough," said Palmer; "you don't look yourself at all to-day, and Margaret is uneasy about you. Your face is white, your hand shakes, and you look older by some years than when I last saw you. When was that?"

"Sunday, father," said Margaret with a sigh.

I assured them that I was too indisposed to accept their kind invitation, and I saw that they believed me. Margaret's brown eyes were fixed anxiously and intently on me. I had been up all night, much worried, that was why I looked older and unwell, but I only said by way of explanation to Palmer, the one magical word 'liver.' When you say that word every man understands you. It touches his heart at once.

As I walked home every person I passed and spoke to said, "How oldened you are!" or "How ill you look!" or "Why, sure-ly that baint you, Mr. George, looking nigher forty than twenty."

I wish Mr. Palmer would not try to thrust Margaret on me. Margaret invites me to dinner. Margaret is concerned at my looks. Margaret remembers when last we met. That is all hyperbola and figure and flower of speech, and means in plain English, I want you to take my eldest daughter off my hands, but I am not going to give more than a trifle with her.

I never was more pleased than on this occasion when I got home again. I unlocked my parlour door, and ran in and up to the clothes basket, and cried in a sort of fond foolish rapture, "Bless it! Bless it!"

The little old woman opened her eyes—they were not clouded with catacact; that must have been a fancy of mine before; she saw me and smiled, and made a sort of crowing noise in her throat. I stooped over to kiss her, when—click! In an instant she had fastened herself to me, and driven her tooth into my chest, and grabbed me with her hands, so that I was held as in a vice. To wrench her off would have been impossible. I believe if torn away the hands would have held to me still, and the arms come off at the wrists. I know that when a ferret fastens on a rabbit you may kill the beast before he will let go, unless you nip his hind foot; then he opens his mouth to squeal, and loosens his grip to defend himself. I did not think of this at the time, or I might have called in someone to pinch Margery's foot; but I doubt, even it I had remembered this, whether I should have had recourse to this expedient. I did not care to have my situation discussed; moreover, I was conscious of a soothing sensation all the time Margery was fast. Besides, I knew by this time that when the little old woman had had enough she would drop off, just as a leech does when full. I would not have you suppose that Margery was sucking my blood. Nothing of the sort; that is, not grossly in the manner of a leech. But she really did, in some marvelous manner to me quite inexplicable, extract life and health, the blood from my veins and the marrow from my bones, and assimilate them herself.

Presently she fell off, as I knew she would when satisfied, and lay in my lap, across my knees. She looked up at me with a smile that had something really pleasant in it. She was positively taller, her skin fresher, her eye clearer than before; her eyelashes were grey, not snowy; and there was actually a down of grey hairs covering her poll, like the feather on a cockatoo. I wrapped a blanket round her, and was about to replace it in the basket, when I found, to me surprise, that it would cramp her limbs; she could not kick out of it. So I got a drawer out of my bureau, fitted it up with pillows, and laid her in that.

I really do think there is something taking about her expression. When you consider her age, she gave wonderfully little trouble. At first it was strange to me to have to do with this sort of little creature—it was my first and only—but I saw that I should soon get used to it. In the afternoon I employed myself in making a pair of rockers, which I adjusted to the drawer, and by this means converted it into a very tolerable cradle. I am handy at carpentering. Indeed there are not many things which I cannot do when put to it. When the emergency arose, as the reader will see, I became really a superior nurse, without any training or experience. Indeed, I feel confident that in the event of this Radical Galdstone-Chamberlain-Bradlaugh Government altering the land laws and robbing me of Brinsabatch, I could always earn my living as a nurse; I could take a baby from the month, if not earlier, or a person of advanced age lapsed into second childhood. Never before have I taken in hand the tools of literature, and yet, I venture to say that—well! There are idiots in the world who don't know the qualities of a cow, and to whom a sample of wheat is submitted in vain. Such persons are welcome to form what opinion they like of my literary style. Their opinion is of no value whatever to me. There is no veneer in my work, it is sterling. There is no padding, as it is called; my literary execution is as substantial and thorough as were the rockers I put on the cradle. The rockers were not put on many days before they were needed. Old Margery became very restless at night, and she would not let me be long out of the house by day. She was cutting her teeth. The back teeth are terribly trying to babies—they have fits sometimes and big heads and water on the brain, all through the molars. If it be so with an infant of a few months, just consider what it must be with an old woman in her three-hundredth year, or thereabouts! I bore with her very patiently, but broken rest is trying to a man. Besudes, about the same time I suffered badly in my jaws, for my teeth, which were formerly perfectly sound, began to decay, break off, and fall out. I may say, approximately, that as Margery cut a tooth I lost one; also that, as her hair grew and darkened, mine came out or turned grey. Moreover, as her eye cleared mine became dim, and as her spirits rose mine became despondent.

In this way, weeks, and even months, passed. It really was a pretty sight to see the havoc of ages repaired in the person of

Margery; the sight would have been one of unalloyed delight, had not the recovery been effected at my expense. The colour came back into her cheek as it left my once so florid complexion; she filled out as I shriveled up, she grew tall as I collapsed; the drawer would now no longer contain her, and a bed was made for her by the fire in the parlour. I noticed a gradual change in the tenor of her talk, as she grew younger. At first she could think and speak of nothing but her ailings, but after, she took to talking scandal, bitter and venomous, of neighbours, that is, of neighbours dead and dropped to dust, whose very tombstones are weathered so as to be illegible. Little by little her talk became less virulent, and softened into harmless prattle, and was all about the things of the farm and house. She was a first-rate worker. I was glad she took such an interest in the farm; she brisked about and saw to everything. I was suffered much from rheumatism and bronchitis. Neighbours came to see me, and all were in the same tale, that I was becoming an old man before my time, that the change in me was something unprecedented and unaccountable. I could not walk without a stick. I stooped. My hair was thin and grey, my limbs so shrunken that my clothes hung on me as on a scarecrow. I was advised to see a doctor; that is—everyone had a special doctor who was sure to cure me; one said I must go to Dr. Budd at North Tawton, and another to Dr. Hingston at Plymouth, and one to this and one to that; they would have sent me flying over the county consulting doctors, and varying them every week. Some said—and I soon found that was the prevailing opinion— that I was bewitched, and advised me strongly to consult the shite witch either in Exeter or Plymouth. I turned a deaf ear to them all. I wanted no doctors. I needed no white witch. I knew well enough what ailed me. I never now went up Brentor to church. Dear life! I could not have climbed such a height if I had wished it! My poor old bones ached at the very thought, and my back was nigh broken when I walked through the shippen one day to the linneye [cattle shed]. Besides, I had grown terribly short of wind, and I had such a rattling on my chest. I almost choked of a night. That was the bronchitic, and when I coughed it shook me pretty well to pieces.

So time passed, and I knew that I was sinking slowly and surely into my grave; there was no real complaint on me to kill me. I was breaking up of old age, and yet was no more that three and twenty. Everyone said I looked as If I was over ninety years. If I could see the hundred, it would be something to be proud of before I was four and twenty. One thought troubled me sorely. Whatever would become of Brinsabatch without a Rosedhu in it? I should die without leaving a lineal descendant in the male line. I would go out of the family. I had not a relation in the world. We Rosedhus always marry late in life, and never have large families. I was the single thread on which the possible Rosedhu posterity depended. I believe that an aunt had once married, and had a lot of children, but she was never named in the family. It was tantamount to a loss of character in Rosedhu eyes. I did not even know her married name. She was dead; but her issue no doubt remained, though I knew nothing of them. They, I suppose would inherit. I found as I grew older that this fretted me more and more. I would soon pass beyond the grave into the world of spirits, and I knew, the moment I turned up there, that the Rosedhus would be down on me for not having left male issue to inherit Brinsabatch, each, with intolerable self-assurance, setting himself up before me as an example I ought to have copied. As if, under my peculiar circumstances, I could help myself. The only one of my ancestors with whom I should eb able to exchange words would be George Rosedhu who had married Mary Cake. I would cast it in his teeth that had he been faithful to his first love, this disastrous contingency would not have occurred.

"Ah!" said I, in a fit of spleen, "it is all very well of you, Margery, to go about the house singing. What is to become of the Rosedhus? To whom will Brinsabatch fall? You have drawn all the flush and health out of me and made yourself young at my charge, – but I get nothing thereby."

"I will nurse you in you decrepitude, dearest George," she answered, and a dimple came to her rosy cheek, the prettiest twinkle in her laughing blue eye. Upon my word she was a bonny buxom wench, and it would have been a delight to be in the house with her, had I been younger. Now I could only gaze on her charms despairingly from afar off, as Moses looked on the Promised Land from Pisgah. What a worker she was, moreover! What a manager! What an organizer! What a housekeeper, cook, diarywoman, rolled into one! Never was the house so neat, the linen so cared for, the brass pans so scoured, the butter so sweet, the dairy so clean. She had been brought up in the old-fashioned, hard-working, sensible ways of farm in the reign of Good Queen Bess. In our days, the women are all infected with your Gladstone-Chamberlain topsy-turvyism, and the farmers' daughters play the piano and murder French, and farmers' wives read Miss Braddon and Ouida and neglect the cows. Her ways were a surprise to all on the estate. The men and the maids had never seen anything like it. Folks could not make Margery out, who she was, and where I had picked her up. Nobody seemed to belong to her; she had never been seen before, and yet she know the names of every tor, and hamlet, and coombe, and moor, as if she had been reared there. But though she knew the places, she did not know the people. She spoke of the Tremaines of Culla-combe, whereas the family had left that house two hundred years ago, and were settled at Sydenham. She talked of the Doidges of Hurlditch, a family that had been gone at least a hundred years. Kilworthy, she supposed, was still tenanted by the Glanvilles, whereas that race is extinct, and the place belongs to the Duke of Bedford, who had turned it into a farm. On the other hand, what was curious was, that Margery hit right now and then on the names of some of the laboring poor; she would salute a man by his right Christian and surname, because he was exactly like an ancestor some two hundred and fity years ago. Though the great families have migrated or disappeared, the poor have stuck to their native villages, and reproduce from century to century the same faces, the same prejudices, the same characteristics. They are almost as unchangeable as the hills.

As I have said, Margery was a puzzle to everyone, and because a puzzle, the workmen and girls looked on her with suspicion. They resented the close way in which they were kept to their work and the rigid supervision exercised over them. Solomon Davy, the clerk, alone suspected who she was. He called several times to see me, and looked hard at me, with an uneasy manner, and seemed as though he wanted to ask me something, but lacked the courage to do so. Margery is always pleasant to Solomon, she knew the Davys that went before him, but he gives her a wide berth; he never lets her come within arm's reach of him. She feels it, I am sure, by her manner; but she is too good-hearted to remark on it.

I cannot deny that she was goodness and attention itself to me, and that I was fond of her. Just as a mother idolizes her baby that draws all its life and growth from her, so was it with me. I begrudged her none of her youth and beauty; I took a sort of motherly pride in her growth and the development of her charms, and for precisely the same reason—they were all drawn out of me.

One day Margery announced that she intended to marry me, and told me I must be prepared to stir my old stumps and go to church with her. She explained her reason candidly to me. She knew that I had a clear business head, and so she consulted me on the subject, which was flattering, and I should have felt more grateful had I not almost reached a condition past acute feeling. She told me that she would nurse me till I expired in her arms, and then, as my widow, would have Brinsabatch. This would secure her future, for with her renewed youth and with her handsome estate she could always command suitors and secure a second husband, from whom she could extract sufficient life and health to maintain her in the bloom of youth. When he was exhausted and withered up and dead, she could obtain a third, and so on ad infinitum. She objected to being again consigned to mummification in the tower of Brentor Church, and this was the simplest and most straightforward solution to her peculiar difficulties. The plan suggested was feasible, and, from her point of view, admirable. I freely, willingly submitted to her proposal. She exercised no undue compulsion on me; she appealed to my reason, and my reason, as far as it remained, told me that her plan was sensible, and in every way worthy of her. She was a handsome woman, with a fine head of brown hair, and the brightest, wickedest, merriest pair of blue eyes. As for her cheeks—quarantines were nothing to them. A man in the prime of life would be proud to have such a woman as his wife, and her selection of me was, in its way, complimentary, even though I knew I was taken for the sake of Brinsabatch.

So I consented, and she herself took the banns to the clerk. Solomon opened his eyes when she told him her purpose, moved uneasily on his seat, and scratched his head. He hardly knew what to make of it. He came to see me, and looked inquiringly at me, but I had one of my fits of coughing on me. When I was sufficiently recovered to speak, I told Solomon how impatient I was for my wedding-day to arrive, and how kind and excellent a nurse Margery was to me. He went away puzzled, and rubbing his forehead. I made but one stipulation with respect to my wedding, that was, that I should be conveyed to the foot of Brentor in a spring-cart, laid on straw, a thence conveyed up the hill to the altar by four strong men, in a litter, laid upon a featherbed, and with hot bottles at my feet and sides. I was entirely incapable of walking.

This was at the beginning of November. Consequently ten months had elapsed since that fatal Christmas Eve on which I had made the acquaintance of Margery of Quether. So the banns were read on the first Sunday in the month at the afternoon service, there being no service that day in the morning at the little church. The banns were published between George Rosedhu, of Brinsabatch, bachelor, and Margaret Palmer, or Quether, spinster. If anyone knew any just cause or impediment why these two should not me joined together in holy matrimony, they were now to declare it. That was the first time of asking.

A pretty sensation the reading of these banns caused. Farmer Palmer's face turned as mottled as brawn, and Miss Palmer blushed as red as a rose and buried her face in her hymn-book. My old Margery had overshot her mark, as the sequel proved. She had not reckoned with your Margaret, her great, great, great, great grand-niece.

When public worship was concluded, Mr. Palmer and his daughter, instead of directing their steps homeward towards Quether, where tea was awaiting them, walked in the opposite direction, and descended on Brinsabatch, to know of me what was meant by the banns—sober earnest or a silly joke.

Margery was not at home. She always frequented S. Mary Tavy church, because she had a dislike to Brentor; it was associated in her mind with two centuries of chilling and repellant associations. Margery was a regular churchgoer. That was part of her bringing up. In her young days, if anyone missed church, he was fined a shilling, and if he did not take the sacrament, was whipped at the cart-tail. These penalties are no longer exacted; nevertheless, Margery is punctual in her attendance. Such is the force of habit early acquired.

Thus it came about that Farmer Palmer and his daughter arrived at Brinsabatch before Margery had returned from church. I am sorry that my hand is not expert at describing things which I neither saw nor heard accurately. I have no imagination, which is a delusive faculty leading to serious error. Palmer and his daughter were attended by Solomon Davy, who I believe endeavoured to explain the situation to them and told them who Margery really was. I had become so dull of hearing, and so cataracted in eye, that I was unable to understand all that went on, and to follow and take part in the somewhat heated and animated conversation. If, like a modern writer of fiction, I were to give the whole of what was said, with description of the attitudes assumed, the inflections of the voices, and the degrees of colours that mantled the several cheeks, I might make my narrative more acceptable, no doubt, to the vulgar many, but it would lose its value to the appreciative few, who ask for a true record of what I observed.

I believe that Solomon in time made it clear to the dull intellects of the Palmers that the banns were for my marriage with the great, great, great, great-aunt of Margaret, and not with herself. What he said of poor Margery I don't know. I strained my ears to catch what he said, but heard only a buzzing as of bees. I doubt not that he spiced the truth with plenty of falsehood.

Farmer Palmer has a loud voice. I heard him say to his daughter, "Wait here a bit, Margaret, along with George Rosedhu, and bide till t'other Margery arrives; I back one woman against another."

"Oh, father!" exclaimed the pretty creature, "where are you a-going to?"

"My dear, I shall be back directly. This be Fifth o' November, and bonfire night. The lads be all colleting faggots for a blaze on the moor. I'll fetch 'em here, and they can have the pleasure o' burning the old witch instead of a man o' straw."

I held out my hands in terror and deprecation. "You durstn't do it!"

"Why not?" asked the farmer composedly. "Her's a witch and no mistake. Her have sucked you dry of life as an urchin [hedgehog] sucks a cow of milk."

"But," protested Solomon, "though that be true enough, what about the laws? I won't say but that it be right and scriptural to burn a witch; for it is written, 'Thou shalt not suffer a witch to live,' but I reckon it be against the laws."

"Not at all," said Palmer. "No man can be had up for burning a person who has no existence."

"But she has existence," I remonstrated. "That is the prime cause of her trouble; she has too much of it; she can't die."

"There is no evidence of her existence," argued Palmer. "You, Solomon, tell me how far back you registers go in Brentor Church."

"Back, I reckon, to about 1680."

"Very well, then they contain no record of her birth and baptism. Now you cannot be hung for killing a person of whose existence there is absolutely no legal evidence. The laws won't touch us if we do burn her."

"But—but," I said, crying and snuffling, "she is your own flesh and blood."

"That may be, but that is no reason against her cremation. My own Margaret stands infinitely nearer to me, and her interests closer to my heart, than the person and welfare of a remote ancestress. As the banns have been called, Brinsabatch shall go to my daughter and to no one else. In three weeks; time Margaret shall be called Mrs. Rosedhu." He spoke firmly.

"Father, dear father, how can you be so cruel to me?" cried Margaret. "Do y' look what an atomy Mr. Rosedhu has be come to?"

The burly yeoman paid no heed to his daughter's protest, knowing, no doubt, its unreality. He said to me, "Look y' here, George Rosedhu, you've had my daughter's name coupled wi' yours in the church today, and read out before the whole congregation, without axing my leave or hers. I won't have her made game of even by a man o' substance like you, so she shall marry you before December comes, whether you like it or not."

"Oh, Mr. Plamer, sir," I pleaded, "how can you think to force your daughter into nuptials which must be distasteful to her?"

"Don't you trouble your head about that. Margaret knows whish side her bread is buttered. She can distinguish between clotted cream and skim milk."

"Besides," I argued, "I am bound by the most solemn engagements to my Margery. I have promised to settle Brinsabatch on her."

"You cannot," shouted the farmer of Quether. "The thing is impossible. You cannot marry a woman who has no existence in the eye of the law. The only Margaret Palmer of Quether of whom the law has cognizance is she who now stands before you. She has been baptized, vaccinated, and confirmed. What more do you want to establish her existence? Whereas, what documentary proof can the other Margery produce that she exists? There is but one Margaret Palmer of Quether in this nineteenth century that's flat." He slapped the table, and then, with the air of one administering a crushing argument, he added, "Now tell me, is it possible for a man to marry a woman from whom he is removed by from two to three centuries? Answer me that."

"Put in that bald way," I said, "it does seem unreasonable; but in these Radical-Galdstone-Chamberlain-Bradlaughian times one does not know where one stands. All the lines of demarcation between the possible and the impossible are wiped out, reason and fact do not jump together."

"I leave you to digest that question," answered Palmer triumphantly. He saw I was pushed into a corner. Then he went out, along with Solomon Davy.

I do not think that Margaret objected to be left to meet Margery. I noticed her pluming and bridling like a game-cock before an encounter. She stroked down the folds of her gown, and pursed up her lips, and now and then shot out her tongue from between her lips, as I have seen a wasp test his sting before stabbing me. I was getting uneasy for Margery, and was myself uncomfortable. I said, "Miss Margaret, will you be so good as to pick my up my handkercher; it is lying there on the floor, and I be so cruel bad took with the lumbagie that I can't bend to take it myself."

She complied with my request somewhat surlily. Then I said, "Would you mind, now, just uncorking that bottle there on the shelf, and putting a drop or two on a lump of sugar, and giving it me. My hands be that shaky O cannot put it in my mouth myself, and I've no teeth to hold it by. The drops be ipecacua-hana, and be good for bronchitis."

"No, I won't do it, you nasty old man."

"Then, miss, will you rub my spine with hartshorn and oil: you'll find a bottle of the mixture on the sideboard, and a bit of flannel in the cupboard?"

"I will do nothing of the sort," she said testily.

"You won't, miss? Then please take me up in your arms and carry me to bed. Margery does it. She is very kind and considerate; she begrudges me no trouble , and feeds me out of a spoon."

"I will do nothing of the sort," she said again, in short, angry tones and with an air of supreme disgust.

"I am sorry for it," I said. That was Gospel truth. I knew that when the two women met such a storm of words would rage as would wreck my poor nerves, and I wanted to be in bed and out of it before the hurricane broke loose.

"You'll have to do all this for me," I said, "when you become Mrs. Rosedhu. A very old person needs just as much attention as a baby. I know that, for I've gone through it myself; I've done the nursing. Why will you not leave me alone, and allow Margery to marry me? She will take care of me; she kisses and fondles me. Will you?"

"You disgusting old scarecrow, certainly not."

"And atomy—scarecrow and atomy—what next will you call me? Yet you want to marry me!"

"You fool!" said Margaret shortly. "I put up with you for the sake of Brinsabatch."

"It's the same with Margery," I said; "but she put it more pleasantly. Her manners are better than yours; but she belongs to the old school—the good old school!" I sighed.

What I said made her angry. She did not like to have comparisons drawn between herself and her remote great aunt, to her own disadvantage.

"I suppose I am to have a voice in the matter," I went on; "and though I have liked you very much, Margaret, yet I like the other Margery better. One thing in her favour is—she is older than you."

"You are not going to have her—who has drained life and spirit out of you. D you think I will allow it? Don't you see I bear her a grudge? She has turned the fresh and hale George who courted me into a shrivelled old man. It would have been a pleasure to have young George, it is a penance to have the old one. I owe her that, and I shall scratch her eyes out when we meet."

Whatever you do," I pleaded, do not hurt her. Your father has made a dreadful threat. I hope he will not execute it."

"There she comes!" exclaimed Margaret Palmer, starting to her feet in a tremor of delight. "I hear her step on the walk."

"Thrown the hearthrug over me," I entreated, "I cannot bear to be agitated. Toss the table-cover above the hearthrug, all helps to deaden the sound."

Margaret complied with my request. Here again my narrative must present an appearance of incompleteness. I cannot describe what I neither saw nor heard during the interview between Margaret and Margery, because I was buried under a heavy sheepskin rug and a think-painted damask table-cover on the top of that. I have no imagination, and I only relate what I actually saw and heard. I saw nothing, and what I heard resembled the hanging of pots and pans when a host of maids are going after a swarm of bees. Of words I could distinguish none, till after a while the hearthrug and table-cover slipped off, owing to my coughing a great deal, the dust out of the hearthrug having got into my bronchial tubes. Then I saw a sight which filled me with dismay.

My room was full of men and boys, with their caps and hats on. Their faces were flushed, and eager, savage delight danced in their eyes. One had a pitchfork, several had sticks, one was armed with a flail. Head and shoulders above the rest stood Farmer Palmer, keeping back the mob that crowded in at the door. In the front of all as if in a cockpit, opposite each other, stood the two Margarets, red in face, blazing in temper, their tongues going, their eyes sparkling, their hands extended. I will say that poor Margery acted solely on the defensive. She held up her arms in self-protection. Margaret had driven her nails into her check and a read streak down the side showed that she had drawn blood.

"See, see!" exclaimed the younger Margaret, "the witch! Her power is broken. The blood is running."

This is a popular belief. If you can draw blood from a witch, her power—at least over you—is at an end.

My poor Margery gazed with alarm at the crowd of red, threatening faces that looked at her. She shrank from the sticks, the clubs, the pitchfork and flail. She drew behind me, as if I, broken down into premature old age, could defend and assist her. I raised my shrill pipe in entreaty, but my words were without effect. Those horrible faces glowered at Margery with the savagery of dogs surrounding a hare they are about to tear into pieces. The fear of witchcraft blotted all human compassion out of their hearts.

Suddenly a red light blazed in at the window. The evening had fallen fast and it was now dark.

"Look! Look there!" shouted Farmer Palmer. "Look there, you witch, at the bed made for you. There are plenty of faggots to heap over you should you complain of the cold."

Mary uttered a scream of terror and clutched my hair, whilst she cowered on the floor behind it.

"Oh, George!" she cried in her agony of dread, "save me! Save me! They cannot kill me, but they can fry and burn me! Then I shall live on-on-on, a scorched morsel, not like a human being."

"My darling," I answered, "I can do nothing against all these men." I, however, made a desperate attempt. "I am master in this hosue," I cried in my shrill old tones; "no one has any right within the doors without my permission, and I order you all to go away peaceably and to leave me alone."

The men and boys, led by Palmer, laughed, and did not budge an inch. There came a shout from outside:

"Bring out the witch, and let her burn!"

There is an innate cruelty in human nature which neither Christianity, nor education, nor teetotalism, will eradicate. I always thought the peasantry of the West of England wonderfully gentle, kindly, and free from brutality, and yet—scratch the man and the beast appears; here were my peaceable, tender-hearted country men ravening for the life of a poor woman , really pretty, and as good-dispositioned and without malice as an angel. I knew that they would gloat over her anguish in the fire, that they would poke up the fuel to make her burn more thoroughly—they would do so without compassion; not really because they thought her a witch, but because Farmer Palmer had told them they might burn her without fear of the law.

A fresh heap of fuel had been tossed upon the pyre, and the fame spouted up to heaven. A roar from the boys without: "Bring her out! Let her burn!"

Poor Margery covered her eyes with her hands and shut out the terrible light.

"Oh, George, George!" she cried, "save me, and I will give you back some of your youth and strength again."

"Stand back," thundered Palmer, as the circle of men contracted about her, and hands were thrust forth to grasp and tear her from my chair. "Do you hear me? She has offered to recover our friend Rosedhu."

"You cannot do it, my poor darling," I said.

"Oh, save me, George, and I will indeed."

"You hear her," shouted Palmer. "Stand back, and let her fulfill what she has undertaken."

Then Margaret put in her voice. She was afraid that her rival would escape. "No, father, do not trust her. She can do nothing. She is a witch, and wants to cast spells over you all. Take her away, boys, and pitch her into the fire. Don't listen to a word she says, however hard she prays to be let go."

"Into the flames with her!" shouted the men, and stepped forward. That is the place for such as she."

"Fair play, my lads," said Palmer, and with his strong arm he drove the rabble back. "As for you, Margaret, don't you interfere. Now then you—Margery—or whatever you call yourself, stand up and come forward. None shall hurt you if you really recover Rosedhu of his age and incapacity. But, mind you, if you fail, I swear that with the cudgel I will break every bone in your body, and then throw you into the fire with my own arms."

Margery quivered and cried out at the threat.

"Are you going to do it or not?" asked Palmer.

Poor Margery, feeling the necessity for prompt action, if she would save herself from terrible torture, rose from her crouching posture and stole tremblingly forward.

"Stand out o' the road, boys," shouted Palmer; "clear away with you," and with his stick he swept a circle round Margery and me.

"Oh, George," she said, with tears of mortification in her blue eyes, "I'm sorry to do it. I wouldn't if I could; I really wouldn't. But I cannot help myself. These cruel men do so scare me. We might have been so comfortable together; I'd have nursed you into your grave quite beautiful and convenient like, then I'd have had Brinsabatch to myself, and it would have gone so well for all parties. But now, you see, that blessed arrangement you managed so nicely for me won't come to nothing because of the wickedness of evil men, who walks about like unto roaming and roaring lions seeking who they may devour. I cannot help myself, George. You'll never doo me the justice to say it were against my will and under compulsion. There, give me your two hands into mine"

She took my hands and stood opposite me, holding them at arm's length, and looking into my eyes. Poor thing! her lips trembled, and the tears stood on her lids and overflowed and trickled down her soft red cheeks. It was a sore trial and disappointment to her, but she bore it like Christian, and never cast a word of bitterness at those who forced her to it. And to think what a sacrifice she was making! Those rude creatures knew nothing of that, and could not appreciate the greatness of her self-sacrifice. I submitted, because I saw in this was only the means of rescuing her.

As she held my hands, I felt as if streams of vital force were flowing from her up my arms into my body. The aching in my bones ceased. My legs became stronger, my head lighter and more erect. I could see better, and hear better. I began to smell the peat burning on the hearth, I felt an inclination to draw Margery on to my knees and kiss her; but when I looked at her, the desire passed, she was waning as I waxed. She grew older, the colour left her cheek, her eyes because dim; then, all at once I sprang to my feet and shook off her hands. "Enough, Margery, enough," I said. "you have restored me sufficient of my strength and health, the rest I freely make over to you. Now for the rest of you." My voice was full and loud as that of Palmer himself. "Everyone of you listen to me. This is my house, and an Englishman's house in his castle. Leave this room, leave my land at once, or I prosecute every man jack of you for burglary and trespass. Good Lord! Do you know where you are? Do you know who I am? This is Brinsabatch, and I am a Rosedhu. Gladstone and Chamberlain and Bradlaugh haven't brought matters quite so far yet that every dirty Radical may come inside and a landed proprietor's doors and snap his fingers under his nose." I snatched the stick out of Palmer's hand and went at the men with it. Not one ventured to show me his face. I saw a sudden change of posture, and a crush and rush out of my door and down my little passage. "You bide here, Palmer," I said; "and Margaret also. But as for all this rag-tag and bob-tail that you have brought in, I'll make a clean sweep of them in a jiffy."

"It is all very well, Rosedhu," said Palmer, folding his arms, and settling his legs wide apart. "You have got rid of this rabble, and you are right to do so if you choose. But you do not get rid of me and Margaret so fast. The banns have been called between my daughter and you; I take no account of the other, she has no legal existence."

I was silent, and looked from Margery to Margaret.

"Besides," Palmer went on, "you may not think so much of her now. In appearance she is old enough to be your grand-mother."

Certainly Margery looked aged, a hale woman, but still old—too old to be thought of as a bride at the hymeneal altar. Margaret was young and pretty; I wish she had not been quite so young and opened such an alarming vista of possibilities. But then I looked at myself in a glass opposite, and saw that I was grey-headed and on the turn down the hill of life. That was an advantage. "There is one thing," I said musingly: "in the matter of amiability there is no comparison. Margery is as good—"

"We will have no comparisons drawn," interrupted Palmer, as the girl darted a look at me that plainly said, "You shall suffer for this some day." "Hold out your fist like a man and say that you will take my daughter for better, for worse, and make her mistress of Brinsabatch within the month. The first time of asking took place today."

"Let us say in another couple or three years," said I, with the principle of the family at heart.

"No," answered Palmer curtly. Within the month, unless you constnet to that—into the fire the old hag goes."

"Oh, Palmer!" I exclaimed. You passed your word to her that she should be spared."

"No, no. I said that unless she restored you I would break every bone of her body and throw her into the flames myself. I will certainly not touch her with my stick, nor commit her myself to the flames, but I will let the men outside deal with her as they like. I see what it is, there is no security for you from the witchcrafts of that old hag till there is another woman in this house. That woman must be my daughter, and when she is here I defy all the witches that dance Cox Tor, and all the pretty wenches of Devonshire to get so much as a foot inside the door."

"Father!" protested Margaret.

"My dear, I know you."

"Well, you need not say it."

"Give me a twelvemonth's grace," I entreated.

"No, not above twenty days."

A howl from without—a fresh faggot was cast on the fire. The pyre was not on my ground but on a bit of waste adjoining the lane, and as I am not lord of the manor I have no rights over it. That the rascals knew.

Poor Margery laid hold of my arm. Margaret at once intervened and thrust her aside. "You do not touch him again."

"You see," laughed the father, "it is as I said. Come, your hand."

I gave it with a sigh.

I have written these few pages to let people know that Margery of Quether is about somewhere—where I do not know for certain, but I believe she has gone off into the remotest parts of Dartmoor, where, probably she will seek herself a cave among the granite tors, in which to conceal herself, where no boys will be likely to find and throw stones at her. I am uneasy now that there is such a rush of visitors to Dartmoor to enjoy the wonderful air and scenery, lest they should come across her and in thoughtlessness or ignorance do her an injury. Now that they know her story, I trust they will give her a wide berth.

I think that what I have gone though has taught me a lesson, but it is not one much recommended thought it is largely followed: Never succour those who solicit succour, or they will suck you dry.

# BRAM STOKER:
## COUNT WAMPYR (1890)

Bram [i.e., Abraham] Stoker (1847-1912) has been eclipsed by his literary creation. *Dracula* has transcended horror per se to become one of the best-selling novels in the world. The following three pages are all that remains of an early draft of his masterpiece.[1]

"Bram Stoker's Original Foundation Notes & Data for His 'Dracula'" consist of 124 pages of hand-written plot notes, hand-written research notes, and typed research notes (which include three photographs and a newspaper clipping). These papers were auctioned at Sotheby, Wilkinson & Hodge in London in 1913—one year after the author's death—for the paltry sum of two pounds, two shillings. They changed hands several times before they were acquired by the Rosenbach Museum & Library in Philadelphia.

The first section of the "Notes" and the first three pages of section two are scribbled on odd scraps of paper. These hand-written notes show how the story evolved from unrecognizable pastiches of people, places and events to a nine-page calendar of events that includes most of the familiar story which has been told and retold in every part of the world since 1897.

The following pages were written when the novel was still titled *The Un-Dead*, and its anti-hero was referred to as "Count Wampyr" from "Styria."[2]

---

1 The photo-facsimiles of pages 38a, 38b and 38c are presented by the courtesy of the Rosenbach Museum & Library in Philadelphia, and may not be reproduced without their written consent.

2 Robert Eighteen-Bisang and Elizabeth Miller provide more details about pages 38a, 38b, 38c and examine every page of Bram Stoker's "Notes" in *Bram Stoker's Notes for Dracula* (Jefferson, NC: McFarland, 2008).

Memo 1 (page 38a) establishes rules that govern Bram Stoker's literary creation and provides details about the vampire's castle. The reference "Salzburg" indicates that, like Joseph Sheridan LeFanu's "Carmilla," the novel was originally set in Austria. The novel opens with "Left Munich at 8.36 PM on 1st May ..." while the story "Dracula's Guest" takes place in Munich.

Not that Stoker always imagined his vampire as a "Count," but he did not find the name "Dracula" until he had drafted most of his novel. On a subsequent page, he wrote "Count Dracula" in the top left-hand corner and scribbled "Dracula" on both sides of the heading.

The last four lines of Memo 1 initiate episodes that were deleted by the time the novel went to press. However, the phrase "face of Count in London" became part of chapter 13. When Jonathan sees Dracula in London he exclaims: "It is the man himself?" Most importantly, these lines prove that before Stoker was seduced by the charms of Whitby, he assumed that his vampire would enter England via Dover, which was the most common portal to London.

Memo 2 (page 38b) continues to explore vampires' strengths and weaknesses. They mention that Dracula is insensitive to music, and he cannot be photographed (or Codaked).

Memo 3 (page 38c) is chock full of events that are not found in the novel. The theme of a dinner party with thirteen guests parodies the "Last Supper," while the "mad doctor" and the segment in which each guest is "asked to tell something strange" echo the celebrated literary gathering at the Villa Diodati, where a ghost-story contest led to the creation of Shelley's *Frankenstein*, Byron's "A Fragment" and, eventually, Polidori's "The Vampyre."

The last line of Memo 3, in which a doctor restores a man to life, is one of the most baffling dead ends in the Notes.

———————

# Vampire

memo(1)

~~no looking glasses, in rooms none~~

never can see him reflected ~~in one — no shadow?~~

light arc angel & give no shadow —

~~never eat, nor drink~~

Carried or led over threshold

~~Enormous strength~~ —

see in the dark

power of getting small or large

Money always old gold — trace it to Salzburg banking house

at Munich ~~dead house~~ see face among

I.2  flowers — ~~think corpse~~ — but is alive

III.—x  (afterwards when white moustache grown is Dane or friend of Count in London

doctor at ~~dinner~~ Custom house sees him or Corpse —

coffins, collected pile taken over — one empty we thought —

## Memo i

no looking glasses in Count's house
never can see him reflected in one—no shadow?
lights arranged to give no shadow—
never eats nor drinks
carried or led over threshold
enormous strength
see in the dark
power of getting small or large
money always old gold—traced to Salzburg banking house
I-2   At Munich Dead House see face among flowers—think
corpse—but is alive
III   Afterwards when white moustache grown is same as face
of Count in London
Doctor at Dover Custom house sees him or corpse
Coffins selected to be taken over—wrong one brought

38 b

Vampire

Mema(?)

II ---      Zoological garden — wolves &c
       cowed — rage of eagle &
       lion &c

II. III      goes through fog by instinct

I. II      white teeth &c

     Crosses river & running water at
     exact slack or flood of tide —

II   influence over rats

II   painters cannot paint his likeness their
     likenesses always like some one else —

II   insensibility to music

II   absolute despisal of death & the dead

II. III   attitude with regard to religion — only moved
     by relics older than own real date over a
     century —

I. II. III   power of Century live thoughts or humanity
     dead ones in others feeling

     could not codlok him — come
     out block or the sepulture
     corpse &c

## MEMO 2

| | |
|---|---|
| II | Zoological garden—wolves hyenas cowed—rage of eagle & lion |
| II. III | goes through fog by instinct |
| I. II | white teeth |
| | crosses river & running water at exact slack or full flood of tide |
| II | influence over rats |
| II | painters cannot paint him—their likenesses always like someone else |
| II | insensibility to music |
| II | absolute despisal of death & the dead |
| II. III | attitude with regard to religion—only moved by relics older than own real date [unreadable] century |
| I. II. III | power of creating evil thoughts or banishing good ones in others present |
| | Could not codak [i.e., photograph] him—come out black or like skeleton corpse |

38 C

Vampire

memma (3)

IV

The dinnerparty at the
mad doctor's.
Thirteen – each has a number.
Each asked to tell something
strange – order of numbers
makes the story complete – at
the end the Count comes in –

_____

the divisional surgeon, being sick the
doctor is asked to see man in coffin –
restores him to life

## MEMO 3

IV  the dinner party at the mad doctor's
thirteen—each has a number
Each asked to tell something strange—order of numbers
makes the story complete—at the end the Count comes in
The divisional surgeon being sick the doctor is asked to see
man in coffin—restores him to life

# Julian Osgood Field:
## A Kiss of Judas (1893)

Julian Osgood Field (1849-1925) used the pseudonym "X. L."
on a handful of weird, diabolic stories.

Field was born in New York, but educated in England. He
lived in France during the 1880s where he became friends with
Victor Hugo, Guy de Maupassant and other writers. He eventually settled in London where "A Kiss of Judas" debuted in the
*Pall Mall Magazine* in July, 1893. The story was accompanied by
Aubrey Beardsley's drawing "The Kiss of Judas. (According to
the Gospels, Judas identified Jesus to the men who arrested and,
eventually, crucified him by means of a kiss.)

"A Kiss of Judas" was reprinted in *Aut Diabolus Aut Nihil: And
Other Stories* (*The Devil or Nothing . . .*) which was published by
Methuen the following year. Its preface states that "The only real
portrait here is that of His Satanic Majesty Himself," while claims
such as "all the characters are sketched from life" and are "intimate friends of mine" convinced many readers that the stories
were factual accounts of European diabolism.

Field became a notorious money lender and confidence man
who involved Lady Ida Sitwell in a financial scandal that led to
her imprisonment for debt in 1912. He was sentenced to eighteen
months' hard labor at Wormwood Scrubs Prison in 1915.

THE KISS OF JVDAS

"Woman of outer darkness, fiend of death,
    From what inhuman cave, what dire abyss,
    Hast thou invisible that spell o'erheard?
    What potent hand hath touched thy quickened corse,
    What song dissolved thy cerements, who unclosed
    Those faded eyes and filled them from the stars?"
Landor: Gebir.

## THE JOURNEY

Towards the end of September, about eight years ago, the steamship Albrecht, under the command of the popular Captain Pellegrini, had on its voyage down the Danube, as far as Rustchuck, the honour of counting among its passengers a gentleman to whom not inaptly might have been addressed the somewhat audacious remark made by Charles Buller to a well-known peer, now deceased, "I often think how puzzled your Maker must be to account for your conduct." And, indeed, a more curious jumble of lovable and detestable qualities than went to the making-up of the personality, labeled for formal purposes Lieutenant-Colonel Richard Ulick Verner Rowan, but familiarly known to Society as 'Hippy' Rowan, it would, we think, have been difficult to find. Selfish almost to cruelty, and yet capable of acts of generous self-sacrifice to which many a better man could not perhaps have risen; famous for his unnecessary harshness in the numerous wars wherein he had distinguished himself, and yet enjoying the well-merited reputation of being the best-natured man in London, Hippy Rowan, thanks to the calm and healthy spirit of philosophy within him, had in the course of his fifty odd years of mundane experiences, never allowed a touch of cynicism to chill his heart. It is not so easy or natural as many may imagine to be content with a great deal; but in the golden days when much had been his—at the meridian of his altogether pleasant life, in which even the afternoon shadows were in no wise indicative of the terrors of the advancing night—Dick Rowan was possessed of the same serene spirit of content which distinguished him in the latter and more troublous times when he found himself forced to look gout and debt in the face on an income barely double the wages he had formerly given to his cordon bleu.

Just before our story opens, he had been invited by his old friend Djavil Pacha, a Turkish millionaire, to spend a few days with him at his palace on the Bosphorus—a summons which Dick Rowan was now steaming down the Danube to obey . . .

He had chosen this particularly monotonous and uncomfortable way of reaching his friend for reasons which do not concern us: but the thought of the unpleasant railway journey from Rustchuck to Varna which awaited him, and then the encounter with the Black Sea, did not tend to assuage the twinges of gout and irritability which assailed him by fits and starts as, during the two dreary days he watched the shores on either side glide slowly by—seeing on the right Hungary at length give place to Servia, and the Servia to Turkey, while perpetual Wallachia, sad and desolate, stretched unceasingly and for ever to the left— walking up and down the deck leaning on the arm of his trusty valet, or rather, Ancient or Lieutenant, Adams by name, a man almost as well known and fully as well informed as his master, a Cockney who, without any control over the aspirates in his native English, spoke eight other different languages, including Arabic, accurately and fluently, and whose knowledge of Oriental countries dated indeed from the days when he had been page- boy to the great Eltchi in Constantinople. There were but few passengers on board—an abnormally small number, in fact—and to this circumstance, doubtless, was it due that Rowan who, as a rule, paid but little attention to his fellow-travelers, happened to remark a mysterious-looking individual—a man, and appar- ently not an old one—who sat quite apart from the others and by himself, muffled up to the eyes in a very voluminous, albeit rather dirty, white silk handkerchief, and who was evidently invalid, judging from the listless way in which he sat, the extreme pallor of the only part of his face which could be seen, and above all, the fever-fed light which glared from between his sore and lashless eyelids. He was dressed entirely in black, and although his clothes were somewhat shabby, they betokened carelessness on the part of their wearer rather than poverty; and Adams had noticed and called his master's attention to the fact that on one finger of the man's thin, yellow, dirty hand, which every now and then he would lift to rearrange still higher up about his face the silken muffler, sparkled a diamond, which the omniscient valet recognized to be a stone of value.

"What an extremely disagreeable-looking man, Adams!" pettishly murmured the Colonel in English, as he and his servant in their perambulations up and down the deck for the twentieth time on the first morning of the journey passed by where the mysterious stranger sat. "And how he stares at us! He has the eyes of a lunatic, and there is evidently something horrible the matter with his face. Perhaps he's a leper. Ask the Captain about him."

But the ever-amiable Captain Pellegrini had not much information to impart, save indeed that the man was certainly neither a madman nor a leper, nor indeed, so far as he knew, an invalid.

He was a Moldavian, Isaac Lebedenko by name, a young man, a medical student or doctor, the Captain thought; but, at all events, a man in very well-to-do circumstances, for he always spent his money freely.

"I have known him off and on for two years, please your Excellency," said the skipper. "Though I must confess I have never seen his face properly, for he's always muffled up in that way. He takes his meals by himself, and of course pays extra for doing so, and in fact he always, so far as I know, keeps entirely to himself and never speaks to any one. But the steward's boy, who has waited on him and seen his face, says there is nothing the matter with him except indeed that he's the ugliest man he ever saw."

"Perhaps he's consumptive," suggested the Colonel. But the all-wise Adams shook his head. That was quite inadmissible. He had seen the man walk, and had noticed his legs. Phthisis could not deceive him, he could recognize its presence at a glance. This man was as strong on his legs as a panther; no consumption there.

"Well," said the Colonel, impatiently, "there's evidently something wrong with him, no matter what, and I'm glad I'm not condemned to remain long in his society; for he certainly has the most unpleasant look in his eyes that I've seen since we left the lepers." And then he turned the current of the conversation, and the subject dropped.

That night, very late, when the Colonel was sitting quite alone on deck, smoking a cigarette, and thinking over his approaching visit to Djavil, wondering what persons his old friend would have invited to his palace to meet him, and a thousand souvenirs thronging to his mind as he dreamily glanced up at the moon which smiled over slowly-receding Servia, a voice close to his ear, a slow, huskily sibilant high-pitched whisper, broke the stillness, saying in lisping French—

"May I ask, Monsieur, by what right you dare to question persons about me?" and, turning, he saw standing by his shoulder that horrible man in shabby black, his eyes glaring with exceptional ferocity from between the red bare lids, and the diamond-decorated, clawlike hand grasping convulsively the soiled white muffler, presumably to prevent the vehemence of his speech from causing it to slip down.

Hippy rose to his feet at once, and, as he did so, his face passed close to the half-shrouded countenance of the man who had addressed him, and the familiar sickening smell of animal musk full of repulsive significance to the experienced traveler assailed his nostrils.

"What do you mean?" he exclaimed, shrinking back, his disgust quite overpowering for the moment every other sentiment. "Stand back! Don't come near me!"

The man said nothing, stood quite still, but Rowan saw plainly in the moonlight the red-encircled eyes gleam with renewed ferocity, the yellow, claw-like hand wearing the diamond ring grasping the dirty muffler agitated by a convulsive spasm, and heard beneath the silken covering the husky breathing caught as in a sob. Hippy recovered himself at once. "Forgive me, Monsieur," he said, coldly. "You startled me. Might I beg you to repeat your question?"

The man said nothing. It was evident that he had perceived the disgust he had inspired, and that his anger, his indignation, mastered him, and that he dared not trust himself to speak.

"You asked me I think," continued the Colonel in a more gentle tone—for his conscience smote him as he reflected that he might perhaps involuntarily have caused pain to one who, notwithstanding his unpleasant aspect, and arrogant, not to say hostile, attitude, was doubtless merely an invalid and a sufferer—"You asked me, I think, Monsieur, by what right I made inquiries concerning you? Pray pardon me for having done so. I have, indeed, no excuse to offer, but I am really sorry if I have offended you. I merely asked the Captain—"

But the man interrupted him, his voice, which was tremulous with passion, coming as a husky wheezy hiss, which rendered the strong lisp with which he pronounced the French the more noticeable and grotesque.

"You asked him—you dared ask him if I were not a leper. He told Hoffmann, the steward's boy, who told me. You can't deny it! Dog of an Englishman!"

Here, gasping for want of breath, and apparently quite over-powered by his anger, the man took a step towards Rowan. This outburst of vituperation came as a great relief to the Colonel. Like most persons of refined feeling, he could stand any wounds better than those inflicted by self-reproach, and the suspicion that perhaps by careless rudeness he had caused pain to the one worthy only of pity had been as gall to him. The man's violent hostility and bad language entirely altered and brightened the aspect of affairs.

"I am sorry," said Hippy, with ironical politeness, "that my nationality should not meet with the honour of your approval. It is not, hélas! the proud privilege of all to be able to boast that they are natives of Moldavia, you know! Pour le reste, all I can do is to repeat my apology for—"But the man interrupted him again.

"Apology!" he echoed, if indeed any word indicative of reso-nance can be applied to the hoarse, damp, lisping whisper in which he spoke—"Apology! Ah, yes! You English curs are all cowards, and only think of apologies. You dare not fight, canaille, but you shall! I'll force you to!" And again he took a step forward, but this time in so menacing a fashion that the Colonel, half amused and half disgusted, thought it prudent to step back.

"Take care!" he said, half raising his stick as if to push the man back as an unclean thing: "keep your distance,"—and then,

speaking quickly, for he feared an assault from the infuriated
Moldavian, and was desirous of avoiding such an absurd compli-
cation, he continued, "If you can prove to me that I ought to meet
you, I shall be happy to do so. You're right, of course, in thinking
duels are no longer the fashion in England. But I'm an exception
to the rule. I've fought two already, and shall be happy to add to
the number by meeting you if it can be arranged. But that's hardly
a matter you and I can properly discuss between ourselves, is it?
Captain Pellegrini knows me. I'll leave my address with him. I
have friends in Turkey, and shall be staying in the neighbourhood
of Constantinople for a fortnight, so if you care to send me your
seconds, I will appoint gentleman to receive them. Allow me to
wish you a good-night!" and Rowan raised his hat with much
formal politeness, and stepped aside as if to depart; but the man
sprang forward like a cat and stood in his way.

"Coward!" he exclaimed, extending both arms as if to bar
Rowan's passage—"Cur! like all your countrymen! You think
to run away from me, but you shall not! You shall go on your
knees and beg my pardon, you accursed Englishman—you
dog—you—"

But just as the enraged Moldavian reached this point in his
fury an awful thing happened. The yellow, claw-like hand having
been withdrawn from clutching the dirty muffler, the vehemence
of the man's speech began gradually to disarrange this covering,
causing it little by little to sink lower and lower and thus to disclose
by degrees to Rowan a sight so strange, so awful, that, impelled
by a morbid curiosity, he involuntarily bent his head forward as
his horror-stricken eyes eagerly noted every step in the infernal
progress of this revelation. And thus, gazing at the slowly slipping
silk, he saw first, beardless, hollow cheeks, twitching with emotion,
but of a most hideous pallor, of indeed that awful hue insepa-
rably associated with the idea of post-mortem changes, then, in
the middle of this livid leanness, lighted only by those fever-fed,
red-lidded eyes, the beginning—the broad base springing from
the very cheekbones as it were—of a repulsive prominence which
apparently went narrowing on to some termination which as yet

the scarf hid, but which the horrified Colonel felt every second surer and yet more sure could not resemble the nasal organ of man, but rather the—ah, yes! the silk fell, and in the moonlight Rowan saw the end he had foreseen, the pointed nose as of a large ferret, and beneath it, far in under it, nervously working, the humid, viscous horror of a small mouth almost round, but lipless, from which came in hurried, husky sibilance the lisping words of hate and menace.

This awful revelation, although partly expected, was so inexpressibly horrible when it came, that, doubtless, the expression of disgust in Rowan's face deepened so suddenly in acuteness and intensity as to arrest the attention of the monster who inspired it, infuriated though he was; for he paused in the lisping tumult of his violence, and, as he paused, became suddenly aware that the muffler had slipped down. Then, rightly interpreting the horror he saw written in the Colonel's countenance, and goaded to a fresh fit of fury, too despairing and violent even for words, he, with an inarticulate moan or whimper, rushed blindly forward with extended arms to attack his enemy. But the Colonel, who had foreseen this onslaught, stepped quickly to one side, and, as he did so, quite overpowered by disgust, he could not resist the temptation of giving the hostile monster a violent push with his heavy walking stick—a thrust of far greater force than he had intended, for it caused the man to totter and fall forward, just as two or three sailors, who, from a distance, had witnessed the last incidents of the dispute, ran up and stood between the adversaries.

"That man," exclaimed the Colonel in German, pointing with his stick to where the Moldavian lay sprawling on his knees, hastily readjusting the muffler around his hideous face. "tried to assault me, and I defended myself. Look after him, but beware of him. He is a wild beast, not a man!" The men looked at the Colonel, whom they knew to be some important grandee held in great honour by their Captain, and then at the shabby mass of black clothes, sprawling on the deck, and then at each other, and marveled greatly, open-mouthed, not knowing what to say or think or do.

"I shall see the Captain about this to-morrow morning," continued Rowan. "But in the meantime, as I say, look after this—this—man, but beware of him!" and so speaking, he turned and strode away in the direction of his cabin.

Just before reaching the stairway he turned and looked back. There in the moonlight stood the man in black, gazing after him, the awful face hidden once more in the dirty muffler, which was now stained on one side with the blood which came trickling down from a wound on the brow. As he saw the Colonel turn, the man raised his clenched fist and shook it very slowly, solemnly, and deliberately—the gesture of a warning and of a curse—and the sailors, fearing further violence, closed around him. Then the Colonel turned and went his way to bed. The following morning Rowan of course made his faithful Adams (who, by the way, was never astonished at anything, having acquired through long residence in the East the stolidity of the Oriental) fully acquainted with the strange events of the preceding night, but charged him to say nothing to anybody.

"I have thought the matter over," said the Colonel, "and have decided merely to tell the Captain that I had a few words with this man, and in a heated moment struck him, and then give Pellegrini his Excellency's address where we shall be for the next fortnight, so that if this man wants to communicate with me in any way, he can. Of course any question of a duel with such a brute is absurd, but I hope he won't attempt to assault me again to-day."

"I'll keep a sharp look-out he doesn't, sir" said Adams.

But such precautions were unnecessary. Nothing more was seen of the Moldavian, who presumably was confined to his cabin by his wound, and the following morning at early dawn the Colonel and his servant left the steamer at Rustchuck and took the train to the Varna and the Black Sea, en route for the splendors of the Bosphorus.

## THE SECOND MEETING

'Hippy' Rowan has arrived at Djavil Pacha's palace on the Bosphorus. Other guests staying with the Turkish millionaire include Lord Melrose ('a well known gambler and breaker and taker of banks'), Emile Bertonneux ('an amusing French news-paper man, of the Paris Oeil de Boeuf') and Tony Jeratczesco (an international bon viveur, 'fond of cards and racing, and with plenty of money to justify his interest in both these expensive forms of speculation'). Jeratczesco has invited the assembled company to join him at his 'mysterious castle' (in the 'Molda-vian Karpaks'). They all agree, and Djavil arranges a spectacular picnic in the country just before their depature. The guests at this function include Leopold Maryx ('the renowned specialist for nervous diseases, who had been summond from Vienna on purpose to see the Sultan'), 'Lord, and especially Lady, Brentford, the champion political bore in petticoats', Leonard P. Beacon, a New York millionaire ('vulgar beyond even the power of dyna-mite to purify') and Lord Malling ('our delightful but impos-sible Ambassador'). The conversation turns to the subject of 'evil spirits'.

Maryx was telling me about the Children of Judas," remarked Hippy Rowan.

"The Children of Judas!" echoed Emile Bertonneux, the Parisian newspaper man, scenting a possible article à sensa-tion—for it is, we suppose, hardly necessary to remind our readers that in so cosmopolitan a gathering the conversation was carried on in French—"Who are they? I had no idea Judas was a père de famille."

"It's a Moldavian legend," replied the great specialist. "They say the Children of Judas, lineal descendents of the arch traitor, are prowling about the world seeking to do harm, and that they kill you with a kiss."

"But how do they get at you to kiss you?" gasped Mr Leonard P. Beacon, his thirst for information leading him to ignore the fact that his mouth was full of loup sauce homard.

"The legend is," said Maryx, "that in the first instance they are here in every shape—men and women, young and old, but generally of extraordinary and surpassing ugliness, but are here merely to fill their hearts with envy, venom, and hatred, and to mark their prey. In order to really do harm, they have to sacrifice themselves to their hatred, go back to the infernal regions whence they came—but go back by the gate of suicide—report to the Chief of the Three Princes of Evil, get their diabolical commission from him, and then return to his world and do the deed. They can come back in any form they think the best adapted to attain their object, or that satisfy their hate: sometimes they come as a mad dog who bites you and gives you hydrophobia—that's one form of the kiss of Judas; sometimes as the breath of pestilence, cholera, or what not—that's another form of the kiss of Judas; sometimes in an attractive shape, and then the kiss is really as one of affection, though as fatal in its effect as the mad dog's bite or the pestilence. When it takes the form of a kiss of affection, however, there is always a mark on the poisoned body of the victim—the wound of the kiss. Last summer, when I was at Sinaia in attendance on the Queen, I saw the body of a peasant girl whose lover had given her the kiss of Judas, and there certainly was on her neck a mark like this:" and Maryx took up his fork and scratched on the tablecloth three X's,—thus, XXX. "Can you guess what that's supposed to signify?" inquired the great physician.

"Thirty," exclaimed Lady Brentford.

"Of course," replied Maryx, "thirty—the thirty pieces of silver, of course—the mark of the price of blood."

"Vous êtes impayable, mon cher!" exclaimed Djavil, grinning. "Whenever you find it no longer pays to kill your patients you can always make money at the foires. Set Hippy Rowan to beat the drum at the door and you sit inside the van telling your wonderful blagues, and you'll make a fortune in no time."

The great Professor paid no attention to these flippant remarks; he was, indeed, notwithstanding his marvelous intelligence and extraordinary science and experience and skill, at heart a very charlatan and mountebank in his love of a gaping crowd; and the interest he saw depicted on the faces of his listeners delighted him.

"Did you say that in the first instance these Children of Judas are supposed to be very ugly?" inquired Colonel Rowan, his thoughts reverting to the awful face of that man Isaac Lebedenko who had assaulted him on the boat. The incident had almost wholly passed away from his memory until then, though he had noted it down in his carefully-kept diary; and he had, by the way, long ago told himself that he must have been mistaken in what he thought that horrible muffler had disclosed to him; that such things could not be, and that he must have been deceived either by some trick of shadow, or by some prank on him by gout astride of his imagination.

"Yes," replied Maryx, "so runs the legend. This physical ugliness betokens, of course, the malignant spirit within. At that stage they may be recognized and avoided, or better still, slain; for they only really become dangerous when their hatred has reached such a pitch that they are prompted to seek a voluntary death and re-incarnation in order to completely satisfy their malignancy; for it is by the gate of suicide alone that they can approach the Arch-Fiend to be fully commissioned and equipped to return to earth on their errand of destruction. So if they are killed in their first stage of development, and not allowed to commit suicide, they are extinguished. When they return fully armed with power from Hell, it is too late; they cannot be recognized, and are fatal; for they have at their command all the weapons and artillery of Satan, from the smile of a pretty woman to the breath of pestilence. This voluntary self-sacrifice of hate in order to more fully satisfy itself by a regeneration, this suicide on the reculer pour mieux sauter principle, is of course nothing but a parody of the Divine Sacrifice of Love on which the Christian religion is based . . ."

When the repast was at length over, every one began strolling about the woods, and Happy Rowan, lighting a cigar, started for a ramble with his old friend Lord Malling. But they had not gone far when their host sent a servant after them to request his lordship to return and speak with him; and so, the Ambassador turning back, Hippy continued his saunter by himself, penetrating by degrees into a somewhat remote and secluded part of the forest, the voice and laugher of the other guests becoming gradually fainter and fainter as he strolled on.

Suddenly, from behind a tree, a man sprang out upon him, and a knife gleamed in the sunlight, swiftly descending upon his heart. Hippy, quick as lightning, leapt to one side, striking up as he did so with his heavy walking-stick at the would be assassin's arm, and with such force that he sent the knife flying out of the man's hand into the air; and then turning, he dealt the villain a blow on the side of the head which brought him to the ground as one dead. It was the Moldavian, Isaac Lebedenko. Hippy had recognised the eyes gleaming over the dirty-white muffler the moment the man sprang out upon him; and now, as he lay on the ground insensible, there could, of course, be no shadow of doubt about his identity, although he had so fallen, on one side, that the wrapper had not been disarranged from his face. We have said that, although enjoying the well-merited reputation of being the best-natured man in London, Dick Rowan had laid himself open to the reproach of having been most unduly harsh and severe in numerous wars in which he had been engaged; and this harshness, not to say cruelty, presumably ever latent in his nature, but which seemed only to be called to the surface under certain special conditions closely connected to peril and the excitement engendered thereby, now made itself apparent. The Moldavian had fallen on his side, and the shock of his fall had been so violent, while one hand lay palm upwards and half open on the trunk of a large fallen tree, the other hand, palm downwards, had been thrown upon its fellow. It was rather a peculiar position for the shock resulting from a fall to have thrown the hands into, and of course indicated that the blow had been so severe that the man had not been able to make any attempt to break his fall, but had sunk to the ground like a doll. Such, at least, was the way Rowan explained the matter as he stood over his prostrate enemy, wondering in his mind how he could possibly contrive to secure the violent would-be assassin until such time as he should be able to obtain assistance and have him handed over to the authorities for punishment; and just as he noticed the position of his hands his eyes caught the gleaming of the knife, which had fallen in the grass a little farther off. Hippy went to where it lay, and picked it up. It was a murderous-looking weapon indeed: broad, double-edged, and very sharp, though rather thick and not long; and fitted with a big round handle of lead, destined, of course, to lend terrible momentum to any blow struck by it. Rowan looked at the knife, and then at the hands of the Moldavian, lying in so diabolically tempting a position; and just then a quivering of the man's legs plainly indicated that he was recovering his senses. If it was to be done at all, there was evidently no time to be lost; so Rowan, taking the sharp instrument, and positioning it point downwards over the man's hands, which were already beginning to twitch with returning consciousness, and using his huge walking-stick as a hammer, with one powerful blow on the broad heavy handle of the knife, drove it through both the hands of the Moldavian and into the trunk of the tree up to the very hilt. A slight and almost inaudible groan came from behind the white wrapper—that was all; but Rowan could see that under the sting of the sudden pain the man had completely recovered consciousness, for the awful eyes, just visible above the muffler, were now open and fixed upon him.

"You miserable scoundrel!" exclaimed Rowan in German, his voice hoarse with anger, "You may think yourself lucky I didn't kill you like a dog when you lay there at my mercy. But I'll have you punished—never fear. Lie quiet there until I have you sent to prison."

The man said nothing: his awful eyes simply looked at Rowan.

"I have been forced, as you see," continued the Colonel, leisurely taking out a cigar and lighting it, "to nail you to the tree to prevent your escaping. Vermin is often treated so, you know. But I shan't inconvenience you for long. In a very few minutes I shall be sending people to unpin you and bind you properly, and have you taken off to prison. We have not seen the last of each other yet, my good friend—believe me, we have not."

Then the man spoke—it was almost in a whisper, but the words came with the horrible liquid lisp Rowan remembered with so much disgust. "No," he murmured, "we have not seen the last of each other yet—we have not."

"There's but little fear, I fancy, of your not being here when I send for you," resumed Rowan, after a moment's pause, during which he and the Moldavian had been steadfastly gazing at each other. "So we needn't waste more time now, and especially as you must be rather uncomfortable. So à bientôt." Then, just as he was turning away, he stopped. "In case," said he very quietly, "you should succeed in wriggling away before I send for you, and prefer mutilating your hands to suffering the very many lashes I shall certainly have administered to you, it's as well you should know, perhaps, that when travelling I invariably carry a revolver. I'm without it to-day—very luckily for you—by the merest accident. But I'm not likely to forget again. So take care."

And then Rowan turned and began strolling leisurely back to where he had left his friends. His last words had not been idly spoken, but were intended to first of all suggest, to the miserable wretch whom he left nailed to the fallen tree, that escape was not altogether impossible, provided he were ready to pay the terrible price of self-mutilation required; and, secondly, to indicate the humiliating nature and severity of the punishment in store for him, that he might decide whether escape at any cost were not preferable to such torture and degradation. For, as a matter of fact, Hippy Rowan, directly the first moment of anger and the accompanying spasm of malignant cruelty had passed away, had decided in his mind to proceed no further in the matter, and by no means to take upon himself the ennui and trouble of having the paltry villain more seriously punished than he had already been. Had he had his revolver with him, he would of course have killed the man; but, as if was, he had nailed him as vermin to a tree in a lonely forest in Asia, and there he would leave him to his fate. He might starve to death there, or escape by a terrible mutilation, or possibly with his teeth remove the knife; or somebody might happen to pass by and relieve him—though this last was hardly likely: but at all events he, Hippy Rowan, having warned the villain what to expect in the event of his again molesting him, would have nothing more to do with the matter, and, indeed, not even mention the disagreeable episode to his friends—at least, not at present.

When Rowan got back to the scene of the picnic, he found the preparations for departure just being completed; and in a few minutes all Djavil's guests were once more comfortably ensconced in the carriages and on their way back to the Bosphorus.

All Djavil's house-guests were tired; so after dinner, a little music and chatting, and some very harmless gambling, they retired to rest much earlier than usual, Rowan being indeed glad when the time came that, unobserved and alone, he could deliver himself up wholly to his reflections, which happened that night to be a strangely melancholy complexion. His rooms were on the ground floor, the windows indeed opening out on to the garden which sloped down to the marble terrace bordering the Bosphorus; and since it was to meditate rather than to sleep that Rowan had sought retirement, the Colonel sent the faithful Adams to bed, lit a cigar and went out, descending to the waterside to enjoy the view. Hardly had he reached the terrace, however, when from its farther end, which lay in shadow, emerged, crawling in the moonlight along the white marble pavement, an awful figure, which he knew but too well—that of Isaac Lebedenko the Moldavian, the man whom he had left but a few hours before nailed to a tree in the forest in Asia. As Rowan saw the man, the man saw him; and as Hippy stepped back and hurriedly felt in his pocket for his revolver, remembering, even as he did so, that he had left that useful weapon on his dressing-table, the Moldavian drew himself up and sprang towards his enemy, pulling, as he did so, with one had the muffler from his face, and disclosing with hideous distinctness in the moonlight the indescribable horror of the countenance of a monster not born of woman, while with the other hand he fumbled in his pocket.

"The only way!" he gasped, in lisping German: "the only way! But I am ready—glad; for I shall come to you now and you cannot escape me! See!" And so saying, and before Rowan could realize what was taking place, the man stabbed himself to the heart, and with a loud groan fell backwards into the waters of the Bosphorus, which closed over him.

"And you say you were not frightened?" exclaimed Bertonneux of the Oeil de Boeuf.

Hippy Rowan shook his head and smiled. "No, of course not," he said. Then he added, lowering his voice lest the others should hear him, "Do you know, it's a strange thing, mon cher, that never in my life have I known what fear is. It's no boast, of course, but a fact; and you can ask any one who's been with me in danger. There are plenty of them about, for I began with Inkermann and only ended with Candahar, not to speak of innumerable little private adventures more or less unpleasant between times, like the one I've just been telling you about, in fact. You know me well enough to feel that I'm neither a fool nor a coxcomb, and as a matter of fact this is not exactly courage, I fancy, but rather an absolute inability to entertain such a sentiment as fear. Just as some people are born blind and deaf and dumb."

The scene was an immense and lofty chamber, luxuriously furnished, half drawing-room, half smoking-room, in Tony Jeratczesco's house in Moldavia, in the Karpak Mountains, and the time about a month after the events recorded in the last chapter had taken place.

To the French journalist Rowan had already told the story of his horrible adventure with Isaac Lebedenko and of the man's suicide—all or which events, together with minutes of what Maryx had said about the Children of Judas, were found carefully noted down in the Colonel's diary after his death—from which source of information and the testimony of Adams the present authentic account of these strange occurrences is taken;

but Mr Leonard P. Beacon not having heard the story before, Hippy had been prevailed upon to repeat it to him.

Hippy had spoken in a low tone, to avoid attracting attention; but he had not been taken into consideration the boisterous nature of his American auditor, who now exclaimed at the top of his voice: "What! do you mean seriously to tell me, Rowan, that you have never known what fear is? that you simply can't be frightened or anything?"

Annoying as it was under the circumstances to have such a question put in so trumpet-tongued a fashion, Hippy plainly saw that the American would insist upon a reply to his thundered query, and that it would in no wise better matters do delay giving it.

"I do," said he simply; and then added, in a half-whisper, "I wish you wouldn't yell so, Beacon." But it was too late. One local gentleman, a certain Prince Valerian Eldourdza, who, owing to the ract of his having been educated at a Lycée in Paris, was looked upon as the Admirable Crichton of that part of Moldavia, pressed Hippy very hard, plying him with most personal and impertinent questions as to his belief in a future life, future punishment, the devil, and so forth, and at last, indeed, going as far as to solemnly declare that not only did he not believe in Colonel Rowan's inability to experience terror, but that he would himself undertake under a penalty of £4,000 to frighten him. This somewhat offensive boast had, in the first instance, fallen from Eldourdza's lips in the heat of excitement, and probably without the speaker himself attaching any very great meaning or importance to his words; but the statement having been received with vociferous approval by the other local Boyards who were present, his Highness had been constrained to repeat the bet, and the second time give it a more specific form. "One hundred thousand francs," he repeated, bringing his very small and very unclean fist down on the table with much violence, "that I frighten you, Colonel, before you leave here— that is, of course, always provided you're not leaving at once."

"My friend is staying with me another month," interposed Jeratczesco, rather angrily. "But I can't allow such bets to be made in my house, Eldourdza. I hate practical jokes—we have quite enough of that kind of folly in England."

"You leave this to me, Tony," said Rowan to his host, speaking quickly, and in English; then, turning to Eldourdza: "Let's understand each other plainly, Prince. What do you mean by fright? Of course you can startle me by jumping out from a dark corner, or by any trick of that kind. I made no bet about that kind of thing, of course; but I'll bet you an even hundred thousand franks, if you like, or a hundred and fifty thousand francs, that you don't make me experience what is generally and by every one understood by the word fright—a sentiment of fear, or of anything even remotely resembling fear. How shall we define it, for we must be clear on this point?"

"Hair standing on end and teeth chattering," suggested Mr Leonard P. Beacon, who was greatly delighted at the turn affairs had taken, foreseeing an adventure and new experience of some kind.

"Exactly," replied Eldourdza, who had been consulting in a whisper with his friends, and absorbing yet another gobletful of champagne strongly laced with brandy. "Let those very words be used if you like—I'll bet you an even hundred and fifty thousand francs—two hundred thousand if you like" (Hippy nodded)— "that before you leave this place, four weeks from to-day, you shall be so frightened that your hair will stand on end, your teeth will chatter, and what's more, you'll call for help."

"Very well," assented Rowan, laughing, "C'est entendu; but I shan't make you go so far as that, my dear Prince. I shall be quite ready to pay up if you do more than merely startle me in the way I spoke of just now—by some sudden noise, or jumping out at me, or some such silly prank. Anything even approaching fear, much less terror, of course, and I pay up at once. "And," he added good-naturedly—for he was fond of winning money, and the certainty of this £8,000 was very pleasant to him—"luckily for you, Eldourdza, I happen to have the money to pay with if

I lose. I was on every winner the last day at Baden—couldn't do wrong—and sent it all on to Gunzburg at once, where it is intact, for I didn't want to be tempted to gamble till I got to St Petersburg."

And so this strange bet was made, and duly noted down with the approval of all, even Jeratczesco withdrawing his objection when he saw the very evident satisfaction with which the Colonel regarded what he felt sure to be the only possible result of this absurd wager.

But if Hippy Rowan had foreseen the wholly unexpected way in which this waiting day by day, night after night, and hour by hour for the surprise—of course of an apparently unpleasant nature—which Eldourdza and his friends must be preparing for him—had he, we say, foreseen the peculiar and unprecedented way in which this really absurd suspense was destined gradually, and by almost imperceptible degrees, to affect his nerves in the course of the next month—he would most assuredly have let the Prince's silly wager pass unnoticed. And what made this never-absent feeling of care, of personal caution, of unceasing vigilance, the more acutely irksome to Hippy, was that these novel sensations could be ascribed but to one altogether disagreeable and detestable cause—namely, the advance of old age. His experience of life had told him that the constitution of a man who had lived as he had lived was apt to break down suddenly, no matter how apparently robust it might be; the supports, the foundation, which kept the structure in its place and seemingly firm and upright, having been little by little, and very gradually but very surely removed in the course of years, the nights of which had been worn to morning in the fatigue of pleasure, and the days of which had been scornful of repose. He had seen innumerable friends of his, apparently as strong and vigorous as himself, suddenly give way to this fashion—fall down like a house of cards, as it were, and be swept away into the outer darkness. Could it be owing to the approach of some such sudden and disastrous conclusion to his mundane affairs, that he found, day to day, as the next four weeks wore on, his nerves, hitherto apparently of steel, becoming more and more unstrung by this suspense, the cause of which was in reality so utterly puerile and contemptible? This was very certainly not his first experience of suspense: he had been in danger of his live very often, and on a few occasions this danger had been imminent for a considerable period of time, and yet never could he recall having felt before this uneasiness of mind, this perpetual questioning of his heart, which he now experienced while merely waiting for these boorish savages to play some more or less gruesome, and even perhaps dangerous practical joke on him. It must be old age; it could be nothing else—old age, and the beginning, perhaps, of a general breaking-up of the system; the first intimation, as it were, of the second and finally payment about to be required of him for those extravagances already alluded to, those prolonged and oft-repeated saunters from midnight to dawn arm-in-arm with Bacchus and baccarat,—such outriders of Death's chariot, Rowan told himself, it must be, that induced him, greatly to his own surprise, to waste so much of his time twisting and turning over in his mind all kinds of possible and impossible speculations as to how these wretched Moldavians were going to try and frighten him. This led him to examine carefully his apartments every night before retiring to rest, and see that his revolver had not been tampered with and was safely under his pillow. Of course this very abnormal condition of mind, which in no wise even remotely resembled fear, and was one merely of perpetual watchfulness, was of very gradual growth, and Hippy Rowan was throughout the whole course of its development, until just before the end, sufficiently master of himself to conceal his feelings, not only from his friends, but even from his valet, the omniscient Adams; and the very visible change in the Colonel's appearance and manner, which by-and-by came to be remarked, was ascribed by all—and in a great measure justly ascribed—to a very severe chill which he caught shortly after the night of the wager, and which confined him to the house, and indeed to his room, for many days. Neither Prince Eldourdza nor any one else had made any allusion whatever, in Rowan's hearing, to the wager since the night of which it had been made and formally noted down; and this fact in itself, this studied silence, became in the course of time, and as Rowan's nervous irritability increased, a source of annoyance to him, and induced him at length, suddenly, one morning, when they were all at breakfast together, to boldly allude to the matter, which was becoming more and more constantly uppermost in his mind.

"Pardon me, Prince," said he, smiling, and with well-assumed carelessness, "if I allude to the matter of our wager, which you see to have forgotten, for you have only ten days left now, and—"

"Plenty of time!" interrupted Eldourdza roughly. "Forgotten it? Not I—have I?" he continued, turning to his friends. "You know whether I have forgotten it or not!" Significant and sinister grins and much shaking of heads in negation responded to this appeal,—a pantomime which excited the Colonel's curiosity not a little.

"Well," said he, "I'm glad to hear it, for I shouldn't like to take your money without your having had some semblance of a run for it. All I wanted to tell you was this, and I feel sure you'll agree with what I now say. Of course I've no idea what kind of prank you're going to play on me, to endeavor to frighten me, but no doubt it will be as horrible and awful a thing as you can concoct, for I suppose you've no intention of making me a present of two hundred thousand francs."

"Certainly not!" laughed Prince Valerian; "if you get it at all you'll have to pay dear for it, believe me."

"Very well," replied Hippy—"anything you like; but that's just what I wanted to speak about. Of course I'm at your disposal to do anything you like with, and to try and frighten in any way and every way you can contrive; but you can easily understand that there must be a limit to my endurance, otherwise you'd make me look like a fool. What I mean is, that you're at perfect liberty, say, to send any ghost or vampire or wild beast or devil, or anything else you can think of, to my room to try and frighten me, and for that purpose I am glad to lend you all the aid in my power. As it is, I leave my door unlocked every night now, as perhaps you know. But there must be some limit to this,—I mean that your endeavor to frighten me must have some limit in time, and can't go on forever. Suppose we put it at one hour—for one hour let your ghost or devil do its worst: then at the end of that time, if it has failed to frighten me, your goblin will become merely a nuisance, and I think I shall be justified in extinguishing it, don't you?"

"Most assuredly," replied Eldourdza. "In less than an hour: we don't ask for an hour—half an hour will do,—after half an hour you are perfectly at liberty to do as you like—provided always," he added grimly, "that by that time you are not half dead with fright."

"Very well, then," rejoiced Hippy. "So that's understood. After half an hour from the time your test, whatever it may be, begins, I shall be free to use any means I care to adopt to put a stop to this test, provided by that time, of course, I have not felt anything even remotely resembling alarm. As in the event of your test being something really offensive and disagreeable to me I should probably use my revolver, I thought it only fair to have this plainly understood, so that what is really only a silly practical joke may not, by a misunderstanding, end in tragedy."

The Prince nodded in acquiescence. "You are quite right," he said. "After half an hour do as you please. But you're mistaken in looking upon this as a practical joke, Colonel Rowan: it will be no joke, and may indeed, even against your will, end in a tragedy."

As may be readily imagined, these few mysterious words of menace from the man pledged, in some way or other, to cause him within ten days' time to experience the novel, but doubtless unpleasant, sensation of terror, did not tend to bring the Colonel to a more restful state of mind; and his never-ending speculation as to what scheme these savages might perchance be planning wherewith to frighten him began again after this conversation to torment his brain with renewed persistency. Of course Eldourdza would do all he could to win his bet—not for the sake of the money, perhaps, for that could be nothing to him, but for the pleasure and delight of triumph; and, equally of course—at least so Hippy told himself, this desired fright the Prince and his friends would only endeavor to bring about by some pseudo-supernatural agency, for they could hardly imagine that any of the vulgar dangers of life—say an attack of many adversaries, whether men or brutes, peril from water, fire, or what not; in fact, any of the thousand-and-one not uncommon evils which threaten human existence—could possibly affright so hardened and experienced a soldier and traveller as he was, a man whose record of perilous adventures was so well known. The supernatural, therefore, the terrors which owe their horror to the fact of their being inexplicable, the power of them unfathomable; the awful enemies which may be lurking crouched behind the last breath of life ready to spring upon us as the heart stops beating; such, or rather the semblance of such, would doubtless be alone the influences which these wild barbarians would seek to bring to bear upon his nerves to try them. And when this probability having been suggested to his imagination, Colonel Rowan began recalling to mind all the gruesome stories he had ever heard of about ghosts, hobgoblins, and the like, his restlessness and nervous watchfulness (to which he only gave way when in the privacy of his own chamber, of course) so increased as the last ten days sped by, that at length Adams, who slept in the next room, remarking his master's condition, arranged, without, of course, the knowledge of any one, to keep watch and ward over the Colonel during these last few nights by means of an aperture high up in the wall, through which he could obtain a perfect view of his master's sleeping apartment, and see all that book place therein.

So it came to pass that on the last night but two Hippy never retired to rest until the dawn, having decided, after mature reflection, that no matter what absurd practical jokes his friends might be going to play on him, he would cut a less ludicrous figure in his dressing-gown than in bed, and that it might indeed be advisable to be thus prepared to follow the tormenting masqueraders from his chamber to punish them elsewhere, and before the whole household, in the event of their conduct proving too outrageous. And so, after having as usual carefully examined every hole and cranny of his sleeping apartment (as the unobserved Adams from his peephole above saw him do very plainly), and lighted many tapers about the old-fashioned and vast chamber, and put many cheering logs upon the fire, the Colonel lit a cigar and began pacing up and down the room, turning over of course in his mind the perpetual question—"What are those uncouth madmen going to do?" and the query for ever followed by the usual reflection—"They can do as they please, provided they don't, by their folly, make me look like a fool." There would probably be the rattling of chains and bones, and some very cleverly contrived apparition; and even, in fact, some real danger, perhaps for these men were really perfect savages, who would stop at nothing to attain their end; and I Iippy would certainly not have been surprised to have found a box of dynamite concealed beneath his bed.

"Luckily, this is the last night but two," he said to himself—"and after all this bet has taught me one thing I never plainly realized before, and in a certain sense I have really lost the wager, for there is one thing I am afraid of, and very much afraid of, more and more afraid of every minute, and that is being made a fool of." Then he stopped in his perambulation and stared at himself in the looking-glass. Yes; he was certainly growing old: the grey hairs he cared nothing about—they were entirely insignificant; and the crows' feet and wrinkles were of no importance—they did not in the least annoy him; but the eyes, ah! the eyes were losing their light—that light that had disported itself over so many beautiful things. But then even a youthful face would look sad in so mystic a mirror—for it was very old, and evidently Venetian, and had doubtless been in that room in that castle in that remote corner of Moldavia for years and years and seen perchance strange strings,—and was destined (who could tell?) before three nights were over to reflect images of even more fantastic terror than had ever darkened it before. What a pity that this old looking-glass could not recall some of the most pleasant images that had been reflected in it in the long ago to keep him company that night! If he stared at it long enough, would he not, perhaps, at length perceive for away, there in the most remote and distant and least lighted corner of the room, reflected the fair sad face of some Moldavian dame who had wept and kissed and loved and lost in the old days of the Hospodars?

Then, drawing up a comfortable armchair before the blazing logs, he seated himself, and taking up Le Rouge et le Noir, which he happened to find lying on the table by his side, ere long had red himself to sleep over the marvellous narrative if the vicissitudes of Julien Sorel, only awaking, indeed, when the

"fair-faced sun,
killing the stars and dews and dreams and desolations of the
    night,"

was plainly visible through the curtains, and the noises of the awakening household warned him that another day had begun. Then he arose and went to bed, fondly believing that by this little comedy he was deceiving the omniscient Adams, who, as a matter of fact, perched on a step-ladder in the adjoining apartment, had kept an unceasing watch over his master. That day, Rowan's last day on earth, passed without any incident worthy of notice. Jeratczesco announced at breakfast that he had engaged a band of laoutari—gypsy minstrels—to enliven his friends, but that, as he only expected them to arrive late that night, his guests would not have the opportunity of enjoying their wild and delightful music until the morning.

"I shall lodge them in your wing of the house, where they'll be quiet," explained Tony to Colonel Rowan later on in the day, when they happened to be alone. "You know how beautiful some of these tsigane women are, and how jealously guarded by their men. I don't want a row here, and there's no knowing what mad folly Eldourdza and his friends might be up to when drunk."

And that the prudent Tony was quite justified in taking all precautionary measures to ensure peace and tranquility during the sojourn of the gypsies beneath his roof was amply proved that very night when they arrived late, for the Moldavian magnates, who, with Eldourdza at their head, would seem to have intentionally got drunk rather earlier than usual that evening, were only with the greatest difficulty restrained by their host from rushing out into the moonlit courtyard and embracing the women of the minstrel band, as they were seen and heard passing and chattering and singing on their way to their quarters. The arrival of these gypsies, and the prospect of the break which their performances would make in the monotony of daily life at the château (which, by the way, all save the most enthusiastic sportsmen would have found intolerably tedious), greatly enlivened Hippy Rowan's spirits; and when he retired for the night—the last night but one of this absurd waiting for surprises, as he reminded himself with a smile—he opened his window and looked out across the quadrangle to the lights in the rooms occupied by the wandering musicians, wondering whether indeed this band contained any of those really beautiful women such as he remembered having remarked among the Strelna gypsy musicians of Moscow,—women unlike any other women to be found in any class or country in the world, and whose peculiar charm is as indescribable as it is indisputable, processing as it does a power partaking of the supernatural, springing as it were from a fountain of infernal fascination. What a splendid night! And nearly Christmas too, the very season for ghostly masquerading, and—But hark! A woman's voice singing.

Hippy leaned out and listened. The voice was low and very sweet, though the woman singing was evidently engaged in some other occupation which absorbed her attention, for there would be careless pauses in her song, the words of which in a Rumanian dialect ran somewhat as follows:

"Love shot his arrow o'er the Sea,
    And all the waters leaped with joy,

Lifting their foam-wreathed arms in glee,
To bid sunlight hold the boy;
But the Sun said
'My beams are shed
To cheer with flowers the lonely dead.'"

Here the singing ceased for a moment, but presently a man's
voice took up the song, singing in the same careless fashion,
stopping every now and then.

"Death spread his pinions o'er the Sea,
And all the waves with storm-thrilled breath
In sobs besought the Moon that she
Might break the tear-plumed wings of Death.
But the Moon cried
'My silver tide
Will only—"

But here a merry burst of laughter interrupted the singer, and
though for some time after Rowan could hear the voices of the
gypsies laughing and talking, he could not distinguish what was
being said, and there was no more singing.

"What a strange people!" murmured Rowan to himself, as the
closed the window, "and what suitable neighbours to have on
such a night as this, when at any moment now I may expect to
see a cavalcade of ghosts come galloping into the room!"

Then the watchful Adams saw his master make his usual
careful inspection of the room, seat himself by the fire, take up
Stendhal again, and read himself to sleep.

Suddenly Rowan awoke, roused by a sound that stole into
his ears very gradually and very gently, but which, when his
drowsy faculties had understood its meaning, stirred them to
instant activity—the sound of weeping. He sprang to his feet
and looked around the room. He was alone; the apartment was
brilliantly illuminated, thanks to two large lamps and several
tapers in girandoles, and he could plainly see into the farthest

corner: nobody—no animated creature was visible. He listened, but not a sound broke the stillness of the night. He must have been dreaming. But no—hark! there it was again, the sound of weeping, of some one in great and bitter distress: it came from the corridor, and not far from his chamber door. Should he go and see what it was? Could this be any part of the Molda-vian's masquerading? Surely not! Hardly would they begin their attempt to frighten a man by such heartrending expressions of anguish, which could evoke but pity and compassion. Again! Oh, what a wealth of woe!

And a woman too: the long-drawn, gasping, tear-clogged suspiration was pitched in a key of peculiar pathos which that treasury of divine tenderness, a woman's heart, alone can find to woo compassion. Again,—yes, certainly a woman: could it perchance be one of the laoutari? The corridor led to the part of the house where they were sleeping, and, so far as he knew, they were the only women in the house except the servants. Surely Eldourdza had nothing to do with this; and even if he had, what then? Had not this drunken Moldavian boor already occupied his mind quite long enough with speculations as to what he might and what he might not be about to do? Let him do as he pleased, and what he liked, and go to the devil!

There was a woman in terrible distress just outside his door, and he, Hippy Rowan, must go to her without delay—that was very clear. So, taking his revolver in his hand in case of need, Rowan advanced, opened the door wide, and looked out into the sombre corridor; Adams, greatly frightened, watching his master the while, and, having heard nothing, was at a loss to understand the Colonel's conduct. Even as he opened the door Rowan saw that he had guessed aright, and that it was a woman who was giving utterance to these most pitiful and heartrending expressions of anguish. There she lay, not very near his door after all, weeping bitterly, her face buried in her hands—as if she had been praying on her knees for mercy, and in a very agony of supplication had fallen forward. Rowan saw at once that those white and shapely hands must belong to a young woman; and so his voice assumed a tone of very special tenderness and compassion, as he said, in the Rumanian dialect in which he had heard the gypsies singing:

"What is it, lady? Can I help you?"

The mourner, who apparently had not remarked the opening of the door, at the sound of Hippy's voice ceased her lamenting; and after a moment's pause slowly raised her head, withdrawing her hands from her face as she did so, and revealing to Rowan's astonished eyes the most faultlessly lovely countenance he had ever gazed upon in living woman—a countenance different to anything Hippy had ever seen. Was it the moonlight pouring in through the uncurtained windows which gave it that ethereal radiance? Who could she be? That she was not a gypsy was very evident, for her skin was of the most fine and delicate fairness, and her hair, which fell in caressing curls over her forehead, of a soft and tender brown. Moreover her dress was entirely unlike that of a tsigane, both in colour and in form, being all black, and fashioned, so far as Rowan could see, as that of a member of some religious order, the beautiful face being, as it were, framed round about in a covering not unlike a cowl. Rowan had heard, he thought, of some sisterhood in the neighbourhood: perhaps this fair mourner belonged to such a community;—at all events she was assuredly a very lonely woman, and it behooved him, both as a man of heart and as a man of taste, to console her in her sorrow. But to attain this desired end, of course the first and most necessary step would be to make himself understood, and that, apparently, he had not so far succeeded in doing. The lustrous violet eyes looked at him, indeed, with startled surprise and fawn-like timidity, though there was assuredly nothing redoubtable in the kind aspect of Hippy's handsome face, and he had instinctively hidden the revolver in his pocket the moment he had seen the pathetic prostrate figure in the corridor; but beyond this half-frightened expression there was nothing to be recognized but sorrow in that lovely countenance: not the slightest indication that his words had conveyed to the mourner's mind any idea of sympathy and compassion. Again he addressed her, this time in no dialect, but in the purest Rumanian and in a still more tender wonder in the sweet Madonna face remained unchanged. Then, feeling that the situation was becoming rather ludicrous, he said, this time speaking in German and beckoning towards the open door of his apartment,—

"Lady, let me beg of you to tell me what troubles you! Come into my room and rest and warm yourself. Believe me, there is nothing I would not gladly do to be of service to you. You have only to command me; I am an Englishman, a gentleman, a soldier—so you may trust me. Let me help you, lady: come, I beg of you." Then, after a pause, as the mourner neither spoke nor moved, Hippy bowed, and, motioning her to follow him, walked slowly into his room, turning every now and then and repeating his gesture of invitation;—she the while remaining upon her knees,—looking after him, indeed, but making no attempt to rise or follow.

Although Adams had at no time lost sight of his master, whose back, as he seemed to be engaged in conversation with some invisible person far down the corridor, had always been within the range of the faithful servant's vision, still it was with a feeling of great relief that he now saw the Colonel come back into the room unharmed, although the expression of tenderness and pity in his master's face rather puzzled the man, as did also the Colonel's conduct in turning when he had reached the fireplace and looking anxiously back towards the door which had left open behind him, as if expecting and indeed longing for the arrival of some visitor. At length, after the lapse of a few minutes—a delay which, though brief, the servant could plainly see his master bore impatiently, the longed-for visitor slowly emerged from the darkness of the corridor until she stood framed in the doorway, against one side of which, as if to support herself, she lightly placed a small white hand. It was thus Adams saw the slender black-robed figure of a sweet girl mourner appear, and the first time in his life was astonished, nay, astounded rather, at the marvellous resemblance in depth of tenderness, in purity of sorrow-hallowed loveliness, between this nocturnal lady visitor to his master and a Madonna from a canvas, say, of Raphael, standing apparently before him clothed in flesh.

Perhaps some such fantastic idea of an incarnation of one of Raphael's Holy Virgins occurred to Rowan as he bowed low and advanced to welcome his fair visitor, for this time he addressed her in Italian, thanking her for the great honour she was doing him, making all kinds of graceful and very Italian protestations of sympathy and respect, and concluding a very pretty speech by begging her not to stay there on the threshold, but to come in and seat herself by the fire; adding that if his presence were in any way distasteful to her he would at once withdraw and leave her in undisturbed possession of the room. But this attempt, clothed in the choicest Tuscan, to inspire confidence, met with no greater measure of success than had attended its Rumanian and German predecessors. The sweetly sorrowful lady stood on the threshold in the same timid attitude, staring at the Colonel with no abatement in the tender melancholy of her face, but apparently in no wise understanding his words, and even, indeed, ignoring his gesture inviting her to enter and be seated.

What was to be done? He could hardly, of course, take this lovely girl–Madonna in his arms and drag her into his room by force; and yet it seemed intolerably absurd, and indeed impossible, to leave her standing there in the doorway. Why had she come even to the threshold of his door, if she had not intended coming farther in the event of her seeing nothing to alarm her? Of course, and beyond all doubt, if he could only make her understand his sympathy and respect, and that she need have no fear of him, and would come in and perhaps tell him the cause of her distress, and let him help her; and on the other hand, knowing so many languages and even dialects and patois as he did, it seemed almost impossible that he should not be able at length to hit upon some form of speech by which he could convey to his most perfect incarnate type of spiritual purity and loveliness the expression of his devoted homage.

So he started off on a wild polyglottic steeplechase, making protestations of respect and sympathy and offers of aid and friendship in e very language and dialect he could remember, from his native English to the patois spoken by the Jews in White Russia. But all to no purpose; and at length he was constrained to pause and acknowledge that he was utterly defeated.

"You're very beautiful," said he at last, with a sigh, speaking in his native English, the inability of his fair auditor to understand him possessing at least the meager and thankless advantage of allowing him to express his admiration in words no matter how impassioned, provided, of course, he took care his face should not betray the significance and ardour of his speech—"the most beautiful woman I think I ever saw; but you're a beautiful riddle, and I don't know how to read you. What language can you speak, I wonder? Only the language of love, perhaps! Were I to kneel down there before you, or take you in my arms and kiss you, in what language would you repulse me, or— ?"

Here he paused, greatly surprised: were his eyes deceiving him, or was at length a change stealing over the Madonna face, and the timidity and sadness in it slowly giving place to an expression of some brighter sentiment? That she could not understand the language he was speaking he felt sure, for he had already addressed her in it, and his words had evidently failed utterly to convey any meaning to her mind. But surely there was a difference now, and something he had said, or some gesture he had made, or some expression in his face, had been pleading to her, for the great shadow of melancholy was slowly passing from her. But between the language, the English he had used before and that which he had just spoken, what difference was there? None, of course, save in the sense: then the words had been of respect and sympathy, now of love and tenderness. Could it be that by some marvelous intuition her woman's instinct had at once divined the more tender words? Or indeed was it not possible, nay, likely, that in speaking them he had involuntarily let their meaning be reflected in his eyes, and that she had read it there?

But then such tenderness and affection were not displeasing to her; and this Mask of the Madonna, this ideal type of womanly purity, could be lighted by the joy of love.

The thought set Rowan's blood coursing through his veins like fire, and made his heart beat as if he had been but twenty. He must see, and at once: he would speak to her again in words of affection, and let his eyes partly and by degrees interpret what he said, carefully of course, and always guided by what he should see her eyes reply to his, lest he should offend her. And so he began telling this lovely woman in very low, quiet and grave tones, but in his words of great tenderness, how fair he found her, and as he spoke his eyes expressed the meaning of his words more and more clearly and ardently as he recognized with ever-growing delight that the Madonna face was being gradually illuminated and transfigured by joy, as word after word of ever-increasing passion, echoed in tender glances from his eyes, fell from his lips.

And as he spoke he did not advance towards her, but only clasped his hands and stood still far from her, looking at her in the doorway; while she, more and more visibly affected by his ever-growing emotion, first withdrew her hand from the side of the door where she had leant it, and pushed back the cowl from her face a little, still further disclosing, by so doing, the wavy wealth of soft brown curls, and then, as the violet eyes became by degrees lighted with great joy and the sweet lips melted to a smile of ineffable rapture, clasped both hands together just beneath her cheek in an attitude of girlish and innocent delight.

So she stood until the fervour of Rowan's words and voice and eyes rose to an ecstasy of passion, and then leaning forward her head, not indeed to hide the sweet blushes which were rising to her cheeks, but as a child eager to rush to a beloved embrace, and her eyes answering the ardour she read in those she gazed into, she half stretched forth her arms and if her longing to twine him in a caress were but restrained by maiden bashful-ness. Rowan saw the gesture, stepped forward, opened wide his arms, and the girl Madonna rushed to his embrace, nestling her blushing face upon his neck, as in rapture of fondness he clasped her to his bosom.

At the same moment a terrible cry rang through the room and through the house, waking the tsiganes, who sprang from their beds in mad terror, and startling the stupid Moldavians, who, despairing of really frightening Rowan, had decided on merely making him look like a fool, and were at that very moment creeping up the staircase, dressed in absurd costumes and armed with monster squirts and all kinds of grotesque instruments—the cry of a strong man in an agony of terror. The horrified Adams saw his master hurl the woman from him with great violence, snatch his revolver from his pocket, discharge three chambers of it at her in quick succession, and then reel and fall forward on his face, while she, rising from the floor apparently unhurt, glided from the apartment by the still open door. When Adams reached his master's side he found him quite dead, the body presenting two most remarkable peculiarities: first a very strong odour of musk—and secondly, on the neck three small wounds shaped like three X's joined together. The medical man, a German, who was immediately called in, ascribed the death of Colonel Rowan to aneurism of the heart, and declined to attach the least importance to the three small wounds or bites on the neck, the post-mortem examination proving that so far as the cause of death was concerned the physician was right in his conjecture.

As for the strange lady with Madonna face, Adams was far too shrewd of a man of the world to make know the extraordinary circumstance to every one. He told Tony Jeratczesco, and inquiries were made; but no such person had been seen or heard of, and so the matter dropped; and it is only within the last few months that Mr. Adams, now retired from his delicate and difficult profession of valet and living in the neighbourhood of Newmarket, could be prevailed upon to give a detailed account of all the strange facts connected with the death of his master, show Hippy Rowan's diary, and complete his story by producing a photograph which he himself had taken of the dead man's neck, on which is plainly visible the imprint of the Kiss of Judas.

# MARY ELIZABETH BRADDON:
## HERSELF (1894)

Mary Elizabeth Braddon (1837-1915) was the most popular and prolific of the Victorian "sensation" novelists. Her best seller, *Lady Audley's Secret*, which was published in 1862, was followed by more than eighty novels. The exact number is not known because her husband, John Maxwell, published some of her work under a variety of pseudonyms.

Braddon was a close friend of Bram and Florence Stoker for many years. Braddon wrote to Bram on 23 June, 1897, to congratulate him on the success of *Dracula*. Her letter concluded: "We will talk of it more anon, when I have soberly read and meditated thereupon. I have done my humdrum little story of transfusion in 'The Good Lady Ducayne'—but your 'bloofer lady. . . .'"

"Good Lady Ducayne" debuted in the *Strand Magazine* in February 1896, and has been reprinted dozens of times. One year earlier, she wrote a grimmer, more atmospheric tale of vampirism that has escaped popular attention. "Herself" was first published in the *Sheffied Weekly Telegraph* on 17 November, 1894. Its protagonist, Lota, is a rebellious and independent woman in the tradition of heroines such as Lucy Audley (who, incidentally, may be one of the models for Bram Stoker's hapless heroine, Lucy Westenra).

———

## CHAPTER I

" A nd you intend to keep the Orange Grove for your own occupation, Madam," interrogates the lawyer gravely, with his downward-looking eyes completely hidden under bushy brows.

"Decidedly," answered my friend. "Why, the Orange Grove is the very best part of my fortune. It seems almost a special Providence, don't you know, Helen," pursued Lota, turning to me, "that my dear old grandfather should have made himself a winter home in the south. There are the doctors always teasing me about my weak chest, and there is a lonely house and gardens and orange groves waiting for me in a climate invented on purpose for weak chests. I shall live there every winter of my life, Mr. Dean."

The eminently respectable solicitor allowed a lapse of silence before he replied.

"It is not a lucky house, Miss Hammond."

"How not lucky?"

"Your grandfather only lived to spend one winter in it. He was in very good health when he went there in December—a strong, sturdy old man—and when he sent for me in February to prepare the will which made you his sole heiress, I was shocked at the change in him—broken—wasted—nerves shattered—a mere wreck.

"That was very sad; but surely you would not blame a lovely villa in Italy," smiling down at a photograph in her lap, the picture of the typical southern villa, French windows, verandah, balconies, tower, terraces, garden, and fountain, "for the sudden break-up of an elderly constitution. I have heard that old men of very active habits and a hardy way of living, like my dear old grandfather, are apt to grow old suddenly."

"It was not merely that he was aged—he was mentally changed—nervous, restless, to all appearance unhappy."

"Well, didn't you ask him why?" demanded Lota, whose impetuous temper was beginning to revolt against the lawyer's solemnity.

"My position hardly warranted my questioning Mr. Hammond on a matter so purely personal. I saw the change, and regretted it. Six weeks later he was gone."

Poor old gran'pa. We were such friend when I was a little thing. And then they sent me to Germany with a governess—poor little motherless mite—and then they packed me off to Pekin where father was Consul and there he died, and then they sent me home again—and I was taken up by the smartest of all my aunts, and had my little plunge in society, and always exceeded my allowance; was up to my eyes in debt—for a girl. I suppose a man would hardly count such bills as I used to owe. And then gran'pa took it into his head to be pleased with me; and here I am—residuary legatee. I think that's what you call me?" with an interrogative glance at the lawyer, who nodded a grave assent, "and I am going to spend the winter months in my villa near Taggia. Only think of that, Helen, Taggia—Tag-gi-a!"

She syllabled the word slowly, ending with a little smack of her pretty lips as if it were something nice to eat, and she looked at me for sympathy.

"I haven't the faintest idea what you mean by Tag-gi-a," said I. "It sounds like an African word."

"Surely you have read Dr. Antonio."

"Surely I have not."

"Then I have done with you. There is a gulf between us. All that I know of the Liguria comes out of that delightful book. It taught me to pine for the shores for the Mediterranean when I was quite a little thing. And they show you Dr. Ruffini's house at Taggia. His actual house, where he actually lived."

"You ought to consider, Miss Hammond, that the Riviera has changed a good deal since Ruffini's time," said the lawyer. "Not that I have anything to say against the Riviera per se. All I would advise is that should winter in a more convenient locality than a romantic gorge between San Remo and Alassio. I would suggest Nice, for instance."

"Nice. Why, someone was saying only the other day that Nice is the chosen rendezvous of all the worst characters in Europe and America."

"Perhaps that's what makes it such an agreeable place," said the lawyer. "There are circles and circles in Nice. You need never breathe the same atmosphere as the bad characters.

"A huge towny place," exclaimed Lota. "Gran'pa said it was not better than Brighton."

"Could anything be better than Brighton?" asked I.

"Helen, you were always a Philistine. It was because of the horridness of Nice and Cannes that gran'pa bought a villa—four times too big for him—in this romantic spot."

She kissed the white house in the photograph. She gloated over the wildness of the landscape, in which the villa stood out, solitary, majestic. Palms, olives, cypress—a deep gorge cutting through the heart of the picture—mountains romantically remote—one white crest in the furthest distance—a foreground of tumbled crags and threads of running water.

"Is it really real?" she asked suddenly, "not a photographer's painted background? They have such odious tricks, those photographers. One sits for one's picture in a tidy South Kensington studio, and they send one home smirking out of a primeval forest, or in front of a stormy ocean. Is it real?

"Absolutely real."

"Very well, Mr. Dean. Then I am going to establish myself there in the first week of December, and if you want to be very careful of me for gran'pa's sake all you have to do is to find me a thoroughly respectable major-domo, who won't drink my wine or run away with my plate. My aunt will engage the rest of my people."

"My dear young lady, you may command any poor services of mine; but really now, is it not sheer perversity to choose a rambling house in a wild part of the country where your ample means would allow you to hire the prettiest bijou-villa on the Riviera?"

"I hate bijou houses, always too small for anybody except some sour old maid who wants to over-hear all her servants say about her. The spacious rambling house—the wild solitary landscape—those are what I want, Mr. Dean. Get me a butler who won't cut my throat, and I ask no more."

"Then madam, I have done. A willful woman must have her way, even when it is a foolish way."

"Everything in life is foolish," Lota answered, lightly. "The people who live haphazard come out just as well at the end as your ineffable wiseacres. And now that you know I am fixed as fate, that nothing you can say will unbend my iron will, do, like a darling old family lawyer whom I have known ever since I began to know one face from another, do tell me why you object to the Orange Grove. Is it the drainage?"

"There is no drainage."

"Then that's all right," checking it off on her forefinger. "Is it the neighbours?"

"Need I say there are no neighbours?"

"Number two satisfactory."

"Is it the atmosphere? Low the villa is not; damp it can hardly be, perched on the side of a hill."

"I believe the back rooms are damp. The hill side comes too near the windows. The back rooms are decidedly gloomy, and I believe damp."

"And how many rooms are there in all?"

"Nearer thirty than twenty. I repeat it is a great rambling house, ever so much too large for you or any sensible young lady."

"For the sensible young lady, no doubt," said Lota, nodding impertinently at me. "She likes a first floor in Regency Square, Brighton, with a little room under the tiles for her maid. I am not sensible, and I like lots of rooms; rooms to roam about in, to furnish and unfurnish, and arrange and rearrange; rooms to see ghosts in. And now, dearest Mr. Dean, I am going to pluck out the heart of your mystery. What kind of ghost is it that haunts the Orange Grove? I know there is a ghost."

"Who told you so?"

"You. You have been telling me so for the last half-hour. It is because of the ghost you don't want me to go to the Orange Grove. You might just as well be candid and tell me the whole story. I am not afraid of ghosts. In fact, I rather like the idea of having a ghost on my property. Wouldn't you Helen, if you had property?"

"No," I answered, decisively. "I hate ghosts. They are always associated with damp houses and bad drainage. I don't believe you would find a ghost in Brighton, not even if you advertised for one."

"Tell me all about the ghost," urged Lota.

"There is nothing to tell. Neither the people in the neighbourhood nor the servants of the house went so far as to say the Orange Grove was haunted. The utmost assertion was that time out of mind the master or the mistress of that house had been miserable."

"Time out of mind. Why, I thought gran'pa built the house twenty years ago."

"He only added the front which you see in the photograph. The back part of the house, the larger part, is three hundred years old. The place was a monkish hospital, the infirmary belonging to a Benedictine monastery in the neighbourhood, and to which the sick from other Benedictine houses were sent."

"Oh, that was ages ago and ages ago. You don't suppose that the ghosts of all the sick monks, who were so inconsiderate as to die in my house, haunt the rooms at the back?"

"I say again, Miss Hammond, nobody has ever to my knowledge asserted that the house was haunted."

"Then it can't be haunted. If it were the servants would have seen something. They are champion ghost-seers."

"I am not a believer in ghosts, Miss Hammond," said the friendly old lawyer; "but I own to a grain of superstition on one point. I can't help thinking there is such a thing as 'luck.' I have seen such marked distinctions between the lucky and unlucky people I have met in my professional career. Now, the Orange Grove has been an unlucky house for the last hundred years. It's bad luck is as old as its history. And why, in the name of all that's reasonable, should a beautiful young lady with all the world to choose from insist upon living at the Orange Grove?"

"First, because it is my own house; next, because I hardly conceived a passion for it the moment I saw this photograph; and thirdly, perhaps because your opposition has given a zest to the whole thing. I shall establish myself there next December, and you must come out to me after Christmas, Helen. Your beloved Brighton is odious in February and March."

"Brighton is always delightful," answered I, "but of course I shall be charmed to go to you."

## CHAPTER II
### AN EARTHLY PARADISE

I was Lota's dearest friend, and she was mine. I had never seen anyone quite so pretty, or quite so fascinating then: I have never seen anyone as pretty or as fascinating since. She was no Helen, no Cleopatra, no superbly modelled specimen of typical loveliness. She was only herself. Like no one else, and to my mind better than everybody else—a delicately-wrought ethereal creature, all spirit and fire and impulse and affection, flinging herself with ardour into every pursuit, living intensely in the present, curiously reckless of the future, curiously forgetful of the past.

When I parted with her at Charing Cross Station on the first of December it was understood that I was to join her about the middle of January. One of my uncles was going to Italy at that time, and was to escort me to Taggia, where I was to be met by my hostess. I was surprised, therefore, when a telegram arrived before Christmas, entreating me to go to her at once.

I telegraphed back: "Are you ill?"

Answer: "Not ill; but I want you."

My reply: "Impossible. Will go as arranged."

I would have given much, as I told Lota in the letter that followed my last message, to have done what she wished; but family claims were too strong. A brother was to marry at the beginning of the year, and I should have been thought heartless had I shirked the ceremony. And there was the old idea of

Christmas as a time for family gatherings. Had she been ill, or unhappy, I would have cancelled every other claim, and gone to her without one hour's delay, I told her; but I knew her a creature of caprices, and this was doubtless only one caprice among many.

I knew that she was well cared for. She had a maiden aunt with her, the mildest and sweetest of spinsters, who absolutely adored her. She had her old nurse and slave, a West Indian half-caste, who had accompanied her from Pekin, and she had—

"Another, and a dearer one still."

Captain Holbrook, of the Stonyshere Regiment, was at San Remo. I had seen his name in a travelling note in the *World*, and I smiled as I read the announcement, and thought how few of his acquaintance would know as well as I knew the magnet which attracted him to quit San Remo rather than to Monte Carlo or Nice. I knew that he loved Violetta Hammond devotedly, and that she had played fast and loose with him, amused at his worship, accepting all his attentions in her light happy manner, and giving no heed to the future.

Yes, my pretty, insouciante Lota was well cared for, ringed round with exceeding love, guarded as faithfully as a god in an Indian temple. I had no uneasiness about her, and I alighted in a very happy frame of mind at the quiet little station at Taggia, beside the tideless sea, in dusk of a January evening.

Lota was on the platform to welcome me, with Miss Elderson, her maternal aunt, in attendance upon her, the younger lady muffled in sealskin from head to foot.

"Why Lota," said I, when we had kissed, and laughed a little with eyes full of tears, "you are wrapped up as if this were Russia, and to me the air feels balmier than an English April."

"Oh, when one has a hundred guinea coat one may as well wear it," she answered carelessly. "I bought this sealskin among my mourning."

"Lota is chillier than she used to be," said Miss Elderson, in her plaintive voice.

There was a landau with a pair of fine strong horses waiting to carry us up to the villa. The road wound gently upward, past orange and lemon groves, and silvery streamlets, and hanging woods, where velvet dark cypresses rose tower-like amidst the silvery grey of the olives, and so to about midway between the valley, where Taggia's antique palaces and church towers gleamed pale in the dusk, and the crest of the hill along which straggled the white houses of a village. The after-glow was rosy in the sky when a turn of the road brought our faces towards the summer-like sea, and in that lovely light every line in Lota's face was but too distinctly visible. Too distinctly, for I saw the cruel change which three months had made in her fresh young beauty. She had left me all the bloom of girlhood, gay, careless, brimming over with the joy of life and the new delight of that freedom of choice which wealth gives to a fatherless and motherless girl. To go where she liked, do as she liked, roam the world over, choosing always the companions she loved—that had been Lota's dream of happiness, and if there had been some touch of self-love in her idea of bliss there had been also a generous and affectionate heart, and unfailing kindness to those whom Fate had not used so kindly.

I saw her now a haggard, anxious-looking woman, the signs of worry written too plainly on the wan pinched face, the lovely eyes larger but paler than of old, and the markings of nervous depression visible in the droop of the lips that had once been like Cupid's bow.

I remember Mr. Dean's endeavour to dissuade her from occupying her grandfather's villa on this lovely hill, and I began to detest the Orange Grove before I had seen it. I was prepared to find an abode of gloom—a house where the foul miasma from some neighbouring swamp crept in at every window, and hung grey and chill in every passage; a house whose too obvious unwholesomeness had conjured up images of terror, the spectral forms engendered of slackened nerves, and sleepless nights. I made up my mind that if it were possible for a bold and energetic woman to influence Lota Hammond I would be that woman, and whisk her off to Nice or Monte Carlo before she had time to consider what I was doing.

There would be a capital pretext in the Carnival. I would declare that I had set my heart upon seeing a Carnival at Nice; and once there I would take care she never returned to the place that was killing her. I looked, with a thrill of anger, at the mild sheep-faced aunt. How could she have been so blind as not to perceive the change in her niece? And Captain Holbrook! What a poor creature, to call himself a lover, and let the girl he loved perish before his eyes.

I had time to think while the horses walked slowly up the hill-road, for neither the aunt nor the niece had much to say. Each in her turn pointed out some feature in the view. Lota told me that she adored Taggia, and doted on her villa and garden; and that was the utmost extent of our conversation in the journey of more than an hour.

At last we drove round a sharpish curve, and on the hill side above us, looking down at us from a marble terrace, I saw the prettiest house I had ever seen in my life; a fairy palace, with lighted windows, shining against a back-ground of wooded hills. I could not see the colours of the flowers in the thickening gloom of night, but I could smell the scent of the roses and the fragrant-leaved geraniums that filled the vases on the terrace.

Within and without all was alike sparkling and lightsome; and so far as I could see on the night of my arrival there was not a corner which could have accommodated a ghost. Lota told me that one of her first improvements had been to install the electric light.

"I love to think that this house is shining like a star when the people of Taggia look across the valley," she said.

I told her that I had seen Captain Holbrook's name among the visitors at San Remo.

"He is staying at Taggia now," she said. "He grew tired of San Remo."

"The desire to be nearer you had nothing to do with the change?"

"You can ask him if you like," she answered, with something of her old insouciance. "He is coming to dinner to-night."

"Does he spend his days and nights going up and down the hill?" I asked.

"You will be able to see for yourself as to that. There is not much for anyone to do in Taggia."

† † † † † †

Captain Holbrook found me alone in the salon when he came; for, in spite of the disadvantages of arrival after a long journey, I was dressed before Lota. He was very friendly, and seemed really glad to see me; indeed, he lost no time in saying as much with a plainness of speech which was more friendly than flattering.

"I am heartily glad you have come," he said, "for now I hope we shall be able to get Miss Hammond away from this depressing hole."

Remembering that the house was perched upon the shoulders of a romantic hill, with an outlook of surpassing loveliness, and looking round at the brilliant colouring of an Italian drawing-room steeped in soft clear light, and redolent of roses and carnations, it seemed rather hard measure to hear of Lota's inheritance talked of as "a depressing hole"; but the cruel change in Lota herself was enough to justify the most unqualified dislike of the house in which the change had come to pass.

Miss Elderson and her niece appeared before I could reply, and we went to dinner. The dining-room was as bright and gracious of aspect as all the other rooms which I had seen, everything having been altered and improved to suit Lota's somewhat expensive tastes.

"The villa ought to be pretty," Miss Elderson murmured plaintively, "for Lota's improvements have cost a fortune."

"Life is so short. We ought to make the best of it," said Lota gaily.

We were full of gaiety, and there was the sound of talk and light laughter all through the dinner; but I felt that there was a forced note in our mirth, and my own heart was like lead. We all went back to the drawing-room together. The windows were open to the moonlight, and the faint sighing of the night wind among the olive woods. Lota and her lover established themselves in front of the blazing pine logs, and Miss Elderson asked me if I could like a stroll on the terrace. There were fleecy white shawls lying about ready for casual excursions of this kind, and the good old lady wrapped one about my shoulders with motherly care. I followed her promptly, foreseeing that she was anxious to talk confidentially with me as I was to talk with her.

My eagerness anticipated her measured speech. "You are unhappy about Lota," I asked.

"Very, very unhappy."

"But why haven't you taken her away from here? You must see that the place is killing her. Or perhaps the dreadful change in her may not strike you, who have been seeing her every day—?"

"It does strike me; the change is too palpable. I see it every morning, see her looking a little worse, a little worse every day, as if some dreadful disease were eating away her life. And yet our good English doctor from San Remo says there is nothing the matter except a slight lung trouble, and that this air is the very finest, the position of this house faultless, for such a case as hers, high enough to be bracing, yet sheltered from all cold winds. He told me that we could take her no better place than Genoa and Marseilles."

"But is she to stop here, and fade, and die? There is some evil influence in this house. Mr. Dean said as much; something horrible, uncanny, mysterious."

"My dear, my dear! Ejaculated the amiable invertebrate creature, shaking her head in solemn reproachfullness, "can you, a good Churchwoman, believe in any nonsense of that sort?"

"I don't know what to believe; but I can see that my dearest friend is perishing bodily and mentally. The three months in which we have been parted have done the work of years of declining health. And she was warned against the house; she was warned."

"There is nothing the matter with the house," that weak-brained spinster answered pettishly. "The sanitary engineer from Cannes has examined everything. The drainage is simply perfect—"

"And your niece is dying!" I said, savagely, and turned my back upon Miss Elderson.

I gazed across the pale grey woods to the sapphire sea, with eyes that scarcely saw the loveliness they looked upon. My heart was swelling with indignation against this feeble affection which would see the thing it loved vanishing off the earth, and yet could not be moved to energetic action.

## CHAPTER III
### SOMETIMES THEY FADE AND DIE

I tested the strength of my own influence the next day, and I was inclined to be less severe in my judgement of the meek spinster, after a long morning in the woods with Lota and Captain Holbrook, in which all my arguments and entreaties, backed most fervently by an adoring lover, had proved useless.

"I am assured that no place could suit my health better," Lota said, decisively, "and I mean to stay here till my doctor orders me to Varese or home to England. Do you suppose I spent a year's income on the villa with the idea of running away from it? I am tired to death of being teased about the place. First it is auntie, and then it is Captain Holbrook, and now it is young Helen. Villa, gardens, and woods are utterly lovely, and I mean to stay."

"But if you are not happy here?"

"Who says I am not happy?"

"Your face says it, Lota."

"I am just as happy here as I should be anywhere else," she answered, doggedly, "and I mean to stay."

She set her teeth as she finished the sentence, and her face had a look of angry resolve that I had never seen in it before. It seemed as if she were fighting against something, defying something. She rose abruptly from the bank upon which she had been sitting, in a sheltered hollow, near the rocky cleft where a ruined oil mill hung mouldering on the brink of a waterfall; and she began to walk up and down very fast, muttering to herself with frowning brows:

"I shall stay! I shall stay!" I heard her repeating, as she passed me.

After that miserable morning—miserable in a climate and a scene of loveliness where bare existence should have been bliss—I had many serious conversations with Captain Holbrook, who was at the villa every day, the most wonderful and devoted of lovers. From him I learnt all that was known of the house in which I was living. He had taken infinite pains to discover any reason, in the house or the neighbourhood, for the lamentable change in Lota, but with the slightest results. No legend of the supernatural was associated with the Orange Grove; but on being questioned searchingly an old Italian physician who had spent his life at Taggia, and who had known Ruffini, confessed that there was a something, a mysterious something, about the villa which seemed to have affected everybody who lived in it, as owner or master, within the memory of the oldest inhabitant.

"People are not happy there. No, they are not happy, and sometimes they fade and die."

"Invalids who come to the South to die?"

"Not always. The Signorina's grandfather was an elderly man; but he appeared in robust health when he came. However, at that age, a sudden break up is by no means wonderful. There were previous instances of decay and death far more appalling, and in some ways mysterious. I am sorry the pretty young lady has spent so much money on the villa."

"What does money matter if she would only go elsewhere?"

She would not. That was the difficulty. No argument of her lover's could move her. She would go in April, she told him, at the season for departure; but not even his persuasion, his urgent prayers, would induce her to leave one week or one day sooner than the doctor ordered.

"I should hate myself if I were weak enough to run away from this place," she said; and it seemed to me that those words were the clue to her conduct, and that she making a martyr of herself rather than succumb to something of horror which was haunting and killing her.

Her marriage had been fixed for the following June, and George Holbrook was strong in the rights of a future husband; but submissive as she was in all other respects, upon this point she was stubborn, and her lover's fervent pleading moved her no more than the piteous entreaties of her spinster aunt.

I began to understand that the case was hopeless, so far as Lota's well-being depended upon her speedy removal from the Orange Grove. We could only wait as hopefully as we could for April, and the time she had fixed for departure. I took the earliest opportunity of confiding my fears to the English physician; but clever and amiable as he was, he laughed all ideas of occult influence to scorn.

"From the moment the sanitary engineer—a really scientific man—certified this house as a healthy house, the last word was said as to its suitableness for Miss Hammond. The situation is perfect, the climate all that one could desire. It would be folly to move her till the spring is advanced well enough for Varese or England."

What could I say against this verdict of local experience? Lota was not one of those interesting and profitable cases which a doctor likes to keep under his own eye. As a patient, her doctor only saw her once in way; but he dropped in at the villa often as a friend, and he had been useful in bringing nice people about her.

I pressed the question so far as to ask him about the rooms at the back of the house, the old monkish rooms which had served as an infirmary in the seventeenth and eighteenth centuries. "Surely those rooms must be cold and damp?"

"Damp, no. Cold, yes. All north rooms are cold on the Riviera—and the change from south to north is perilous—but as no one uses the old monkish rooms their aspect can make little difference."

"Does not Miss Hammond use those rooms sometimes?"

"Never, I believe. Indeed, I understood Miss Elderson to say that the corridor leading to the old part of the house is kept locked, and that she has the key. I take it the good lady thinks that if the rooms are haunted it is her business to keep the ghosts in safe custody—as she does the groceries."

"Has nobody ever used these rooms since the new villa was built?" I asked.

"Mr. Hammond used them, and was rather attached to that part of the house. His library is still there, I believe, in what was once a refectory."

"I should love to see it."

"You have only to ask Miss Elderson."

I did ask Miss Elderson without an hour's delay, the first time I found myself alone with her. She blushed, hesitated, assured me that the rooms contained nothing worth looking at, and fully confessed that the key was not comepatible.

"I have not lost it," she said. "It is only mislaid. It is sure to turn up when I am looking for something else. I put it in a safe place."

Miss Elderson's places of safety had been one of our stock jokes ever since I had know Lota and her aunt; so I was inclined to despair of ever seeing those mysterious rooms in which the monks had lived. Yet after meditating upon the subject in a long ramble on the hill above the villa I was inclined to think that Lota might know more about that key than the good simple soul who mislaid it. There were hours in every day during which my friend disappeared from the family circle, hours in which she was supposed to be resting inside the mosquito curtains in her own room. I had knocked at her door once or twice during this period of supposed rest; and there had been no answer. I had tried the door softly, and had found it locked, and had gone away believing my friend fast asleep; but now I began to wonder whether Lota might not possess the key of those uninhabited rooms, and for some strange capricious motive spend some of her lonely hours within those walls. I made an investigation at the back of the villa the following day, before the early coffee and the rolls, which we three spinsters generally took in the verandah on warm sunny mornings, and most of our mornings were warm. I found the massive Venetian shutters firmly secured inside, and affording not a glimpse of the rooms within. The windows looked straight upon the precipitous hill, and these northward-facing rooms must needs be dark and chilly at the best of times. My curiosity was completely baffled. Even if I had been disposed to do a little house-breaking there was no possibility of opening those too solid looking shutters. I tugged at the fastenings savagely, but made no more impression than if I had been a fly.

## CHAPTER IV
### SUNSHINE OUTSIDE, BUT ICE AT THE CORE

For the next four days I watched Lota's movements.

After our morning saunter—she was far too weak now to go further than the terraced paths near the villa, and our sauntering was of the slowest—my poor friend would retire to her room for what she called her afternoon rest, while the carriage, rarely used by herself, conveyed her aunt and me for a drive, which our low spirits made ineffably dreary. Vainly was that panorama of loveliness spread before my eyes—I could enjoy nothing; for between me and that romantic scene there was the image of my perishing friend, dying by inches, and obstinately determined to die.

I questioned Lota's maid about those long afternoons which her mistress spent in her darkened room, and the young woman's answers confirmed my suspicions.

Miss Hammond did not like to be disturbed. She was a very heavy sleeper.

"She likes me to go to her at four o'clock every afternoon to do her hair, and put on her teagown. She is generally fast asleep when I go to her."

"And her door locked?"

"No, the door is very seldom locked at four. I went an hour earlier once with a telegram, and then the door was locked, and

Miss Hammond was so fast asleep that she couldn't hear me knocking. I had to wait till the usual time."

On the fourth day after my inspection of the shutters, I started for the daily drive at the accustomed hour; but when we had gone a little way down the hill, I pretended to remember an important letter that had to be written, and asked Miss Elderson to stop the carriage, and let me go back to the villa, excusing my desertion for this afternoon. The poor lady, who was as low-spirited as myself, declared she would miss me sadly, and the carriage crept on, while I climbed the hill by those straight steep paths which shortened the journey to a five minutes' walk.

The silence of the villa as I went softly in at the open hall doors suggested a general siesta. There was an awning in front of the door, and the hall was wrapt in shadow, the corridor beyond darker still, and at the end of this corridor I saw a flitting figure in pale grey—the pale Indian cashmere of Lota's neat morning frock. I heard a key turn, then the creaking of a heavy door, and the darkness had swallowed that pale grey figure.

I waited a few moments, and then stole softly along the passage. The door was half open, and I peered into the room beyond. It was empty, but an open door facing the fireplace showed me another room—a room lined with bookshelves, and in this room I could hear footsteps pacing slowly to and fro, very slowly, with the feeble tread I knew too well.

Presently she turned, put her hand to her brow as if remembering something, and hurried to the door where I was standing.

"It is I, Lota!" I called out, as she approached me, lest she should be startled by my unexpected presence.

I had been mean enough to steal a march upon her, but I was not mean enough to conceal myself.

"You here!" she exclaimed.

I told her how I had suspected her visits to these deserted rooms, and how I had dreaded the melancholy effect which their dreariness must needs exercise upon her mind and health.

"Do you call them dreary?" she asked, with a curious little laugh. "I call them charming. They are the only rooms in the house that interest me. And it was just the same with my grandfather. He spent his declining days in these queer old rooms, surrounded by these queer old things."

She looked round her, with furtive, wandering glances, at the heavy old bookshelves, the black and white cabinets, the dismal old Italian tapestry, and at a Venetian glass which occupied a narrow recess at the end of the inner room, a glass that reached from floor to ceiling, and in a florid carved frame, from which the gilding had mostly worn away.

Her glance lingered on this Venetian glass, which to my uneducated eye looked the oldest piece of furniture in the room. The surface was so clouded and tarnished that although Lota and I were standing opposite it at a little distance, I could see no reflection of ourselves or of the room.

"You cannot find that curious old glass very flattering to your vanity," I said, trying to be sprightly and careless in my remarks, while my eyes were watching that wasted countenance with its hectic bloom, and those too brilliant eyes.

"No, it doesn't flatter, but I like it," she said, going a little nearer the glass, and then suddenly drawing a dark velvet curtain across the narrow space between the two projecting bookcases.

I had not noticed the curtain till she touched it, for this end of the long room was in shadow. The heavy shutters which I had seen outside were closed over two of the windows, but the shutters had been pushed back from the third window, and the casements were open to the still, soft air.

There was a sofa opposite the curtained recess. Lota sank down upon it, folded her arms, and looked at me with a defiant smile.

"Well, what do you think of my den?" she asked.

"I think you could not have chosen a worse."

"And yet my grandfather liked these rooms better than all the rest of the house. He almost lived in them. His old servant told me so."

"An elderly fancy, which no doubt injured his health."

"People choose to say so, because he died sooner than they expected. His death would have come at the appointed time. The day and hour were written in the Book of Fate before he came here. The house had nothing to do with it—only in this quiet old room he had time to think of what was coming."

"He was old, and had lived his life; you are young, and life is all before you."

"All!" She echoed, with a laugh that chilled my heart.

I tried to be cheerful, matter of fact, practical. I urged her to abandon this dismal library, with its dry old books, airless gloom and northern aspect. I told her she had been guilty of an unworthy deceit in spending long hours in rooms that had been especially forbidden her. She made an end of my pleading with cruel abruptness.

"You are talking nonsense, Helen. You know that I am doomed to die before the summer is over, and I know that you know it."

"You were well when you came here; you have been growing worse day by day."

"My good health was only seeming. The seeds of disease were here," touching her contracted chest. "They have only developed. Don't talk to me, Helen; I shall spend my quiet hours in these rooms till the end, like my poor old grandfather. There need be no more concealment or double dealing. This house is mine, and I shall occupy the rooms I like."

She drew herself up haughtily as she rose from the sofa, but the poor little attempt at dignity was spoilt by a paroxysm of coughing that made her glad to rest in my arms, while I laid her gently down upon the sofa.

The darkness came upon us while she lay there, prostrate, exhausted, and that afternoon in the shadow of the steep hill was the first of many such afternoons.

From that day she allowed me to share her solitude, so long as I did not disturb her reveries, her long silences, or brief snatches of slumber. I sat by the open window and worked or read, while she lay on the sofa, or moved softly about the room, looking at the books on the shelves, or often stopping before that dark Venetian glass to contemplate her own shadowy image.

I wondered exceedingly in those days what pleasure or interest she could find in surveying that blurred shadow of her faded beauty. Was it in bitterness she looked at her altered form, the shrunken features—or only in philosophical wonder such as Marlborough felt, when he pointed to the withered old form in the glass—the poor remains of peerless manhood and exclaimed: "That was once a man."

I had no power to withdraw her from that gloomy solitude. I was thankful for the privilege of being with her, able to comfort her in moments of physical misery.

Captain Holbrook left within a few days of my discovery, his leave having so nearly expired that he had only just time enough to get back to Portsmouth, where his regiment was stationed. He went regretfully, full of fear, and his last anxious words were spoken to me at the little station on the sea shore.

"Do all you can to bring her home as soon as the doctor will let her come," he said. "I leave her with a heavy heart, but I can do no good by remaining. I shall count every hour between now and April. She has promised to stay at Southsea till we are married, so that we may be near each other. I am to find a pretty villa for her and her aunt. It will be something for me to do."

My heart ached for him in his forlorness, glad of any little duty that made a link between him and his sweetheart. I knew that he dearly loved his profession, and I knew also that he had offered to leave the army if Lota liked—to alter the whole plan of his life rather than be parted from her, even for a few weeks. She had forbidden such a sacrifice; and she had stubbornly refused to advance the date of her marriage, and marry him at San Remo, as he had entreated her at Ventnor, where he believed she would be better than in her Italian paradise.

He was gone, and I felt miserably helpless and lonely without him—lonely even in Lota's company, for between her and me there were shadows and mysteries that filled my heart with dread. Sitting in the same room with her—admitted now to constant companionship—I felt not the less that there were secrets in her life which I knew not. Her eloquent face told some sad story which I could not read; and sometimes it seemed to me that between her and me there was a third presence, and that the name of the third was Death.

She let me share her quiet afternoons in the old rooms, but though her occupation of these rooms was no longer concealed from the household, she kept the privilege of solitude with jealous care. Her aunt still believed in the siesta between lunch and dinner, and went for her solitary drives with a placid submission to Lota's desire that the carriage and horses should be used by somebody. The poor thing was quite as unhappy as I, and quite as fond as Lota; but her feeble spirit had no power to struggle against her niece's strong will. Of these two the younger had always ruled the elder. After Captain Holbrook's departure the doctor took his patient seriously in hand, and I soon perceived a marked change in his manner of questioning her, while the stethoscope came now into frequent use. The casual weekly visits became daily visits; and in answer to my anxious questions I was told that the case had suddenly assumed a serious character.

"We have something to fight against now," said the doctor; "until now we have had nothing but nerves and fancies."

"And now?"

"The lungs are affected."

This was the beginning of a new sadness. Instead of vague fears, we had now the certainty of evil; and I think in the dreary days and weeks that followed, the poor old aunt and I had not one thought or desire, or fear, which was not centred in the fair young creature whose fading life we watched. Two English nurses, summoned from Cannes, aided in the actual nursing, for which trained skill was needed; but in all the little services which love can perform Miss Elderson and I were Lota's faithful slaves.

I told the doctor of her afternoons spent in her grandfather's library; and I told him also that I doubted my power, or his, to induce her to abandon that room.

"She has a fancy for it, and you know how difficult fancies are to fight with when anyone is out of health."

"It is a curious fact," said the doctor, "that in every bad case I have attended in this house my patient has had an obstinate preference for that dull, cold, room."

"When you say every bad case, I think you must mean every fatal case," I said.

"Yes. Unhappily the three or four cases I am thinking of ended fatally; but that fact need not make you unhappy. Feeble, elderly people come to this southern shore to spin out the frail thread of life that is at breaking point when they leave England. In your young friend's case sunshine and balmy air may do much. She ought to live on the sunny side of the house; but her fancy for her grandfather's library may be indulged all the same. She can spend her evenings in that room, which can be made thoroughly warm and comfortable before she enters it. The room is well built and dry. When the shutters are shut and the curtains drawn, and the temperature carefully regulated, it will be as good a room as any other for the lamp-light hours; but for the day let her have all the sunshine she can."

I repeated this little lecture to Lota, who promised to obey.

"I like the queer, old room," she said, "and, Helen, don't think me a bear if I say that I should like to alone there sometimes, as I used to be before you hunted me down. Society is very nice for people who are well enough to enjoy it, but I'm not up to society, not even yours and auntie's. Yes, I know what you are going to say. You sit like a mouse, and don't speak till you are spoken to; but the very knowledge that you are there, watching me and thinking about me, worries me. And as for the auntie, with her little anxious fidgettings, wanting to settle my footstool, and shake up my pillows, and turn the leaves of my books, and always making me uncomfortable in the kindest way, dear soul—well, I don't mind confessing that she gets on my nerves, and makes me feel as if I should like to scream. Let me have one hour or two of perfect solitude sometimes, Helen. The nurse don't count. She can sit in the room, and you will know that I am not going to die suddenly without anybody to look on at my poor little tragedy."

She had talked longer and more earnestly than usual, and the talking ended in a fit of coughing which shook the wasted frame. I promised that all should be as she wished. If solitude were more restful than even our quiet companionship, she should be sometimes alone. I would answer for her aunt, as for myself.

The nurses were two bright, capable young women, and were used to the caprices of the sick. I told them exactly what was wanted: a silent unobtrusive presence, a watchful care of the patient's physical comfort by day and night. And henceforth Lota's evenings were spent for the most part in solitude. She had her books, and her drawing-board, on which with light, weak hand she would sketch faint remembrances of the spots that had charmed us most in our drives or rambles. She had her basket overflowing with scraps of fancy work, beginnings of things that were to have no end.

"She doesn't read very long, or work for more than ten minutes at a time," the nurse told me. "She just dozes away most of the evening, or walks about the room now and then, and stands to look at herself in that gloomy old glass. It's strange that she should be so fond of looking in the glass, poor dear, when she can scarcely fail to see the change in herself."

"No, no, she must see, and it is breaking her heart. I wish we could do away with every looking-glass in the house," said I, remembering how pretty she had been in the fresh bloom of her happy girlhood only six months before that dreary time.

"She is very fond of going over her grandfather's papers," the nurse told me. "There is a book I see her reading very often—a manuscript book."

"His diary, perhaps," said I.

"It might be that; but it's strange that she should care to pore over an old gentleman's diary."

Strange, yes; but all her fancies and likings were strange ever since I had entered that unlucky house. In her thought of her lover she was not as other girls. She was angry when I suggested that we should tell him of her illness, in order that he might get leave to come to her, if it were only for a few days.

"No, no, let him never look upon my face again," she said. "It is bad enough for him to remember me as I was when we parted at the station. It is ever so much worse now—and it will be—oh, Helen, to think of what must come—at last!"

She hid her face in her hands, and the frail frame was convulsed with the vehemence of her sobbing. It was long before I could soothe her; and this violent grief seemed the more terrible because of the forced cheerfulness of her usual manner.

## CHAPTER V
## SEEK NOT TO KNOW

We kept early hours at the villa. We dined at seven, and at eight Lota withdrew to the room which she was pleased to call her den. At ten there was a procession of invalid, nurse, aunt, and friend to Lota's bedroom, where the night nurse, in her neat print gown and pretty white cap, was waiting to receive her. There were many kisses and tender good-nights, and a great show of cheerfulness on all sides, and then Miss Elderson and I crept slowly to our rooms—exchanging a few sad words, a few sympathetic sighs to cry ourselves to sleep, and to awake in the morning with the thought of the doom hanging over us.

I used to drop in upon Lota's solitude a little before bed-time, sometimes with her aunt, sometimes alone. She would look up from her book with a surprised air, or start out of her sleep.

"Bedtime already?"

Sometimes when I found her sleeping, I would seat myself beside her sofa, and wait in silence for her waking. How picturesque, how luxurious, the old room looked in the glaring light of the wood, which brightened even the grim tapestry, and glorified the bowls of red and purple anemones and other scentless flowers, and shining brown floor. It was a room that I too could have loved were it not for the shadow of fear that hung over all things at the Orange Grove.

I went to the library earlier than usual one evening. The clock had not long struck since when I left the drawing room. I had seen a change for the worse in Lota at dinner, though she had kept up her pretence of gaiety, and had refused to be treated as an invalid, insisting upon dining as we dined, scarcely toughing some things, eating ravenously of other dishes, the least wholesome, laughing to scorn all her doctor's advice about dietary. I endured the interval between eight and nine, stifling my anxieties, and indulging the mild old lady with a game of bezique, which my wretched play allowed her to win easily. Like most old people her sorrow was of a mild and modified quality, and she had, I believe, resigned herself to the inevitable. The careful doctor, the admirable nurses, had set her mind at ease about dear Lota, she told me. She felt that all was being done that love and care could do, and for the rest, well, she had her church services, her prayers, her morning and evening readings in the well-worn New Testament. I believe she was almost happy.

"We must all die, my dear Helen," she said, plaintively.

Die, yes. Die when one had reached that humdrum stage on the road of life where this poor old thing was plodding, past barren fields and flowerless hedges—the stage of grey hairs, and toothless gums, and failing sight, and dull hearing—and an old fashioned, one dead intellect. But to die like Lota, in the pride of youth, with beauty and wealth and love all one's own! To lay all this down in the grave! That seemed hard, too hard for my understanding or my patience.

† † † † † †

I found her asleep on the sofa by the hearth, the nurse sitting quietly on guard in her armchair, knitting the stocking which was never out of her hands unless they were occupied in the patient's service. To-night's sleep was sounder than usual, for the sleeper did not stir at my approach, and I seated myself in the low chair by the foot of the sofa without waking her.

A book had slipped from her hand, and lay on the silken coverlet open. The pages caught my eye, for they were in manuscript, and I remembered what the nurse had said about Lota's fancy for this volume. I stole my hand across the coverlet, and possessed myself of the book, so softly that the sleeper's sensitive frame had no consciousness of my touch.

A manuscript volume of about two hundred pages in the neat firm hand, very small, yet easy to read, so perfectly were the letters formed and so evenly were the lines spaced.

I turned the leaves eagerly. A diary, a business man's diary, recording in commonplace phraseology the transactions of each day, Stock Exchange, Stock Exchange—railways—mines—loans—banks—money, money, money, made or lost. That was all the neat penmanship told me, as I turned leaf after leaf, and ran my eye over page after page.

The social life of the writer was indicated in a few brief sentences. "Dined with the Parkers: dinner execrable; company stupid; talked to Lendon, who has made half a million in Mexican copper; a dull man."

"Came to Brighton for Easter; clear turtle at the Ship good; they have given me my old rooms; asked Smith (Suez Smith, not Turkish Smith) to dinner."

What interest could Lota possibly find in such a journal—a prosy commonplace record of losses and gains, bristling with figures?

This was what I asked myself as I turned leaf after leaf, and saw only everlasting repetition of financial notes, strange names of loans and mines and railways, with contractions that reduced them to a cipher. Slowly, my hand softly turning the pages of the thick volume, I had gone through about three-fourths of the book when I came to the heading, "Orange Grove," and the brief entries of the financier gave place to the detailed ideas and experiences of the man of leisure, an exile from familiar scenes and old faces, driven back upon self-commune for the amusement of his lonely hours.

This doubtless was where Lota's interest in the book began, and here I began to read every word of the diary with closest attention. I did not stop to think whether I justified in reading the pages which the dead man had penned in his retirement, whether a license which his grand-daughter allowed herself might be taken by me. My one thought was to discover the reason of Lota's interest in the book, and whether its influence upon her mind and spirits was as harmful as I feared.

I slipped from the chair to the rug beside the sofa, and, sitting there on the ground, with the full light of the shaded reading-lamp upon the book, I forgot everything but the pages before me.

The first few pages after the old man's installation in his villa were full of cheerfulness. He wrote of this land of the South, new to his narrow experience, as an earthly paradise. He was almost as sentimental in his enthusiasms as a girl, as if it had not been for the old-fashioned style in which his raptures expressed themselves these pages might have been written by a youthful pen.

He was particularly interested in the old monkish rooms at the back of the villa, but he fully recognized the danger of occupying them.

"I have put my books in the long room which was used as a refectory," he wrote, "but as I now rarely look at them there is no fear of my being tempted to spend more than an occasional hour in the room."

Then after an interval of nearly a month—

"I have arranged my books, as I find the library the most interesting room in the house. My doctor objects to the gloomy aspect, but I find a pleasing melancholy in the shadow of the steep olive-clad hill. I begin to think that this life of retirement, with no companions but my books, suits me better than the pursuit of money making, which has occupied so large a portion of my later years."

Then followed pages of criticism upon the books he read—history, travels, poetry—books which he had been collecting for many years, but which he was now only beginning to enjoy.

"I see before me a studious old age," he wrote, "and I hope I may live as long as the head of my old college, Martin Routh. I have made more than enough money to satisfy myself, and to provide ample wealth for the dear girl who will inherit the greater part of my fortune. I can afford to fold my hands, and enjoy the long quiet years of old age in the companionship of the master spirits who have gone before. How near, how living they seem as I steep myself in their thoughts, dream their dreams, see life as they saw it! Virgil, Dante, Chaucer, Shakespeare, Milton, and all those later lights that have shone upon the dullest lives and made them beautiful—how they live with us, and fill our thoughts, and make up the brightest part of our daily existence."

I read many pages of comment and reverie in the neat, clear penmanship of a man who wrote for his own pleasure, in the restful solitude of his own fire-side.

Suddenly there came a change—the shadow of the cloud that hung over that house.

"I am living too much alone. I did not think I was of the stuff which is subject to delusions and marbled fancies—but I was wrong. I suppose no man's mind can retain its strength of fibre without the friction of intercourse with other minds of its own calibre I have been living alone with the minds of the dead, and waited upon by foreign servants, with whom I hardly exchange half a dozen sentences in a day. And the result is what no doubt any brain-doctor would have foretold.

"I have begun to see ghosts.

"The thing I have seen is so evidently an emanation of my own mind—so palpably a materialization of my own self-consciousness, brooding upon myself and my chances of long life—that it is a weakness even to record the appearance that has haunted me during the last few evenings. No shadow of dying monk has stolen between me and the lamplight; no presence from the vanished years, revisiting places. The thing which I have seen is myself—not myself as I am—but myself as I am to be in the coming years, many or few.

"The vision—purely self-induced as I know it to be—has not the less given a shock to the placid contentment of my mind, and the long hopes which, in spite of the Venusian's warning, I had of late been cherishing.

"Looking up from my book in yesterday's twilight my casual glance rested on the old Venetian mirror in front of my desk; and gradually, out of the blurred darkness, I saw a face looking at me.

"My own face as it might be after the wasting of disease, or the slow decay of advancing years—a face at least ten years older that the face I had seen in my glass a few hours before—hollow cheeks, haggard eyes, the loose under-lip drooping weakly—a bent figure in an invalid chair, an aspect of utter helplessness. And it was myself. Of that fact I had no shadow of doubt.

"Hypochondria, of course—a common form of the malady,—perhaps this shaping of the imagination into visions. Yet, the thing was strange—for I had been troubled by no apprehensions of illness or premature old age. I had never even thought of myself as a old man. In the pride bred of long immunity from illness I had considered myself exempt for the ailments that are wont to attend declining years. I had pictured myself living to the extremity of human life, and dropping peacefully into the centenarian's grave.

"I was angry with myself for being affected by the vision and I locked the door of the library when I went to dress for dinner, determined not to re-enter the room till I had done something—by out-door exercise and change of scene—to restore the balance of my brain. Yet when I had dined there came upon me so feverish a desire to know whether the glass would again show me the same figure and face I have the key to my major-domo, and told him to light the lamps and make up the fire in the library.

"Yes, the thing lived in the blotched and blurred old glass. The dusky surface, which was too dull to reflect the realities of life, gave back that vision of age and decay with unalterable fidelity. The face and figure came and went, and the glass was often black—but whenever the thing appeared it was the same—the same in every dismal particular, in all the signs of senility and fading life.

"'This is what I am to be twenty years hence,' I told myself; 'a man of eighty might look like that.'

"Yet I had hoped to escape that bitter lot of gradual decay which I had seen and pitied in other men. I had promised myself that the reward of a temperate life—a life free from all consuming fires of dissipation, all tempestuous passions—would be a vigorous and prolonged old age. So surely as I had toiled to amass fortune so surely also had I striven to save up for myself long years of health and activity, a life prolonged to the utmost span."

† † † † † †

There was a break of ten days in the journal, and when the record was resumed the change in the writing shocked me. The neat firm penmanship gave place to weak and straggling characters, which, but for marked peculiarities in the formation of certain letters, I should have taken for the writing of a stranger.

"The thing is always there in the black depths of that damnable glass—and I spend the greater part of m life watching for it. I have struggled in vain against the bitter curiosity to know the worst which hthe vision of the future can show me. Three days ago I flung the key of this detestable room into the deepest well on the premises; but an hour afterwards I sent to Taggia for a blacksmith, and had the lock picked, and ordered a new key, and a duplicate, lest in some future fit of spleen I should throw away a second key, and suffer agonies before the door could be opened.

"'*Tu ne quaesieris, scire nefas*—'

"Vainly the poet's warning buzzes and booms in my vexed ear—repeating itself perpetually, like the beating of a pulse in my brain or like the ticking of a clock that will not let a man sleep.

"'*Scire nefas—scire nefas,*'

"The desire to know more is no stranger than reason.

"Well, I am at least prepared for what is to come. I live no longer in a fool's paradise. The thing which I see daily and hourly is no hallucination, no materialization of my self-consciousness, as I thought in the beginning. It is a warning and a prophesy. So shalt though be. Soon, soon, shalt thou resemble this form which it shocks thee now to look upon.

"Since first the shadow of myself looked at me from the darker shadows of the glass I have felt every indication of the approaching doom. The doctor tries to laugh away my fears, but he owns that I am below par—meaningless phrase—talks of nervine decay, and suggests my going to St. Moritz. He doubts if this place suits me, and confesses that I have changed for the worse since I came here."

Again an interval, and then in writing that was only just legible.

"It is a month since I wrote in this book—a month which has realized all that the Venetian glass showed me when first I began to read its secret.

"I am a helpless old man, carried about in an invalid chair. Gone my pleasant prospect of long tranquil years; gone my selfish scheme of enjoyment, the fruition of a life of money-getting. The old Eastern fable has been realized once again. My gold has turned to withered leaves, so far as any pleasure that it can buy for me. I hope that my grand-daughter may get some good out of the wealth I have toiled to win."

Again a break, longer this time, and again the handwriting showed signs of increasing weakness. I had to pore over it closely in order to decipher the broken, crooked lines penciled casually over the pages.

"The weather is insufferably hot; but too ill to be moved. In library—coolest room—doctor no objection. I have seen the last picture in glass—Death—corruption—the cavern of Lazarus, and no Redeemer's hand to raise the dead. Horrible! Horrible! Myself as I must be—soon, soon! How Soon?"

And then scrawled in a corner of the page, I found the date—June 24, 1889.

I knew that Mr. Hammond died early in the July of that year.

† † † † † †

Seated on the floor, with my head bent over the pages, and reading more by the light of the blazing logs than by the lamp on the table above me, I was unaware that Lota had awoke, and had raised herself from her reclining position of the sofa. I was still absorbed in my study of those last horrible lines when a pale hand came suddenly down upon the open book, and a laugh which was almost a shriek ran thought the silent spaces around us. The nurse started up and ran to her patient, who was struggling to her feet and staring wildly into the long narrow glass in the recess opposite her sofa.

"Look, look!" she shrieked. "It has come—the vision of Death! The dreadful face—the shroud—the coffin. Look, Helen, look!"

My gaze followed the direction of those wild eyes, and I know not whether my excited brain conjured up the image that appalled me. This alone I know, that in the depths of that dark glass, indistinct as a form seen through turbid water, a ghastly face, a shrouded figure, looked out a me—

"As one dead in the bottom of a tomb."

A sudden cry from the nurse called me from the horror of that vision to stern reality, to see the life-blood ebbing from the lips I had kissed so often with all a sister's love. My poor friend never spoke again. A severe attack of hemorrhage hastened the inevitable end; and before her heart-broken lover could come to clasp the hand and gaze into her fading eyes, Violetta Hammond passed away.

# Prof. P. Jones:
# The Priest and His Cook (1895)

"The Priest and His Cook" is excerpted from Prof. P. Jones'
*The Probatim: A Slav Novel* (London: H. S. Nichols, 1895) which
contains a number of Slavic folktales. In "The Story of Jella and
the Macic" (pages 11–22), the villains are punished by a cemetery
full of vampires.

The following story, which is taken from Chapter 16, "The
Vampire," is preceded by the phrase:

"The old man complied willingly, above all as Vranic had
brought a bukara of wine with him, so he at once began the
story of . . . "

---

In the village of Steino there lived an old priest who was
exceedingly wealthy, but who was, withal, as miserly as he
was rich. Although he had fields which stretched farther than
the eyes could reach, fat pastures, herds and flocks; although his
cellars were filled with mellow wine, his barns were bursting
with the grace of God; although abundance reigned in his house,
still he was never known to have given a crust of bread to a
beggar or a glass of wine to a weary old man.

He lived all alone with a skinflint of an old cook, as stingy as
himself, who would rather by far have seen an apple rot than give
it to a hungry child whose mouth watered for it.

Those two grim old fogeys, birds of one feather, cared for
no one else in this world except for each other, and, in fact, the
people in Steino said—, but people in villages have bad tongues,
so it's useless to repeat what was said about them.

The priest had a nephew, a smith, a good-hearted, bright-eyed,
burly kind of a fellow, beloved by all the village, except by his

uncle, whom he had greatly displeased because he had married a bonny lass of the neighbouring village of Smarje, instead of take as a wife the—,well, the cook's niece, though, between us and the wall, the cook was never known to have had a sister or a brother either, and the people—, but, as I said before, the people were apt to say nasty things about their priest.

The smith, who was quite a pauper, had several children, for the poorer a man is the more babies his wife presents him with—women everywhere are such unreasonable creatures—and whenever he applied to his uncle for a trifle, the uncle would spout the Scriptures in Latin, saying something about the unfitness of casting pearls before pigs, and that he would rather see him hanged than help him.

Once—it was in the middle of winter—the poor smith had been without any work for days and days. He had spent his last penny; then the baker would not give him any more bread on credit, and at last, on a cold, frosty night, the poor children had been obliged to go to bed supperless.

The smith, who had sworn a few days before never again to put his foot in the priest's house, was, in his despair, obliged to humble himself, and go and beg for a load of bread, with which to satisfy his children on the morrow.

Before he knocked at the door, he went and peeped in through the half-closed shutters, and he saw his uncle and the cook seated by a roaring fire, with their feet on the fender, munching roasted chestnuts and drinking mulled wine. Their shining lips still seemed greasy from the fat sausages they had eaten for supper, and, as he sniffed the window, he fancied the air was redolent with the spices of black-pudding. The smell made his mouth water and his hungry stomach rumble.

The poor man knocked at the door with a trembling hand; his legs began to quake, he had not eaten the whole of that long day; but then he thought of his hungry children, and knocked with a steadier hand.

The priest, hearing the knock, thought it must be some pious parishioner bringing him a fat pullet or perhaps a sleek sucking-pig, the price of a mass to be said on the morrow; but when, instead, he saw his nephew, looking as mean and as sheepish as people usually do when they go a-begging, he was greatly disappointed.

"What do you want, bothering here at this time of the night?" asked the old priest, gruffly.

"Uncle," said the poor man, dejectedly.

"I suppose you've been drinking, as usual; you stink of spirits."

"Spirits, in sooth! When I haven't a penny to bless me."

"Oh, if it's only a blessing you want, here, take one and go!"

And the priest lifted up his thumb and the two fingers, and uttered something like "Dominus vobiscum," and then waved him off; whilst the old shrew skulking near him uttered a croaking kind of laugh, and said that a priest's blessing was a priceless boon.

"Yes," replied the smith, "upon a full stomach; but my children have gone to bed supperless, and I haven't had a crust of bread the whole of the day."

"'Man shall not live by bread alone,' the scriptures say, and you ought to know that if you are a Christian, sir."

"Eh? I daresay the Scriptures are right, for priests surely do not live on bread alone; they fatten on plump pullets and crisp pork-pies."

"Do you mean you bully me, you unbelieving beggar?"

"Bully you, uncle!" said the burly man in a piteous tone. "Only, think of my starving children."

"He begrudges his uncle the grub he eats," shrieked the old cat of a cook.

"I'd have given you something, but the proud man should be punished," said the wrathful priest, growing purple in the face.

"Oh, uncle, my children!" sobbed the poor man.

"What business has a man to have a brood of brats when he can't earn enough to buy bread for them?" said the cook, aloud, to herself.

"Will you hold your tongue, you cantankerous old cat?" said the smith to the cook.

The old vixen began to howl, and the priest, in his anger, cursed his nephew, telling him that he and his children could starve for all he cared.

The smith thereupon went home, looking at piteous as a tail-less turkey-cock; and while his children slept and, perhaps, dreamt of kolaci, he told his wife the failure he had met with.

"Your uncle is a brute," said she.

"He's a priest, and all priests are brutes, you know."

"Well, I don't know about all of them, for I heard my great-grandmother say that once upon a time there lived— "

"Oh, there are casual exceptions to every rule!" said her husband. "But, now, what's to be done?"

"Listen," said the wife, who was a shrewd kind of woman, "we can't let the children starve, can we?"

"No, indeed!"

"Then follow my advice. I know of a grass that, given to a horse, or an ox, or a sheep, or goat, makes the animal fall down, looking as if it were dead."

"Well, but you don't mean to feed the children with this grass, do you?" said the smith, not seeing the drift of what she meant.

"No; but you could secretly go and give some to your uncle's fattest ox."

"So," said the husband, scratching his head.

"Once the animal falls down head, he'll surely give it you, as no butcher'll buy it; we'll kill it and thus be provided with meat for a long time. Besides, you can sell the bones, the horns, the hide, and get a little money besides."

"And for tomorrow?"

"I'll manage to borrow a few potatoes and a cup of milk."

On the next day the wife went and got the grass, and the smith, unseen, managed to go and give it to his uncle's fattest ox. A few hours afterwards the animal was found dead.

On hearing that his finest ox was found in the stable lying stiff and stark the priest nearly had a fit; and his grief was still greater when he found out that not a man in the village would offer him a penny for it, so when his nephew came he was glad enough to give it to him to get rid of it.

The cook, who had prompted the priest to make a present of the ox to his nephew, hoped that the smith and all his family would be poisoned by feeding on carrion flesh.

"But," said the uncle, "bring me back the bones, the horns, and the hide."

To everyone's surprise, and to the old cook's rage, the smith and his children fed on the flesh of the dead ox, and throve on it. After the ox had all been eaten up, the priest lost a goat, and then a goose, in the same way, and the smith and his family ate them up with evident gusto.

After that, the old cook began to suspect foul play on the part of the smith, and she spoke of her suspicions to her master.

The priest got into a great rage, and wanted to go at once to the police and accuse his nephew of sorcery.

"No," said the cook, "we must catch them on the hip, and then we can act."

"But how are we to find them out?"

After brooding over the matter for some days, the cook bethought herself that the best plan would be to shut herself up in a cupboard, and have it taken to the nephew's house.

The priest, having approved of her plan, put it at once into execution.

"I have," said the uncle to the nephew, "an old cupboard which needs repairing; will you take it into your house and keep it for a few days?"

"Willingly," said the nephew, who had not the slightest suspicion of the trap laid to catch him.

The cupboard was brought, and put in the only room the smith possessed; the children look at it with wonder, for they have never seen such a big piece of furniture before. The wife had some suspicion. Still, she kept her own counsel.

Soon afterwards the remains of the goose was brought on the table, and, as the children licked the bones, the husband and wife discussed what meat they were to have for the forthcoming days—was it to be pork, veal, or turkey?

As they were engrossed with this interesting topic, a slight, shrill sound came out of the cupboard.

"What's that?" said the wife, whose ears were on the alert.

"I didn't hear anything," said the smith.

"Apshee," was the sound that came again from the cupboard.

"There, did you hear?" asked the wife.

"Yes; but from where did that unearthly sound come?"

The wife, without speaking, winked at her husband and pointed to the cupboard.

"Papshee," was now heard louder than ever.

The children stopped gnawing the goose's bones; they opened their greasy mouths and their eyes to the utmost and looked scared.

"There's someone shut in the cupboard," said the smith, jumping up, and snatching up his tools.

A moment afterwards the door flew open, and to everyone's surprise, except the wife's, the old cook was found standing bolt upright in the empty space and listening to what they were saying.

The old woman, finding herself discovered was about to scream, but the smith caught her by the throat and gave her such a powerful squeeze, that before knowing what he was doing, he had choked the cook to death.

The poor man was in despair, for he had never meant to commit a murder—he only wanted to prevent the old shrew from screaming.

"Bog me ovary! What is to become of me now?"

"Pooh!" said the wife, shrugging her shoulders; "she deserves her fate; as we make our bed, so we must lie."

"Yes," quoth the smith, "but if they find out that I've strangled her, they'll hang me."

"And who'll find you out?" said she. "Let's put a potato in her mouth and lock up the cupboard again; they'll think that she choked herself eating potatoes."

The smith followed his wife's advice, and early on the morrow the priest came again and asked for his press.

"Talking the matter over with the cook," said he, "I've decided not to have my cupboard repaired, so I've come to take it back."

"Your cook is right," said the smith's wife. "She's a wise old woman, your cook is."

"Very," said the priest, uncomfortably.

"There's more in her head than you suppose," said the wife, thinking of the potato.

"There is," said the priest.

"Give my kind respects to your cook," said the wife as the men were taking the cupboard away.

"Thank you," said the priest, "I'll certainly do so."

About an hour afterwards the priest came back, ghastly pale, to his nephew, and taking him aside, said:

"My dear nephew—my only kith-and-kin—a great misfortune has befallen me."

"What is it, uncle?" asked the smith.

"My cook," said the priest, lowering his voice, "has—eating potatoes—somehow or other—I don't know how—choked herself."

"Oh!" quoth the smith, turning pale, "it is a great misfortune; but you'll say masses for her and have her properly buried."

"But the fact is," interrupted the priest, "she looks so dreadful, with her eyes starting out of their sockets, and her mouth wide open, that I'm quite frightened of her, and besides, if the people see her they'll say that I murdered her."

"Well, and how am I to help you?"

"Come and take her away, in a sack if you like; then bury her in some hole, or throw her down a well. Do whatever you like, as long as I'm ride of her."

The smith scratched his head.

"You must help me; you are my only relation. You know that whatever I have'll go to you some day, so— "

"And when people ask what has become of her?"

"I'll say she's gone to her—her niece."

"Well, I don't mind helping you, as long as I don't get into a scrape myself."

"No, no! How can you get into trouble?"

The priest went off, and soon afterwards the smith went to his uncle's house, and taking a big sack, shoved the cook into it and tied the sack up, put it on his shoulders and trudged off.

"Here," said the uncle, "take this florin to get a glass of wine on the way, and I hope I'll never see her any more—nor," he added to himself—"you either."

It was a warm day, and the cook was heavy. The poor man was in great perspiration; his throat was parched; the road was dusty and hilly. After an hour's march he stopped at a roadside inn to drink a glass of wine. He quaffed it down at a gulp and then he had another, and again another, so that when he came out everything was rather hazy and blurred. Seeing some carts of hay at the door which were going to the next town, he asked permission to get on top of one of the wagons. The permission was not only granted, but the carter even helped him to hoist his sack on top. The smith, in return, got down and offered the man a glass of wine for his kindness. Then he again got on the cart and went off to sleep. An hour or two afterwards, when he awoke, the sack was gone. Had it slipped down? Had it been stolen from him?—he could not tell.

He did not ask for it, but he only congratulated himself at having so dexterously got rid of the cook, and at once went back home.

That evening his children had hardly been put to bed when the door was opened, and his uncle, looking pale and scared, came in panting.

"She's back, she's back!" he gasped.

"Who is back?" asked the astonished smith.

"Why, she, the cook."

"Alive?" gasped the smith.

"No, dead in the sack."

"Then how the deuce did she get back?"

"How? I ask you how?"

"I really don't know how. I dug a hole ten feet deep, half filled the hole with lime, then the other half with stones and earth, and I planted a tree within the hole, and covered the earth all around with sods. It gave me two days' work. I'll take and show you the place if you like."

The priest looked at his nephew, bewildered.

"But, tell me," continued the smith, "how did she come back?"

"Well they bought me a wagon of hay, and on the wagon there was a sack, which I thought must contain potatoes or turnips which some parishioner sent me, so I had the sack put in the kitchen. When the men had gone I undid the sack, and to my horror pops the cook's ugly head, staring at me with her jutting goggle-eyes and her gaping mouth, looking like a horrid jack-in-the-box. Do come and take her away, or she'll drive me out of my senses; but come at once."

The smith went back to the priest's house, tied the cook in the sack, and then putting the sack on his shoulders, he carried his load away. He had made up his mind to go and chuck her own one of those bottomless shafts which abound in the stony plans of the Karst.

He walked all night; at daybreak he saw a man sleeping on the grass by the high way, having near him a sack exactly like the one he was carrying.

"What a good joke it'll be," thought he, "to take that sack and put in its stead."

He at once stepped lightly on the grass, put down the cook, took up the other sack, which was much lighter than his own, and scampered back home as fast as his weary legs could carry him.

An hour afterwards the sleeping man, took up his sack, which he was surprised to find much heavier than it had been when he had gone off to sleep, and then went on his way.

That evening the priest came back to his nephew's house, looking uglier and more ghastly, if possible, than the evening before. Panting and gasping, with a weak and broken voice:

"She's back again," he said in a hoarse whisper.

The smith burst out laughing.

"It's no laughing matter," quoth the priest, with a long face.

"No indeed, it isn't," replied the nephew. "Only, tell me how she came back."

"A pedlar, an honest man whom I sometimes help by lending him a trifle on his goods—merely out of charity—brought me a sack of shoes, begging me to keep it for him till he found a stall for tomorrow's fair. I told him to put the sack in the kitchen, and he did so. When he had gone, I thought I'd just see what kind of shoes he had for sale, and I almost fainted when I saw the frightful face of the cook staring at me."

"And now," asked the smith, "am I to carry her away again, for you know uncle, she is rather heavy; and besides—"

"No," replied the priest; "I'll go away myself for a few days; during that time drown her, burn or bury her; in fact, do what you like with her, as long as you get rid of her. Perhaps, knowing I'm not at home, she'll not come back. In the meanwhile, as you are my only relation, come and live in my house and take care of my things as if they were your own; and they'll be yours soon enough, for this affair has made an old man of me."

The priest went home, followed by his nephew. Arriving there, he went to the stable, saddled the mare, got on her, gave his nephew his blessing, bade him take care of his house, and trotted off. No sooner had he gone than the smith saddled the stallion, then went and took the cook out of the sack, tied her on the stallion's saddle, then let the horse loose to follow the mare.

The poor priest had not gone a mile before he heard a horse galloping behind him, and fearing that it was police coming to bring him back, he spurred the mare and galloped on; but the faster he rode, the quicker the stallion galloped after him.

Looking round, the priest, to his horror and dismay, saw his cook, with her eyes starting wildly out of their sockets, and her horrid mouth gaping as black as the hole of hell, chasing him, nay, she was only a few yards behind.

The terrified priest spurred on the mare, which began to gallop along the highway; but withal she flew like an arrow, the stallion was gaining ground at every step. The priest, fainting with fear, lost all his presence of mind; he then spurred the mare across country. The poor animal reared at first, and then began to gallop over the stony plain; no obstacles could stop her, she jumped over bushes and briars, stumbling almost at every step.

The priest, palsied with terror, as ghastly pale as a ghost, could not help turning around; alas! The cook was always at his heels. His fear was such that he almost dropped from his horse. He lashed the poor mare, forgetful of all the dangers the plains of the Karst presented, for the ground yawned everywhere—here in huge, deep clefts, there in bottomless shafts; or it stank in cup-like hollows, all bordered with sharp, jagged rocks, or concealed in the bushes that surround them. His only thought was to escape from the grim spectre that pursued him. The lame and bleeding mare had stopped on the brink of one of these precipes, trembling and convulsed with terror. The priest, who had just turned around, dug his spurs into the animal sides; she tried to clear the cleft, but missed her footing, and rolled down in the abyss. The stallion, seeing the mare disappear, stopped short, and uttered a loud neigh, shivering with fear. The shock the poor beast had got burst the bonds which held the corpse on his back, and the cook was thus chucked over his head on the prone edge of the pit.

A few days afterwards some peasants who happened to pass by found the cook sitting, stiff and stark, astride on a rock, seemingly staring, with eyes starting from their sockets and her black mouth gaping widely, at the mangled remains of her master's corpse.

As the priest had told the clerk that he was going away for a few days, everybody came to their conclusion that his cook, having followed him against his will, had frightened the mare and thus caused her own and her master's death.

The smith having been left in possession of his uncle's house, as well as all of his money and estates, and being, moreover the only legal heir, thus found himself all at once the richest man in the village. As he was beloved by everybody, all rejoiced at his good luck, especially all those who owed money to the priest and whose debts he cancelled.

"You liked this story?" said the old man to Vranic, as soon as he had finished.

"Yes," replied the tailor, thinking of the ghastly, livid corpse, with grinning, gaping mouth, and glassy, goggle eyes, galloping after the priest, and wondering whether she was like the vampire. "Yes, it's an interesting story, but rather gruesome."

"Well, but it's only a story, and, whether ghastly or lively, it's only words—which—as the proverb says—are evanescent as soap-bubbles. Now," continued he, "if you want to go off to sleep, look at this," and he gave him a bit of cardboard, on which were traced several circles; "look at it till you see all these rings wheeling round. When they disappear, you'll be asleep."

The old man put the bit of cardboard before Vranic, who leaned his elbows on the table and his head between the palms of his hands, and stared at the drawing. Five minutes afterwards he was fast asleep.

When he awoke the next morning, his head was not only aching, but his weakness had so much increased that he had hardly strength enough to stand on his feet. He, therefore, made up his mind to go to the parish priest, and lay the whole matter before him.

Priests are everywhere but fetich men; therefore, if they have burnt witches for using charms and philters, it is simply because these women trespassed on their own domains, and were more successful than they themselves. Of what use would a priest be if he could not pray for rain, give little sacré cœur bits of flannel as talismans against pestilence, or brass medals to scare away the devil? A priest who can do nothing for us here below, must and will soon fall into discredit. The hereafter is so vague and indefinite that it cannot inspire us with half the interest the present does.

The priest whom Branic consulted was of the same opinion as the tailor. He, too, believed that probably his brother had become a vampire, who nightly left the tomb to go and suck his blood. For his own sake, as well as for that of the whole town, it would be well to exorcise the ghost. The matter, however, had to be kept a profound secret, as the Government had put its veto on vampire-killing, and looked upon all such practices as illegal.

It was, therefore, agreed that Vranic, together with his relations and some friends, should go to the curate's about ten o'clock at night; there the curate would be waiting for them with another priest; from there the little party would stealthily proceed to the cemetery where the ceremony was to be held.

The Friday fixed upon arrived. The night was dark, the weather sultry; a storm had been brooding in the heavy clouds overhead and was not ready to burst every moment.

As soon as the muffled people got to the gate of the burying ground the mortuary chapel was opened to them by the sexton. The priests put on their officiating robes, recited several orisons appropriate to the occasion; then, with the Cross carried before them, bearing a holy-water sprinkler in their hands, followed by Vranic and his friends—all with blessed tapers—they went up to the murdered man's tomb. The priest then bade the sexton dig up the earth and bring out the coffin.

The smell, as the pit was being dug lower down, became always more offensive; but when, at last, the rotting deal coffin was drawn out and opened, it became overpoweringly loathsome. The corpse, however, being found in a good state of preservation, there could be no doubt that the dead man was a vampire. It is true that the tapers which everyone held gave but a dim and flickering light; moreover, that the stench was so sickening that all turned at once their heads away in disgust; still, they had all seen enough of the corpse to declare it to be but seemingly dead. The priest, standing as far from it as he possible could, began at once to exorcise it in the name of the Trinity, the Virgin and all the Saints; to sprinkle it with holy water, commanding it not to move, not to jump out of its box and run away—for these ghouls are cunning devils, and if one is not on the alert they skedaddle the moment the coffin is opened. Our priest, however, was a match even for the dead man, and his holy-water sprinkler was uplifted even before the lid of the loathsome chest was loosened.

The storm which had been threatening the whole of that day broke out at last. No sooner had the sexton begun to dig the grave than the wind, which had been moaning and wailing round the stones and wooden crosses, began to howl with a sinister sound. Then, just as the priest uttered the formula of the exorcism—when the coffin was uncovered and the uncanny corpse was seen—a flash of lurid lightning gleamed over its livid features, and the rumbling thunder ended in a tremendous crash; the earth shook as if with the throes of childbirth; hell seemed to yawn and yield forth its fulsome dead. As the priest sprinkled the corpse with holy water, the rain came down in torrents as if to drown the world.

Although the noise was deafening, still some of the men affirm that they heard the corpse lament and entreat not to be killed; but the priest, a tall, stalwart man of great strength and courage, went on perfectly undaunted, paying no heed to the vampire, mumbling his prayers as if the man prostrate before him was some ordinary corpse and this was a commonplace, every-day funeral.

The priest, having reached in his orisons the moment when he uttered the name of Isukrst, of God the son, Josko Vranic, who stood by, shivering from head to foot, and looking like a cat extracted from a tub of soap-suds, drew out a dagger from under his coat, where it had been carefully concealed from the ghost's sight, and stabbed the corpse. It was, of course, a black steel stiletto, for only such a weapon can kill a vampire. He should have stabbed the dead man in his neck and through the throat, but he was so sick that he could hardly stand; besides, his candle that instant went out, and, moreover, he was terribly frightened, for although he was stabbing but a corpse, still that corpse was his own brother.

A flash of lightning which followed that instant of perfect darkness showed him that the dagger, instead of being stuck in the dead man's neck, was thrust in the right cheek.

The ceremony being now over, the priests and their attendants hastened back to the chapel to take shelter from the rage of the storm, as well as to escape from the pestilential stench.

The sexton alone remained outside to heap up the earth again on the uncanny corpse, and shut up the grave.

"Are you sure you stabbed the corpse in the neck, severing the throat, and thus preventing it from ever sucking blood again?" asked the priest.

"Yes, I believed I have," answered Vranic, with a whining voice.

"I don't ask you what you believe; have you done it—yes, or no?" asked the ecclesiastic, sternly.

"Well, just as I lifted my knife to stab, the candle went out. I couldn't see at all; the night was so dark; you all were far from me. Besides, as I bent down, the smell made me so sick that—"

"You don't know where you stabbed?" added the priest, angrily.

"He stabbed him in the cheek!" said the sexton, coming in.

"Fool!" burst out the priest, in a stentorian voice.

"I was sure this would be the case," cried out one of the party. "Vranic has always been a bungler of a tailor."

"You have done a fine piece of work, you have, indeed, you wretch!" hissed the priest, looking at Vranic scornfully.

"You have endowed that cursed brother of yours with everlasting life," said the other priest, "and now the whole town will be infested with another vampire for ever!"

"Do you really think so?" asked Vranic, ready to burst out crying.

"Think so!" said all the other men, scornfully. "To bring us here in the middle of the night with this storm, to stifle us with this poisonous stench, and this is the result!"

"But really—" stammered Vranic.

"Anyhow, he'll not leave you till he has sucked the last drop of blood from your body."

The storm having somewhat abated, all the company wended their way homewards, taking no notice of the tailor, who followed them like a mangy cur which everyone avoids.

That night, Vranic had not a wink of sleep. No one would have him in his house; nobody would sleep with him, for fear of falling afterwards a prey to the vampire. As soon as he lay down and tried to shut his eyes, the terrifying sight appeared before him. The festering ghost with the horrible gash in the cheek, just over the jaw-bone, was ever present to his eyes; nor could he get rid of the loathsome, sickening stench with which his clothes, nay, his very body, seemed saturated. If a mouse stirred he fancies he could see the ghost standing by him. He hid his head under the bed-cover not to see, not to hear, until he was almost smothered, and every now and then he felt a human laid on his head, on his shoulder, on his legs, and his teeth chattered with fear.

The storm ceased; still, the sky remained overcast, and a thin, drizzling rain had succeeded the interrupted showers. The dreadful night came to an end; he was happy to see the grey light of dawn succeed the appalling darkness. Daylight brought with it happier thoughts.

"Perhaps," said he to himself, "my brother was no vampire, after all! Perhaps the blade of the dagger, driven in the cheek, had penetrated slantingly into the neck, severed the throat, and thus killed the vampire; for something must have happened to keep the ghost away."

On the next day, Vranic remained shut up at home. He felt sure that his own relations would henceforth hate him, and his acquaintances would stone him if they possibly could. Nothing makes a man not only unjust, but even cruel, like fear, and no fear is greater than the vague dread of the unknown. That whole day he tried to work, but his thoughts were always fixed either on the festering corpse he had stabbed or on the coming night.

Would the ghoul, reeking of hell, come and suck up his blood?

As the light wanted his very strength began to flow away, his legs grew weak, his flesh shivered, the beating of his heart grew ever more irregular.

He lighted his little oil-lamp before it was quite dark, looked about stealthily trembling lest he should see the dreaded apparition before its time, started and shuddered at the slightest noise.

He was weary and worn out by the emotions of the former sleepless night; still, he could not make up his mind to go to bed. He placed his elbows on the board, buried his head within his hands, and remained there brooding over his woes. Without daring to lift up his eyes or look around, he at times stretched out his hand, clutched a gourd full of spirits and took a sip. Time passed, the twilight had faded away into soft, mellow darkness without; but in the tailor's room the little flickering light only rendered the shadows grim and gruesome.

Drink and lassitude at last overpowered the poor man; his head began to get drowsy, his ideas more confused; the heaviness of sleep weighed him down.

All at once he was aroused from his lethargy by a sound of rushing winds. He hardly noticed it when it blew from afar, like the slight breeze that ruffles the surface of the sea; but, now that it came nearer, he remembered having heard it some evenings before. He grew pale, panted, and then his breath stopped, convulsed as he was by fear.

As upon the previous night, the wind was lost in the distance, and then in the stillness of the night he heard the low, hushed sound of footsteps coming from afar; but they drew nearer and ever nearer, with a heavy, slow, metrical step. The nightwalker was near his house, at his door, on his threshold. The loathsome, sickening smell of corruption grew stronger and stronger. Now it was as overpoweringly nauseous as when he had bent down to stab his dead brother. The sound of footsteps was now within his room; the spectre must surely be by his side. He kept his eyes tightly shut and his head bent down. A cold perspiration was trickling from his forehead and through his fingers onto the table.

All at once, something heavy and metallic was thrown in front of him. Although his eyes were tightly shut, he knew that it was the black dagger that his brother had come to bring him back, and he was not mistaken.

Was there a chuckle just then?

Almost against his will he opened his eyes, lifted his head, and looked at his guest. The vampire was standing by his side, grinning at him hideously, notwithstanding the gash in his right cheek.

"Thank you brother," said he, in a hollow, mocking voice, "for what you did yesterday; you have, in fact, given me everlasting life; and, as one good turn deserved another, you soon will be a vampire along with me. Come, don't look so scared, man; it's a pleasant life, after all. We sleep soundly during the day, and, believe me, no bed is so comfortable as the coffin, no house so quiet as the grave; but at night, when all the world sleeps and only witches are awake, then we not only live, but we enjoy life. No cankering care, no worry about the morrow. We have only fun and frolic, for we suck, we suck, we suck."

Vranic heard the sound of smacking lips just by his neck, the vampire had already laid his hands upon him.

He tried to rise, to struggle, but his strength and senses forsook him; he uttered a choked, raucous sound, then his breath again stopped spasmodically, his face grew livid, he gasped for breath, his face and lips got to be of a violet hue, his eyes shut themselves, as he dropped fainting in his chair.

# Dick Donovan: The Woman with the "Oily Eyes" (1899)

"Dick Donovan" was the pseudonym of the prolific author, James Edward Muddock (1843-1934). He was born in Hampshire near the English Channel but, in 1857, joined his father in India. He wrote several stories about the "Indian Mutiny," which erupted the day he arrived in Calcutta. Over the next few years he travelled extensively and recorded local legends and folktales.

His fictional author-detective, "Dick Donovan"—who debuted in *The Man-Hunter: Stories from the Note-Book of a Detective* (1888)—was almost as well known as Sherlock Holmes. Donovan contributed several "Romances from a Detective's Casebook" to the *Strand* magazine, where they appeared next to the Holmes stories.

Muddock's best horror stories were presented in two volumes: *Stories Weird and Wonderful* (1899; by J. E. Muddock) and *Tales of Terror* (1899; by Dick Donovan). Both books were published by Chatto & Windus. The latter collection contains two tales about one of the most frightening female vampires in literature. The sub-title of the second story suggests that it is a "sequel," but most modern readers would call it a "pre-quel."

---

Although often urged to put into print the remarkable story which follows I have always strenuously refused to do so, partly on account of personal reasons and partly out of respect for the feelings of the relatives of those concerned. But after much consideration I have come to the conclusion that my original objections can no longer be urged. The principal actors are dead. I myself am well stricken in years, and before very long must pay the debt of nature which is exacted from everything that lives.

Although so long a time has elapsed since the grim tragedy I am about to record, I cannot think of it even now without a shudder. The story of the life of every man and woman is probably more or less a tragedy, but nothing I have ever heard of can compare in ghastly, weird horror with all the peculiar circumstances of the case in point. Most certainly I would never have put pen to paper to record it had it not been from a sense of duty. Long years ago certain garbled versions crept into the public journals, and though at the time I did not consider it desirable to contradict them, I do think now that the moment has come when I, the only living being fully acquainted with the facts, should make them known, otherwise lies will become history, and posterity will accept it as truth. But there is still another reason I may venture to advance for breaking the silence of years. I think in the interest of science the case should be recorded. I have not always held this view, but when a man bends under the weight of years, and he sniffs the mould of his grave, his ideas undergo a complete change, and the opinions of his youth are not the opinions of his old age. There may be exceptions to this, but I fancy they must be very few. With these preliminary remarks I will plunge at once into my story.

It was the end of August 1857 that I acted as best man at the wedding of my friend Jack Redcar, C.E. It was a memorable year, for our hold on our magnificent Indian Empire had nearly been shaken loose by a mutiny which had threatened to spread throughout the whole of India. At the beginning of 1856 I had returned home from India after a three years' spell. I had gone out as a young medico in the service of the H.E.I.C., but my health broke down and I was compelled to resign my appointment. A year later my friend Redcar, who had also been in the Company's service as a civil engineer, came back to England, as his father had recently died and left him a modest fortune. Jack was not only my senior in year, but I had always considered him my superior in every respect. We were at a public school together, and both went up to Oxford, though not together, for he was finishing his final year when I was a freshman.

Although erratic and a bit wild he was a brilliant fellow; and while I was considered dull and plodding, and found some difficulty in mastering my subjects, there was nothing he tackled that he failed to succeed in, and come out with flying colours. In the early stage of our acquaintance he made me his fag, and patronized me, but that did not last long. A friendship sprang up. He took a great liking to me, why I know not; but it was reciprocated, and when he got his Indian appointment I resolved to follow, and by dint of hard work, and having a friend at court, I succeeded in obtaining my commission in John Company's service. Jack married Maude Vane Tremlett, as sweet a woman as ever drew God's breath of life. If I attempted to describe her in detail I am afraid it might be considered that I was exaggerating, but briefly I may say she was the perfection of physical beauty. Jack himself was an exceptionally find fellow. A brawny giant with a singularly handsome face. At the time of his wedding he was thirty or thereabouts, while Maude was in her twenty-fifth year. There was a universal opinion that a better matched couple had never been brought together. He had a masterful nature; nevertheless was kind, gentle, and manly to a degree.

It may be thought that I speak with some bias and prejudice in Jack's favour, but I can honestly say that at the time I refer to he was as fine a fellow as ever figured as hero in song or story. He was the pink of honour, and few who really knew him but would have trusted him with their honour, their fortunes, their lives. This may be strong, but I declare it's true, and I am the more anxious to emphasise it because his after life was in such marked contrast, and he presents a study in psychology that is not only deeply interesting, but extraordinary.

The wedding was a really brilliant affair, for Jack had troops of friends, who vied with each other in marking the event in a becoming manner, while his bride was idolized by a doting household. Father and mother, sisters and brothers, worshipped her. She was exceedingly well connected. Her father held an important Government appointment, and her mother came from the somewhat celebrated Yorkshire family of the Kingscotes. Students of history will remember that a Colonel Kingscote figured prominently and honourably as a royalist during the reign of the unfortunate Charles I.

No one who was present on that brilliant August morning of 1857, when Jack Redcar was united in the bonds of wedlock to beautiful Maude Tremlett, would have believed it possible that such grim and tragic events would so speedily follow. The newly-married pair left in the course of the day for the Continent, and during their honeymoon I received several charming letters from Jack, who was not only a diligent correspondent, but he possessed a power of description and a literary style that made his letter delightful reading. Another thing that marked this particular correspondence was the unstinted—I may almost say florid—praise he bestowed upon his wife. To illustrate what I mean, here is a passage from one of his letters:—

'I wish I had command of language sufficiently eloquent to speak of my darling Maude as she should be spoken of. She has a perfectly angelic nature; and though it may be true that never a human being was yet born without faults, for the life of me I can find none in my sweet wife. Of course you will say, old chap, that this is honeymoon gush, but, upon my soul, it isn't. I am only doing scant justice to the dear woman who has linked her fate with mine. I have sometimes wondered what I have done that the gods should have blest me in such a manner. For my own part, I don't think I was deserving of so much happiness, and I assure you I am happy—perfectly, deliciously happy. Will it last? Yes, I am sure it will. Maude will always be to me what she is now, a flawless woman; a woman with all the virtues that turn women into angels, and without one of the weaknesses or one of the vices which too often mar an otherwise perfect feminine character. I hope, old boy, that if ever you marry, the woman you choose will be only half as good as mine.'

Had such language been used by anyone else I might have been disposed to add a good deal more than the proverbial pinch of salt before swallowing it. But, as a matter of fact, Jack was not a mere gusher. He had a thoroughly practical, as distinguished from a sentimental, mind, and he was endowed with exceptionally keen powers of observation. And so, making all the allowances for the honeymoon romance, I was prepared to accept my friend's statement as to the merits of his wife without a quibble. Indeed, I knew her to be a most charming lady, endowed with many of the qualities which give the feminine nature its charm. But I would even go a step farther than that, and declare that Mrs. Redcar was a woman in ten thousand. At that time I hadn't a doubt that the young couple were splendidly matched, and it seemed to me probable that the future that stretched before them was not likely to be disturbed by any of the commonplace incidents which seemed inseparable from most lives. I regarded Jack as a man of such high moral worth that his wife's happiness was safe in his keeping. I pictured them leading an ideal, poetical life— a life freed from all the vulgar details which blight the careers of so many people—a life which would prove a blessing to themselves as well as a joy to all with whom they had to deal.

When they started their tour Mr. and Mrs. Redcar anticipated being absent from England for five or six weeks only, but for several reasons they were induced to prolong their travels, and thus it chanced I was away when they returned shortly before Christmas of the year of their marriage. My own private affairs took me to America. As a matter of fact a relative had died leaving me a small property in that country, which required my personal attention; the consequence was I remained out of England for nearly three years.

For the first year or so Jack Redcar wrote to me with commendable regularity. I was duly apprised of the birth of a son and heir. This event seemed to put the crown upon their happiness; but three months later came the first note of sorrow. The baby died, and the doting parents were distracted. Jack wrote:

'My poor woman is absolutely prostrated, but I tell her we were getting too happy, and this blow has been dealt to remind us that human existence must be chequered in order that we may appreciate more fully the supreme joy of that after-life which we are told we may gain for the striving. This, of course, is a pretty sentiment, but the loss of the baby mite has hit me hard. Still, Maude is left to me, and she is such a splendid woman, that I ought to feel I am more than blest.'

This was the last letter I ever received from Jack, but his wife wrote at odd times. Hers were merely gossipy little chronicles of passing events, and singularly enough she never alluded to her husband, although she wrote in a light, happy vein. This set me wondering, and when I answered her I never failed to inquire about her husband. I continued to receive letters from her, though at long intervals, down to the month of my departure from America, two years later.

I arrived in London in the winter, and an awful winter it was. London was indeed a city of dreadful night. Gloom and fog were everywhere. Everybody one met looked miserable and despondent. Into the public houses and gin palaces such of the poor as could scratch a few pence together crowded for the sake of the warmth and light. But in the streets sights were to be seen which made one doubt if civilization is the blessing we are asked to believe it. Starving men, women and children, soaked and sodden with the soot-laden fog, prowled about in the vain hope of finding food and shelter. But the well-to-do passed them with indifference, too intent on their own affairs, and too wrapped in self-interests to bestow thought upon the great city's pariahs.

Immediately after my arrival I penned a brief note to Jack Redcar, giving him my address, and saying I would take an early opportunity of calling, as I was longing to feel once more the hearty, honest grip of his handshake. A week later a note was put into my hand as I was in the very act of going out to keep an appointment in the city. Recognizing Mrs. Redcar's handwriting I tore open the envelope, and read, with what feelings may be best imagined, the following lines:

'For God's sake come and see me at once. I am heart-broken and am going mad. You are the only friend in the world to whom I feel I can appeal. Come to me, in the name of pity.

'Maude Redcar.'

I absolutely staggered as I read these brief lines, which were so pregnant with mystery, sorrow, and hopelessness. What did it all mean? To me, it was like a burst of thunder from a cloudless summer sky. Something was wrong, that was certain; what that something was I could only vaguely guess at. But I resolved not to remain long in suspense. I put off my engagement, important as it was, and hailing a hansom directed the driver to go to Hampstead, where the Redcars had their residence.

The house was detached and stood in about two acres of ground, and I could imagine it being a little Paradise in brilliant summer weather; but it seemed now in the winter murk, as if a heavy pall of sorrow and anguish enveloped it.

I was shown into an exquisitely furnished drawing room by an old and ill-favoured woman, who answered my knock at the door. She gave me the impression that she was a sullen, deceptive creature, and I was at a loss to understand how such a woman could have found service with my friends—the bright and happy friends of three years ago. When I handed her my card to convey to Mrs. Redcar she impertinently turned it over, and scrutinized it, and fixed her cold bleared grey eyes on me, so that I was induced to say peremptorily, 'Will you be good enough to go to your mistress at once and announce my arrival?'

'I ain't got no mistress,' she growled. 'I've got a master'; and with this cryptic utterance she left the room.

I waited a quarter of an hour, then the door was abruptly opened, and there stood before me Mrs. Redcar, but not the bright, sweet, radiant little woman of old. A look of premature age was in her face. Her eyes were red with weeping, and had a frightened, hunted expression. I was so astounded that I stood for a moment like one dumb-founded; but as Mrs. Redcar seized my hand and shook it, she gasped in a nervous, spasmodic way:

'Thank God, you have come! My last hope is in you.'

Then, completely overcome by emotion, she burst into hysterical sobbing, and covered her face with her handkerchief.

My astonishment was still so great, the unexpected had so completely paralysed me for the moment, that I seemed incapable of action. But of course this spell quickly passed, and I regained my self-possession.

'How is it I find this change?' I asked. It was a natural question, and the first my brain shaped.

'It's the work of a malignant fiend,' she sobbed.

This answer only deepened my mystery, and I began to think that perhaps she was literally mad. Then suddenly, as if she divined my thoughts, drew her handkerchief from her face, motioned me to be seated, and literally flung herself on to a couch.

'It's an awful story,' she said, in a hoarse, hollow voice, 'and I look to you, and appeal to you, and pray to you to help me.'

'You can rely upon my doing anything that lies in my power,' I answered. 'But tell me your trouble. How is Jack? Where is he?'

'In her arms, probably,' she exclaimed between her teeth; and she twisted her handkerchief up rope-wise and dragged it backward and forward through her hand with an excess of desperate, nervous energy. Her answer gave me a keynote. Jack had swerved from the path of honour, and allowed himself to be charmed by other eyes to the neglect of this woman whom he had described to me as being angelic. Although her beauty was now a little marred by tears and sorrow, she was still very beautiful and attractive, and had she been so disposed she might have taken an army of men captive. She saw by the expression on my face that her remark was not an enigma to me, and she added quickly: 'Oh, yes, it's true, and I look to you, doctor, to help me. It is an awful, dreadful story, but mind you, I don't blame Jack so much; he is not master of himself. This diabolical creature has enslaved him. She is like the creatures of old that one reads about. She is in possession of some devilish power which enables her to destroy men body and soul.'

'Good God! This is awful,' I involuntarily ejaculated; for I was aghast and horror-stricken at the revelation. Could it be possible that my brilliant friend, who had won golden opinions from all sorts and conditions of men, had fallen from his pedestal to wallow in the mire of sinfulness and deception.

'It is awful,' answered Mrs. Redcar. 'I tell you, doctor, there is something uncanny about the whole business. The woman is an unnatural woman. She is a she-devil. And from my heart I pity and sorrow for my poor boy.'

'Where is he now?' I asked.

'In Paris with her.'

'How long has this been going on?'

'Since a few weeks after our marriage.'

'Good heavens, you don't say so!'

'You may well look surprised, but it's true. Three weeks after our marriage, Jack and I were at Wiesbaden. As we were going downstairs to dinner one evening, we met this woman coming up. A shudder of horror came over me as I looked at her, for she had the most extra-ordinary eyes I have ever seen. I clung to my husband in sheer fright, and I noted that he turned and looked at her, and she also turned and looked at him.

'"What a remarkable woman," he muttered strangely, so strangely that it was as if some other voice was using his lips. Then he broke into a laugh, and, passing his arm around my waist, said: "Why, my dear little woman, I believe you are frightened."

'"I am," I said; "that dreadful creature has startled me more than an Indian cobra would have done."

'"Well, upon my word," said Jack, "I must confess she is a strange-looking being. Did ever you see such eyes? Why, they make one think of the fairy-books and the mythical beings who flit through their pages."

'During the whole of the dinner-time that woman's face haunted me. It was a strong, hard-featured, almost masculine face, every line of which indicated a nature that was base, cruel, and treacherous. The thin lips, the drawn nostrils, the retreating chin, could never be associated with anything that soft, gentle, or womanly. But it was the eyes that were the wonderful feature—they absolutely seemed to exercise some magic influence; they were oily eyes that gleamed and glistened, and they seemed to have in them that sinister light which is peculiar to the cobra, and other poisonous snakes. You may imagine the spell and influence they exerted over me when, on the following day, I urged my husband to leave Wiesbaden at once, notwithstanding that the place was glorious in its autumn dress, and was filled with a fashionable and light-hearted crowd. But my lightest wish then was law to Jack, so that very afternoon we were on our way to Homburg, and it was only when Wiesbaden was miles behind me that I began to breathe freely again.

'We had been in Homburg for a fortnight, and the incident of Wiesbaden had passed from my mind, when one morning, as Jack and I were on our way from the Springs, we came face to face with the woman with the oily eyes. I nearly fainted, but she smiled a hideous, cunning, cruel smile, inclined her head slightly in token of recognition, and passed on. I looked at my husband. It seemed to me he was unusually pale, and I was surprised to see him turn and gaze after her, and she had also turned and was gazing at us. Not a word was uttered by either of us, but I pressed my husband's arm and we walked rapidly away to our apartments.

'"It's strange," I remarked to Jack as we sat at breakfast, "that we should meet that awful woman again."

'"Oh, not at all," he laughed. "You know at this time of the year, people move about from place to place, and it's wonderful how you keep rubbing shoulders with the same set."

'It was quite true what Jack said, nevertheless, I could not help the feeling that the woman with the oil eyes had followed us to Homburg. If I had mentioned this then it would have been considered ridiculous, for we had only met her once, and had never spoken a word to her. What earthly interest, therefore, could she possibly take in us who were utter strangers to her. But, looked at by the light of after events, my surmise was true. The creature had marked Jack for her victim the moment we unhappily met on the stairs at Wiesbade. I tell you, doctor, that that woman is a human ghoul, a vampire, who lives not only by sucking the blood of men, but by destroying their souls.'

Mrs. Redcar broke down again at this stage of her narrative, and I endeavoured to comfort her; but she quickly mastered her feelings sufficiently to continue her remarkable story.

'Some days later my husband and I moved along with the throng that drifted up and down the promenade listening to the band, when we met a lady whom I had known as a neighbor when I was at home with my parents. We stopped and chatted with her for some time, until Jack asked us to excuse him while he went to purchase some matches at a kiosk; he said he would be by the fountain in ten minutes, and I was to wait for him.

'My lady friend and I moved along and chatted as women will, and then she bade me good-night as she had to rejoin her friends. I at once hurried to the rendezvous at the fountain, but Jack wasn't there. I waited some time, but still he came not. I walked about impatiently and half frightened, and when nearly three-quarters of an hour had passed I felt sure Jack had gone home, so with all haste I went to our apartments close by, but he was not in, and had not been in. Half distracted, I flew back to the prom-enade. It was nearly deserted, for the band had gone. As I hurried along, not knowing where to go to, and scarcely knowing what I was doing, I was attracted by a laugh—a laugh I knew. It was Jack's, and proceeding a few years further I found him on a seat under a linden tree with the woman with the oily eyes.

'"Why, my dear Maude," he exclaimed, "wherever have you been to? I've hunted everywhere for you."

'A great lump came in my throat, for I felt that Jack was lying to me. I really don't know what I said or what I did, but I am conscious in a vague way that he introduced me to the woman, but the only name I caught was that of Annette. It burnt itself into my brain; it has haunted me ever since.

'Annette put out her white hand veiled by a silk net glove through which diamond rings sparkled. I believe I did touch the proffered fingers, and I shuddered, and I heard her say in a silvery voice that was quite of keeping with her appearance:

'"If I were your husband I should take you to task. Beauty like yours, you know, ought not to go unattended in a place like this."

'Perhaps she thought this was funny, for she laughed, and then patted me on the shoulder with her fan. But I hated her from that moment—hated her with a hatred I did not deem myself capable of.

'We continued to sit there, how long I don't know. It seemed to me a very long time, but perhaps it wasn't long. when we rose to go to the promenade was nearly deserted, only two or three couples remained. The moon was shining brilliantly; the night wind sighed pleasantly in the trees; but the beauty of the night was lost upon me. I felt ill at ease, and, for the first time in my life, unhappy. Annette walked with us nearly to our door. When the moment for parting came she again offered me the tips of her fingers, but I merely bowed frigidly, and shrank from her as I saw her oily eyes fixed upon me.

'"Ta, ta!" she said in her fatal silvery voice; "keep a watchful guard over your husband, my dear; and you, sir, don't let your beautiful little lady stray from you again, or there will be grief between you."

'Those wicked words, every one of which was meant to have its effect, was like the poison of asps to me; you may imagine how they stung me when I tell you I was seized with an almost irresistible desire to hurl the full weight of my body at her, and, having thrown her down, trample upon her. She had aroused in me such a feeling of horror that very little more would have begotten in me the desperation of madness, and I might have committed some act which I should have regretted all my life. But bestowing another glance of her basilisk eyes upon me she moved off, and I felt relieved; though, when I reached my room, I burst into hysterical weeping. Jack took me in his arms, and kissed and comforted me, and all my love for him was strong again; as I lay with my head pillowed on his breast I felt once more supremely happy.

'The next day, on thinking the matter over, I came to the conclusion that my suspicions were unjust, my fears groundless, my jealousy stupid, and that my conduct had been rude in the extreme. I resolved, therefore, to be more amiable and polite to Annette when I again met her. But, strangely enough, though we remained in Homburg a fortnight longer we did not meet; but I know now my husband saw her several times.

'Of course, if it had not been for subsequent events, it would have been said that I was a victim of strong hysteria on that memorable night. Men are so ready to accuse women of hysteria because they are more sensitive, and see deeper than men do themselves. But my aversion to Annette from the instant I set eyes upon her, and the inferences I drew, were not due to hysteria, but to that eighth sense possessed by women, which had no name, and of which men know nothing. At least, I mean to say that they cannot understand it.

Again Mrs. Redcar broke off in her narrative, for emotion had got better of her. I deemed it advisable to wait. Her remarkable story had aroused all my interest, and I was anxious not to lose any connecting link of it, for from the psychological point of view it was a study.

'Of course, as I have begun the story I must finish it to its bitter end,' she went on. 'As I have told you, I did not see Annette again in Homburg, and when we left all my confidence in Jack was restored, and my love for him was stronger than ever if that were possible. Happiness came back to me. Oh! I was so happy, and thinking I had done a cruel, bitter wrong to Jack in even supposing for a moment that he would be unfaithful to me. I tried by every little artifice a woman is capable of to prove my devotion to him.

'Well, to make a long story short, we continued to travel about for some time, and finally returned home, and my baby was born. It seemed to me then as if God was really too good to me. I had everything in the world that a human being can reasonably want. An angel baby, a brave, handsome husband, ample means, hosts of friends. I was supremely happy. I thanked my Maker for it all every hour of my life. But suddenly amongst the roses the hiss of the serpent sounded. One day a carriage drove up to our door. It brought a lady visitor. She was shown into our drawing-room, and when asked for her name made some excuse to the servant. Of course, I hurried down to see who my caller was, and imagine my horror when on entering the room I beheld Annette.

"'My dear Mrs. Redcar," she gushingly exclaimed, emphasizing every word, "I am so delighted to see you again. Being in London, I could not resist the temptation to call and renew acquaintances."

'The voice was as silvery as ever, and her awful eyes seemed more oily. In my confusion and astonishment I did not inquire how she had got our address; but I know that I refused her proffered hand, and by my manner gave her unmistakably to understand that I did not regard her as a welcome visitor. But she seemed perfectly indifferent. She talked gaily, flippantly. She threw her fatal spell about me. She fascinated me, so that when she asked to see my baby I mechanically rang the bell, and as mechanically told the servant to send the nurse and baby in. when she came, the damnable woman took the child from the nurse and danced him, but he suddenly broke into a scream of terror, so that I rushed forward; but the silvery voice said:

"'Oh, you silly little mother. The baby is all right. Look how quiet he is now."

'She was holding him at arm's length, and gazing at him with her basilisk eyes, and he was silent. Then she hugged and fondled him, and kissed him, and all the while I felt as if my brain was on fire, but I could neither speak nor move a hand to save my precious little baby.

'At last she returned him to his nurse, who at once left the room by my orders, and then Annette kept up a cackle of conversation. Although it did not strike me then as peculiar, for I was too confused to have any clear thought about anything—it did afterwards—she never once inquired about Jack. It happened when he was out. He had gone away early that morning to the city on some important business in which he was engaged.

'At last Annette took herself off, to my intense relief. She said nothing about calling again; she gave no address, and made no request for me to call on her. Even had she done so I should not have called. I was only too thankful she had gone, and I fervently hoped I should never see her again.

'As soon as she had departed I rushed upstairs, for baby was screaming violently. I found him in the nurse's arms, and she was doing her utmost to comfort him. But he refused to be comforted, and I took him and put him to my breast, and he still fought, and struggled, and screamed, and his baby eyes seemed to me to be bulging with terror. From that moment the darling little creature began to sicken. He gradually pined and wasted, and in a few weeks was lying like a beautiful waxen doll in a bed of flowers. He was stiff, and cold, and dead.

'When Jack came home in the evening of the day of Annette's call, and I told him she had been, he did not seem in the least surprised, but merely remarked:

'"I hope you were hospitable to her."

'I did not answer him, for I had been anything but hospitable. I had not even invited her to partake of the conventional cup of tea.

'As our baby boy faded day by day, Jack seemed to change, and the child's death overwhelmed him. He was never absolutely unkind to me at that period, but he seemed to have entirely altered. He became sullen, silent, even morose, and he spent the whole of his days away from me. When I gently chided him, he replied that his work absorbed all his attention. And so things went on until another thunderbolt fell at my feet.

'One afternoon Jack returned home and brought Annette. He told me that he had invited her to spend a few days with us. When I urged an objection he was angry with me for the first time in our married life. I was at once silenced, for his influence over me was still great, and I thought I would try and overcome my prejudice for Annette. At any rate, as Jack's wife I resolved to be hospitable, and play the hostess with grace. But I soon found that I was regarded as of very little consequence. Annette ruled Jack, she ruled me, she ruled the household.

'You will perhaps ask why I did not rise up in wrath, and, asserting my position and dignity, drive the wicked creature out of my home. But I tell you, doctor, I was utterly powerless. She worked some devil's spell upon me, and I was entirely under the influence of her will.

'Her visit stretched into weeks. Our well-tried and faithful servants left. Others came, but their stay was brief; and at last the old woman who opened the door to you was stalled. She is a creature of Annette's, and is a spy upon my movements.

'All this time Jack was under the spell of the charmer, as I was. Over and over again I resolved to go to my friends, appeal to them, tell them everything, and ask them to protect me; but my will failed, and I bore and suffered in silence. And my husband neglected me; he seemed to find pleasure only in Annette's company. Oh, how I fretted and gnawed my heart, and yet I could not break away from the awful life. I tell you, doctor, that that woman possessed some strange, devilish, supernatural power over me and Jack. When she looked at me I shriveled up. When she spoke, her silvery voice seemed to sting every nerve and fibre in my body, and he was like wax in her hands. To me he became positively brutal, and he told me over and over again that I was spoiling his life. But, though she was a repulsive, mysterious, crafty, cruel woman, he seemed to find his happiness in her company.

'One morning, after a restless, horrible, feverish night, I arose, feeling strangely ill, and as if I were going mad. I worked myself up to almost a pitch of frenzy, and, spurred by desperation, I rushed into the drawing-room, and where my husband and Annette were together, and exclaimed to her:

'"Woman, do you not see that you are killing me? Why have you come here? Why do you persecute me with your devilish wiles? You must know you are not welcome. You must feel you are an intruder."

'Overcome by the effort this had cost me, I sank down on the floor on my knees, and wept passionately. Then I heard the silvery voice say, in tones of surprise and injured innocence:

"'Well, upon my word, Mrs. Redcar, this is an extra ordinary way to treat your husband's guest. I really thought I was a welcome visitor instead of an intruder; but, since I am mistake, I will go at once."

'I looked at her through a blinding mist of tears. I met the gaze of her oily eyes, but only for a moment, and felt powerless again. I glanced at my husband. He was standing with his head bowed, and, as it seemed to me, in a pose of shame and humiliation. But suddenly he darted at me, and I heard him say: "What do you mean by creating such a scene as this? You must understand I am master here." Then he struck me a violent blow on the head, and there was a long blank.

'When I came to my senses I was in bed, and the hideous old hag who opened the door to you was bending over me. It was some little time before I could realize what had occurred. When I did, I asked the woman where Mr. Redcar was, and she answered sullenly:

"'Gone."

"'And the—Annette; where is she?" I asked.

"'Gone, too," was the answer.

'Another blank ensued. I fell very ill, and when my brain was capable of coherent thought again I learnt that I had passed through a crisis, and my life had been in jeopardy. A doctor had been attending me, and there was a professional nurse in the house; but she was a hard, dry, unsympathetic woman, and I came to the conclusion—wrongly so, probably—she, too, was one of Annette's creatures.

'I was naturally puzzled to understand why none of my relatives and friends had been to see me, but I was to learn later that many had called, but had been informed I was abroad with my husband, who had been summoned away suddenly in connection with some professional matters. And I also know now that all my letters coming for me were at once forwarded to him, and that any requiring answers he answered.

'As I grew stronger I made up my mind to keep my own counsel, and not let any of my friends know of what I had gone through and suffered; for I still loved my husband, and looked upon him as a victim to be pitied and rescued from the infernal wiles of the she-demon. When I heard of your arrival in England, I felt you were the one person in the wide world I could appeal to with safety, for you can understand how anxious I am to avoid a scandal. Will you help me? Will you save your old friend Jack? Restore him to sanity, doctor, bring him back to my arms again, which will be wide open to receive him.'

I listened to poor Mrs. Redcar's story patiently, and at first was disposed to look upon it as a too common tale of human weakness. Jack Redcar had fallen into the power of an adventuress, and had been unable to resist her influence. Such things had happened before, such things will happen again, I argued with myself. There are certain women who seem capable of making men mad for a brief space; but under proper treatment they come to their senses quickly, and blush with shame as they think of their foolishness. At any rate, for the sake of my old friend, and for the sake of his poor suffering little wife, I was prepared to do anything in reason to bring back the erring husband to his right senses.

I told Mrs. Redcar this. I told her I would redress her wrongs if I could, and fight her battle to the death. She almost threw herself at my feet in her gratitude. But when I suggested that I should acquaint her family with the facts, she begged of me passionately not to do so. Her one great anxiety was to screen her husband. One thing, however, I insisted upon. That was, the old woman should be sent away, the house shut up, and that Mrs. Redcar should take apartments in an hotel, so that I might be in touch with her. She demurred to this at first, but ultimately yielded to my persuasion.

Next, I went to the old woman. She was a German Suisse— her name was Grebert. I told her to pack up her things and clear out at once. She laughed in my face, and impertinently told me to mind my own business. I took out my watch and said, 'I give you half an hour. If you are not off the premises then, I will call in the police and have you turned out. Any claim you have on Mrs. Redcar, who is the mistress here—shall be settled at once.'

She replied that she did not recognize my authority, that she had been placed there by Mr. Redcar, who was her master, and unless he told her to go she should remain. I made it plain to her that I was determined and would stand no nonsense. Mr. Redcar had taken himself off, I said; Mrs. Redcar was his lawful wife, and I was acting for her and on her behalf.

My arguments prevailed, and after some wrangling the hag came to the conclusion that discretion was the better part of valor, and consented to go providing we paid her twenty pounds. This we decided to do rather than have a scene, but three hours passed before we saw the last of the creature. Mrs. Redcar had already packed up such things as she required, and when I had seen the house securely fastened up I procured a cab, and conveyed the poor little lady to a quiet West-end hotel, close to my own residence, so that I could keep a watchful eye upon her.

Of course, this was only the beginning of the task I had set myself, which was to woo back the erring husband, if possible, to his wife's side, and to restore him to the position of happiness, honour, and dignity from which he had fallen. I thought this might be comparatively easy, and little dreamed of the grim events that were to follow my interference.

Three weeks later I was in Paris, and proceeded to the Hotel de l'Univers, where Mrs. Redcar had ascertained through his bankers her husband was staying. But to my chagrin, I found he had departed from his companion, and the address he had given for his letters at the post-office was Potes, in Spain. As I had taken up the running I had no alternative but to face the long, dreary journey in pursuit of the fugitives, or confess defeat at the start.

It is not necessary for me to dwell upon that awful journey in the winter time. Suffice to say I reached my destination in due course.

Potes, it is necessary to explain, is a small town magnificently situated in the Liebana Valley, in the Asturian Pyrenees, under the shadow of Pico de Europa. Now, what struck me as peculiar was the fugitives coming to such a place at that time of the year. Snow lay heavily everywhere. The cold was intense. For what reason had such a spot been chosen? It was a mystery I could not hope to solve just then. There was only one small hotel in the village, and where Annette and Redcar were staying. My first impulse was not to let them know of my presence, but to keep them under observation for a time. I dismissed that thought as soon as formed, for I was not a detective, and did not like the idea of playing the spy. But even had I been so disposed, there would have been a difficulty about finding accommodation. Moreover, it was a small place, and the presence of a foreigner at that time of year must necessarily have caused a good deal of gossip. The result was I went boldly to the hotel, engaged a room, and then inquired for Redcar. I was directed to a private room, where I found him alone. My unexpected appearance startled him, and when he realized who I was, he swore at me, and demanded to know my business.

He had altered so much that in a crowd I really might have had some difficult in recognizing him. His face wore a drawn, anxious, nervous look, and his eyes had acquired a restless, shifty motion, while his hair was already streaked with grey.

I began to reason with him. I reminded him of our old friendship, and I drew a harrowing picture of the sufferings of his dear, devoted, beautiful little wife.

At first he seemed callous; but presently he grew interested, and when I referred to his wife he burst into tears. Then suddenly he grasped my wrist with a powerful grip, and said:

'Hush! Annette mustn't know this—-mustn't hear. I tell you, Peter, she is a ghoul. She sucks my blood. She has woven a mighty spell about me, and I am powerless. Take me away; take me to dear little Maude.'

I looked at him for some moments with a keen professional scrutiny, for his manner and strange words were not those of sanity. I determined to take him at his word, and, if possible, remove him from the influence of the wicked siren who had so fatally lured him.

'Yes,' I said, 'we will go without a moment's unnecessary delay. I will see if a carriage and post-horses are to be had, so that we can drive to the nearest railway station.'

He assented languidly to this, and I rose with the intention of asking of making inquiries of the hotel people; but simultaneously with my action the door opened and Annette appeared. Up to that moment I thought that Mrs. Redcar had exaggerated in describing her, therefore I was hardly prepared to find that so far from the description being an exaggeration, it had fallen short of the fact.

Annette was slightly above the medium height, with a well-developed figure, but a face that to me was absolutely repellent. There was not a single line of beauty nor a trace of womanliness in it. It was hard, coarse, cruel, with thin lips drawn tightly over even white teeth. And the eyes were the most wonderful eyes I have ever seen in a human being. Maude was right when she spoke of them as 'oily eyes'. They literally shone with a strange, greasy, luster, and were capable of such a marvelous expression that I felt myself falling under their peculiar fascination. I am honest and frank enough to say that, had it been her pleasure, I believe she could have lured me to destruction as she had lured my poor friend. But I was forearmed, because forewarned. Moreover, I fancy I had a much stronger will than Redcar. Any way, I braced myself up to conquer and crush this human serpent, for such I felt her to be.

Before I could speak, her melodious voice rang out with the query, addressed to Jack:

'Who is this gentleman? Is he a friend of yours?'

'Yes, yes,' gasped Jack, like one who spoke under the influence of a nightmare.

She bowed and smiled, revealing all her white teeth, and she held forth her hand to me, a delicately shaped hand, with clear, transparent skin, and her long lithe fingers were bejeweled with diamonds.

I drew myself up, as one does when a desperate effort is needed, and, refusing the proffered hand, I said:

'Madame, hypocrisy and deceit are useless. I am a medical man, my name is Peter Haslar, and Mr. Redcar and I have been friends from youth. I've come here to separate him from your baneful influence and carry him back to his broken-hearted wife. That is my mission. I hope I have made it clear to you?'

She showed not the slightest sign of being disturbed, but smiled on me again, and bowed gracefully and with the most perfect self-possession. And speaking in a soft gentle manner, which in such startling contrast to the woman's appearance, she said:

'Oh, yes; thank you. But, like the majority of your countrymen, you display a tendency to arrogate too much to yourself. I am a Spaniard myself, by birth, but cosmopolitan by inclination, and, believe me, I do not speak with any prejudice against your nationality, but I have yet to learn, sir, that you have any right to constitute yourself Mr. Redcar's keeper.'

Her English was perfect, though she pronounced it with just a slight foreign accent. There was no anger in her tones, no defiance. She spoke softly, silvery, persuasively.

'I do not pretend to be his keeper, madame; I am his sincere friend,' I answered. 'and surely I need not remind you that he owes a duty to his lawful wife.'

During this short conversation Jack had sat motionless on the edge of a couch, his chin resting on his hands, and apparently absorbed with some conflicting thoughts. But Annette turned to him, and, still smiling, said:

'I think Mr. Redcar is quite capable of answering for himself. Stand up, Jack, and speak your thoughts like a man.'

Although she spoke in her oily, insidious way, her request a peremptory command. I realized at once, and I saw as Jack rose he gazed at her, and her lustrous eyes fixed him. Then he turned upon me with a furious gesture and exclaimed, with a violence of expression that startled me:

'Yes, Annette is right. I am my own master. What the devil do you mean by following me, like the sneak and cur that you are? Go back to Maude, and tell her that I loathe her. Go; relieve me of your presence, or I may forget myself and injure you.'

Annette, still smiling and still perfectly self-possessed, said:

'You hear what your friend says, doctor. Need I say that if you are a gentleman you will respect his wishes?"'

I could no longer contain myself. Her calm, defiant, icy manner, maddened me, and her silvery voice seemed to cut down on to my most sensitive nerves, for it was so suggestive of the devilish nature of the creature. It was so incongruous when contrasted with her harsh, horribly cruel face. I placed myself between Jack and her, and meeting her weird gaze, I said, hotly:

'Leave this room. You are an outrage on your sex; a shame and a disgrace to the very name of woman. Go, and leave me with my friend, whose reason you have stolen away.'

She still smiled and was still unmoved, and suddenly I felt myself gripped in a grip of iron, and with terrific force I was hurled into a corner of the room, where, huddled up in a heap, I lay stunned for some moments. But as my senses returned I saw the awful woman smiling still, and she was waving her long white bejeweled hand before the infuriated Jack, as if she were mesmerizing him; and I saw him sink on to the sofa subdued and calmed. Then addressing me she said:

'That is a curious way for your friend to display his friendship. I may be wrong, but perhaps as a medical man you will recognize that your presence has an irritating effect on Mr. Redcar, and if I may suggest it, I think it desirable that you should part at once and see him no more.'

'Devil!' I shouted at her. 'You have bewitched him, and made him forgetful of his honour and of what he owes to those that are dear to him. But I will defeat you yet.'

She merely bowed and smiled, but deigned no reply; and holding her arm to Jack, he took it, and they passed out of the room. She was elegantly attired. Her raven hair was fascinatingly dressed in wavy bands. There was something regal in her carriage,

and gracefulness in her every movement; and yet she filled me
with a sense of indefinable horror; a dread to which I should
have been ashamed to own to a little while ago.

I tried to spring up and go after them, but my body seemed
a mass of pain, and my left arm hung limp and powerless. It was
fractured below the elbow. There was no bell in the room, and I
limped out in search of assistance. I made my way painfully along
a gloomy corridor, and hearing a male voice speaking Spanish, I
knocked at a door, which was opened by the landlord. I addressed
him, but he shook his head and gave me to understand that he
spoke no English. Unhappily, I spoke no Spanish. Then he smiled
as some idea flitted through his mind, and bowing me into
the room he motioned me to be seated, and hurried away. He
returned in about five minutes accompanied by Annette, whom
he had brought to act as interpreter. I was almost tempted to fly
at her and strangle her where she stood. She was undisturbed,
calm, and still smiled. She spoke to the man in Spanish, then she
explained to me that she had told him I had just slipped on the
polished floor, and falling over a chair had injured myself, and
she had requested him to summon the village surgeon if need be.

Without waiting for me to reply she swept gracefully out
of the room. Indeed, I could not reply, for I felt as if I were
choking with suppressed rage. The landlord rendered me physical assistance and took me to my bedroom, where I lay down
on my bed, feeling mortified, ill, and crushed. Half an hour later
a queer-looking old man, with long hair twisted into ringlets,
was ushered into my room, and I soon gathered that he was the
village surgeon. He spoke no English, but I explained my injury
by signs, and he went away, returning in a little while with the
necessary bandages and splints, and he proceeded to rather clum-
sily bandage my broken arm. I passed a cruel and wretched night.
My physical pain was great, but my mental pain was greater.
The thought forced itself upon me that I had been defeated, and
that the fiendish, cunning woman was too much for me. I felt
no resentment against Jack. His act of violence was the act of
a madman, and I pitied him. For hours I lay revolving all sorts

of schemes to try and get him away from the diabolical influence of Annette. But though I could hit upon nothing, I firmly
resolved that while my life lasted I would make every effort to
save my old friend, and if possible restore him to the bosom of
his distracted wife.

The case altogether was a very remarkable one, and the question naturally arose, why did a man so highly gifted and so intel-
ligent as Jack Redcar desert his charming, devoted, and beautiful wife, to follow an adventuress who entirely lacked physical
beauty. Theories without number might have been suggested
to account for the phenomenon, but not one would have been
correct. The true answer is, Annette was not a natural being.
In the ordinary way she might be described as a woman of
perverted moral character, or as a physiological freak, but that
would have been rather a misleading way of putting it. She was,
in short, a human monstrosity. By that I do not mean to say her
body was contorted, twisted, or deformed. But into her human
composition had entered a strain of the fiend; and I might go
even further than this and say she was more animal than human.
Though in whatever way she may be described, it is certain she
was an anomaly—a human riddle.

The morning following the outrage upon me found me prostrated and ill. A night of racking pain and mental distress had told
even upon my good constitution. The situation in which I found
myself was a singularly unfortunate one. I was a foreigner in an
out-of-the-way place, and my want of knowledge of Spanish, of
course, placed me at a tremendous disadvantage.

The landlord came to me and brought his wife, and between
them they attended to my wants, and did what they could for my
comfort. But they were ignorant, uncultivated people, only one
remove from the peasant class, and I realized that they could be of
little use to me. Now the nearest important town to this Alpine
village was Santander, but that was nearly a hundred miles away.
As everyone knows who has been in Spain, a hundred miles, even
on a railway, is a considerable journey; but there was no railway
between Santander and Potes. An old ramshackle vehicle, called
a diligence, ran between two places everyday in the summer and

twice a week in the winter, and it took fourteen hours to do the journey. Even a well-appointed carriage and pair could not cover the distance under eight hours, as the road was infamous, and in parts was little better than a mule track. I knew that there was a British consul in Santander, and I was hopeful that if I could communicate with him he might be able to render me some assistance. In the meantime I had to devise some scheme for holding Annette in check and saving my friend. But in my crippled and prostrate condition I could not do much. While lying in my bed, and thus revolving all these things in my mind, the door gently opened and Annette glided in—'glided' best expresses her movement, for she seemed to put forth no effort. She sat down beside the bed and laid her hand on mine.

'You are ill this morning,' she said softly. 'This is regrettable, but you have only yourself to blame. It is dangerous to interfere in matters in which you have no concern. My business is mine, Mr. Redcar's is his, and yours is your own, but the three won't amalgamate. Jack and I came here for the sake of the peace and quietness of these solitudes; unhappily you intrude yourself and disaster follows.'

Her voice was as silvery as ever. The same calm self-possessed air characterized her; but in her oily eyes was a peculiar light, and I had to turn away, for they exerted a sort of mesmeric influence over me, and I am convinced that had I not exerted all my will power I should have thrown myself into the creature's arms. This is a fact which I have no hesitation in stating, as it serves between than any other illustration to show what a wonderful power of fascination the remarkable woman possessed. Naturally I felt disgusted and enraged, but I fully recognized that I could not fight the woman openly; I must to some extent meet her with my own weapons. She was cunning, artful, insidious, pitiless, and the basilisk-like power she possessed not only gave her a great advantage but made her a very dangerous opponent. At any rate, having regard to all the circumstances and my crippled condition, I saw that my only chance was in temporizing with her. So I tried to reason with her, and I pointed out that Redcar had been guilty of baseness in leaving his wife, who was devoted to him.

At this point of my argument, Annette interrupted me, and for the first time she displayed something like passion, and her voice became hard and raucous.

'His wife,' she said with a sneer of supreme contempt. 'A poor fool, a fleshly doll. At the precise instant I set my eyes upon her for the first time I felt that I should like to destroy her, because she is a type of woman who make the world commonplace and reduce all men to a common level. She hated me from the first and I hated her. She would have crushed me if she could, but she was too insignificant a worm to do that, and I crushed her.'

This cold, brutal callousness enraged me; I turned fiercely upon her and exclaimed:

'Leave me, you are a more infamous and heartless wretch than I believed you to be. You are absolutely unworthy the name of a woman, and if you irritate me much more I may even forget that you have a woman's shape.'

She spoke again. All trace of passion had disappeared. She smiled the wicked insidious smile which made her so dangerous, and her voice resumed its liquid, silvery tones:

'You are very violent,' she said gently, 'and it will do you harm in your condition. But you see violence can be met with violence. The gentleman you are pleased to call your friend afforded you painful evidence last night that he knows how to resent unjustifiable interference, and to take care of himself. I am under his protection, and there is no doubt he will protect me.

'For God's sake, leave me!' I cried, tortured beyond endurance by her hypocrisy and wickedness.

'Oh, certainly, if you desire it,' she answered, as she rose from her seat. 'But I thought I might be of use. It is useless your trying to influence Mr. Redcar—absolutely useless. His destiny is linked with mine, and the human being doesn't exist who can sunder us. With this knowledge, you will do well to retrace your steps; and, if you like, I will arrange to have you comfortable conveyed to Santander, where you can get a vessel. Anyway, you will waste your time and retard your recovery by remaining here.'

'I tend to remain here, nevertheless,' I said, with set teeth. 'And, what is more, madame, when I go my friend Redcar will accompany me.'

She laughed. She patted my head as a mother might pat the head of her child. She spoke in her most insidious silvery tones.

'We shall see, mon cher—we shall see. You will be better to-morrow. Adieu!'

That was all she said, and she was gone. She glided out of the room as she had glided in.

I felt irritated almost into madness for some little time; but as I reflected, it was forced upon me that I had to deal with a monster of iniquity, who had so subdued the will of her victim, Redcar, that he was a mere wooden puppet in her hand. Force in such a case was worse than useless. What I had to do was to try and circumvent her, and I tried to think out some plan of action.

All that day I was compelled to keep my bed, and, owing to the clumsy way in which my arm had been bandaged, I suffered intolerable pain, and had to send for the old surgeon again to come and help me to reset the fracture. I got some ease after that, and a dose of chloral sent me to sleep, which continued for many hours. When I awoke I managed to summon the landlord, and he brought me food, and a lantern containing a candle so that I might have light. And, in compliance with my request, he made me a large jug of lemonade, in order that I could have a drink in the night, for I was feverish, and my throat was parched. He had no sooner left the room than Annette entered to inquire if she could do anything for me. I told her that I had made the landlord understand all that I desired, and he would look after me, so she wished me good-night and left. Knowing as I did that sleep was very essential in my case, I swallowed another, though smaller, dose of chloral, and then there was a blank.

How long I slept I really don't know; but suddenly, in a dazed sort of way, I saw a strange sight. The room I occupied was a long, somewhat meagerly furnished, one. The entrance door was at the extreme end, opposite the bed. Over the doorway hung a faded curtain of green velvet. By the feeble light of the candle lantern I saw this curtain slowly pulled on one side by a white hand; then a face peered in; next Annette entered. Her long hair was hanging down her back, and she wore a nightdress of soft, clinging substance, which outlined her figure. With never a sound she moved lightly towards the bed, and waved her hand two to three times over my face. I tried to move, to utter a sound, but couldn't; and yet what I am describing was no dream, but a reality. Slightly bending over me, she poured from a tiny phial she carried in the palm of her hand a few drops of a slightly acrid, burning liquid right into my mouth, and at that instant, as I believe, it seemed to me as if a thick, heavy pall over my eyes, for all was darkness.

I awoke hours later. The winter sun was shining brightly into my room. I felt strangely languid, and had a hot, stinging sensation in my throat. I felt my pulse, and found it was only beating at the rate of fifty-eight beats in one minute. Then I recalled the extraordinary incident of the previous night, which, had it not been for my sensations, I might have regarded as a bad dream, the outcome of a disturbed state of the brain. But as it was, I hadn't a doubt that Annette had administered some subtle and slow poison to me. My medical knowledge enabled me to diagnose my own case so far, that I was convinced I was suffering from the effects of a potent poisonous drug, the action of which was to lower the action of the vital forces and weaken the heart. Being probably cumulative, a few doses more or less, according to the strength of that subject, the action of the heart would b e so impeded that the organ would cease to beat. Although all this passed through my brain, I felt so weak and languid that I had neither energy nor strength to arouse myself, and when the landlord brought me in some food I took no notice of him. I knew that this symptom of languor and indifference was very characteristic of certain vegetable poisons, though what it was Annette had administered to me I could not determine.

Throughout that day I lay in a drowsy, dreamy state. At times my brain was clear enough, and I was able to think and reason; but there were blanks, marked, no doubt, by periods of sleep.

When night came I felt a little better, and I found that the heart's action had improved. It was steadier, firmer, and the pulse indicated sixty-two beats. Now I had no doubt that if it was Annette's intention to bring about my death slowly she would come again that night, and arousing myself as well as I could, and summoning all my will power, I resolved to be on the watch. During the afternoon I had drunk milk freely, regarding it as an antidote, and when the landlord visited me for the last time that evening I made him understand that I wanted a large jug of fresh milk from the cow, if he could get it. He kept cows of his own; they were confined in a chalet on the mountain side, not far from his house, so that he was able to comply with my request. I took a long draught of this hot milk, which revived my energies wonderfully, and then I waited for developments. I had allowed my watch to run down, consequently I had no means of knowing the time. It was a weary vigil, lying there lonely and ill, and struggling against the desire for sleep.

By-and-by I saw the white hand lift the curtain again, and Annette entered, clad as she was on the previous night. When she came within reach of me I sprang up in the bed and seized her wrist.

'What do you want here?' I demanded angrily. 'Do you mean to murder me?'

Her imperturbability was exasperating. She neither winced nor cried out, nor displayed the slightest sign of surprise. She merely remarked in her soft cooing voice, her white teeth showing as her thin lips parted in a smile:

'You are evidently restless and excited to-night, and it is hardly generous of you to treat my kindly interest in such a way.'

'Kindly interest!' I echoed with sneer, as, released her wrist, I fell back on the bed.

'Yes; you haven't treated me well, and you are an intruder here. Nevertheless, as you are a stranger amongst strangers, and cannot speak the language of the country, I would be of service to you if I could. I have come to see if you have everything you require for the night.'

'And you did the same last night,' I cried in hot anger, for, knowing her infamy and wickedness, I could not keep my temper.

'Certainly,' she answered, coolly; 'and I found you calmly dozing, so left you.'

'Yes—after you poured poison down my throat,' I replied.

She broke into a laugh—a rippling laugh, with the tinkle of silver in it—and she seemed hugely amused.

'Well, well,' she said; 'it is obvious, sir, you are not in a fit state to be alone. Your nerves are evidently unstrung, and you are either the victim of a bad dream or some strange delusion. But there, there; I will pardon you. You are not responsible just at present for your language.'

As she spoke she passed her soft white hand over my forehead. There was magic in her touch, and it seemed as if all my will had left me, and there stole over me a delightful sense of dreamy languor. I looked at her, and I saw her strange eyes change color. They became illumined, as if it were, by a violet light that fascinated me so that I could not turn from her. Indeed, I was absolutely subdued to her will now. Everything in the room faded, and I saw nothing but those marvelous eyes glowing with violet light which seemed to fill me with a feeling of ecstasy. I have a vague idea that she kept passing her hand over my face and forehead; that she breathed upon my face; then that she pressed her face to mine, and I felt her hot breath in my neck.

Perhaps it will be said that I dreamed all this. I don't believe it was a dream. I firmly and honestly believe that every word I have written is true.

Hours afterwards my dulled brain began to awake to things mundane. The morning sun was flooding the room, and I was conscious that somebody stood over me, and soon I recognized the old surgeon, who had come to see that the splints and bandages had not shifted. I felt extraordinarily weak, and I found that my pulse was beating very slowly and feebly. Again I had the burning feeling in the throat and a strange and absolutely indescribable sensation at the side of the neck. The old doctor must have recognized that I was unusually feeble, for he went to the landlord, and returned presently with some cognac which he made me swallow, and it picked me up considerably.

After his departure I lay for sometime, and tried to give definite shape to vague and dreadful thoughts that haunted me, and filled me with a shrinking horror. That Annette was a monster in human form I hadn't a doubt, and I felt equally certain that she had designs upon my life. That she had now administered poison to me on two occasions seemed to me beyond question, but I hesitated to believe that she was guilty of the unspeakable crime which my sensations suggested.

At last, unable to endure the tumult in my brain, I sprang out of bed, rushed to the looking-glass, and examined my neck. I literally staggered back, and fell prostrate on the bed, overcome by the hideous discovery I had made. It had the effect, however, of calling me back to life and energy, and I had a mental resolution that I would, at all hazards, save my friend, though I clearly recognized how powerless I was to cope with the awful creature single-handed.

I managed to dress myself, not without some difficulty; then I summoned the landlord, and made him understand that I must go immediately to Santander at any cost. My intention was to invoke the aid of the consul there. But the most I insisted, the more the old landlord shook his head. At length, in desperation, I rushed from the house, hoping to find somebody who understood French or English. As I almost ran up the village street I came face to face with a priest. I asked him in English if he spoke my language, but he shook his head. Then I tried him with French, and to my joy he answered me that he understood a little French. I told him of my desire to start for Santander that very day, but he said that it was impossible, as, owing to the unusual hot sun in the daytime there had been a great melting of snow, with the result that a flooded river had destroyed a portion of the road; and though a gang of men had been set to repair it, it would be two or three days before it was passable.

'But is there no other way of going?' I asked.

'Only by a very hazardous route over the mountains,' he answered. And he added that the risk was so great it was doubtful if anyone could be found who would act as a guide. 'Besides,' he went on, 'you seem very ill and weak. Even a strong man might fail, but you would be certain to perish from exhaustion and exposure.'

I was bound to recognize the force of his argument. It was a maddening disappointment, but there was no help for it. Then it occurred to me to take the old priest into my confidence and invoke his aid. Though, on second thoughts, I hesitated, for was it not possible—nay, highly probable—that if I told the horrible story he and others would think I was mad. Annette was a Spanish woman, and it was feasible to suppose she would secure the ear of those ignorant villagers sooner than I should. No, I would keep the ghastly business to myself for the present at any rate, and wait with such patience as I could command until I could make the journey to Santander. The priest promised me that on the morrow he would let me know if the road was passable, and, if so, he would procure me a carriage and make all the preparations for the journey. So, thanking him, for his kindly services, I turned towards the hotel again. As I neared the house I observed two persons on the mountain path that went up among the pine trees. The sun was shining brilliantly; the sky was cloudless, the air crisp and keen. The two persons were Annette and Redcar. I watched them for some minutes until they were lost to sight amongst the trees.

Suddenly an irresistible impulse to follow them seized me. Why I know not. Indeed, had I paused to reason with myself it would have seemed to me then a mad act, and that I was risking my life to no purpose. But I did not reason. I yielded to the impulse, though first of all I went to my room, put on a thicker pair of boots, and armed myself with a revolver which I had brought with me. During my extensive travelling about America a revolver was a necessity, and by force of habit I put it up with my clothes when packing my things in London for my Continental journey.

Holding the weapon between my knees, I put a cartridge in each barrel, and, providing myself with a stick in addition, I went forth again and began to climb the mountain path. I was by no means a sanguinary man; even my pugnacity could only be aroused after much irritation. Nevertheless, I knew how to defend myself, and in this instance, knowing that I had to deal with a woman who was capable of any crime, and who, I felt sure, would not hesitate to take my life if she got the chance, I deemed it advisable to be on my guard against any emergency that might arise. As regards Redcar, he had already given me forcible and painful evidence that he could be dangerous; but I did not hold him responsible for his actions. I regarded him as being temporarily insane owing to the internal influence the awful woman exercised over him. Therefore it would only have been in the very last extremity that I should have resorted to lethal weapons as a defence against him. My one sole aim, hope, desire, prayer, was to rescue him from the spell that held him in thrall and restore him to his wife, his honour, his sanity. With respect to Annette, it was different. She was a blot on nature, a disgrace to humankind, and, rather than let her gain complete ascendency over me and my friend I would have shot her if I had reason to believe she contemplated taking my life. It might have involved me in serious trouble with the authorities at first, for in Spain the foreigner can hope for little justice. I was convinced, however, that ultimately I should be exonerated.

Such were the thoughts that filled my mind as I painfully made my way up the steep mountain side. My fractured arm was exceedingly painful. Every limb in my body ached, and I was so languid, so weak that it was with difficult I dragged myself along. But worse than all this was an all but irresistible desire to sleep, the result, I was certain, of the poison that had been administered to me. But it would have been fatal to have slept. I knew that, and so I fought against the inclination with all my might and main, and allowed my thoughts to dwell on poor little Maude

Redcar, waiting desolate and heartbroken in London for news.
This supplied me with the necessary spur and kept me going.

The trees were nearly all entirely bare of snow. It had, I was
informed, been an unusually mild season, and at that time the
sun's rays were very powerful. The path I was pursuing was
nothing more than a rough track worn by the peasants passing
between the valley and their hay chalets dotted about the mountain. Snow lay on the path where it was screened from the sun
by the trees. I heard no sound, saw no sign of those I was seeking
save here and there footprints in the snow. I frequently paused
and listened, but the stillness was unbroken save for the subdued
murmur of falling water afar off.

In my weakened condition the exertion I had endured had
greatly distressed me; my heart beat tumultuously, my pulses
throbbed violently, and my breathing was stertorous. I was far
above the valley now, and the pine trees were straggling and
sparse. The track had become very indistinct, but I still detected
the footsteps of the people I was following. Above the trees I
could discern the snow-capped Picoo de Europa glittering in the
brilliant sun. It was a perfect Alpine scene, which, under other
circumstances, I might have reveled in. But I felt strangely ill,
weak, and miserable, and drowsiness began to steal upon me,
so that I made a sudden effort of will and sprang up again, and
resumed the ascent.

In a little time the forest ended, and before me stretched a
sloping plateau which, owing to its being exposed to the full glare
of the sun, as well as to all the winds that blew, was bare of snow.
The plateau sloped down for probably four hundred feet, then
ended abruptly at the end of a precipice. How far the precipice
descended I could not tell from where I was, but far far below I
could see a stream meandering through a thickly wooded gorge.
I took the details of the scene in with a sudden glance of the
eye, for another sight attracted and riveted my attention, and
froze me with horror to the spot. Beneath a huge boulder which
had fallen from the mountain above, and lodged on the slope,
were Annette and Redcar. He was lying on his back, she was

stretched out beside him, and her face was buried in his neck. Even from where I stood I could see that he was ghastly pale, his features drawn and pinched, his eyes closed. Incredible as it may seem, horrible as it sounds, it is nevertheless true that that hellish woman was sucking away his life blood. She was a human vampire, and my worst fears were confirmed.

I am aware that an astounding statement of this kind should not be made lightly by a man in my position. But I take all the responsibility of it, and I declare solemnly that it is true. More-over, the sequel which I am able to give to this story more than corroborates me, and proves Annette to have been one of those human problems which, happily for the world, are very rare, but of which there are several well authenticated cases.

As soon as I fully realized what was happening I draw my revolver from the side pocket of my jacket and fired, not at Annette, but in the air; my object being to startle her so that she would release her victim. It had the desired effect. She sprang up, livid with rage. Blood—his blood—was oozing from the side of her mouth. Her extraordinary eyes had assumed that strange violet appearance which I had seen once before. Her whole aspect was repulsive, revolting, horrible beyond words. Rooted to the spot I stood and gazed at her, fascinated by the weird, ghastly sight. In my hand I still held the smoking revolver, leveled at her now, and resolved if she rushed towards me to shoot her, for I felt that the world would be well rid of such a hideous monster. But suddenly she stooped, seized her unfortunate victim in her arms, and tore down the slope, and when the edge of the precipice was reached they both disappeared into space.

The whole of this remarkable scene was enacted in the course of a few seconds. It was to me a maddening nightmare. I fell where I stood, and remembered no more until hours afterwards, I found myself lying in bed at the hotel, and the old surgeon and the priest sitting beside me. Gradually I learnt that the sound of the shot from the revolver, echoing and re-echoing in that moun-tain region, had been heard in the village, and some peasants had set off for the mountain to ascertain the cause of the firing. They found me lying on the ground still grasping the weapon, and thinking I had shot myself they carried me down to the hotel.

Naturally I was asked for explanations when I was able to talk, and I recounted the whole of the ghastly story. At first my listeners, the priest and the doctor, seemed to think I was raving in delirium, as well as they might, but I persisted in my statements, and I urged the sending out of a party to search for the bodies. If they were found my story would be corroborated.

In a short time a party of peasants started for the gorge, which was a wild, almost inaccessible, ravine through which flowed a mountain torrent amongst the debris and boulders that from time to time had fallen from the rocky heights. After some hours of searching the party discovered the crushed remains of Jack Redcar. His head had been battered to pieces against the rocks as he fell, and every bone in his body was broken. The precipice over which he had fallen was a jagged, scarred, and irregular wall of rock at least four thousand feet in height. The search for Annette's body was continued until darkness compelled the searchers to return to the village, which they did bringing with them my poor friend's remains. Next day the search was resumed, and the day after, and for many days, but with no results. The woman's corpse was never found. The theory was that somewhere on that frightful rock face she had been caught by a projecting pinnacle, or had got jammed into a crevice, where her unhallowed remains would moulder into dust. It was as fitting end for so frightful a life.

Of course an official inquiry was held—and officialism in Spain is appalling. It was weeks and weeks before the inevitable conclusion of the tribunal was arrived at, and I was exonerated from all blame. In the meantime Redcar's remains were committed to their eternal rest in the picturesque little Alpine village churchyard, and for all times Potes will be associated with that grim and awful tragedy. Why Annette took her victim to that out of the way spot can only be guessed at. She knew that the death of her victim was only a question of weeks, and in that primitive and secluded hamlet it would arouse no suspicion, she being a native of Spain. It would be easy for her to say that she had taken her invalid husband there for the benefit of his health, but unhappily the splendid and bracing air had failed to save his life. In this instance, as in many others, her fiendish cunning would have enabled her to score another triumph had not destiny made me its instrument to encompass her destruction.

For long after my return to England I was very ill. The fearful ordeal I had gone through, coupled with the poison which Annette had administered to me, shattered my health; but the unremitting care and attention bestowed upon me by my old friend's widow pulled me through. And when at last I was restored to strength and vigour, beautiful Maude Redcar became my wife.

NOTE BY THE AUTHOR—The foregoing story was suggested by a tradition current in the Pyrenees, where a belief in ghouls and vampires is still common. The same belief is no less common throughout Syria, in some parts of Turkey, in Russia, and in India. Sir Richard Burton deals with the subject in his 'Vikram and the Vampire.' Years ago, when the author was in India, a poor woman was beaten to death one night in the village by a number of young men armed with cudgels. Their excuse for the crime was that the woman was a vampire, and had sucked the blood of many of their companions, whom she had first lured to her by depriving them of their will power by mesmeric influence.

# Dick Donovan: The Story of Annette (From Official Records): Being the Sequel to "The Woman with the Oily Eyes"

At the time the inquiry was held into the circumstances of Jack Redcar's death, the authorities deemed it their duty to find out something of Annette's past history. In this they were aided by certain documents discovered amongst her belongings, and, by dint of astute and patient investigation, they elicited the following remarkable facts. Her real name was Isabella Ribera, and she was born in a little village in the Sierra Nevada, of Andalusia. Her mother was a highly respectable peasantwoman, of a peculiarly romantic disposition, and fond of listening to and reading weird and supernatural stories. Her father was also a peasant, but intellectual beyond his class. By dint of hard work, he acquired a considerable amount of land and large numbers of cattle, and ultimately became the mayor of his village.

There were two peculiarities noticed about Isabella Ribera when she was born. She had an extraordinary amount of back hair, and she lids of her eyes remained fast sealed until she was a year old. An operation was at first talked about, but the child was examined by a doctor of some repute in the nearest town, and he advised against the operation, saying that it was better to let nature take her course. When the girl was in her thirteenth month she one day suddenly opened her eyes, and those who saw them were frightened. Some people said that they were seal's eyes, others that they were the eyes of a snake, and others, again, that 'the devil looked through them.' The superstitious people in the village urged the parents to consult the priest, and this was done, with the result that the infant was subjected to a religious ceremony, with a view to exorcising the demon which was supposed to have taken possession of her.

As the girl grew she displayed amazing precocity. When she was only four she was more like a grown woman in her acts and ways than a child, and the intuitive knowledge she exhibited only served to increase the superstitious dread with which she inspired people. One day, when she was nearly five, her father had a pig killed. The girl witnessed the operation, and seemed to go almost mad with delight. And suddenly, to the horror and consternation of those looking on, she threw herself on the dying animal and began to drink the blood that flowed from the cut throat. Somebody snatched her up and ran screaming with her to her mother, who was distracted when she heard the story.

The incident, of course, soon became known all over the village, and indeed far beyond it, and a fierce hatred of the child seized upon the people. The consequence was, the parents had to keep a very watchful eye over her. They were seriously advised to have the girl strangled, and her body burnt to ashes with wood that had been blessed and consecrated by the priests. Fearing that an attempt would be made upon her life by the villagers, Isabella's parents secretly conveyed her away and took her to Cordova, where she was placed in the care of the mother superior of a convent.

At this place she was carefully trained and taught, but was regarded as an unnatural child. She seemed to be without heart, feeling, or sentiment. Her aptitude for learning was looked upon as miraculous, and a tale of horror or bloodshed afforded her an infinite amount of enjoyment.

When she was a little more than twelve she escaped from her guardians and disappeared.

For a long time no trace of her was forthcoming, then it became known that she had joined a band of gipsies, and gained such a dominating influence and power over them, that she was made a queen and married a young man of the tribe. A month afterwards he was found dead one morning in his tent. The cause of his death remained a mystery, but it was noticed that there was

a peculiar blue mark at the side of his neck, from which a drop
or two of blood still oozed.

A few weeks after her husband's death, Isabella, queen of
the gipsies, announced to her tribe that she was going to sever
herself from them for a tie and travel all over Europe. Where
she went to during the succeeding two years will never be
known; but she was next heard of in Paris, where she was put
upon her trial, charged with having caused the death of a man
whom she alleged was her husband. She was then known as
Madame Ducoudert. The husband had died in a very mysterious
manner. He seemed to grow bloodless, and gradually faded away.
And after his death certain signs suggested poison. An autopsy,
however, failed to reveal any indications of recognized poisons.
Nevertheless madame was tried, but no evidence was forthcoming to convict her, and she was acquitted.

Almost immediately afterwards she quitted Paris with plenty
of money, her husband, who was well off, having left her all his
property. The Paris police, through their agents and spies, ascertained that she proceeded direct to Bordeaux, where, in a very
short time, she united herself to a handsome young man, the
only son of an exceedingly wealthy Bordeaux wine merchant.
She had changed her name at this stage to Marie Tailleux. She
had a well-developed figure, an enormous quantity of jet black
hair, and perfect teeth. In other respects she was considered to be
ugly, by some even repulsive. And yet she exercised a fatal fascination over men, though women feared and hated her.

She went through Bordeaux to London with the wine-
merchant's son, and six months later the English people were
treated to a sensation. 'Madame and Monsieur Tailleux' travelled
extensively about England and Scotland. Monsieur fell ill, soon
after arriving, of some nameless disease. His illness was characterized by prostration, languor, bloodlessness. He consulted several
doctors, who prescribed for him without effect.

The pair at last took up their residence at a very well-known
metropolitan hotel, where they lived in great style, spent money
lavishly, and were supposed to be people of note. But one morning

monsieur was found dead in bed, and as no doctor had been treating him for some time, and the cause of death could not be certified, an inquest was ordered and a post-mortem became necessary. Those who made the examination had their suspicions aroused. They believed there had been foul-play—at any rate, the man had died of poison. The police were communicated with result, the arrest of madame, and columns and columns of sensational reports in the papers.

Amongst madame's belongings was found a little carved ebony box containing twelve receptacles for twelve tiny phials. Some of these phials were empty, others full of liquid that varied in colour; that is, in one phial it was yellow, in another red, in another green, in another blue, and yet another held what seemed to be clear water.

The chemical analysis of the contents of the stomach quite failed to justify the suspicions of poison. But the blood had a peculiar, watery appearance; the heart was flabby and weak. Madame accounted for possession of the phials by saying they contained gipsy medicine of great efficacy in certain diseases. There was such a small quantity in each phial as to make analysis practically impossible; certain animals, however, were treated with some of the contents, and seemed actually to improve under the treatment. Under the circumstances, of course, there was nothing for it but to release madame, as the magistrate said there was no case to go before a jury.

It is worth while to quote the following description of the woman at this time. It appeared in a report in the Times.

'The prisoner is a most extraordinary looking woman, and appears to be possessed of some wonderful magnetic power, which half fascinates one. It is difficult to say wherein this power lies, unless it be in her eyes. They are certainly remarkable eyes, that have a peculiar, glistening appearance like oil. Then her voice is a revelation. Until she speaks one would be disposed to say the voice of such a harsh-featured woman would be hard, raucous, and raspy. But its tones are those of a silver bell, or a sweet-toned flute. Her self-possession is also marvelous, and she smiles sweetly and fascinatingly. Somehow or another she gives one the impression that she has some of the attributes of the sirens of old, who were said to lure men to their destruction. Possibly this is doing the woman an injustice; but it is difficult to resist the idea. Her hands, too, are in striking contrast to her general physique. They are long, thin, lithe, and white. Taken altogether, she cannot certainly be described as an ordinary type of woman, and we should be disposed to say that, allied to great intelligence, was a subtle cunning and cruelty of disposition that might make her dangerous.'

This description was written during the time the woman was a prisoner. The writer showed that he had a keen insight, and had he but known some of her past history he would probably have written in a much more pronounced way.

'Madame Tailleux' was discharged for the want of legal evidence, and Madame Tailleux soon afterwards left England and went to America, where she became 'Miss Anna Clarkson'; and though nobody knew anything at all about her, she had no difficulty in making her way into so-called Society; but not as an associate and companion of women, who shunned and hated her as she hated them; but men followed her, as men are alleged to have followed Circe. Indeed, in some respects, the classical description of Circe with her magic and potions might apply to Isabella Ribera, with the many aliases.

In a very little while Phineas Miller fell a victim to her potent spells. Phineas was a young man, a stockbroker, and rich. The twain journeyed to Florida, from whence Phineas wrote to an intimate friend that he was strangely ill, and he believed the climate was affecting him. He looked like a corpse, he said. He was languid. He took no interest in anything. He suffered from a peculiar prostration, and found a difficulty in moving about. Yet he experienced no pain, and at times sank into a dreamy state that was pleasant. He thought, however, as soon as he left that part of the country he would be all right.

He was doomed, however, never to leave that part of the country. He went out one day with Miss Anna Clarkson, and an

242 / DICK DONOVAN: THE STORY OF ANNETTE

old negro, to shoot in the swamps. They had a boat which was in charge of the negro. That evening, Miss Clarkson returned alone. She was drenched and covered with slime and mud. There had been an accident. The boat had capsized by striking against a sunken tree. They were all thrown into the water. She managed to cling to the boat, and ultimately to right it, but her companions disappeared. The negro, she thought, was taken by a crocodile.

A search-party went out to try and recover the bodies. The negro was never found, Miller was. He presented an extraordinary appearance, and those who examined him said he had not died by drowning. This theory, however, found no favour. Men were often drowned in the swamps, which swarmed with alligators and crocodiles, huge snakes, and other repulsive things. When a man once got into the water he had no chance. It was a perfect miracle how Miss Clarkson escaped. 'Poor thing, she must have had an awful time of it.'

It is true that crocodiles, alligators, and snakes did swarm in the swamps, and the remarkable thing was that Miller's body was recovered. Much sympathy was shown for Miss Clarkson; Miller was duly buried and forgotten in a week.

Amongst the lady's most pronounced sympathizers was a Mr. Lambert Lennox, an Englishman engaged in fruit-farming. He was about forty-five, a widower with two daughters and a son. It was generally agreed that he was one of the finest men in Florida. He was an athlete. He stood six feet two in his stockings. His health was perfect. It was his boast that he had never been laid up a day with illness.

Mr. Lennox had some business to transact in Jamaica, West Indies, and sailed for that island in one of the trading vessels. In the same vessel went, 'poor' Miss Clarkson. A month or two later Mr. Lennox, Jun., received from Mr. Lennox, Sen., a letter dated from Jamaica, in the West Indies. Amongst much other news the writer told his son that he had not been well. He had a strange aenemic appearance, felt weak and languid, had no energy, suffered from unquenchable thirst, and was constantly falling asleep suddenly, often at the most inopportune moments. He had consulted a doctor, who was of opinion that the climate of Jamaica didn't suit him, and he advised him to get away as soon as possible. 'I shall therefore be home in about six weeks,' Mr. Lennox added. But in the meantime he departed for his long home. Mr. Lambert Lennox died somewhat suddenly one morning, and was buried in the evening. The doctor who had been attending him certified that he had succumbed to low fever. The next mail that went out bore the sad intelligence to his family, and people marveled much when they heard that handsome Lambert Lennox, the man with the iron constitution, had slipped away so quickly, more particularly as long residence in Florida had inured him to a hot climate and miasma.

It was found difficult to trace Miss Clarkson's movements during the next two or three years, but there were grounds for believing that she travelled extensively, and amongst other places visited India, and in this connection there was a somewhat vague and legendary story told. At a hill station a strange and mysterious women put in an appearance. She was thought to be either a Spaniard or a Portuguese. She was known as Mademoiselle Sassetti, though why 'Mademoiselle,' if Spanish or Portuguese, was not explained. But that is a detail.

This mysterious lady claimed to have occult powers. She could read anyone's future. She could perform miracles. The women kept away from her because they were afraid of her, thought there was no definite statement as to how this fear arose. But the men showed no fear, as became them, and amongst others who consulted her was a handsome, much beloved young military officer. His frequent visits to the sorceress caused a good deal of talk, as it was bound to do in an Indian hill station. Grey-bearded men shook their heads sadly, and wise and virtuous women turned up their noses and muttered mysterious interjections such as 'Ah!' 'Oh!' 'Umph.'

One day the station was startled by a report that the young officer had been found dead in a jungle in one of the valleys. He had been bitten by a cobra, so the report said, for there was a peculiar little blue mark at the side of his neck.

If the virtuous ones didn't actually it served him right, they thought it; and mumbled that the young officer had been dining somewhere not wisely but too well, and had mistaken the jungle for his bedroom, and gone to sleep, otherwise how did the cobra manage to bite him in the neck.

It seemed a plausible theory. Anyway it got over a difficulty, and it brought an unpleasant little scandal to a tragic and abrupt end. So the virtuous ones went about their many occupations again, and the atmosphere was purer when it was known that the sorceress had disappeared as mysteriously as she had come.

The next direct evidence we got was that under the name of Isabella Rodino the adventuress turned up in Rome, where she rented a small but expensive villa in the fashionable Via Porta Pia. Everyone who knows Rome knows how exclusive society is, but while Isabella Rodino made no attempt to be received by Roman society she attracted to her villa some of the male representatives of the best families in the city. Amongst these gentlemen was the scion of one of the oldest Roman houses.

Now it may be said boldly here, and that without any reflections, that the young gentleman of Rome, as of most other continental cities, are allowed a good deal more latitude than would be accorded to the same class in, say, cold-blooded, unromantic, prosaic, and commonplace London, whose soot and grime, somehow, seem to grind their way into people's brains and hearts. Anyway the young gentleman referred to, whose baptismal name was Basta, did not at first provoke any very severe criticism, but he was destined ultimately to give the Romans a sensation to talk about for the proverbial nine days, for one Sunday morning a humble fisherman, having some business on the Tiber, fished out of that classic river the stark body of the scion. Over Rome flew the news, and those who loved him, and looked to him to uphold the honour and dignity of his family, were horror stricken.

Now, it's a very curious thing that his distracted relatives firmly believed that the young prodigal had in a moment of remorse, after a night's debauch, flung himself into eternity via the Tiber, and so mighty was their pride that they used their wealth, their influence, and their power to stifle inquiry, and caused a report to be circulated that Basta had met his end through accident. It is not less curious that the family doctor who examined the body was of opinion that there was something mysterious about the lad's death, for he certainly had not died by drowning, and on one side of the neck was a peculiar little bluish puncture. But as the family persisted in their view, the doctor, not wishing to lose their influential patronage, observed a discreet silence.

A week later, however, an agent of the police called on Isabella Rodino, and did something more than hint that it was desirable that within twenty-four hours she should leave Rome as quietly and unobtrusively as possible. The result of this functionary's call was Isabella Rodino journeyed to Florence by that night's mail train. It was known that she only sojourned two days in the fair city on the Arno.

After that there is another hiatus of something like two years in her known career, and it is not easy to fill up. And this brings us to that fatal night in Wiesbaden, when ill-starred Jack Redcar met the enchantress on the hotel stairs. From that point to the moment when, her role being finished, she disappeared for ever from the ken of men, the reader of the story can fill in for himself. She played out her last act under the name of Annette. In selecting her many names she seemed actuated by a fine sense of poetic euphony, and in selecting her victims she was guided by a 'damnable' discrimination.

'Annette,' as we will now call her, was a human riddle, and she illustrates for the millionth time the trite adage that 'Truth is stranger than Fiction,' besides which she presents the world with an object lesson in the study of the occult.

# Hugh McCrae:
## The Vampire (1901)

Hugh Raymond McCrae (1876-1958) was the son of Australian poet George Gordon McRae. He was educated at Hawthorn Grammar School and grew up in his father's literary circles, which he described in *My Father and My Father's Friends* (1935).

McCrae, who belonged to an artists' club called "The Prehistoric Order of Cannibals," lived a Bohemian existence. He wrote "The Vampire" under the pseudonym "W. W. Lamble" for the November 1901 edition of *The Bulletin*, which had published his first poem in 1896.

———————

How well I remember my first love,—with her stuffed busks and her stuffed hair! We did not meet in the summer, nor in the green grass near running water, but in winter, under the pale glare of gas, in the wet street and among people.

She was complexionless, her face so bleached that her black eyes and red lips positively glared; yet she had a silky fascination for me. And her smooth, evil hands brought not only flesh into contact, but mind.

She said she was hungry. I had just drawn my month's earnings, and we went arm-in-arm to a little green-curtained restaurant. It was sufficiently evil-looking, the gas low, and the solitary waiter unobstreperous.

I was drunk. The fumes of the cheap Burgundy started an orchestra in my ears, and swelled the veins of my brain. The wind lifted the blind and blew my cigarettes in a whirring covey off the table. I stooped to pick them up, but the blood-strings in my throat stood out, and the room darkened to my eyes. The waiter noiselessly came to my assistance, replacing them on a plate and retaining a few slyly up his sleeve. But I said nothing, only looking at Marguerite and her long, folded fingers.

She ordered some oysters and, when they had come, I watched her squeeze a lemon-quarter into the shells and over the firm fish.

† † † † † †

I seemed to be in a garden with Marguerite. The garden was full of lilies—tall, white lilies without a speck or mark; and everywhere amongst them were blue flies, trumpeting a buzzing with pleasure. Here and there a rich bee, with powdered legs, swayed on a flower, like a jewel in snow. The air was warm and soft as down, while the rounded sound of bubbling water poppled in the moss, between the bars of lily-stalks. A delicious sweetness of earth and honey mounted to my brain. I watched a butterfly, winged in old-gold and grey, as he flickered on a red tile under the steady shadow of a fern.

Gradually I grew aware of the subtle electrical hand upon my wrist—then of the eyes that made my mind hers, nay, my very soul. The small, piercing eyes, whose pupils diminished and enlarged, and enlarged and diminished, like the flame of a dying lamp. And every time the pupils diminished, they seemed to me two miser hands that gripped my brain and squeezed myself from me, like a water from cloth, opening only to grip again.

But the woman, in the body, was tall, and breasted like a young girl; her back was straight as an arrow, and her neck reared white as a rock-wave carrying the magnificent head on its summit. She had a broad brow, but somewhat slanting; a long, slight nose, an eagerly insolent mouth, and the eyes I have spoken of. Her hair, where it was loose, shimmered and shook as though over a heat-mist.

Presently she lifted her hands from my wrists, and I felt her fingers thrill through my temples, as she drew me towards her and kissed me on the lips. A song seemed to set up in the garden, and the lilies shot up like stars, swayed in the sky, meeting in an arch, and crossed in stormy rushes over our heads. The noise of the water rose clamorously, and a flight of coloured birds brushed my shoulder. A soft sensation went over the whole of my skin, like the dropping of a delicate veil.

And still she drew me closer.

I tried to resist, but, as in a nightmare, my arms remained limp and paralysed. Neither could I cry out. All at once, in the midst of a million kisses, she drew back her head, and, with a gasping laugh, pushed her red lips at my throat and bit me deep, even to blood.

In vain I beat her about the face, and plucked at her cheeks. She hung like a dog. With horrible little laughs and gurgles she greeted my impotent rage.

I put both hands to her forehead, and made to thrust her from me; but again my muscles failed. And she bit deeper.

Then the lilies withered down from the skies and lay stained and yellow on the earth. The butterfly lost its old-gold, and its wings and whole form broadened into a bat's. The soft ripple of the water changed to the purring of a flame, and bale fires leapt from every corner.

Still the woman tore at my throat.

My breath shortened, and I felt as though my skull were contracting and injuring my brain. Spasm after spasm shot through my head. Goaded to madness, I hurled my tormenter away, and as she returned to me, bloody-mouthed, I saw that she too had changed. Her eyes had sunk, her teeth were old and wasted to an appearance of cloves; her nose seemed flattened, and her hair thin. Her face was almost simian.

My strength failed me, and I staggered on my feet. "Marguerite," I cried. "Woman! Devil! Vampire!"

And I fell clean to the ground, like a tree in a storm.

A great coldness rushed upon me, and an icy breath fanned my forehead. I could feel a pair of hands beneath my arm-pits. I was smothering. There was a bandage round my mouth.

I opened my eyes. There were stars—thousands of them—blinking and blinking, but below, turbid and swollen, lay the river without a light for miles.

The hands withdrew suddenly; and a man darted from me, fleeing up the steep stoned bank. It was the waiter of the restaurant. The bandage dropped off my jaw, and I could now understand the sweet scent of my garden dream.

My pockets were empty as the day when my clothes were made; that was a foregone conclusion.

Marguerite never again crossed my path. Yet I know that green-curtained restaurant, and some day I shall see her standing in the doorway. If she beckons, I must go to her.

Because I dare not refuse.

# Phil Robinson:
# Medusa (1902)

Philip Stewart Robinson (1847-1902), who was born in Chunar, India, pioneered Anglo-Indian studies. He was a journalist by trade who was best-known for his books about natural history. His most popular works include *In My Indian Garden* (1878), *Tigers at Large* (1884) and *The Valley of the Teetotum Tree* (1886).

In addition to the following vampire tale, he wrote two pseudo-vampire stories: "The Man-Eating Tree" appeared in his collection, *Under the Punkah* (1881), while "The Last of the Vampires" debuted in the *Contemporary Review* (March 1893) and was reprinted in 1889, along with "Medusa."

"Medusa" debuted in *Tales by Three Brothers* (London: Ibister & Co., Ltd., 1889) which contains stories by Philip and his brothers Edward Kay Robinson and [Sir] Harry Perry Robinson, K.B.E. None of the fables are attributed to specific authors, but it is assumed that Philip wrote the following story.

———

It was on the 17th of June that the world read in its morning paper that James Westerby had died suddenly in his office at Whitehall on the preceding day. The world may still, if its memory be jogged a little, be able to remember that the cause of death was said to have been heart disease, the crisis having been accelerated by overwork. As to the sadness of the event, the newspapers of all political shades agreed.

James Westerby would have been a prominent man, even if he had not been an Under Secretary and one of the pleasantest speakers in the House of Commons. He was of the Westerbys of Oxfordshire, the last, I fear, of a fine old line. "Hotspur" Westerby, of revolutionary fame, was one of his ancestors, and the

Under Secretary prided himself not a little on his resemblance to the old hero, whom Cromwell hated so cordially. His father's place is secure in the world of letters. James Westerby promised to be worthy of his blood. Still young (he died when he was thirty-nine), he had borne himself admirably in public position; and when he died there were not wanting some who spoke of his loss as a national calamity.

To me his death was a personal sorrow. I was, and had been since his appointment, fifteen months before, his private secretary; and, previous to that again, for the twelve years since I came down from the 'Varsity we had been intimate friends, though he was some years my senior.

On the morning of that 16th day of June I was sitting at my desk as usual, between the ante-room and his private office. The last person who had been admitted to his presence was a lady, who, dressed in black and closely veiled, made at the time no distinct impression on my mind. The Under Secretary had refused admittance to some ten or twelve people that morning, but, on my handling him this lady's card, he told me to admit her. She was with him for, perhaps, half an hour. It must have been about 11 o'clock when she passed out. It was just 11:30 when I went into his office and found him dead in his chair.

Some of these facts—with many more or less imaginative details—were presented to the world by the morning papers, as already mentioned, of the 17th. But in no paper was any mention made of the veiled lady, for the altogether sufficient reason that no representative of any paper knew of the veiled lady's existence.

At about a quarter before twelve we were standing—two or three others of the higher employees of the department and myself—in my office, waiting for the arrival of the doctor. The door of the Under Secretary's private room was closed. In the excitement the doorkeeper in the ante-room had presumably deserted his post, for, seeing those to whom I was talking glance toward the outer door, I turned and found myself again confronting the veiled lady.

"Can I see Mr. Westerby once more?" she asked.

"Mr. Westerby, madam," I answered, "is dead."

She did not reply at once, but with both hands raised her veil as if to obtain a clearer view of my face, to see if I spoke the truth. In doing so, she showed me the most beautiful face that I have ever seen, or ever expect to see. One dreams of such eyes. Perhaps Endymion looked into them. But I have never hoped to see them in a woman's face. I scarcely remember that she murmured in a low, incredulous voice, the one word—

"Dead?"

"He died, madam, suddenly, less than an hour ago."

We had been standing as we spoke, within earshot of the others. She now drew back to where my desk stood, in the further corner of the room, whither I followed her.

"Was any one with him after I left, can you remember?" she asked.

"No madam, I had no occasion to go into his room for some little time after you went. When I did so, he was dead."

It was some time before she spoke again; then—

"Excuse me," she said, hesitatingly, "but I hope I shall not have to appear in connection with this. You can understand how very much I should dislike"—this with the faintest smile—"to have my name in all of the newspapers. Of course, if there is an inquest, and if my evidence can be of service, I shall have to give it. But it does not seem to me that anything I can say could be of importance. He was well when I saw him—that is all."

Then, after a pause, during which I was silent: "If you can manage it so that my name will not be mentioned, I shall be very grateful to you," she said. As she spoke, she drew one of her cards from a small black card case and handed it to me, adding, "and I hope you will call and let me have the pleasure of thanking you."

I took the card and assured her that I would do what I could in her behalf. She lowered her veil again and left the room. I read the card now with more interest than I had the former one when taking it to my chief. It said:

## MRS. WALTER F. TIERCE,
19, Grasmere Crescent, W.

Mrs. Tierce had hardly gone when the doctor came in, followed a moment later by a police inspector.

"Heart disease," the doctor said. The inspector asked me a few questions and said that no inquest would be necessary.

I was hardly conscious at the time, I think, that I was telling the officer that no one had been with the Under Secretary for an hour before his death. Nor when it was over and I recognized what I had done, did my conscience disturb me much. It was a mere courtesy to a woman, such as any man would do if he had it in his power. Why should she be made to suffer because he chanced to die about the time that she happened to call upon him?

So the world next morning heard nothing of the veiled lady.

Within a month I was back in my old chambers in Lincoln's Inn trying to gather up the interrupted threads of legal studies—a task which would, perhaps, have progressed more rapidly if it had received my entire attention. As it was, however, work had to be content to divide my thoughts somewhat unequally with another subject—Mrs. Walter Tierce.

`Mrs. Tierce was a widower. When I called at her home immediately after the funeral, she met me with delightful cordiality.

I called frequently after my first visit, and never met any other visitor at the house. It was difficult to understand how so charming a woman could live in a fashionable quarter of London in such complete isolation. But I had no desire that it should be otherwise.

At the age of thirty-five I had settled down, more or less reconciled to the belief that I should never marry. In theory, I have always maintained that it is the duty to himself and to society of every healthy man to take to himself a wife and assume the responsibilities of a householder before he is thirty years of age. A bachelor's life is an inchoate existence; a species of half-life at best—"like the odd half of a pair of scissors," as Benjamin

Franklin said. It is as the head of a family alone, with the care of others on his shoulders, that a man arrives at the possibility of his best development. This was my loudly proclaimed belief. And still I was unmarried. If one could only wake some morning and find himself married—in his own house, with a charming and domestic wife—perhaps with children! But the necessary preliminaries to arriving at that state terrified me. The difficulty of a selection (in the face of an apparently incurable incapability of falling seriously in love with any one individual) was appalling.

But now the picture of a home rose frequently before me, altogether pleasant to contemplate—a home in which two wonderful black eyes smiled at me across the breakfast tablecloth in the morning and were waiting to meet mine as I looked up from my reading in our library at night.

In fact, I was in love—at times. But there were also times when my condition seemed, on analysis, curiously unsatisfactory to myself, curiously contradictory. Especially was this the case immediately after being in Mrs. Tierce's presence, when there was a certain reaction. On leaving her home, I never failed to ask myself wonderingly, if I really loved her as a man should love a woman before asking her to be his wife. She filled all my thoughts by day and a large share of my dreams by night. Those eyes haunted me. In her presence I was helpless—intoxicated—a blind worshipper. I longed to touch her with my hands, to stroke the fabric of her dress or any object which her hands had recently touched. My whole being ached with very tenderness to approach more nearly to her—to be in contact with her—to caress her. The physical attraction of her presence was overmastering.

Fifteen minutes after leaving her, however, I would be dimly wondering if this was really love—the love that a husband should feel for a wife. This absolute submission of my individuality to hers—would it last through days and weeks and months of constant companionship? Through all the stress of years of wedded life? And if it did not, if my individuality asserted itself, and I became critical of her, what then?

Not that her beauty was her only attraction. On the contrary, few women whom I have ever met have impressed me more distinctly with their intellectuality.

But her most charming characteristic was a certain admirable self-possession and self-control. She seemed so thoroughly to understand herself and to know what was her right relation to things around her; and this without a suspicion of masculinity or of the business air. Never for a moment was there danger of her losing either her mental or emotional equilibrium.

In fact, she was adorable. But, though there was no point of view from which she did not seem to me to be entirely the most delightful thing that I had ever seen, I never failed to experience that same misgiving immediately after quitting her presence. It was as short-lived as it was regular in its recurrence. An hour later, as I sat in my chambers alone, her eyes haunted me once more.

Though I had never spoken of my love, she must have read it in my eyes a hundred times, nor apparently was the perusal distasteful to her.

I had been back in Lincoln's Inn now five months, and was sitting in my chambers one dark mid-afternoon in December. Had I been reading, I must have lit the gas. But there was light enough to sit and dream of her; light enough to see those eyes in the shadow of my book-case. My one clerk was away and would not return for an hour. So I dreamed uninterruptedly until a shuffling outside my office door recalled me to myself. It would have looked more business-like in the eyes of a client to have light enough in the room to work by, and I made a movement toward the matchbox. But there was no time. A knock at the door sounded and the door itself was thrown wide open. There was an interval of some seconds and then a figure entered, moving heavily and painfully with the aid of a crutch—a man and crippled, that was all that I could see.

The figure moved laboriously half way across the floor toward me. Then, standing on one foot, the visitor placed his crutch against the wall and allowed himself to drop heavily into a chair a few feet away from me, while I stood looking on, mutely anxious to render assistance but not knowing how to offer it.

After a short silence he spoke, simply pronouncing my name; not interrogatively, but as if to inform me that he knew to whom he was speaking and that his business was with me. I bowed in response, and with matter-of-fact business suavity asked what I could do for him.

He was silent for some moments, and as he sat fronting the window to which my back was turned, and through which came what small light there was in the office, I could see his face plainly enough. Not an old man, by any means, probably younger than myself, with features that must once have been handsome, and would be still but for the deep lines of sorrow or of pain. The figure, too, as he sat, looked full and healthy with nothing but a certain stiffness of pose to tell of its infirmity. At last he spoke, hurriedly, and in a hard, feverish-sounding voice.

"Nothing, thank you. You can do nothing for me. I have come to do something for you, instead." I bowed in acknowledgement.

"I have come to warn you," he went on, still hurriedly and shifting uneasily in his seat, like one who has an unpleasant thing to tell and is anxious to be over with it. The strangeness of his voice and manner, and the intentness—almost the fierceness— with which he looked at me, made me uneasy in my turn. I doubted his sanity, and wished there was more light or that my clerk was present.

"I came to warn you," he said again, and I saw his hands moving nervously as he leaned toward me and spoke harshly and quickly. "You are in love with her—Mrs. Tierce. No; don't deny it. I know, I know, and before heaven, if I can save you I will."

The heaviness of his breathing told the intensity of the excitement under which he was laboring as he went on, edging further forward on his chair and reaching out his hands towards me;

"She is not a woman; she is not human. Yes, I know how beautiful she is; how helpless a man must be before her. I have known it for six years; and had I not known it I should not now be what I am. You will think me mad," he said. "You probably think me so now. I do not wonder at it. What else should you think when a stranger comes into your chambers and tells you that in these matter-of-fact nineteenth-century days there exist beings who are not human—who have more than human attributes, and that one of these beings is the woman whom you love?"

He was quieter now, more serious, and spoke almost argumentatively, as one who seeks only to convince, while he almost despaired of doing it.

"You are laughing at me now—or pitying me; but I call the Almighty God to witness that I speak the truth—if a God can be almighty and let her live. I tell you, sir, that to know her is death. If you do not believe me you will become worse than I am—as her husband is who died at her feet here in London—as the American is who died before her in the café at Nice—as heaven only knows how many more are who have crossed her path."

Of course I had no doubt of his madness; but his earnestness—the utter strength of conviction with which he spoke—was strangely moving. That he, poor fellow, believed what he said, it was impossible to doubt.

"It is six years since I saw her first at Havre, in France. I chanced to be seated at the next table to her at Frascati's, and I knew that I loved her then. The American was with her. I followed her to Cannes, to Trouville, to Monaco, to Nice; and where she went the American went, too. There was no impropriety in their companionship, but he followed her as I did; only that he had her acquaintance and I had not. And I knew, or thought I knew, that it would be useless for me to try and win her while he was there. He evidently worshipped her, and she—for he was a handsome fellow (Reading was his name)—seemed to care for him. So I watched her from a distance, waiting and hoping; and as I have told you my turn came.

"It was in the Café Royal, and nobody it happen but herself. Suddenly she rushed out from the corner where they were sitting and called for help. Every one crowded around, and he was dead—dead in his chair, with his face upturned and his eyes fixed, staring like one suddenly terrified. They said it was heart disease. Heart disease!"

It had grown almost dark, and he drew his chair close to me. The paling light from the window just showed me the worn face and the sunken, feverish eyes.

"Then I came to know her," he continued, after a pause. "I hung upon her as he had done, and for three months I believed that I was the happiest man in Europe. In Venice, in Florence, in Paris, in London, I was constantly with her, day after day. She seemed to love me, and in the Bois or in Hyde Park how proud I was to be seen by her side! Then she went to stay for a month at Oxford, and I, with her permission, followed her there, and would call for her at the Mitre every morning. Under the shadow of the grey college walls and in the well-trimmed walks and gardens, it seemed that her face put on a new and holier beauty in keeping with the place. There it was that I told her that I loved her and asked her to be my wife, as we stood for a minute to rest in the cloisters of Christ Church."

His voice was very sad. It had lost its harshness, and as he remembered—or did he only imagine?—the sweetness of those days of love-making, there was more of a soft regretfulness than of anger in his tones.

"She did not refuse me," he said, "nor did she explicitly accept me. But I was idiotically happy—happy for three whole days—until that afternoon in the Magdalen Walks, when in ten minutes I became, from a healthy, strong man, the wreck you see me now."

The regretfulness was all gone, and the hard, fierce ring was in his voice again as he went on:

"It was on one of the benches in Addison's Walk, as they call it, and I pressed her for some more definite promise than she had yet given me. She did not seem to listen to me, to heed me, as she leaned back, her hands lying idly in her lap and her great, grave eyes looking out across the meadow. I grew more passionate; clasped her hands and begged for an answer. At last she turned her face towards me. I met her eyes—"

His voice broke and he stopped speaking. For a minute or more we sat in silence in the twilight, his face buried in his hands. Then he raised his head again, and in slow, unimpassioned accents, continued:

"As our eyes met, hers looked lusterless, hardly as if she saw me or was looking at me, but as I gazed into them they changed. Somewhere inside them, or behind them, a flame was lit. The pupils expanded, black and brilliant as eyes never shone before. What was it? Was it love? And leaning still closer, I gazed more intensely into the eyes that seemed now to blame before me. And as I looked the spell came upon me. It was as though I swooned. Dimly I became aware that I was losing my power of motion, of speech, of thought. The eyes engulfed me. I was vaguely conscious that I must somehow disengage myself from the spell that was upon me; but I could not. I was powerless, and she—it was as if she fed upon my very life. I cannot phrase it otherwise. I was numb, and, though I tried to speak, could not move one muscle. Then consciousness began to leave me, and I was on the point of—God knows what—swoon or death—when the crunching of feet on the gravel path came sharply to my ears.

"Who was it that passed I do not know. I know not how long I sat there. I remember that she rose without a word and left me. When I moved it was evening. The sun was behind the college walls, and the walk was dark. With my brain hardly awake and my lower limbs still benumbed, slowly I made my way out of the college gates and up the High Street to the Clarendon Hotel, where I was staying. Next morning I awoke what you see me now—a cripple, paralytic for life."

During all this narrative I had sat silent, engrossed in the madman's tale. As a piece of dramatic elocution, it was magnificent. When he finished I cast about for some commonplace remark to make, but in the state of my feelings it was not easy to find one, and it was he who again broke the silence:

"Tierce, poor fool! I warned him as I am warning you. It was two years afterward that she married him, and in two weeks more he was dead—dead in their house in Park Lane—died of heart disease! Heart disease!"

And as he said it, I could not help thinking of James Westerby.

My visitor was about to speak again when a football sounded on the stairs outside, the door opened, and my clerk stood in the entrance, astonished at the darkness.

"Come in, Jackson," I called, to let him know that I was there, and "light the gas, please."

My visitor rose painfully, and again took his crutch.

"I have told you all that is vital to the case," he said in the matter-of-fact voice of a client addressing his attorney, "and you will, of course, do as you think best."

Jackson, about to light the gas, with a burning match in his hand, held the door open for the stranger to pass out, and without another word the cripple moved laboriously away. It was not until he had gone that it occurred to me that I had not asked nor been told his name.

"Has that gentleman ever called before, Jackson?"

"I think not, sir."

But probably I should meet him again.

And now, my thoughts reverted to her. He was mad, of course: and his story was absurd. But as I walked home from the office, those eyes were before me, blazing with the passion which he had lit in them. What eyes they were in truth! How lovely, and how I loved them! And how easy, too, it was to imagine them dilating and engulfing one's senses until he swooned!

I had not hoped to see her again that day, having spent part of the morning in "helping her to shop," and expecting to escort her to the theatre on the evening following. So after a solitary dinner at a restaurant, I climbed up to my chambers to dream away the evening alone.

The story which I had heard a few hours before certainly had not in any way altered my feelings towards Mrs. Tierce. Indeed, I hardly thought of the story, except to pity the poor fellow who told it and to speculate upon his history. Who was he? Had he loved her and gone mad for love of her? And should I tell her of his visit? It might pain her by bringing up unpleasant memories; but on the other hand I should like to know something more of the cripple's history.

But I was restless, and my rooms seemed more than ever lonely and unhomelike that evening; so about nine o'clock, I put on my hat and overcoat and went out into the street.

It was a cold night, damp and raw, with no sign of starlight or moonlight overhead, and a heavy, misty atmosphere through which the street lights shone blurred and twinkling.

Instinctively I turned westward, and, as a matter of course, set my face towards Grasmere Crescent, not with any intention of calling at the house, but with a lover's longing to see it and to be near to her. I passed the house on the opposite side of the street. No. 19 had a large bow-window in the drawing room, on the first floor, and as I approached, the blind of the narrow side-window facing me being raised some few inches gave a glimpse of the brightly lighted, daintily furnished room, with which I was so familiar, within. I had hoped to catch a glimpse of her, but in the small segment of the room that was visible through the aperture, no figure was to be seen.

After passing on to the end of the street I made a circuit round some by-streets and so back to Grasmere Crescent. As I approached now from the north the house looked dark, save for a narrowest chink of light which outlined the edge of the bow-window. When I had passed I turned to look back at the window of which the blind was raised; and doing so, I saw a curious thing.

It was only instantaneous; but just for that instant I saw two figures standing, herself and one of the servants, whom I recognized. They were facing one another, each, it seemed, leaning slightly forward. But even as I looked, the servant suddenly threw up her hands and fell—fell straight backward, rigidly, as if in a fit. Mrs. Tierce started towards the falling girl, as if to catch her. The movement took her out of my range of vision, the projecting woodwork of the window intervening.

It all happened so suddenly that I stood for a moment bewildered and irresolute. Had I really seen it? It was more like some tableau on a stage, or the flash of a slide from a magic lantern, than a reality.

Recovering my senses, my first impulse was to cross the street and offer my services. But why? The girl had but slipped suddenly upon the polished floor, and doubtless they were laughing over it now. It would be an impertinence for me to thrust myself in with a confession of having been playing spy. So, after standing and gazing at the window for a few moments, during which I once saw Mrs. Tierce pass quickly across the room and back, I moved on to my rooms.

The next morning as I sat at breakfast, a note was brought to me.

"I am very sorry," she wrote, "to interfere with your theatre party this evening, but a dreadful thing happened here last night. One of my servants—Mary, you know her—died very suddenly. I was talking to her, when she simply threw up her hands and fell down before me, dead. Regretting that I must ask you to excuse me, I am,

> "Yours cordially,
> "EDITH TIERCE."

I wished now that I had obeyed my first impulse on the preceding evenings and had rung at the door to volunteer my services. I would certainly go and see her immediately after breakfast.

Fortunately my theatre party included only two other persons besides Mrs. Tierce and myself, and I was on sufficiently intimate terms with John Bradstreet and his wife to have no fear of offending them. So I wrote Mrs. Bradstreet a short note explaining the situation briefly, enclosing the tickets and hoping she would use the box or not, as she saw fit. Then I drove at once to Grasmere Crescent.

In her quiet, self-possessed way Mrs. Tierce had already done all that was necessary, and I found that there was little excuse for thrusting my services upon her. Still I saw her frequently during the next two days, though never for any length of time and rarely to talk of things not associated immediately with the melancholy ceremony that was impending. The dead girl seemed to have had no family connections, and the funeral was conducted under Mrs. Tierce's directions. I accompanied her to the church and cemetery, and left her at her own door afterwards, accepting an invitation to call again that evening.

I have spoken before of the curious self-possession, an imperturbable self-reliance, which Mrs. Tierce possessed and which sat very becomingly upon her delicate grave face. Never had this quality in her seemed more admirably perfect to me than during those days when the shadow of death hung over her home.

On the evening of the day of the funeral, she was even more reposeful than usual, in a dreamy mood in which I had seen her before more than once, and in which she seemed hardly conscious of—or rather inattentive to—what passed around her. This mood of hers the cripple had recalled to me when describing the scene in the Oxford walk.

It may have been that the events and scenes of the last few days, with all their appeals to the emotions, had predisposed us both to tenderness. Certainly from the time of my entry when our greeting had been only a hand-clasp, with hardly an audible word on either side, we had spoken constrainedly, in undertones and on personal topics. Though more than once I strove desperately to be matter-of-fact, my voice in spite of myself would sink, and wherever the conversation started from, it ended in herself.

At last some chance word of hers made me broach a subject which I had never approached before, and which she rarely alluded to—her late husband. Before I was conscious of what I was doing, I had said:

"It is not, by any means, I know, your first contact with death. You have told me very little of Mr. Tierce."

"No," she said dreamily, "there is little to tell. We were only married a few weeks."

And then:

"And is it not possible that you might marry again? Could you not?" and I crossed from my chair to take a seat on the sofa by her side, "could you not—is there any hope for me?"

Instead of replying, she sat silent and inattentive, her large swimming eyes looking far into either the past or the future—I wondered which.

"Tell me," I urged, laying my hand on one of hers, as it rested in her lap, "tell me, is there any hope?"

She did not move, did not answer me. Again I implored her, and at last she spoke, but with seeming irrelevance.

"Did you ever hear of the Court of Love?" she asked, "the court over which the Countess Ermengarde presided in the tenth or eleventh century?"

No, I knew nothing of the Court of Love or the Countess Ermengarde, though I have since looked them up.

"The Court decided, and the decision was affirmed by a later Court composed of half the queens and duchesses of Europe, that true love could not exist between married persons."

"But you do not believe it? That was nice centuries ago; and how should queens and duchesses know anything of love?"

"I do not know whether I believe it or not," she murmured, and turned her head as it lay on the cushions of the sofa, to look at me with eyes that still seemed strangely dreamy and far away.

"But you do know," I urged impulsively, leaning forward till my face was dangerously close to hers. "You know that you do not believe it. You know that I should always love you—that I must always love you. And if I may love you as my wife—"

She smiled faintly, charmingly, but did not answer me.

"My darling," I whispered, "say something! Am I to be utterly happy?"

And still she did not answer; but leaned back with the faint half-smile on her lips, and her great inscrutable eyes looking into and through mine. Then in the silence and suspense, the cripple's story came into my mind. No wonder that he should believe that he had been fascinated in some mysterious way—spell-bound, benumbed—by those eyes! No wonder! And still I looked into them; and still they looked through mine. I forgot the nearness of her lips; forgot that I held her hand. I thought only of, saw only, those eyes. And still I thought only of the cripple and vaguely pitied him.

But somehow—when it began I knew not—I found that the expression of the eyes had changed. They were no longer dreamy and far away, but intensely earnest, with a passion in them that was almost hunger.

"Yes," I thought to myself (and I must have smiled in thinking it), "this is what he described. No wonder that they seemed to him to flame. They are not looking at my eyes now, but through, into my brain, into me. My eyes are no more than two pieces of glass in the path of her vision." And I felt a curious, half-gratified recognition of the accuracy of the other's description. And still the eyes seemed to expand until they were many times larger than my own; till I could see nothing but them.

Have you ever, in a half-darkened room, set your face close against a mirror and looked into your own eyes and seen what terrible things they are; how the view of everything else is shut out and all your sense is drawn into the pupils confronting you? So I felt my whole being concentrating itself in—merging itself into—drowning in—her eyes. A strange feeling of intoxication possessed me; of ecstacy. I could have laughed aloud, but that it seemed as if to do it I would somehow have to summon my faculties from too far away.

At what point this strange calmness gave way to conscious fear, I do not know. I saw the pupils of her eyes expanding and contracting, as if with the regular beats of a passionate pulse behind them. I saw, or rather I was aware, that the colour flushed into her cheeks and died again, that her breath, which was warm on my face, came short and gasping. Her lips closed and parted, moist and glistening, suggesting to me somehow the craving of some animal in the presence of food which it could not reach.

Her nostrils dilated, quivering, and her whole being strained with a passion which seemed carnivorous.

"It was as if she preyed upon my very life," he had said, and I understood him now. But the memory of the cripple was fading from me. I was conscious only of myself and of her; of the terror of her fierce hunger and my own helplessness. The power of motion was gone from me; even volition seemed slipping away. The burning of her eyes was in my brain which was as if laid open before her; as a hollow dish set open to the scorching sun. I was utterly at her mercy, without power of resistance; and as her breath grew yet more rapid and more heavy, I knew that she was in some way inhaling my very life.

Suddenly a flash of fear passed across her face—a spasm of agonised disappointment. For a moment it was as if she would, in one long, indrawn breath, draw the last of my strength from me; and then a man's voice sounded in my ear.

"I hope I am in time!"

She had fallen reclining against the cushions of the sofa. I looked up dazedly, and the cripple stood in the centre of the room, his hat in his hand.

"You had better let me take you away," he said, and I heard it half consciously. Turning to look at her, I saw her lie panting and exhausted. I cannot tell the horror of her appearance. Her eyes still sought mine hungrily as before. Her hands, lying in her lap, fumbled each other, her fingers knotting and intertwining. Her lips moved, and all her body quivered with passion. It was a dreadful fancy, but I could liken her to nothing but some blood-sucking thing; some human leech or vampire, torn from its prey, quivering dumbly with its unsated appetite.

At the time I only half understood what passed around me. I knew that the danger was over and what escape lay before me. I saw the cripple waiting for me to rise and was conscious of the horror with which she inspired me. But I was bewildered. My brain seemed numb, and when I endeavoured to stand up my limbs refused their office. Seeing my powerlessness the cripple moved forward and with his healthy arm assisted me. It was with difficulty I stood, for there was no sensation in my feet or legs and it was only by leaning on my companion that I made my way laboriously to the door.

No word had been spoken beyond the two sentences which the cripple had uttered. Reaching the door of the room I turned to look at her once more, supporting myself against the door-post. She had not moved. Under the influence of the passion that was upon her she evidently had no thought or emotion. There was no sign of shame or confusion on her face; nothing but the blind craving for the prey that was being taken from her. Even there, across the full width of the room, her eyes sought mine with the same despairing longing. But she only made me shudder now. The cripple still supporting me, we passed together from the house.

Of the remainder of that evening my memory is confused and faint. I know that I was helping to my chambers and that there, with the assistance of the cripple and some third person, though who, or whence he joined us, I know not, I was put to bed. That night was one long, half-waking swoon, and far into the next afternoon I lay motionless upon my back without speaking or wishing to speak, save only to tell the woman who took care of my rooms that I needed no help or food. As the twilight fell the same good woman came again, and yet again late at night. But I was scarcely conscious, and had no wishes. Even speech was an effort.

For seven days, all through the Christmas holidays, I lay in this state, taking little nourishment; hardly speaking, hardly thinking clearly. At last, on the day after Christmas, I found courage and strength to attack the mail which had been accumulating on my sick-room table. I had expected to find her handwriting on one at least of the envelopes. In this I was disappointed. But some instinct led me to open first one envelope the address of which was written in a hand that was strange to me. It contained nothing but a newspaper clipping:

"A sad accident occurred last night at 19 Grasmere Crescent, W. The house was inhabited by Mrs. Walter Tierce, the widow of the late Walter Tierce, Esq. Last evening Mrs. Tierce, who was twenty-six years of age, retired to rest as usual. This morning she failed to answer the knock of the servant at the door, and on the maid entering the room she noticed a strong and peculiar odour. She was frightened and went out and fetched another servant. The two entered the room and found Mrs. Tierce dead, and an overturned bottle of chloroform by the pillow. It was evidently an accident, and no inquest will be held. A curious coincidence in connection with the sad affair is that this is the second death in the same house within a week. On Monday last, a maid in the service of Mrs. Tierce died suddenly of heart disease. Her funeral occurred yesterday afternoon, when Mrs. Tierce attended it."

Attached to this clipping with a pin was the date line of the evening newspaper from which it was taken—"Friday, December 19th." That was the day after that terrible evening, and a week ago now. The funeral must have already taken place.

Though, as I have said, the handwriting on the envelope was unfamiliar to me, I had my conjecture as to whom the message was from, and after keeping the envelope for all these years, the clue has come which shows that the conjecture was correct. Six weeks ago I received information that I had been appointed executor of the estate of the late James Livingston, of Hereford. James Livingston? The name was unknown to me. Thinking that there might be some mistake, I called at the solicitor's office from which the intimation came. No, there was no mistake, the solicitor informed me; he had drawn up the will, and Mr. Livingston had given him special instructions how to communicate with me.

"And you say you never knew him at all?" he asked musingly, "that is certainly curious for he seemed to know you. But you could not well have forgotten him. He was a cripple—almost entire paralysed in his right side."

# R. Murray Gilchrist:
## The Lover's Ordeal (1905)

Robert Murray Gilchrist (1867–1917) is an anomaly. He wrote several novels about rural life in the Peakland District of Derbyshire, but he is remembered today for his decadent fiction; including his contributions to Aubrey Beardsley's *The Yellow Book*—which published his vampire tale "The Crimson Weaver" in July of 1895.

His first collection, *The Stone Dragon and Other Tragic Romances* (London: Methuen, 1894) is treasured for its contents and is extremely rare. Charon Press published a facsimile edition of *The Stone Dragon* in 1998, while Ash Tree Press collected all of Gilchrist's horror stories in a limited edition titled *The Basilisk: And Other Tales of Dread* in 2003.

"The Lover's Ordeal" first appeared in *The London Magazine* (June 1905), which often carried supernatural stories by the likes of Richard Marsh and H. G. Wells.

---

Mary Padley stood near the leaden statue of Diana on the terrace at Calton Dovecote, gazing towards the stone-arched gate that barred the avenues of limes—sweet scented, with their newly opened bloom—from the dusty high-road.

She wore white—a mantua of thin silk, a stiff petticoat spread over a great hoop, and a quaint stomacher, lilac in colour, and embroidered with silver beads.

Her hair was cushioned and powdered, Madam Padley, her grandmother and guardian, insisting that, since she would probably soon change her estate, she must cease playing the hoyden, and devote herself to a careful study of such fashions as leaked from town to the Peak Country.

It may be stated, however, that the dame, in calling her a hoyden, spoke tenderly enough, since she knew that her sole living descendent had sterling and admirable qualities, combined with a physical loveliness that promised to make her a reigning toast after her union with Mr Endymion Eyre, heir-presumptive to my Lord Newburgh.

Madam, herself being high-spirited, doted upon—though she outwardly condemned—the maid's too fervent love of the romantic and uncommon.

But, at the present moment, Madam Padley had very kindly fallen asleep beside her embroidery-frame, and Mary had stolen from the house to watch for Mr Eyre's coming.

She held in her right hand a folded sheet. A ray of the westering sun touched the words: 'The Spectator, No. 557. Wednesday, June 23, 1714.'

The minutes dragged. She opened the first page, and began to peruse, for the twentieth time, a letter which her lover, who was gifted with some literary power, had addressed to Addison, partly for the sake of eliciting one of that master's wise disquisitions.

'Mr Spectator,' she read softly—'Since the decline of chivalry, a man has no opportunity of proving his devotion to the lady of his choice. Why not permit her to name some ordeal through which he must pass, and by whose performance he might win her from the fullest trust and faith, without which a true marriage is impossible—'

She read no more, for she heard the sound of his mare's hoofs in the distance. A bright smile lighted her face; her colour rose faintly. 'Here comes my author,' she said, 'speeding to hear my yea or nay. Heigho! I wish my heart would not beat so wildly! For all the world 'tis as if I'd stolen a fledgling and prisoned it in my bosom!'

He dismounted at the foot of a mossy staircase. A groom came forward to take the bridle. Mary curtsied her prettiest, then gave him her hand to lift to his lips.

'This evening,' he said laughingly, 'this evening you promised to tell me whether you'd marry me or no. Of course, the asking's but a formality, for I'm fully resolved to make you.'

'Alack,' she cried, 'you've a pretty fashion of showing me that I've met my master! Well, good Mr Eyre, you have courted me for a full year, and I've known you all my life, and, as you are aware, I've no aversion for your person. Yes—yes, I'll marry you—on one condition.'

'And that—' he began.

'You've set my heart upon making you pass through an ordeal. Don't suspect for a moment that I'm ignorant as to who wrote this.' She held her Spectator aloft. 'You've asked to be tested—'

'The deuce upon my scribblings!' he exclaimed. 'Well, mistress, whatever you wish I'll do with the utmost expedition, on one condition—that being that it does not take me long from you. Tell me the ordeal, sweet. I'm eager to pass through it—to have you swear that I'm a worthy man.'

Their eyes met fondly.

'I ne'er doubted that,' she said; 'but all girls have their whimsies. Come down into the park. 'Tis a night made for lovers.'

Then she gave him her hand again; and they went together through the narrow walk of the rosary, where the beautiful flowers were all wet with dew, to a knoll about half a mile from Dovecote, whence one could see almost forty miles of rough moorland and wood passing upwards towards the North Country.

A crescent moon hung overhead. There was no sound save the sighing of the wind and the churring of the moth-hawks.

Mary paused when they reached the summit, and pointed to another hill about three miles away—a strange conical place covered with great trees, from whose tops rose several stacks of twisted chimneys.

'You wish, then, to pass through the ordeal?' she said. 'You are no coward, and that which I set you to do needs a brave spirit. 'Tis—'tis to spend a night at Calton Hall, where no living creature has been after dark since my folk left it eighty years ago. The place is haunted—or so 'tis said—and 'twill require all your courage to pass the midnight hours in those deserted suites.'

He interrupted her by taking her into his arms, quite in an informal fashion, and silencing her lips by the pressure of his own.

'May it be done tonight?' he asked. 'Let me perform this valorous deed at once, and so become a hero in your eyes.'

'Ay,' responded Mary. 'I have the key of the door—I took it unseen from my grandmother's basket. If I had asked for it, be sure she'd not have consented. There's none has a keener belief than she in the mystery that haunts the place o' nights. So, since you sup with us, I'd have you say naught concerning the ordeal, or she'd at once forbid it.'

They returned to the house now. Madam Padley, who had awakened some minutes before, met them in the hall.

She was a stately old woman, still comely despite her seventy years. In youth she had been a lady-in-waiting to the Duchess of York; and her manner still suggested the atmosphere of a Court. As she possessed both fine wit and intuition, she read aright the radiance of the lovers' faces.

'I offer my profound congratulations,' she said. 'Mr Eyre, I'm vastly proud that you're to enter our family. In short, there's no gentleman I've e'er met whom I'd liefer receive as grandson. But, putting the blind god aside, supper is already served; and I am amazingly hungry. Your arm, Endymion. Young miss shall walk behind.'

Throughout the elaborate meal she talked incessantly, preaching a dainty homily on the duties of married folk.

Afterwards Mary and Endymion confessed to each other that they remembered nothing of what she had said, their own thoughts being engaged in rosy pictures of the future.

When the meal was over, they passed to the withdrawing-room, where Mary sat to the new harpsichord and played sweet songs from Purcell's operas.

At ten o'clock Madam Padley rose from her chair and signified courteously that 'twas time for the gentleman to retire, but cordially invited him to spend the following evening in the same fashion.

Mary accompanied him to the courtyard, where a groom waited with his mare. Now that he was starting for the ordeal, the girl's heart failed of a sudden; and she begged him to forget her words. He laughed merrily, and shook his head.

'Too late,' he said. 'I go now to Calton. Not for the world would I renounce the adventure. When I see you again, I shall have wonderful stories of ghosts for your ear alone. If they be harmless things, why, you and I'll go together afterwards to pay 'em a visit of ceremony! Now, adieu, mistress. Sleep well, and dream pretty dreams.'

He turned thrice in his saddle, and waved his hand. She stood watching until he was out of sight. Then she went back very sadly to the house, and, finding that her grandmother had already retired, sought her own chamber, where, instead of undressing, she sat in a deep window-recess, peering through an open case- ment at the moonlit chimneys of the distant house.

Meanwhile, Eyre rode on leisurely over moor and through copse until he reached the neglected pleasance, where the under- growth had matted together until there was scarce space to reach the stairs leading to the colonnade.

He left the mare in a small courtyard, where dock and nettles had covered the stones with a thick carpet; then, making his way to the front, opened the door and entered the musty hall.

There he took out his tinder-box, and struck a light, finding, much to his relief, a tall wax candle standing in a sconce near the mantel. This he lighted, and, holding it high above his head, made his way up the oaken stairs, and through a long gallery, at whose further end stood an open doorway that led to the suite of state-rooms. These were hung with moth-eaten tapestry. In places the decayed canvases of ancient portraits trailed from their frames to the floor. The movement of the light brought around him clouds of evil-smelling bats; two owls on the sill of a broken oriel hooted loudly, then fluttered out into the night.

On and on, through countless chambers whose antique magnificence was veiled with dust and cobwebs, until he came to another and greater door, which stood slightly ajar. And as he pressed the panel with his palm he saw that the place beyond was lighted with a curious radiance—greenish, cold—not unlike the moonlight on a frosty evening.

The door fell back easily. He found himself in a great chamber, the walls adorned with coloured bas-reliefs; the ceiling, still bright and vivid, covered with a gorgeous fresco wherein one saw the gods at play. On the two hearths fires burned—inaudible fires with greedy, lambent flames whose tongues licked the mantel stone.

'By the Lord!' he exclaimed, 'there are folk living here! This is no place for ghosts! As handsome a—'

His voice died, for something had moved at the further end—something hidden in the shadow of a canopy of velvet embroidered with gold thread.

The muscles of his heart tightened. He moved forward, almost unsteadily, holding the candle at arm's length, until he came to the lowest step of a low platform, whereon, in a lacquered chair, rested a form shrouded in a veil of black gauze. And, as he paused there, this veil stirred again, disclosing the figure of a young woman, whose long, white hands moved slowly from her face.

Her eyes opened. They were large and luminous, gleaming as if a steady fire burned behind the pupils. She was wondrously beautiful; her loveliness was greater than that of any woman he had ever dreamed of—greater even than that of the maiden to whom he had given his heart. She was strangely pale, the only colour—a vivid scarlet—being in the plump, curved lips.

'I bid you welcome, signor,' she said. 'The long, long sleep has not been wasted since you are the awakener. Your hand! Weariness is still in my body. I'd fain rise and walk.'

Her voice was exquisitely soft, exquisitely glad. 'Twas not the voice of an Englishwoman. There was a quaint accent, as if she had come from a Southern country. And the hand Endymion took was cold and damp at first—as cold and damp as the hand of one prepared for burial; but, as it lay lightly in his own, it became warm, and the fingers closed tenderly upon his own.

'Your name, signor of whom I have dreamed?' she said.

The blood began to run quickly through his veins.

'Endymion, madam, at your service,' he replied.

'And mine shall be Diana,' she said. 'Diana, who kissed Endymion in the night. Prythee, now, your arm. I'll lean upon you, being but a weak creature. Ah me, but your country's sad! I'd give all for the warm skies of Tuscany—for the vineyards under the hot sun! I like not the moonlight.'

Something impelled him to talk foolishly.

''Tis not the warmth of skies or the sight of vineyards that makes for perfect happiness,' he said. 'There's a rarer warmth—the warmth of love.'

She laid her right palm upon his lips.

'Hush!' she said. 'At this our first meeting why should you talk of love? Doubtless there's some cold, pretty girl living for you alone in the world—some green creature who dotes upon you—who looks to the day when she may call you spouse, unless 'tis so already.'

Then, with a swift movement of the left arm, she drew aside the tapestry from a great window that stretched from floor to pargeting. Beyond, through glass clear as crystal, he could see the moor, white in the moonlight, as if covered with hoar-frost.

'Behold the winter!' said the lady. 'Behold the cruelty of your country! Alas, I am outdone with the cold! Let's to yonder fire for warmth.'

The curtain fell back again. Together they went across the chamber.

Not once in all that time did he bestow one thought upon the girl he loved—the girl whose promise he had won that very night. Past and future were blotted from his mind. He lived solely in the present.

The beauty chose a great chair, covered with crimson silk—a chair with carved arms and legs and padded face-screens

'I sit here, my cavalier,' she said; 'and you rest at my feet. Yonder's a stool. Your head shall lie upon my knee.'

She drew from a tissue bag that hung from her girdle a handful of dried petals, and flung them between the andirons. The fire engulfed them silently. A blood-coloured flame rose high up the chimney.

A strange commingling of luxury and dread came over Endymion. He sank to her feet.

She drew his face, with both hands, to her lap. The she bowed her head until her soft lips touched his neck.

Mary found herself unable to sleep—unable even to prepare for bed.

In less than an hour after Endymion's departure her disquietude became so painful that she left her chamber and hastened to Madam Padley's bedside.

The old lady was sleeping placidly. Her white horsehair headdress had been replaced by a decent cap of plaited linen.

The girl laid a trembling hand upon her shoulder.

'Waken, grandmother,' she said. 'Waken, I am miserable. I have done something that I had no right to do. I am bewildered. Some evil thing is happening!'

The dame started, and sat up.

'What is't child?' she said. 'Art troubled with a nightmare?'

Mary spoke disconnectedly. Madam listened, piecing the broken sentences together; then she flung aside the bedclothes.

'My God,' she cried, 'you have done wrongly! I had never wished to tell you, but the reason—the reason why yonder house is deserted is that your great-grandfather wooed and wed for second wife a foreign woman, who fed upon human blood! And the place grew foul with strange crimes!'

She rang for her Abigail; but before the worthy woman could appear Mary had fled from the chamber and from the house. In another minute the great firebell of the Dovecote was clanging wildly, and the servants leaping from their beds. Madam Padley could not speak for excitement. Her gestures alone bade them follow with all speed in the girl's tracks.

Mary reached the hall long before the others, and, entering through the open doorway, ran up the gallery and passed from room to room, calling passionately upon her lover's name. The moonlight shone now through the latticed windows. Every-where she saw bats flying into the corners. At last she reached the great chamber, not lighted now with mysterious fires, but dark and dusty, and fetid of odour.

Endymion lay prone upon the floor; beside him crouched a woman's figure, the head pressed close to his own. And Mary took the thing madly by the shoulders and thrust it aside, and linked her arms around the young man's waist.

His eyes opened; she heard the sound of his breathing.

'There's naught for it save that I drag you from the place,' she whispered. 'Who knows that she may not bring others stronger than I?'

'I have dreamed terribly,' he muttered; 'dreamed of things that I dare not tell.'

In the gallery he rose awkwardly to his feet, and, leaning heavily against her, stumbled to the staircase.

'Had you not come, dearest one,' he said, 'all the blood had left my body.'

There the servants mat them, and prepared a rough litter, in which he was carried back to the Dovecote. Mary followed, but not until after she had done something that ere another night had blotted Calton Hall out of existence. As she left the place she set fire to the tapestries, and the woodwork took flame almost instantly. Since 'twas her own heritage none could complain. When Madam Padley and Endymion heard they said nothing; but it was easy to see that they approved.

And when, two days afterwards, he was permitted to leave his room and sit with Mary in the sunlit garden, and she took his hand and held it to her bosom, and begged him to forgive her for submitting to such a weird ordeal, he put his disengaged arm around her neck and begged her to be silent.

'For, sweet,' he said, 'there's shame in my happiness. That night hath shown me how nobler is your love than mine.'

# Lionel Sparrow:
# The Vengeance of the Dead (1907)

Lionel Sparrow (1867-1936) lived most of his life in Linton where he owned the local newspaper, *The Grenville Standard*. He wrote more than two dozen stories for *The Australian Journal*.

James Doig, who has taken on the task of educating readers about the richness of early Australian horror fiction, discovered the following story. He reprinted it in *Australian Gothic: An Anthology of Australian Supernatural Fiction: 1867-1939* (Mandurah, WA, Australia: Equilibrium Books, 2007), and has been kind enough to share it with us.

---

## I.

The disappearance of Martin Calthorpe—"that wonderful man", as his admirers called him, "that arch-impostor," as he was stigmatised by others—was something more than a nine days' wonder, and it has not yet quite faded out of the recollection of those who are attracted or impressed by such mysteries. These will have no difficulty in recalling the circumstances, so far as they were known, of his evanishment. The mystery, however, was so complete that little was left to feed the curiosity of the quidnuncs. When it is stated that he had an appointment with a "client" in his chambers in Brunswick-street on an afternoon of November, 1892, and was waited for in vain, and that he was not seen or heard of afterwards by anyone who could or would admit the fact, the available information (outside of these memoirs) is pretty well exhausted. Some particulars, however, may be added concerning his antecedents preliminary to the well-nigh incredible story of how the mystery was subsequently revealed.

"Professor" Calthorpe was apparently one of those strange beings who, finding themselves possessed of powers outside the cognisance of material science, set about turning them to pecuniary account, without seeking to probe their inner meaning, without realising their legitimate uses. (I say "apparently" for a reason which will be developed later.)

Calthorpe described himself as a hypnotist, a psychometrist, and one or two other "ists"; also as a Clairvoyant. In some or all of these capacities he was remarkably successful, to judge by the number of people who were willing to pay him liberally for whatever services he rendered them. Indeed, the house in Brunswick-street was daily besieged by the many who believe in occult phenomena. The professor had a wife, who was a noted spiritualistic medium, and who also drew a handsome income from her "profession."

It was suggestive of the irony of fate that I, who looked upon such people as Professor and Mrs. Calthorpe as little better than criminal impostors, and their clients as mere gulls, should find my destiny involved with theirs. So, at least, I thought then. Later events have changed my opinions considerably, but they have not increased my respect for the crew who seek to tamper with the mysteries of life and death for their personal profit. However, I must not anticipate.

The professor, as I have said, disappeared. He failed to keep his appointment; and the clients waited in vain. The man of mystic powers was not again seen in his usual sphere of life, and all efforts made to trace him failed. His wife could throw no light upon the mystery— —or would not. She seemed greatly agitated—overcome by a sort of terror rather than by natural grief. My friend, Detective Mainspray, who was engaged in the matter, gave me these particulars. Mrs. Calthorpe did not long survive her husband. From the day of his disappearance she gave up her "work," if so it might be called, and fell into a kind of lethargy of horror, like one obsessed, making no effort to arouse herself, though by no means resigning herself to the thought of death. Her bodily vigour (which had been great) declined with remarkable rapidity, but as the end approached a frantic rebellion seemed to rise within her. The final scenes were made memorable by circumstances in the highest degree calculated to unnerve those who witnessed them. I, of course, was not present, but I was told that the dying woman's appearance and demeanour were fan from being marked by that tranquillity with which those who are at peace with conscience usually approach the solemn portals of death.

The appalling intensity of her despair shocked the few friends who stood around her death-bed. She seemed to be struggling in the tolls of an adversary invisible to them, but only too tangibly present to herself. This death-agony was attributed by some of those who witnessed it to an exaggerated horror of the common fate; the more thoughtful, however, accepted this view with extreme reluctance. Later developments, in which I had part, threw a light upon the mystery. The cause of her death was given as heart disease, accelerated by abnormal neurotic conditions connected with the practice of her "profession" as a medium. A circumstance which greatly puzzled not only her friends, but also the physicians who attended her, was her excessive appetite for rich foods during the last few weeks of her life: this appetite, increasing with a rapid loss of flesh, seemed wholly inexplicable. Those who, knowing the quantities of food she had daily assimilated, looked at last upon a body bloodless and emaciated to an incredible degree, were stricken dumb with wonderment and horror.

## II.

Neither the disappearance of Martin Calthorpe nor the death of his wife would have interested me to any considerable degree, but for the fact that I knew my parents to have been acquainted with the man. My father, moody, reticent as he had always been within my memory of him, was not likely to divulge any secrets concerning his past life. Through my friend Mainspray, however, I had glimpses of his early career, which taught me that the book of a man's life may contain pages which it is not wise nor well for a son to turn; and, apart from the bald fact that many years earlier a powerful hatred had been engendered between the two men, through some wrong committed by Calthorpe, I knew little, and sought no further knowledge. When the hypnotist disappeared, however, it became plain to me that my father's gloom had sensibly deepened, and I could not help wondering if this had any connection with the matter. My mother had died only a few months before, after a lingering illness, however, and her death would seem to supply a sufficient and more natural cause for the change observable in the bereaved husband.

My father at first neglected, then finally resigned his business affairs into my charge, and thenceforth lived a very secluded life. I saw but little of him, for he seemed hardly aware at times of my existence. Nothing could exceed, however, the moody intensity of the affection he lavished upon his two daughters, Constance and Winifred. Winnie, the younger, was (if he had any preference) his favourite, for her eyes were startlingly like her mother's. We lived in a rather large house near the St. Kilda-road, about two miles from the city. He owned another house in South Yarra, which should have brought in a substantial sum in rent, but it was out of repair, and, for some reason, he would not allow it to be touched.

Not long after the strange death of Mrs. Calthorpe, my father sought medical advice for our Winnie. We all, Winnie included, were rather surprised, for we could see no cause for alarm in her appearance. Winnie herself protested that she felt well enough, except that she found it rather a bore to cycle or play tennis, and much preferred to go out driving with our friends, the Thorntons, in their new motor car. Old Dr. Gair found nothing the matter with her, except that perhaps she was just a trifle less buxom than a girl of her age and build might be. I think he prescribed some sort of tonic. My father received his optimistic verdict with a gloomy contempt, and it was plain that he was by no means satisfied. The incident passed, and for the time we thought no more about it.

Some weeks later, however, I happened to enter the drawing room, where my sisters were talking, and Winnie was saying –

"No; I can't explain it. And I have such strange dreams, too."

"What sort of dreams, sis?" I asked, lightly; but a glance at her serious face told me that she was in no mood for banter.

"Father seems to have been right, after all," said Connie, in her quiet tones; "Win is getting run down."

I looked at the girl more intently. She was paler than I had ever noticed her to be, and her hands had certainly rather a fragile appearance. She was about eighteen at this time, and should have been flushed with exuberant health. Indeed, a few months before she had been full of a somewhat hoydenish energy and vigour. Now all was changed.

Next week my father took her away to the Blue Mountains. They returned towards the fall of the year, but the girl had not improved. In fact, she had barely held her own. My father called in the best specialists, but they were evidently puzzled by the very simplicity of the case. There was no organic disease, either acute or chronic—no disease of any sort; only a growing weakness, an increasing languor; days darkened by a strange weariness, and nights poisoned by dreams which she would not tell.

To me Winnie was a child—"the baby"; and thus I was on more intimate terms with Connie, who was then in her early twenties. We talked the matter over many times, and discussed the expediency of taking the girl away for a more extended trip.

"It would do you good also, Con," I said; "you're not looking too well."

I said this without attaching much meaning to the words, but Connie gave something of a start.

"Do you think so?" she said; "perhaps I've been worrying about Win. But, really, I don't feel quite myself lately."

This made me look at her closely, and I saw that there was indeed a noticeable change. But the summer had been very trying, and, as she said, the anxiety about Winnie was enough to account for a certain lowering of physical tone.

## III.

My father did not fall in with the proposed trip. He only laughed bitterly when it was mooted, and said, in a harsh voice –

"What's the use? There's no hope."

"No hope." I shall never forget the note of tragic despair in those final words. It was as if a fiat had gone forth—as if in some strange way Irrevocable Fate had spoken with his voice.

In these councils of ours Harry Thornton had borne no part. For some reason or other Connie, who had at this time been engaged to him for nearly a year, was unwilling to take him into her confidence in the matter, and as time went on and her own health did not improve, she became even less inclined to talk about it with him.

Thornton was a strange young fellow in many ways. Whilst he was fond of an outdoor life, excelling in all kinds of athletics, I knew him to be equally inclined to intellectual pursuits; in fact, he took up branches of study quite foreign to ordinary taste Some years before, he had rather startled his friends by becoming the intimate of one Ravana Dâs, a Hindu pundit of the highest caste (Brahmans), and reputed to possess an extraordinary degree of erudition, both Western and Oriental. Thornton made what we chaffingly called a "pilgrimage" to his Eastern friend, and on his return it was plain that: he took his "master", as he called him, with intense seriousness. He continued to correspond with this man, whose portrait had an honoured place on the wall of his study. The face was a remarkable one. It was as clearly and delicately cut as a bronze medallion of a proud, yet gentle, expression, and gave one the idea of a learned ascetic. A certain power, also, seemed to breathe from those features. Anyone studying the portrait (which was done in a sepia by an Indian artist) could readily understand the fascination which the man might exercise over impressionable natures.

The Thorntons were wealthy people, and the young man had license to gratify his fancies. But he lived an extremely simple and blameless life, and I knew of no one more eligible as a husband for Connie, whose tastes, moreover, had much in common with his own.

Harry was not long in perceiving Connie's decline in health; and, connecting it, as I imagined, with that of her sister, grew very anxious. One day, after having taken them for an outing in his motor car, he asked me to accompany him to his rooms in the city.

He said little on the way, but once in his "den" he spoke abruptly of Winnie's illness, which was at this time rapidly progressing.

"What do you think of it?" he asked.

"The doctors advise a complete change of climate," I said, vaguely.

"Humbug!" he muttered.

"It seems the only chance," I said; "but my father has set his face against it. Says there's no hope; but, or course—"

"The girl will die," he said, in a decisive tone. "The only man who could save her is away in the Himalayas, and could not be reached within I don't know how many months."

"You mean -"

"Ravana Dâs—yes. He might do it . . . or tell us how."

"Is he a physician, then?"

"More than that. But it is not exactly a physician that is needed, Burford. There is nothing, I think, vitally wrong with Winnie. But there are possibilities that medical science knows nothing of. This vague talk about 'going into a decline' is merely a veil for ignorance."

"Well, old man, it you can supply a better hypothesis, one that we can work on, I shall be very grateful," I said, a trifle ironically.

"I can't do that—yet." he said, "I don't know enough; and what I fear is too awfully improbable to spring upon an old sceptic like yourself . . . Tell me," he added abruptly, "did your father know that man Calthorpe, the hypnotist, who disappeared about a year ago?"

"Yes—why?" I answered, staring at him in a sort of terror, for which I could not account.

"What was the nature of this acquaintance?" he asked.

"Its nature? Well, I know very little. My father suffered at his hands in some way, and I believe that in a less law abiding country their enmity would have had a tragic ending."

"Burford, your father killed that man!"

"You are mad, my boy—stark, staring mad!"

"Not a bit of it. Oh! If only my master were accessible!"

He stared in a sort of yearning rapture at the portrait on the wall, as if to draw inspiration from it.

"Why do you connect this man Calthorpe with the matter?" I asked. "In the first place, it is not known whether the man is alive or dead."

"Your father's fate is bound up with that man's, Frank," he said, gloomily. "I don't know how. But I can dimly perceive possibilities that horrify me. I did not remark Winnie's extreme weakness till quite lately—unobservant ass that I am! . . . After all, I may be mistaken—the thing seems altogether too hideous—too incredible!"

"This is some beastly superstition your precious master has been filling you up with," I said, impatiently. "Winnie is not the first girl who has gone into a decline. I don't see how Hindu philosophers can help her any more than European physicians."

He made no reply. He was apparently absorbed in the face of the Hindu pundit, and did not seem to hear me. I saw no profit in staying longer, so, with an abrupt 'Good-night!' to which I got no reply, I left him.

The next day Winnie did not rise till late in the evening; and, after that, not at all. She declined with an accelerated rapidity, and in ten days passed to her long rest. The close of her life was very peaceful; even the dreams, which had been 'too dreadful to tell,' left her on the seventh day from her decease. She had long intervals of trance-like sleep, from which she brought back vague memories at an indescribable bliss—as though the spirit, impatient of its fleshly tabernacle, could with difficulty be held to earth by the feeble thread of life.

I need not dwell upon our sorrow. That of my father found some doubtful relief in alcohol and drugs; and only the solicitude and devotion of his surviving daughter saved him, for the time, from utter despair.

"For her sake," he said to me, "I will try and keep up; but she also is doomed—my boy—she also is doomed."

"Why do you talk like this?" I demanded.

His eye grew wild. "There are devils," he said, thickly: "or men with devilish arts. You may stab them through and through with knives—you may spatter their brains on the wall with bullets—no use! They come back in the night and mock you: they rob you of your dearest ones . . . "

I thought of Thornton's words, and said—

"Had you anything to do with the disappearance of that man Calthorpe?"

He started as if stung then broke into a harsh laugh.

"The devil should claim his own, one would think," he muttered. "But what are you driving at?" he asked, suddenly raising his head and meeting my eye sternly. "What should I know about Calthorpe's disappearance?"

"I had the idea that in some way—hypnotism or something—the man may have had a hand in—"

"Her death? Nonsense, boy! You rave!"

He would say no more.

## IV.

By some process of unconscious reasoning, I had evolved the idea that Calthorpe, dead though he was, was exerting a hypnotic power over my sisters, thus striking at my father through his loved ones. It may seem strange that I, a hard-headed man of the world, should have given any attention to such occult hypotheses. But I had lost one beloved sister through a most mysterious malady, and now that malady threatened the other.

Having questioned orthodox science in vain, however, in my extremity, I lent an ear to the suggestions of an alleged knowledge of forces lying outside the range of ordinary experience—a knowledge I had hitherto denied and ridiculed, as the pretension of predatory quacks and impostors. The drowning man catches at straws, and every straw seems a plank of safety.

Connie very soon developed all the symptoms which had marked her sister's decline: and she, too, had mysterious dreams, which no argument or persuasion could induce her to disclose, and which evidently filled her with a conviction that she was doomed.

One day she came to me front her father's room, in a state of wild agitation.

"You must watch him," she said. "He is very near madness. I think he will destroy himself."

"What has he said?"

"Oh, his talk is very wild—I can make little of it. He is possessed with the idea of some enemy—someone who is dead. 'I must seek him in his own place,' he keeps on saying; 'I will find him, and drag him down—down!' Oh, the wildest language! It terrifies me."

I soothed her as best I could; and then, obeying some impulse, for which I could not account, I went to Thornton's rooms, though not expecting to see him. I found him there, however, and he greeted me with an intense earnestness.

"I am glad you have come," he said; I have received a communication."

"From whom?"

"My master. He came to me last night, in his—but you would not understand. Let us call it a dream. He knows our trouble, and will help us. That was impressed upon me beyond all doubt. He will help us! Isn't that glorious, Burford?"

"He has left it pretty late," I said, grimly; and I spoke of my father's condition.

"He should be pacified. To pass on to the next plane in his present state would be extremely perilous, unless he was specially guarded."

"I can't follow your ideas, Harry," I said, with some impatience. "But about your friend, Ravana Dâs. You tell me he is away among the Himalayas. How, then, can he help us?"

"He can easily do so, if he be permitted. Though I have the honour to call him master, he is himself a pupil—the disciple of a still higher teacher. Of course, you don't understand these things. But it was made known to me last night that he will help us, and that he will soon be with us."

"What do you call soon? Unless be travels in some impossible airship, I don't see how. And poor Connie is evidently following her sister. She herself seems to feel it. Only to-day—"

A fixed and startled expression on my friend's face froze the words on my lips. He seemed to see or bear something which I could not. Suddenly the look turned to one of supreme joy and peace, and he sank back in his chair like one relieved of all anxiety.

Involuntarily I turned, and saw that there was a stranger in the room. He was near the door, and must of course, have entered thereby, though I had not seen it open. One glance told me that it was the Hindu, the pundit, Ravana Dâs. There were the delicate, finely-carved, ascetic features, with their grave, gentle, yet lofty expression, as of one who knew all that philosophy could teach, and had renounced all that the world could give. To conceive of this man having a single evil thought was impossible. I remembered afterwards that he was dressed in ordinary clothes, such as we wore ourselves; but I did not remark this at the time.

"I am with you, as you see," he said, in a low, musical voice, which seemed just a trifle muffled; "and I will give you what help I can. But time is limited."

"My dear master," said Thornton, with the utmost reverence; "you have saved us all. This is my friend, Mr. Burford."

"Yes. Well? You are troubled about your sister, Mr. Burford; and your father, too? Is it not so?"

His accent was pure enough, but there was a strange intonation or expression difficult to describe. I was completely subdued by the sheer personality of the man, yet I found courage to say -

"You have come here all the way from the Himalayas?"

Yes. But that is not our present business. There was one known to you as Martin Calthorpe, whom you suppose to be in some way connected with the death of your younger sister, and the illness of the one still living. Tell me briefly all you know about this man."

I told him the little that I knew, and also what I guessed. His chiselled face remained impassive during my speech. He was silent for some moments; then he turned to Thornton.

"The man is not unknown to us," he said. "He took the darker path many years ago, and developed some powers. By the unbridled use of those powers he finally wrenched away his lower personality from the higher self, and when the time came he passed from earth suddenly. Doubtless he was what you call killed. Being so utterly evil, he found it necessary—you understand."

Thornton act bolt upright, deadly pale.

"Of course," he stammered: "I—I should have known; but—but these things are so incredible—"

"You were always of the sceptical ones," said Ravana Dâs, with his gentle smile. "This being is happily one of the last of his kind. We must destroy him."

"Destroy him?" I repeated. "But you say he has already been killed!"

"He has been what you call killed. That is probable. Words are misleading. Our task now is to put it out of his power to do further harm; and I think that can be done."

I was silent, pondering these enigmatical words. When I looked up the Hindu had gone. I turned to Thornton, but he grasped my hand, and said, "Come again to-night, Frank. I promise you the end of all this horror."

I understood that I had to leave, and went away in a confused and dissatisfied state of mind, yet with a growing hope struggling to rise in my heart.

On my return home, I found the house in a commotion. The cause was soon made known to me. My father had shot himself. Connie was prostrated by the shock and could not be seen. A note was handed to me.

"My Dear Frank" it read, "I can bear up no longer. I killed that man's body and now I go to find his black soul. If the wretch's own beliefs are correct, I shall meet him in some sphere of troubled or erring spirits, and there our lifelong war shall he renewed. It is my fate. He and I are bound together. He is striking at me through my loved ones, but the end has not yet come. Farewell!"

A madman's letter? So I should have thought, but for the meeting with the Hindu mystic. Now, to my bewildered mind, all things seemed possible. In some strange realm "out of space, out of time"—I pictured two unhappy, crime stained, earth-bound spirits, grappling with each other, entangled in an awful conflict for a supremacy that should be eternal.

V.

The requirements of the law having been hastily complied with, I tried to pull myself together for the night's appointment. In a few hours Connie had recovered sufficiently to see me, and I found her, though prostrated in body, calm in mind.

"These are cruel things that have come upon us, Frank," she said, in a tone of gentle resignation, "and I am afraid you will soon be left alone—"

"No, no, Connie!" I said "It's all unutterably strange, but I have a feeling that something is being done for us even now, when all seems at the blackest. My dearest, you must not lose heart!"

She looked at me strangely. My careless, man-of-the-world attitude in religious matters had often pained her devotional nature, and perhaps she took my words as indicating a reviving trust in the mercy of Providence.

"I feel that I would rather be with dear Winnie," she murmured: "yet I would not like to leave you, Frank."

"Harry wouldn't like to lose you either, sis," I replied, with some faint effort at cheerfulness, at which the ghost of a smile appeared on her pallid lips.

As noon as darkness came I hurried away to Thornton's rooms. He was waiting for me.

"There is work for us to-night, Burford," he said. "My master has traced the whole thing from the beginning."

"An Indian Sherlock Holmes?" I muttered.

"No, nothing of that sort. These men work on different lines—not, perhaps, so very different, though, If the truth were known. He has only to change his centre of consciousness, and read what we call the akashic records—pictures automatically photographed, as it were, upon the ether by all the events that have ever happened—and—But what's the matter? Anything new?"

He had noticed a change in me. I told him of the tragedy at home. Though greatly shocked, he did not seem very much surprised. He read my father's last words with attention.

"It's a great misfortune, old fellow; but don't let these lines disturb you. The vibrations set up by your father's last thoughts will take him into very unpleasant states of consciousness for a time, no doubt; but he will never meet Calthorpe again—that gentleman goes to his own place to-night. And your father will be helped—there is no doubt of that."

"You seem to know all about it," I said wearily. "But where is your master, as you call him?"

"He is here!" said the young man, gravely.

I turned. The Hindu was seated on a chair beside me. This time I was positive that he had not entered by the door, and a moment before the chair had been empty.

"We must go," said Ravana Dâs, ignoring my amazement. My time is precious."

"Come!" said Thornton.

We went into the street and boarded a South Yarra tram, just like a trio of ordinary mortals. The Hindu was silent until Domain-road was reached, then he said to me—

"Whatever happens, friend Burford, you must not let your nerve desert you. You have a house in a street called Caroline?"

"Caroline Street—yes. But it is empty."

"Assuredly there are no ordinary tenants there. Yet we shall find someone. I think it will be necessary to destroy your house."

"As you please; but it's rather a fine property."

"Property—wealth—all Illusion!" muttered Ravana Dâs: and he spoke a few words to Thornton which I did not catch.

We alighted at Park Street, near the gates of the Botanical Gardens, and walked thence to the street in which the house stood. Together we entered the empty house. Thornton produced an electric torch, and we passed along a passage and reached a store-room or pantry, from which we descended some steps into a cellar, the Hindu guiding us. Except for some lumber, the cellar was quite empty.

"Whatever you see," whispered Thornton, "be silent until he speaks!"

The Hindu stood with folded arms gazing intently at the wall opposite the entrance. Several minutes passed in profound silence. Suddenly a brick fell to the floor. It seemed to come from near the top. It was followed by others in quick succession, till in a few moments an opening was made revealing a small, inner cell, from which came the acrid odour of cement mingled with that of long pent-up air. The Hindu, of whom I now stood in the utmost awe, but in nowise feared, signed us to enter.

Raising aloft his torch, Thornton went first, and I followed. There was but one object in the cell, and that was the dead body of a man; and there needed no ghost from the grave to tell me that it was the mortal remains of Martin Calthorpe. It was stretched upon the earthen floor, and stared with glassy eyes at the low, cemented ceiling.

The body was that of a man in the prime of life—a portly, well-nourished body that might have been merely asleep, but for the staring eyes and a bullet-hole in the centre of the forehead. There was not the least appearance of decay—no more than if the man had just been killed. There was even colour in the cheeks. I thought of another corpse lying at my almost desolated home, and a dull, deadly rage began to swell up within my heart.

Then wonder and horror possessed me. How could this body have been preserved so long? Had Calthorpe met his rate so recently? Or had the walling-up of the cell -

"He has been thus a year or more," said Ravana Dâs, answering my thoughts. "But to your work," he added, taking the torch from Harry.

Signing to me, Thornton took the body by the shoulders, a hand under each; I took the ankles, and we essayed to lift it. Harry is an athlete, and my own strength is above the average, but our utmost efforts quite failed to move the corpse.

"It's no use," said the young man, with a gasp, and we fell back, I in a state of speechless amazement.

"Use your blade, then!" said the Hindu.

Thornton drew from under his coat a heavy Goorkha sword, and approached the body, as though that lifeless clay were a living toe. My feeling of hatred had returned, and I set my teeth.

Thornton bent his knee, and aimed a powerful blow at the dead man's neck. To my unutterable horror the blade stopped within a few inches of its mark and flew from the striker's hand. He retreated, dazed.

The Hindu turned to me.

"Take the weapon," he said, calmly. "After all, it is the son who should avenge his father." He gave the torch to Harry, and stood at the feet of the corpse. One glimpse I caught of bin bronze features, and it was no longer a living man I saw. It was incarnate Will!

Nerved with a power not my own, I grasped the sword and aimed a deadly blow. It was stopped as before, and my arm tingled an though I had struck a log of wood.

"Again!" cried the Hindu, raising his two hands, and thrusting them forward over the body.

It was like an order to the soldier in battle. I struck; and this time the heavy blade met with no resistance. The head rolled aside, and there gushed from the trunk torrents of rich, red blood, until the body seemed literally to swim in it.

"It is done!" said the voice of Ravana Dâs. "You know the rest. Farewell!"

He was gone.

† † † † † †

The work of carrying the corpse (which was easily lifted now) to one of the upper rooms was accomplished in silence. Fifteen minutes later we stood amongst a rapidly increasing crowd of people, watching a dense mass of flames spurting from all quarters of the wooden house. The roof fell in, and when it became certain that no part of the building could be saved, we left.

† † † † †

It was not yet very late, though it seemed to me that ages had passed since I left home. We returned to Harry's rooms, for I was thirsting for some explanation of the things I had seen

I was feverish with excitement, but Thornton seemed to have acquired something of his master's self-control; and when we were comfortably seated in his little den, with the pictured, pale-bronze features of the Indian occultist gazing benignantly down upon us, my friend entered into an explanation which, I must confess, only increased my amazement.

"This Calthorpe," he began, "was a man who had given himself up entirely to evil."

"That much seems to be abundantly evident," I interjected.

"You must try and realise, however, what to meant by the absolute rejection of the good in every shape and form. Ordinarily, evil is relative, not absolute—we seldom meet the aristocrat of crime. The fatal grandeur, the awful eminence of a 'Satan' is rarely revealed to us. Had this man been gifted with intellect in proportion to his wickedness, he could easily have made himself a national—ay, even a world-wide scourge."

"Yet he was not of a low type of intellect?"

"Too low to flee to the grander conceptions of crime. What he has accomplished we shall never know, for he wielded powers that enabled him to laugh at human justice, as your friend Detective Mainspray understands it."

"I have heard you say that the development of these occult powers depends on entire purity of thought and deed?"

"The full development—yes. You have seen how easily my master (who is himself only a disciple as yet) overcame by force of will the etheric resistance which Calthorpe was able to interpose between my sword and his precious neck. Yes, occult powers are, at their highest, united with great loftiness of character and nobility of aim; sometimes they are associated, in a limited form, with a grovelling and sordid nature; and, again, as in Calthorpe's case, they are seen in combination with positive malevolence and tendencies of an altogether evil kind. The so-called 'black magicians' of the middle ages were, no doubt, men of the stamp of Calthorpe. Such beings, gifted with powers which, though limited on their own plane, are superior to the workings of physical science as commonly known, must possess, as you will see, potentialities for active evil before which the imagination may well stand appalled."

"And this power—whatever it may be—how could this wretch carry it with him to the next world?"

"The power really belongs to the 'next world,' as you call it, and can be more readily exerted there. But let me explain. This man had literally thrown away the immortal part of himself, since be was all evil, and nothing that is evil can live. He was doomed to a sort of slow disintegration—the gradual conscious decay and death of the animal personality that had wilfully wrenched itself away from its immortal essence."

"You mean the soul? And what becomes of that?"

"It rests on its own plane, so to speak, till the time arrives for its next incarnation on earth."

"Very well. Go on."

"We know that Calthorpe was killed. Having some occult knowledge, he was aware that a soulless entity, deprived or its physical vehicle, was doomed to perish. The ordinary man, after the death of the body, remains for a time in a state the Hindus call 'Pretaloka' until his thoughts are entirely freed from earthly concerns. Pretaloka is the scientific fact behind the dogma of purgatory. While living, Calthorpe could, in trance, visit the lower levels of Pretaloka, and roam about there at will—that is, his thought could vibrate in unison with the vibrations of the spirit-matter of those levels, and thus function there."

"But this was only on condition, I understand, that he had a living body to return to?"

"Exactly. Being without a soul to which he could cling, he needed a body as a sort of point of support. Losing his physical life utterly, he would sink by a natural and inevitable law to a lower state even than Pretaloka, there to suffer, as I have said, the horrors of disintegration and decay, ending in the complete annihilation of the human personality."

"But what use could his body be when he was shot dead?"

"The effect of the bullet would be merely to transfer his consciousness to Pretaloka. By occult arts he could preserve his remains from decomposition as long as they were not disturbed. Evidently your father played into his hands by walling up the body in that cell. If he had only thought of destroying it, as we did, by burning down the house, thus severing the magnetic line of communication, so to speak, depended on by Calthorpe for mere existence, that worthy would have gone to his own place almost immediately."

"And that place is—"

"We will not speak of it," said Thornton, with a shiver. "As it was, in order to remain in the state called Pretaloka (for it is not a place), he was compelled to preserve his late vehicle—his body— in a sort of cataleptic trance, and that he could only do by stealing vitality front the living and transferring it to the corpse."

I shuddered as I recalled the scene in the cell—the torrents of fresh blood.

"Then," I muttered, "this—this creature was nothing but a vampire?"

"A vampire, indeed—glutting his vengeance and serving his necessity at the same time. Remember how his wife died—she was his first victim; and her fate was the more terrible because she knew what was happening. Calthorpe was a 'black occultist' of inferior powers, or he would probably have been better known to my master, in which case help might have come sooner."

"His powers seem to have been sufficient for his purposes," I said, bitterly.

"Yes. Yet, with a deeper knowledge, he could have demateri- alised his body, and removed it to some inaccessible place; and, again with wider powers, he could have kept it alive by extracting the necessary vitality from the physical air, which contains all that is needed for human sustenance. But his fate was decreed, and he himself was the instrument of his own undoing."

"That may be very well, old man, but it doesn't bring back Winnie and the poor, old dad."

"They are far better off where they are, Frank. Religion and occultism agree on that point, as on so many others. The grief of friends for those gone before only harms them, for it attracts their thoughts earthward during their stay in that realm of illusion I have called Pretaloka, and so delays them on their journey heavenward. Thus we should not grieve, but rather, in the words of the poet –

"'Waft the angel on her flight with a paean of old days.'"

"And—and is the creature finally disposed of? Is Connie entirely freed from all further peril?"

"You shall see!" said the young man, his voice vibrating with confidence and joy. "We have slain the cockatrice. Its power for evil is now confined to its own plane. The thing is perishing with its self-created poison. Let us think of it no further."

"One more question," I said. "How did your Indian teacher get here if he were away in the Himalayas only the day before?"

"What we saw was not his physical body at all. The body is the prison of the soul for ordinary mortals. We can see merely what comes before its windows. But the occultist has found the, key of his prison, and can emerge from it at pleasure. It is no longer a prison for him—merely a dwelling. In other words, he can project his ego, his soul, his true self—whatever name you choose to give it—out of his body to any place he pleases with the rapidity of thought"

"He seemed a substantial enough body, as far as I could see."

"Doubtless. Thought is creative in a deeper sense than we dream. Science tells us that all the materials that constitute our physical bodies exist in the air we breathe. An advanced occultist can draw thence by the power of will all he needs for a temporary vehicle in which to function; or, if he so prefers he can produce by illusion all that he wishes people to believe they see."

We talked on till daylight neither of us feeling any desire for sleep. Thornton went deeply into his strange teachings, and I heard for the first time a great deal that was wildly incredible; but I had to confess that, if it was madness, there was no lack of method in it.

Early in the morning, feeling the need of fresh air and action, we set out on foot for my home, still discussing the tremendous questions of man's life and destiny.

Arrived at the house, a servant informed us that Connie was in the morning-room, and that breakfast was served there. Somewhat surprised, and forgetting our unwashed and unkempt condition, we entered. Connie was seated at the table, with a liberal repast before her.

She arose hurriedly, a bright flush suffusing her cheeks.

"I—I felt so hungry," she said; "you really must excuse me—"

A rush of terrible memories surged up within my heart, and I fell into a seat, giving way to a fit of hysterical weeping. And Harry, for all his assumed calmness, incontinently joined in my sudden emotion, and the scene was at once ludicrous and tragic. Two strong young men crying like children, and a delicate girl— whom they had helped in a humble degree to rescue from the clutches of a monster—doing her utmost to soothe them.

It was some time before we could join Connie at her breakfast, but when we did I felt that the meal inaugurated a new period of health and happiness for the dear girl and her devoted lover, and formed a peace and resignation such as I had lately despaired of.

# MORLEY ROBERTS:
## THE BLOOD FETISH (1909)

Morley Charles Roberts (1857–1942) was born in London and educated at the Bedford School for boys in Bedford and Owens College in Manchester.

He was a prodigious author who penned more than fifty novels. Roberts travelled extensively and wrote about his adventures in places such as California, Canada, Rhodesia, the Orient and the South Seas. His best-known work may be *The Private Life of Henry Maitland* (1912), a fictionalized biography of his friend, George Gissing.

The following curiosity is from his collection *Midsummer Madness*, which was published by Eveleigh Nash in 1909.

———

In the early years preceding the First World War, vampire stories set in even more remote parts of the world saw the genre develop still further. The great explorer, Sir Richard Burton, for instance, offered an entire collection of stories from India entitled, *Vikram the Vampire* (1893); while George Soulie's translation of 'The Corpse The Blood Drinker' from a Chinese book, *Strange Stories From The Lodge of Leisures* (1913) indicated that the vampire had been a part of that great nation's history for centuries. The fact that the tradition also existed in that other vast continent, Africa, was demonstrated by this next story, 'The Blood Fetish' by Morley Roberts which is not only highly unusual, but has also never been anthologised before. If I indicate no more than it is the grisly tale of a severed hand that resorts to vampirism in order to sustain itself, I think the reader will be in no doubt that the word unusual is an understatement if anything! I have a feeling, too, that the story must have had quite an impact on the readers of the *Strand* magazine when it appeared in October 1908. Sadly, though, this famous magazine which gave the world Sherlock Holmes and made Sir Arthur Conan Doyle a household name, did little for Morley Roberts who contributed just as frequently and sometimes every bit as ingeniously as the creator of the Great Detective. He is today virtually forgotten, except among those collectors who treasure the rare volumes of his novels and short stories.

Morley Roberts (1857-1942) was born in London, the son of an income tax inspector, but spent much of his early life traveling around the world which accounts for the variety of settings of his stories. In 1876, for instance, he was helping to rebuild railways in Australia. This was followed by cattle ranching in America, projects in India, Africa, the South Seas and Central America, not to mention a period at sea, before he finally returned home and devoted the rest of his life to fiction writing. His first success as a novelist was with The Adventures of the Broad Arrow (1897), a 'lost race' story set in Australia which contains a vivid picture of the Australian outback that is obviously drawn from personal experience. This was followed by similar tales of fantasy and the macabre including 'The Colossus' (1899), 'The Degradation of Geoffrey Alwith' (1908), 'The Serpent's Fang' (1930), and 'The White Mamaloi' (1931), plus a string of weird stories for the Strand and Pearson's Magazine like 'A Thing of Wax', 'Out of the Great Silence', 'The Man With The Nose', 'The Fog' (a notable tale about London being threatened with a horrible doom) and 'The Blood Fetish' which he indicated was inspired by a curious incident that happened to him while he was living in Africa. It is, I think, one of his very best short fictions and certainly unique among all the vampire stories I have read . . .

Outside the tent the forest was alive and busy, as it is for ever in the tropics of Africa. Birds called with harsh strange notes from dark trees, for, though the forest was even more full of creeping shadows, the sun had not yet sunk beyond the western flats through which the Kigi ran to the sea. Monkeys chattered and howled: and beneath this chorus was the hum of a million insects, that voice of the bush which never ceases. The sick man in the tent moved uneasily and looked at his companion.

'Give me something to drink, doctor,' he said.

The doctor supported his head while he drank.

'Were there any of your drugs in it?' asked the patient.

'No, Smith,' said the doctor.

'My taste is morbid,' said Smith. 'I shan't last long, old chap.'

Dr Winslow looked out into the forest, into the night, for now it was night very suddenly.

'Nonsense,' said Winslow. 'You'll live to take your collection home and be more famous than you are now.'

'Am I famous?' asked Simcox Smith. 'I suppose I am in my way. I'm thought to know more than most about this country and the devilish ways of it. Every one acknowledges that, or everyone but Hayling.'

He frowned as he mentioned the name.

'He's no better than an ignorant fool,' he remarked. 'But we see strange things here, doctor.'

The doctor sighed.

'I suppose so,' he said, 'but what fools we are to be here at all.'

The dying man shook his head.

'No, no, I've learnt a lot, old chap. I wish I could teach Hayling. I meant to, and now I can't. He'll spend all his time trying to discredit my—my discoveries.'

'Lie quiet,' said the doctor, and for long minutes Simcox Smith and the anthropologist said nothing. He lay thinking. But he spoke at last.

'I've not bought that thing from Suja,' he said.

'Don't,' said Winslow.

'You think it's fraud?'

'I'm sure of it,' said Winslow.

Simcox Smith laughed.

'You are as bad as Hayling.'

He put out his hand and drew Winslow closer to him.

'Suja showed me what it did,' he said. 'I saw it myself.'

'On what?' asked Winslow quickly.

'On a prisoner, one who was killed when you were away.'

'And it did—'

'Did something! My God, yes,' said the anthropologist, shivering.

'What?' asked the doctor curiously, but with drawn brows.

'He grew pale and it got red. I thought I saw the wrist,' said Simcox Smith. 'I thought I saw it. I did see it.'

Winslow would have said it was all a delusion if Smith had been well. He knew how men's minds went in the rotten bush of the West Coast. He had seen intellects rot, and feared for his own.

'Oh,' said Winslow.

The sick man lay back in his bed.

'I'll buy it and send it to Hayling.'

'Nonsense,' said Winslow; 'don't.'

'You don't believe it, so why shouldn't I send it? I will. I'll show Hayling! He's a blind fool, and believes there are no devilish things in this world. What is this world, old chap, and what are we? It's all horrible and ghastly. Fetch Suja, old chap.'

'Nonsense, lie down and be quiet,' said Winslow.

'I want Suja, the old rascal, I want him,' said Smith urgently. 'I must have it for Hayling. I'd like Hayling or some of his house to grow pale. They'll see more than the wrist. Oh God! What's the head like?'

He shivered.

'I want Suja,' he said moaning, and presently Winslow went out and send a boy for Suja, who came crawling on his hands and knees, for he was monstrously old and withered and weak. But his eyes were alive. They looked like lamps in a gnarled piece of wood. He kneeled on the floor beside Smith's bed. Smith talked to him in his own tongue that Winslow could not understand, and the two men, the two dying men, talked long and eagerly while Winslow smoked. Suja was dying, had been dying for twenty, fifty years. His people said they knew not how old he was. But Smith would die next day, said Winslow. Suja and Smith talked, and at last they came to an agreement. And then Suja crawled out of the tent.

'Get me a hundred dollars out of my chest,' said Smith. 'And when I am dead you will give him my clothes and blankets; all of them.'

'All right if you say so,' said Winslow. He got the hundred dollars out, and presently the old sorcerer came back. With him he brought a parcel done up in fibre and a big leaf, and over that some brown paper on which was as label in red letters,' With great care'. It was a precious piece of paper, and not a soul thereabouts but Suja would have touched it. The red letters were some dreadful charm, so Suja had told the others.

'This is it,' said Suja.

'Give him the money,' said Smith eagerly.

He turned to Suja and spoke quietly to him in his own tongue.

'It's not mine, Suja, but John Hayling's. Say it.'

Winslow heard Suja say something, and then he heard the words, 'Shon 'Aylin'.'

Simcox Smith looked up at Winslow.

'He gives it to Hayling, Winslow,' he said triumphantly.

'Is that part of the mumbo jumbo?' asked Winslow, half contemptuously. But somehow he was not wholly contemptuous. The darkness of the night and the glimmer of the lamp in the darkness, and the strange and horrible aspect of the sorcerer affected him.

'Shon 'Aylin',' mumbled Suja, as he counted his dollars.

'Yes, it's part of it,' said Smith. 'It won't work except on the one who owns it and on his people. It must be transferred. We have it to the slave who died.'

'It's a beastly idea,' said Winslow.

'You'll send it for me,' said Smith. 'You must.'

'Oh, all right,' said Winslow.

With trembling hands Smith put the packet into a biscuit tin. Old Suja crept out into the darkness.

'I believe anything with that old devil in the tent,' said Winslow. Smith giggled.

'It's true, and it's Hayling's. I always meant to send it to him, the unbelieving beast,' he said. 'I wish I was going to live to see it. You'll send it, Winslow?'

'Yes.'

'You promise on your word of honour?' insisted Smith.

Reluctantly enough, Winslow gave his word of honour, and Smith was satisfied. And at ten o'clock that night he died in his sleep.

Winslow packed up all his papers and collections, and sent him down to the coast by carriers and canoe. The packet containing the fetish which Smith had bought from the ancient sorcerer he sent by post to England. He addressed it to A.J. Hayling, 201 Lansdown Road, St John's Wood. By this time Winslow had recovered his tone. He believed nothing which he could not see. He was angry with himself for having been affected by what Smith and old Suja had said and done.

'It's absurd, of course,' said Winslow, with bend brows. He added, 'but it's a beastly idea.'

When he sent the fetish away he wrote a letter to go with it, saying that Simcox Smith had often spoken to him of his rival in England. He described briefly what had occurred at the time of Smith's death, and gave some brief details of old Suja. He was obviously very old, and all the natives for miles round were frightened of him. Nevertheless, there was, of course, nothing in the thing. Latterly the climate and overwork had obviously affected Smith's mind. 'I should not sent it if he had not made me promise to do so on my word of honour,' wrote Winslow.

He dismissed the matter from his mind, and the parcel and letter went home by the next Elder Dempster boat.

Mr Hayling was rather pleased than otherwise to hear of Simcox Smith's decease, although he said 'poor fellow,' as one must when a scientific enemy and rival dies. They had quarreled for years when they met at the Societ's rooms, and had fought in the scientific journals. Hayling was an anthropological Mr Gradgrind. He wanted facts, and nothing but facts. He believed he was a Baconian, as he knew nothing of Bacon. It had never occurred to him that there was any mystery in anything. There was nothing but ignorance, and most men were very ignorant.

The existence of men, of things, of the universe, of matter itself, were all taken for granted by him, in the same way they were taken for granted by the average man. What made Simcox Smith (who had a penchant for metaphysics) once jokingly called the Me-ness of the Ego was an absurdity. It was idiocy. When a man begins to think what made himself an Ego and what constitutes 'Me', he is on the verge of insanity unless he is a great philosopher.

'Simcox Smith is an ass,' said Hayling, quite oblivious to the fact that Smith had done good work in many directions and offered some conjectural hypotheses to the world which had much merit and might some day rank as theories. 'Simcox Smith is an ass. He believed in occultism. He believed, I am prepared to swear, in witchcraft. He mistook the horrible ideas of a savage race for realities. Would you believe it, he even said that everything believed in utter and simple faith had a kind of reality? He said this was a law of nature!'

Obviously Simcox Smith had been mad. But some easily affected and imaginative people said it was a dreadful idea, just as Winslow had said the notion of Suja's blood fetish was a beastly one. Imagine for an instant that the idea was true! It meant that the frightful imaginations of madmen had a quasi existence at least! It meant that there was a dreadful element of truth (for who knew what truth was?) in any conceived folly. A man had but to imagine something to create it. One of Smith's friends really believed this. He was an atheist, he said, but he believed (in a way, he added, as he laughed) that mankind had really created a kind of anthropomorphic deity, with the passions and feelings attributed to him by belief and tradition. No wonder, said this friend of Smith's, that the world was a horrible place to anyone who could grasp its misery and had ears for its groans.

It must be acknowledged that this idea of Simcox Smith's was a horrible one. It really affected some men. One tried it on a child (he was very scientific, and believed in his experiments he could more or less control) and the child saw things which threw it into a fit and injured it for life. Nevertheless, it was a very interesting experiment, for something happened to the child (there were odd marks on it) which looked like something more than suggestion, unless it all true that we hear of stigmata. Perhaps it is, but personally I have an idea (I knew Smith) that there is something in his damnable creating theory.

But to return to Hayling. He got the parcel from the Coast, and he read Winslow's letter.

'Poor fellow,' said Hayling; 'so he's dead at last. Well, well! And what is this that he sends? A blood fetish? Ah, he thinks he can convert me at the last, the poor mad devil.'

He opened the parcel, and inside the matting and the leaves, which smelt of the West Coast of Africa (the smell being muddy and very distinctive to those who have smelt it), he found a dried black hand, severed at the wrist joint. There was nothing else, only this hand.

'Humph,' said Hayling, who had nerves which had never been shaken by the bush and the fevers of the bush, and had never heard black men whispering dreadfully of the lost soulds of the dead. 'Humph.'

He picked it up and looked at it. It was an ordinary hand, a right hand, and there was nothing remarkable about it at first. On a further look the nails seemed remarkably long, and that gave the hand a rather cruel look. Hayling said 'humph,' again. He examined it carefully and saw that it was very deeply marked on the palm.

'Very interesting,' said Hayling. Curiously enough (or rather it would have been curious if we didn't know that the strongest of us have our weak spots), he had a belief or some belief in palmistry. He had never acknowledged it to a soul but a well-known palmist in the west of London. 'Very interesting. I wonder what Sacconi would say of these lines?'

Sacconi was the palmist. He was an Irishman.

'I'll show it to Sacconi,' said Hayling. He packed it up in its box again and put it in a cupboard, which he locked up. He dismissed the matter, for he had a good deal to do. He had to write something about Simcox Smith, for instance, and he was working on totemism. He hardly thought of the dried hand for some days.

Hayling was a bachelor, and lived with a niece and a house-keeper. He was a nice man to live with unless one knew anything about anthropology and totems and such like, and Mary Hayling knew nothing about them whatever. She said 'Yes, uncle dear,' and 'No, uncle dear,' just as she ought to do, and when he abused Simcox Smith, or Robins-Gunter, or Williams, who were rivals of his, she was always sympathetic and said it was a shame.

'What's a shame?' said Hayling.

'I don't know, dear uncle,' said Mary Hayling.

And Hayling laughed.

Then there was the housekeeper. She was fair, stout and ruddy, and very cheerful in spite of the fact that skulls and bones and specimen things in bottles made her flesh creep. She knew nothing whatever about them, and wondered what they mattered. Why Mr Hayling raged and rumbled about other men's opinions on such horrid subjects she didn't know. However, she took every-thing easily, and only remonstrated when the fullness of the house necessitated skulls being exposed to public view. The passage even had some of them and the maids objected to dusting them, as was only natural. Hayling said he didn't want'em dusted, but what would any housekeeper who was properly constituted think of that? She made the girls dust them, though she herself shivered. She even saw that they wiped glass bottles with awful things inside them. She and the housemaid cleaned up Mr Hayling's own room and opened the cupboard where the hand was. The girl gave a horrid squeak as she put her hand in and touched it.

'O, law, ma'am, what is it?' asked Kate.

'Don't be a fool, girl,' said Mrs Farwell, with a shiver. 'It's only a hand.'

'Only—oh Lord! I won't touch it,' said the girl. 'There's a dead mouse by it.'

'Then take out the dead mouse,' said the housekeeper. The girl did so, and slammed the cupboard door to and locked it. The mouse was a poor shriveled little thing, but how interesting it would have been to dead Simcox Smith neither Kate nor the housekeeper knew. It went into the dustbin as if it did not bear witness to a horror.

That afternoon Mrs Farwell spoke to Hayling.

'If you please, sir, there's a hand in that cupboard, and I couldn't get Kate to clean it out.'

'A hand! Oh yes, I remember,' said Hayling. 'The girl's a fool. Does she think it will hurt her? How did she know it was there? I wrapped it up. Some one's been meddling.'

'I don't think so, sir,' said Mrs Farwell, with dignity. 'She is much too frightened to meddle, and so am I.'

'Mrs Farwell, you are a fool,' said Hayling.

'Thank you, sir,' said Mrs Farwell. When Mrs Farwell had sailed out of the room Hayling opened the cupboard and found the hand out of its package.

'Some one has been meddling,' growled Hayling. 'They pretend that they are frightened and come hunting here to get a sensation. I know 'em. They're all savages, and so are all of us. Civilization!'

He gave a snort when he thought of what civilization was. That is an anthropological way of looking at it. It's not a theological way at all.

He looked at the hand. It was a curious hand.

'It's contracted a little,' said Hayling. 'The fist has closed, I think. Drying unequally. But it's interesting; I'll show it to Sacconi.'

He put the hand into its coverings, and took it that very afternoon to Sacconi.

Personally Hayling believed in chiromancy. As I have said, it really was his only weakness. I never used to believe it when he argued with me, but now I have my doubts. When Sacconi took the thing into his own white and beautiful hands and turned it over to look at the palm, his eyebrows went up in a very odd way. Hayling said so.

'This, oh, ah,' said Sacconi. His real name was Flynn. He came from Limerick. 'This is very odd—very –'

'Very what?' asked Hayling.

'Horrible, quite horrible,' said Sacconi.

'Can you read it, man?'

Sacconi grunted.

'Can I read the Times? I can, but I don't. I've half the mind not to read this. It's very horrible, Hayling.'

'The devil,' said Hayling; 'what d'ye mean?'

'This is a negro's hand.'

'Any fool can see that,' said Hayling rudely.

'A murderer's hand.'

'That's likely enough,' said Hayling.

'A cannibal's hand.'

'You don't say so!' said Hayling.

'Oh, worse than that.'

'What's worse?'

Sacconi said a lot that Hayling denounced as fudge. Probably it was fudge. And yet—

'I'd burn it,' said Sacconi, with a shiver, as he handed it back to Hayling, and went to wash his hands. 'I'd burn it.'

'There's a damn weak spot in you, Sacconi,' said the anthropologist.

'Perhaps,' said Sacconi, 'but I'd burn it.'

'Damn nonsense,' said Hayling. 'Why should I?'

'I believe a lot of things you don't,' said Sacconi.

'I disbelieve a lot that you don't,' retorted Hayling.

'You see, I'm a bit of a clairvoyant,' said Sacconi.

'I've heard you say that before,' said Hayling, as he went away.

When he got home again he put the hand in the cupboard. He forgot to lock it up. And he locked the cat up in his room when he went to bed.

There was an awful crying of cats, or a cat, in the middle of the night. But cats fight about that time.

And when Kate opened the door of Hayling's working-room in the morning she saw the hand upon the hearthrug, and gave a horrid scream. It brought Mrs Farwell out of the drawling room, and Hayling out of the bathroom in a big towel.

'What the devil—' said Hayling.

'What is it, Kate?' cried Mrs Farwell.

'The hand! the hand!' said Kate. 'It's on the floor.'

Mrs Farwell saw it. Hayling put on his dressing-gown, and came down and saw it, too.

'Give that fool a month's notice,' said Hayling. 'She's been meddling again.'

'I haven't,' said Kate, sobbing. And then Mrs Farwell saw the cat lying stretched out under Hayling's desk.

'It was the cat. There she is,' said Mrs Farwell.

'Damn the cat,' said Hayling. He took Kate's broom and gave the cat a push with it.

The cat was dead.

'I don't want a month's notice,' said Kate, quavering. 'I'll go now.'

'Send the fool off,' said Hayling angrily. He took up the cat, of which he had been very fond, and put it outside, and shut the door on the crying girl and Mrs Farwell. He picked up the hand and looked at it.

'Very odd,' said Hayling.

He looked again.

'Very beastly,' said Hayling. 'I suppose it's my imagination.'

He looked once more.

'Looks fresher,' said Hayling. 'These fools of women have infected me.'

He put the hand down on his desk by the side of a very curious Maori skull, and went upstairs again to finish dressing.

That morning the scientific monthlies were out, and there was much of interest in them that Hayling forgot all about the hand. He had an article in one of them abusing Robins-Gunter, whose views on anthropology were coloured by his fanaticism in religion. 'Imagine a man like that thinking he is an authority on anything scientific,' said Hayling. It was a pleasure to slaughter him on his own altar, and indeed this time Hayling felt he had offered Robins-Gunter up to the outraged deity of Truth.

'It's a massacre,' said Hayling; 'it's not a criticism—it's a massacre.'

He said 'Ha-ha!' and went to town to hear what others had to say about it. They had so much to say that he remained at the club till very late, and got rather too much wine to drink. Or perhaps it was the whisky-and-soda. He left his working-room door open and unlocked.

Kate had gone, sacrificing a fortnight's wages. Mrs Farwell said she was a fool. Kate said she would rather be a fool outside that house. She also said a lot of foolish things about the hand, which had a very silly effect upon the housekeeper. For how else can we account for what happened that night? Kate said that the beastly hand was alive, and that it had killed the cat. Uneducated superstitious girls from the country often say things as silly. But Mrs Farwell was a woman of nerves. She only went to sleep when heard her master come in.

She woke screaming at three o'clock, and Hayling was still so much under the influence of Robins-Gunter's scientific blood and the club whisky that he didn't wake. But Mary Hayling woke and so did the cook, and they came running to Mrs Farwell's room. They found her door open.

'What's the matter? What's the matter?' screamed Mary Hayling. She brought a candle and found Mrs Farwell sitting up in bed.

She was as white as a ghost, bloodlessly white. 'There's been a horrible thing in my room,' she whispered.

The cook collapsed on a chair; Mary Hayling say on the bed and put her arms round the housekeeper.

'What?'

'I saw it,' whispered Mrs Farwell. 'A black man, reddish black, very horrible—'

She fainted, and Mary laid her down.

'Stay with her,' said Mary. 'I'll go and wake my uncle.'

The cook whimpered, but she lighted the gas and stayed, while Mary hammered on Hayling's door. He thought it was thunderous applause at a dinner given him by the Royal Society. Then he woke.

'What is it?'

Mary opened the door and told him to get up.

'Oh, these women,' he said.

His head ached. He went upstairs cursing and found Mrs Farwell barely conscious.

The cook was shaking like a jelly, and Hayling thrust her aside. He had some medical training before he turned to anthropology, and he took hold of the housekeeper's wrist, and found her pulse a mere running thread.

'Go and bring brandy,' said Hayling, 'and fetch Dr Sutton from next door.'

He was very white himself. So far as he could guess she looked as if she were dying of loss of blood. But she didn't die. Sutton, when he came in, said the same.

'She's not white only from fainting, she's blanched,' he declared.

He turned back her nightgown, and found a very strange red patch on her shoulder. It was redder than the white skin, and moist. He touched it with a handkerchief, and the linen was faintly reddened. He turned and stared at Hayling.

'This is very extraordinary,' he said, and Hayling nodded.

He tried to speak and could not. At last he got his voice. It was dry and thick.

'Don't you think the patch is the shape of a hand?' asked Hayling.

'Yes, rather,' replied Sutton; 'somewhat like it, I should say.'

They were all in the room then: Mary Hayling and the cook. There was no other person in the house. They could have sworn that was a fact. They heard a noise below.

'What's that?' asked Hayling.

'Someone gone out the front door, sir,' said the trembling cook.

'Nonsense,' said Hayling.

But the door slammed. When he ran down he found no one about. He went upstairs again shaking. For he had looked for something in his own room and had not found it.

The next day there was a curious paragraph in all the evening papers.

'The freshly severed hand of a negro was picked up early this morning in Lansdown Road, St John's Wood, just outside the residence of the well-known anthropologist, Mr A.J. Hayling. The police are investigating the mystery.'

But Hayling destroyed the article in which he proposed to massacre the poor credulous Simcox Smith.

# Appendix: Charles Dickens, Jr.: Vampyres and Ghouls (1871)

Charles Dickens (i.e., Charles John Huffman Dickens) founded the weekly literary magazine *All the Year Round* in 1859. Many important novels, including Dicken's *A Tale of Two Cities*, were serialized in this publication.

Following his death in 1870, his son Charles Culliford Boz Dickens (1837-1896), became the owner and editor of the magazine. He remained in charge of it until the magazine ceased publication in 1895.

Most of the anonymous articles that appeared in *All the Year Round* were written by Charles Dickens and his son, so it can be assumed that Dickens, Jr. wrote the essay "Vampyres and Ghouls," which appeared on the 20th of May, 1871.

---

These gentry are not yet quite dead. At least the belief in them still lingers in some country districts; while in South-Eastern Europe, and South-Western Asia, the credence prevails among whole tribes, and even nations. There appears to be no essential difference between the European vampyre and the Asiatic ghoul – a sort of demon, delighting to animate the bodies of dead persons, and feed upon their blood. It is believed that the superstition has existed in the Levant since the time of the ancient Greeks; but among that artistic people the vampyre was a lamia, a beautiful woman, who allured youths to her, and then fed upon their young flesh and blood. Be that as it may, the Byzantine Christians, after the time of Constantine, entertained a belief that the bodies of those who died excommunicated were kept by an emissary of the Evil One, who endowed them with a sort of life, sufficient to enable them to go forth at night from their graves, and feast on other men. The only way to get rid of these passive agents of mischief was to dig the bodies up from the graves, dis-excommunicate them, and bury them.

William of Newbury, who lived in the twelfth century, narrates that in Buckinghamshire a man appeared several times to his wife after he had been buried. The archdeacon and clergy, on being applied to, thought it right to ask the advice of the bishop of the diocese, as to the proper course to be pursued. He advised that the body should be burned – the only cure for vampyres. On opening the grave, the corpse was found to be in the same state as when interred; a property, we are told, generally possessed by vampyres.

The most detailed vampyre stories belong to the Danubian and Greek countries. Tournefort describes a scene that came under his personal notice in Greece. A peasant of Mycone was murdered in the fields in the year 1701. He had been a man of quarrelsome, ill-natured disposition: just the sort of man, according to the current belief of the peasantry, to be haunted by vampyres after death. Two days after his burial, it was noised abroad that he had been seen to walk in the might with great haste, overturning people's goods, putting out their lights, pinching them, and playing them strange pranks. The rumour was so often repeated, that at length the priests avowed their belief in its truth. Masses were said in the chapels, and ceremonies were performed, having for their object to drive out the vampyre that inhabited the dead man. On the tenth clay after the burial, a mass was said, the body was disinterred, and the heart taken out. Frankincense was burned to ward off infection; but the bystanders insisted on the smoke of the frankincense being a direct emanation from the dead body – a sure sign, according to popular belief, of vampyrism. They burned the heart on the sea-shore, the conventional way of getting rid of vampyres. Still this did not settle the matter. Positive statements went the round of the village that the dead man was still tip to all kinds Of mischief, beating people in the night, breaking down doors, unroofing houses, shaking windows. The matter became serious. Many of the inhabitants were so thoroughly frightened and panic-stricken as to flee; while those who remained nearly lost all self-control. They debated, they fasted, they made processions through the village, they sprinkled the doors of the houses with holy water, they speculated as to whether mass had been properly said, and the heart properly burned. At length they resolved to burn the body itself; they collected plenty of wood, pitch, and tar, and carried out their plan. Tournefort (who had found it necessary to be cautious as to expressing his incredulity), states that no more was heard of the supposed vampyre.

In the year 1725, on the borders of Hungary and Transylvania, a vampyre story arose, which was renewed afterwards in a noteworthy way. A peasant of Madveiga, named Arnold Paul, was crushed to death by the fall of a waggon-load of hay. Thirty days afterwards, four persons died, with all the symptoms (according to popular belief) of their blood having, been sucked by vainpyres. Some of the neighbours remembered having heard Arnold say that he had often been tormented by a vampyre; and they jumped to a conclusion that the passive vampyre had now become active. This was in accordance with a kind of formula or theorem on the subject: that a man who, when alive, has had his blood sucked by a vampyre, will, after his death, deal with other persons in like manner. The neighbours exhumed Arnold Paul, drove a stake through the heart, cut off the head, and burned the body. The bodies of the four persons who had recently died were treated in a similar way, to make surety doubly sure. Nevertheless, even this did not suffice. In 1732, seven years after these events, seventeen persons died in the village near about one time. The memory of the unlucky Arnold recurred to the viilagers; the vampyre theory was again appealed to: he was believed to have dealt with the seventeen as be had previously dealt with the four; and they were therefore disinterred, the heads cut off, the hearts staked, the bodies burned, and the ashes dispersed. One supposition was that Arnold bad vampyrised some cattle, that the seventeen villagers had eaten of the beef, and had fallen victims in consequence. This affair attracted much attention at the time. Louis the Fifteenth directed his ambassador at Vienna to make inquiries in the matter. Many of the witnesses attested on oath that the disinterred bodies were full of blood, and exhibited few of the usual symptoms of death: indications which the believers in vampyres stoutly maintained to be always present in such cases. This has induced many physicians to think that real cases of catalepsy or trance were mixed up with the popular belief, and were supplemented by a large allowance of epidemic fanaticism.

In Epirus and Thessaly there is a belief in living vampyres, men who leave their shepherd dwellings by night, and roam about, biting and tearing men and animals. In Moldavia the traditional priccolitsch, and in Wallachia the murony, must be somewhat remarkable beings. They are real living men, who become dogs at night, with the backbone prolonged to form a sort of tail, they roam through the villages, delighting to kill cattle.

Calmet, in his curious work relating to the marvels of the phantom world, quotes a letter which was written in 1738, and which added one to the long list of vampyre stories belonging to the Danubian provinces. "We have just had in this part of Hungary a scene of vampyrism, duly attested by two officials of the tribunal of Belgrade, who went down to the places specified; and by an officer of the emperor's troops at Graditz, who was an ocular witness of the proceedings. At the beginning of September there died in the village of Kisilony, three leagues from Graditz, a man sixty-two years of age. Three days after his burial he appeared in the night to his son, and asked for something to eat. The son having given him something, he ate and disappeared. The next day the son recounted to his neighbours what had occurred. That night the father did not appear; but on the following night he showed himself, and asked again for food. They do not know whether the son gave him any on that occasion or not; but on the following day the son was found dead in his bed. On that same day five or six persons in the village fell suddenly ill, and died one after another in a few days." The villagers resolved to open the grave of the old man, and examine the body; they did so, and declared that the symptoms presented were such as usually pertain to vampirism – eyes open, fresh colour, &c. The executioner drove a stake into the heart, and reduced the body to ashes. All the other persons recently dead were similarly exhumed; but as they did not exhibit the suspicious symptoms, they were quietly reinterred.

One theory in that part of Europe is, that an illegitimate son of parents, both of whom are illegitimate, is peculiarly likely to become a vampyre. If a dead body is supposed to be vampyrised it is taken up; should the usual symptoms of decay present themselves, the case is supposed to be a natural one, and the body is sprinkled with holy water by the priest; but should the freshness above adverted to appear, the ordeal of destruction is at once decided on. In some parts of Wallachia, skilled persons are called in to prevent a corpse from becoming a vampyre, by various charms, as well as by the rougher and coarser plan of driving a nail through the head. One charm is to rub the body in various places with the lard of a pig killed on St. Ignatius's Day; another is to lay by the side of the body a stick made of the stem of a wild rose. Some of the vampyrised persons are believed, when they emerge from their graves at night, not to go about in human form, but as dogs, cats, frogs, toads, fleas, lice, bugs, spiders, &c. sucking the blood of living persons by biting them in the back or neck. This belief forcibly suggests one remark: that as the peasantry in those parts of Europe are wofully deficient in cleanliness of person, clothing, and bedding, nothing is more likely than that they are bitten at night by some of the smaller creatures above named, without the assistance of any vampyre.

Mr. Pashley, in his Travels in Crete, states that when he was at the town of Askylo, he asked about the vampyres or katakhanadhes, as the Cretans called them of whose existence and doings he had heard many recitals, stoutly corroborated by the peasantry. Many of the stories converged towards one central fact, which Mr. Pashley believed had given origin to them all. On one occasion a man of some note was buried at St. George's Church at Kalikrati, in the island of Crete. An arch or canopy was built over his grave. But he soon afterwards made his appearance as a vampyre, haunting the village, and destroying men and children. A shepherd was one day tending his sheep and goats near the church, and on being caught in a shower, went under the arch to seek shelter from the rain. He determined to pass the night there, laid aside his arms, and stretched himself on a stone to sleep. In placing his fire-arms down (gentle shepherds of pastoral poems do not want fire-arms; but the Cretans are not gentle shepherds), he happened to cross them. Now this crossing was always believed to have the effect of preventing a vampyre from emerging from the spot where the emblem was found. Thereupon occurred a singular debate. The vampyre rose in the night, and requested the shepherd to remove the fire-arms in order that he might pass, as he had some important business to transact. The shepherd, inferring from this request that the corpse was the identical vampyre which had been doing so much mischief, at first refused his assent; but on obtaining from the vampyre a promise on oath that he would not hurt him, the shepherd moved the crossed arms. The vampyre, thus enabled to rise, went to a distance of about two miles, and killed two persons, a man and a woman. On his return, the shepherd saw some indication of what had occurred, which caused the vampyre to threaten him with a similar fate if he divulged what he had seen. He courageously told all, however. The priests and other persons came to the spot next morning, took up the corpse (which in daytime was as lifeless as any other) and burnt it. While burning, a little spot of blood spurted on the shepherd's foot, which instantly withered away; but otherwise no evil resulted, and the vampyre was effectually destroyed. This was certainly a very peculiar vampyre story; for the coolness with which the corpse and the shepherd carried on their conversation under the arch was unique enough. Nevertheless, the persons who narrated the affair to Mr. Pashley firmly believed in its truth, although slightly differing in their versions of it.

Modern vampyres in Western Europe seldom trouble society, so far as narratives tell; but across the Atlantic something of the kind has occupied public attention within the limits of the present generation. In 1854, the Times gave an extract from an American newspaper, the Norwich Courier, concerning an event that had just occurred. Horace Ray, of Griswold, died of consumption in 1846; two of his children afterwards died of the same complaint; eight years afterwards, in 1854, a third died. The neighbours, evidently having the vampyre theory in their thoughts, determined to exhume the bodies of the first two children, and burn them; under the supposition that the dead had been feeding on the living. If the dead body remained in a fresh or semi-fresh state, all the vampyre mischief would be produced. In what state the bodies were really found we are not told; but they were disinterred and burned on the 8th of June in the above-named year.

This superstition appears to be closely connected with that of the were-wolf, which sometimes presents very terrible features. Medical men give the name of lycanthropy to a kind of monomania which lies at the bottom of all the were-wolf stories. In popular interpretation, a were-wolf is a man or woman who has been changed into the form of a wolf, either to gratify a taste for human flesh and blood, or as a Divine punishment. The Reverend Baring Gould narrates the history of Marshal de Retz, a noble, brave, and wealthy man of the time of Charles the Seventh in France. He was sane and reasonable in all matters save one; but in that one he was a terrible being. He delighted in putting young and delicate children to death, and. then destroying them, without (so far as appears) wishing to put the flesh or the blood to his lips. In the course of a lengthened trial which brought his career to an end, the truth came to light that he had destroyed eight hundred children in seven years. There was neither accusation nor confession about a wolf here; it was a man afflicted with a morbid propensity of a dreadful kind. Somewhat different was the case of Jean Grenier, in 1603. He was a herd-boy, aged fourteen, who was brought before a tribunal at Bordeaux on a most extraordinary charge. Several witnesses, chiefly young girls, accused him of having attacked them under the guise of a wolf. The charge was strange, but the confession was still stranger; for the boy declared that he had killed and eaten several children, and the fathers of those children asserted the same thing. Grenier was said to be half an idiot; if so, his idiocy on the one hand, and the superstitions ignorance of the peasantry on the other, may perchance supply a solution to the enigma. One of the most extraordinary cases on record occurred in France in 1849, the facts being brought to light before a court-martial, presided over by Colonel Manselon. Many of the cemeteries near Paris were found to have been entered in the night, graves opened, coffins disturbed, and dead bodies strewed around the place in a torn and mangled condition. This was so often repeated, and in so many cemeteries, that great anguish and terror were spread among the people. A strict watch was kept. Some of the patrols or police of the cemeteries thought they saw a figure several times flitting about among the graves, but could never quite satisfy themselves on the matter. Surgeons were examined, to ascertain whether it was the work of the class of men who used in England to be called resurrectionists, or body-snatchers; but they all declared that the wild reckless mutilation was quite of another character. Again was a strict watch kept; a kind of man-trap was contrived at a part of the wall of Père la Chaise cemetery, which appeared as if it had been frequently scaled. A sort of grenade connected with the man-trap was heard to explode; the watch fired their guns; someone was seen to flee quickly; and then they found traces of blood, and a few fragments of military clothing, at one particular spot. Next day, it became publicly known that a non-commissioned officer of the Seventy-fourth Regiment had returned wounded to the barracks in the middle of the night, and had been conveyed to a military hospital. Further inquiry led to a revelation of the fact that Sergeant Bertrand, of the regiment here named, was the unhappy cause of all the turmoil. He was in general demeanour kind and gentle, frank and gay; and nothing but a malady of a special kind could have driven him to the commission of such crimes as those with which he was charged, and which his own confession helped to confirm. He described the impulse under which he acted as being irresistible, altogether beyond his own control; it came upon him about once a fortnight. He had a terrible consciousness while under its influence, and yet he could not resist. The minute details which he gave to the tribunal of his mode of proceeding at the cemeteries might suit those who like to sup on horrors, but may be dispensed with here. Suffice it to say that he aided by his confession to corroborate the charge; that he was sentenced to twelve months' imprisonment; and that eminent physicians of Paris endeavoured to restore the balance of his mind during his quiet incarceration.

Fifty years ago, vampyre literature had a temporary run of public favour. The Vampyre, or the Bride of the Isles, a drama, and The Vampyre, a melodrama in two acts, were presented at the theatres: the hero being enacted by some performer who had the art of making himself gaunt and ghastly on occasions. There was also a story under the same title, purporting to be by the Right Honourable Lord Byron, which attracted notice. The form of the superstition chiefly prevalent in modern Greece is that vampyres, notwithstanding all the means used to destroy their bodies, will resume their shape, and recommence their mischievous wanderings, as soon as the rays of moonlight fall on their graves. This serves as the foundation of the tale in question. But Lord Byron repudiated it. In a characteristic letter to Galignani, he said; "If the book is clever, it would be base to deprive the real writer, whoever he may be, of his honours; if stupid, I desire the responsibility of nobody's dullness but my own." The authorship was afterwards claimed by another writer, who stated that the idea of the tale had been suggested to his mind by something he had met with in Byron.

All the stories of vampyres, ghouls, and were-wolves, we may safely assert, can find their solution in a combination of three causes — a sort of epidemic superstition among ignorant persons; some of the phenomena of trance or epileptic sleep; and special monomaniac diseases which it is the province of the physician to study.